# THE LONG LOST

## Tor/Forge books by Ramsey Campbell

*Ancient Images*
*Cold Print*
*The Count of Eleven*
*Dark Companions*
*The Doll Who Ate His Mother*
*The Face That Must Die*
*Fine Frights* (editor)
*The Hungry Moon*
*Incarnate*
*The Influence*
*The Long Lost*
*Midnight Sun*
*The Nameless*
*Obsession*
*The Parasite*
*Waking Nightmares*

# THE LONG LOST

## Ramsey Campbell

A TOM DOHERTY ASSOCIATES BOOK
NEW YORK

THE LONG LOST

Copyright © 1993 by Ramsey Campbell

First published in Great Britain in 1993 by Headline Book Publishing PLC.

A Tor Book
Published by Tom Doherty Associates, Inc.
175 Fifth Avenue
New York, N.Y. 10010

Tor® is a registered trademark of Tom Doherty Associates, Inc.

ISBN 0-312-85825-6

First Tor edition: October 1994

Printed in the United States of America

0 9 8 7 6 5 4 3 2 1

for Kristina and Dennis Etchison, with love:
something old . . .

# Acknowledgements

The usual culprits, of course, for being with me while the book was growing: Jenny, Tammy and Matt.

Among the works of music I listened to while writing was a tape sent to me by Yves Sauriol and Fooyi of Montreal, to whom special thanks.

And to Anne Slee and John Wilson for advising me on issues I needed to research, though neither person should be held responsible for inventions I had to make.

Not to mention the entire Welsh nation for allowing themselves to be used as a literary device or several.

Nor let me forget the staff of Barclays Bank in New Brighton, who took care of the only manuscript of this novel while the family and I were in Hisaronu.

# One

As soon as David ordered drinks for himself and Joelle, everybody in the bar stopped speaking English. A man who removed his well-worn pipe from his mouth only to sip his beer emitted a slow puff of smoke to hover above his cloth-capped head, a thought balloon which faded before its sense could be filled in. His friend, who had been complaining amiably at him across the low plump-walled roughly plastered room, leaned down to drum on his sheepdog's ribs with the flat of his hand. Two young bank clerks, their first names pinned to the lapels of their blouses, left off discussing holidays in Tenerife over quarter-bottles of something like champagne and were all at once shrilly Welsh. The barman, whose shoulders were so straight they gave him the look of having forgotten to remove a hanger from his jacket, placed Joelle's half of lager in front of David and David's pint of tarry stout in front of her, and seemed pleased with himself. 'Shall we sit outside?' David said.

'More room for us out there, you think?' said Joelle.

She'd raised her head on her long neck so as to jerk her red hair away from her ears. Anger made the greenish flecks in her brown eyes appear to sparkle. 'You could be finding a table out there while I pay,' David suggested.

'There's plenty, and none of them looked reserved for the natives.'

David paid, and was debating whether to ask for his pint to be topped up now that its wad of foam had shrunk when one of the bank clerks made a remark that sounded like several species of spitting. 'Excuse me, was that about us?' Joelle said, raising her voice to compete with a pop song that had started in all four corners of the room, an American girl singing with the unforced slightly metallic purity of a synthesiser.

The bank clerk only went on staring at Joelle while her colleague said 'Not looking for a second home, are you?'

'Is that what Gladys said, Myfanwy?' Joelle seldom stayed angry

1

for long, and when neither angular young face responded except with a stare she grew conversational. 'We're always interested in houses.'

'None for sale round here.'

'Only to the folk who need them.'

'We don't buy,' David said, 'we build.'

'Home-makers, that's us,' Joelle said.

'Got children, have you?' Myfanwy demanded.

'Only Cuthbert, and you wouldn't want to know him.'

'He's locked in his room for the weekend,' David said.

'With a loaf and some water.'

'Maybe that'll teach him not to empty tins of paint into the bath.'

Now the clerks were staring because they'd been struck dumb in any language. It wasn't until David shut the door behind himself and Joelle that he heard them burst out babbling, a flood of words in which Welsh and English ground together. He blew the pockmarked disc of foam into the token flowerbed and set the tankard with a clang on the nearest of the round tin tables before sitting on a bony white chair opposite Joelle. 'Welcome to Wales, isn't it,' he said.

'I expect they'll like us better on the coast.'

'It's a wonder those two can bear to handle English money in their bank.'

'Maybe they use old Celtic coins.'

'It's the old ways are best, look you,' David declared, adopting a hideous Welsh lilt, then buried his mouth and his mirth in his stout, because the two clerks had emerged from the pub. 'Sorry,' he spluttered, wiping his upper lip, when they glared at him. 'With a name like Owain I thought I was entitled to, er, expose my roots.'

'We've none of that name round here,' Gladys snapped.

'You must have exported us all.'

'We couldn't have been enough of a tourist attraction,' Joelle suggested sweetly.

Gladys compressed her lips, turning them a paler pink, and Myfanwy parted hers, displaying perfect teeth white as neon in the June sunlight; then the clerks marched away along the lorry-laden tree-lined winding road. 'I suppose we're having a kind of fun,' Joelle said. 'Especially you, exposing your root to young women.'

'Don't say things like that or you'll be giving me evil thoughts.'

'The sooner you drink up the sooner we can be on our way to doing something about them,' Joelle said, balancing her chair on its hind legs while she tilted her head back to catch the last of her lager. As the amber drops fell between her generous lips the hem of her thin white skirt whispered higher on her thighs, and David gulped his stout. 'Ready for action?' Joelle said.

David groaned. 'Give this a chance to go down.'

'I see what you mean. I'll drive if you like.'

'Better let me to keep me occupied.'

Joelle took his hand and pressed her lips to his palm. By the time the sensation faded he was able to walk, bow-legged to begin with, to the Volvo. Joelle closed her eyes and arched her back against the front passenger seat and stretched out her limbs as he started the engine. He swung the vehicle off the patch of gravel that served as a car park, and resisted the temptation to squawk his horn as he overtook Myfanwy and Gladys. Beyond the narrow elongated village the last of a convoy of lorries wriggled over a hill at the limit of his vision, and then there was only the shimmering road.

It was early afternoon. The Owains had been well into Wales for a couple of hours, passing through towns where LLAFUR in windows denoted allegiance to the Labour Party and where at one point David had wondered what a LLEGE sign signified until he saw that a tree was getting in the way of its saying COLLEGE. They would have set off last night if Herb Crantry's front-room radiator hadn't sprung a leak. By now they were more than halfway to the lonely coast of the Lleyn Peninsula. Since they'd turned inland at Bangor the long-winded road had been oppressed by green, which hid the hills and mountains whenever the ferns and trees and vines that overhung the route doled out a view. When David found himself tempted to speed up and catch one of the streams across the tarmac to see how an illusion of water could reflect real trees, he took advantage of a layby where a perspiring brawny balding cook was serving hamburgers from a caravan. 'I could nod if you want to take over,' David told Joelle.

The warmth of her body was waiting for him in the passenger seat. When she changed gear the back of her hand brushed his leg, and the old snake raised its head again. Not bad after ten years of marriage, he thought – she wasn't, nor what he felt for her. He gripped his knees while the aching weight subsided. His eyes closed rather than watch the road avoiding trees and black cows planted in the fields, and he imagined the sea beyond the coast receding as Joelle drove towards it, the waves dwindling like the mirages on the tarmac. A breeze through the open windows stroked his face and fluttered Joelle's skirt against his hand between the seats. He seemed to try for hours to lift his eyelids, not that there was any hurry, until suddenly they sprang up. 'Are we there?'

'Maybe nearly, but I don't think this is anywhere.'

'Didn't you just say something?'

'If I did I mustn't have been listening. Such as what?'

'I don't know – my name.' He must have dreamed it while wakening; it had sounded more like Dafydd, which was daft. He peered over his shoulder, twingeing his neck, in an attempt to recapture the view he'd glimpsed through a gap in a wall – a cluster of white buildings against a misty sunlit seascape at the foot of a cliff. Clumps of wall and their ferny cockscombs had already obscured it, making him feel like a child robbed of somewhere that distance rendered magical. Here came a signpost for Port-unpronounceable, the village where he and Joelle meant to stay, though there was no longer any sign pointing along a side road to the sea. A glance down that lane showed him shaggy hedges and a distant glint of water; then the signpost was past, launching a blackbird after the car.

Ten minutes of enforced wandering between fields brought the car to the edge of Portmouthful, a fishing village that seemed too small to have streets at so many different angles, the steepest leading down to a pebbly beach and a lazy dance of boats. Above the main street – a post office selling beach toys, an ice-cream shop and a fish-and-chip, an antique shop leaned against by a cartwheel – half a dozen whitewashed houses offered bed and breakfast. Joelle parked the Volvo outside the lowest, the car's headlights several inches higher than its rear, and David lifted the overnight bag off the back seat. 'Let's find a room and then see about lunch,' Joelle said, 'or whatever you're hungry for.'

She hadn't rung the doorbell of the nearest house when the woman sitting in the lounge among potted plants and long tables strewn with magazines stubbed out her cigarette and hurried to open the front door. 'Mrs Thomas,' she said, and shook their hands. 'Plenty of room till the kids finish school.'

'We'd just be staying overnight.'

'Mustn't complain,' Mrs Thomas said as if David had, and placed a cough on the back of her hand. 'Fifteen pounds each out of season.'

'Shall we pay you now?' Joelle said.

'Whatever you think best,' the landlady said, unpacking her chins as she raised her broad face to gaze straight at Joelle and then at David, and preceded them along the hall to a room which barely contained a desk and a chair and a board hung with keys. The doorframe was warped by old settlement, and a wedge had been glued to the top of the door to make it snug. 'What name would it be?'

'Owain.'

'Both, is that?'

'Decidedly,' Joelle said in her turn.

'Whereabouts from?'

'Chester.'

'Quite a long way just to come for a bed for the night.'

Despite her manner of disinterested worldly scepticism David felt compelled to respond 'One way of tiring ourselves out.'

'A handful, is he? Put yourselves in the register. A double, was it?'

'Unless that's a problem,' David said, picking up the cracked bandaged ballpoint pen that was strung to the book.

'I don't know why it should be, I'm sure,' Mrs Thomas said, and in the same tone 'I expect you'll both want a good breakfast.'

The point of the pen was so unsteady it made him appear to be forging his name and address. Mrs Thomas gazed at this and said 'I'll give you number three. That's the best view out of the doubles.'

Did he hear her implying that they mightn't have time to spare for the view? 'Shall we take our key now?' he said with as little urgency as he could manage.

'Can you wait an hour or so? The girl's gone over to her aunt with the flu.'

'Not to deliver it, I hope.'

'He's a handful all right,' Mrs Thomas said briskly, and to David 'Your bag'll be safe if you want to go out.'

Despite Joelle's sidelong grin at him he didn't say 'That's no way to talk about my wife', nor indeed anything until they were outside on the street which smelled sunlit, where he unbuttoned his shirt as far as his navel. 'Shouldn't we have asked to see the room?'

'Whatever it's like I can stand it for one night if you can. Shall we track down that lunch?'

'Maybe I should just call the machine first in case there are any messages.'

'You'll have a job.'

'You've never left the what's it called, the remote interrogator at home.'

'He who doesn't pack can't complain. Maybe Cuthbert flushed it down the loo.'

5

'Then I wish he hadn't. If anyone's after us I could at least have called them back.'

'I should think even Herb can survive without us for one weekend. We're here for you to catch up on your sleep, remember.'

'That was one reason,' David admitted, and set his mind on lunch.

The nearest, and possibly the only, meal for sale in the village was at the fish and chip shop. Walking while eating out of a newspaper felt like a return to innocence, to a way you weren't supposed to act in public once you grew up. They strolled down to the beach, where two cats too hot to fight each other lazed at length on the sea wall as though waiting for a fisherman to spill his catch. David had been hoping for a sight of the village he'd glimpsed from the coast road, but it was hidden by the cliff to the left of the bay. The beach shrank to nothing at the foot of the cliff, and he didn't think there would be a safe path along the top, since chunks of the edge had fallen into the sea. 'How about a drive?' he said.

'Another one?'

'There's somewhere I saw just before we got here.'

'All right,' Joelle said with her usual impulsiveness, 'surprise me.'

They dropped their pages of incomprehensibly Welsh news in a concrete bin on the way to the Volvo. As Joelle slammed her door Mrs Thomas jumped up to look out of the front room, her mouth sprouting hairgrips as she bunned her greying hair. David held up one forefinger and tapped it with the other, then bent it in half and tapped it again. 'I just hope that wasn't a rude sign in Welsh,' he said as he started the car.

As the determined whiteness of the village gave way to the haphazard green which crowded onto the verges of the road, a buoy tolled out on the water. Just beyond the village sign a chunky flood of sheep, directed by a farmer and his dog, blocked the road for minutes. A black horse was studiously cropping grass in a field, advancing its front legs one step and waiting several seconds before shifting its hind legs. Otherwise the road and its surroundings were deserted as far as the signpost. David steered the Volvo into the lane which the signpost failed to designate, and felt the surface beneath the wheels grow rougher. 'Here's hoping you know what you're doing,' Joelle said.

'Don't I always?'

6

After a mile or so David wondered if an arm of the signpost had been removed because there was no longer any point to the route. Thorny hedges too high to see over were on their way to meeting across it, and scratched the car whenever he swerved to stay out of an overgrown ditch. Wasps hovered like dangerous seeds above the hedges. At least the obsessively winding lane tended in the direction of the buildings he'd glimpsed from the main road. It also sloped downhill, steeply enough that David adopted a lower gear. After most of another mile Joelle said 'This certainly is mysterious.'

'Just be thankful we've got good brak—' David said, and stamped on them. Past an unpredictably sharp curve the lane both widened and came to an abrupt end, beyond which the misty sea exploded its dazzle into his eyes. He felt the car slewing towards the collapsed edge of a stony patch perhaps less than three times wide as the car was long, he heard stones dislodged by the wheels scattering rapidly down a cliff which sounded both steep and high. The rear wheels were skidding uncontrollably towards the cliff, and it was the greatest act of faith he had ever made in his life to release the brakes for a second in order to minimise the skid. He slammed the car into first with a screech of gears, praying that would send it away from the drop, but it lurched towards the far end of the cliff edge. His foot recoiled from the accelerator pedal and fumbled for the brake, and the car stalled in the middle of the barren patch.

'That was exciting,' Joelle said several breaths later. 'Was that my surprise? Can I open my eyes now?'

'Sorry about the ride. It wasn't quite what I had in mind.'

'I'm glad to hear it. What was?'

'I'll show you.'

He didn't begin shaking until he was out of the car. He was leaning his wet palms on the hot dusty roof when he saw Joelle was shaky too. His legs almost let him down as he went around the vehicle to her. They clung to each other, David stroking her hair while his fingers ceased trembling. Eventually she gave him a quick kiss and stepped back. 'Where's the surprise?' she said, picking her way over stones to a cleft in the edge.

It was the start of a path which zigzagged down a jagged limestone slope like a crystallisation of the mist which blurred the sea. About two hundred yards below, in a cove at the foot of the cliff, was a village larger than David had expected. Perhaps half a mile out from the cluster of several dozen slate roofs and walls white as dough, a long narrow greenish island was stranded on the ribbed sand by the tide towards which it was pointing. Joelle held onto David's arm with one hand and shaded her eyes with the other. 'How did you know this was here?'

'I saw it from the main road.'

'I can't see how.'

'Neither can I, now you mention it, but I did. Was it worth the drive?'

'I don't know if anything could be worth that drive,' Joelle said, kissing him to show she didn't mean it. 'We won't know unless we go and look.'

Though David had no fear of heights, he felt happier on ladders than on the crumbling frequently steep path. By the time he was halfway down, where Joelle had perched on a rock embroidered with moss to wait for him, his eyes were stinging with sweat and he was muttering curses at the treacherous rubble. 'You can,' he panted, 'see why the people moved away.'

'All this exertion should give us an appetite.'

'For what?'

'We'll have to see,' she told him, kicking a large pebble over the edge of the path as she slipped off the rock.

The village wasn't as deserted as it appeared, for although the pebble clattered down no further than the next stretch of path, it seemed to have awakened a larger stone where the path led between the first cottages. As Joelle slithered down, the object expanded and flapped into the air, and she halted, pressing one hand to her heart. 'Pigeon,' David called.

'Post.'

'Horn.'

'Porn.'

'Hard.'

'Easy.'

'I wish it was.'

'More than one word. You lose.'

'It's my body talking,' David said, sliding down the last few uneven yards to her. 'Well, this is it, I'm afraid.'

'I'm glad you brought me. You know I like mysteries. What do you think happened?'

'I expect people couldn't face the climb.'

'Wouldn't you like to think it was something stranger?'

'It doesn't matter what I'd like to think.'

He was following her along the street, which was a maze of

lumps of fallen walls. Through the glassless windows of the single-storey buildings the slate roofs looked patched with blue sky. Sunlight exposed interiors pale and bare as the insides of old skulls. In some rooms David saw pieces of wood that might have been the remains of furniture, or timber that had collapsed onto the rubble, but otherwise the only sign of life was the dry grass which sprouted in the rooms and whispered in the sandy breeze. 'I don't think anyone's been here for a long time,' Joelle murmured.

'Because . . .'

'No signs of civilisation. No broken bottles or empty cans or signs of amorous activity.' The ruined street angled to the right, showing the Owains the beach and the island, and Joelle shivered as a breeze hinted at the chill of the mist which hung above the sea. 'Not even any graffiti,' she said.

'It's a long way down just to leave your name.'

They stepped out from between the cottages, sending a few pebbles stumbling across the beach. Apart from fallen slabs of the cliff, it was featureless. Beyond the island the margin of the sea looked artificial, a virtually straight line of stillness erasing the long waves. 'Ready for some more exertion?' Joelle said.

'Any time.' David moved in front of her and glanced up the deserted cliff before running his hands down from her shoulders to the back of her skirt and lifting it gradually as he stroked her bottom. 'Let's see if we can bring some life back to the village.'

For a moment she seemed doubtful, then she raised one leg and rubbed it along the outside of his thigh. She brushed her hands over his face and took hold of his head while her mouth opened on his, but then she grabbed his hands. 'I hate to interrupt, but I think someone wants us,' she said.

# Two

At first David could see nothing different when he turned to look. The waves petered out on the sand beyond the island, the sky had expunged itself of everything except pure blue. Even the pigeon had gone, unless that was the bird fluttering on a branch of a stunted tree on the crest of the island. Or was the shape a tree? He narrowed his eyes so as to focus on the silhouette against the restless glittering of the sea, and managed to satisfy himself that it had two branches, one raised on each side of the trunk. 'You think someone's waving to us?'

'More like beckoning.'

David shaded his eyes with one hand and waved the other. He still hadn't focused when the silhouette vanished like a twig consumed in an instant by the fire of the sea. 'What happened?' he protested. 'Where did it go?'

'I couldn't see. Did they fall?'

The outline of the island was confused with the surrounding glitter, and David could distinguish nothing within it other than overgrown greyish rock. 'Shouldn't we go and see?' Joelle said. 'They might have thought that was what you were waving to tell them.'

'Did you really see a person? It looked more like a scarecrow to me. Maybe it got blown over.'

'What would a scarecrow be doing on that little lump?'

'What would anyone?'

'I do think we ought to go and look.'

'I'd like to find out what we saw as long as the tide's out. It shouldn't take more than an hour.'

David thought he was exaggerating. Foreshortened as it was, the island looked incapable of hiding anything. As he stepped forward it seemed to inch across the sand, which shone with silver ripples left behind by the ebb tide, to meet him. Sand spurted from beneath his heels as he gave himself a head start. 'Race you,' he called to Joelle.

'Cheat,' she cried.

The arms of the cove opened on either side of him, so that he had the impression of running straight out to sea. He felt himself breasting the air, an increasingly palpable medium bearing a chill that failed to cool him down as the distance to the island grew more stubborn and the colours intensified ahead of him, brownish sand sown with the tints of broken shells, the pigeon greys and dabs of green on the island, which looked so implacably present it was almost unnatural, as though its underside had been sliced off clean so that it could stand on the beach. He heard Joelle panting behind him, and threw himself into a sprint which almost tripped him up. He splashed through a long pool shaped like a giant teardrop, sandy water gritting between his sandals and the soles of his bare feet, and forced himself to run across the last hundred yards of blackened sand to the island. 'Careful,' Joelle gasped, more urgently than seemed appropriate, as he jumped over a patch of glistening black seaweed onto the rock.

David stumbled upwards several feet to regain his balance and supported himself with one hand on a clump of brown ferns, which crumbled under his palm. 'Of what?' he said breathlessly.

'I thought you might fall.'

'Where was I going to fall to?'

'All right, so I was being stupid.'

'No more than me,' he said, reaching his free hand down to help her climb.

'That's not saying much. Whose idea was it to have a half-mile race?' She kissed him on coming level with him, but when he took hold of her shoulders she disengaged herself gently. 'Not here, David. It's too cold, for one thing.'

He grasped a rock above his head in preparation for hauling himself up the spiky slope. At the top, some twenty feet away, grass-blades scraped together against the sky. 'What were you anxious about really?' he said.

'To tell you the truth, I don't really know. I didn't want you hurting yourself on the rocks when we've all that way back to the car.' She frowned at herself and shrugged or shivered. 'Come on, let's see if there was anyone and then we can go.'

David clambered to the top and helped Joelle over the edge. From up here the island appeared more solitary than ever, a mountain ridge robbed of its landscape, a backbone without a body, a stone snake bloated in places as though as though by feeding, surrounded by a glistening stain. A few patches of nondescript vegetation clung to rocks despite the winds that must scour the island with salt and sand. Some kind of tree stood at the highest point, about halfway along the island. 'Was that what we saw?' Joelle said, her voice flattened by the openness.

'It could be.'

That seemed increasingly unlikely as they progressed step by step along the ridge. The object was beginning to look to David like a transplanted signpost or a cross. The ridge bent sharply, changing the angle of his vision, and he saw it was a stunted tree, no taller than a sapling but cracked and grey with age. The left-hand branch was at least a foot longer than the other, and a single fruit hung from it. As David scrambled within reach of the tree he lost his footing and grabbed at the branch. 'Don't touch it,' Joelle cried, 'it might be poisonous.'

'I wasn't going to pick it,' David assured her, grasping the crotch of the branch and the trunk. Perhaps the dangling shrivelled veinous object wasn't a fruit but another of the fibrous swellings which were visible in at least a dozen places on the otherwise scrawny trunk. He let go as soon as he'd steadied himself, because the wrinkled bark felt like old skin on the bone of the tree. 'Would that down there have been for anything?' he wondered aloud.

Below the rise on which the tree stood was a roughly circular hollow almost as wide as the island and about twenty feet deep. The side to his right had partially collapsed into a sloping mound of grey rock scattered with barren earth. Opposite the mound was the largest patch of vegetation they had seen on the island. 'That's strange,' Joelle said. 'I wonder if someone lived here.'

'Because . . .'

'That looks as if it could have been a herb garden.'

'Want to have a pick while we're here?'

As David made to place one foot on the topmost of a series of steps which were either natural or very unevenly hacked out of the rock, Joelle gripped his arm. 'I thought we were seeing if anyone was in trouble.'

'If there was anyone we'd have seen them by now,' David said with a wave at the deserted narrowing stretch of rock beyond the hollow.

When he stepped below the edge he found himself descending into silence. As well as the subdued breathing of the sea, a sound he'd scarcely noticed until it was suppressed, the hollow cut off the wind, so that he was suddenly hotter. By the time he reached the bottom of the steps he was mopping his forehead. 'Perfectly safe,' he told Joelle, and crossed the flat cracked floor, which seemed barren even of colour.

Perhaps she was right about the herb garden; he couldn't judge. The tangle of vegetation did appear artificial by comparison with the rest of the island. Dust and larger fragments of rock ground together under his sandals, a sharp close sound trapped by the hollow, as he went nearer. 'Joelle, come and have a—' he called, and halted in the act of turning to her. 'Well, will you look at that. Good God.'

She leaned forward, teetering halfway down the steps. 'What have you seen?'

'Don't worry, nothing terrible. Only I've been standing down here without realising there was a house.'

Under the mound of rock beside the steps was a squat cottage with two squarish windows, one gaping in the side nearest the steps, the other overlooking the possible garden from beside a stout wooden door in an unadorned frame. The cottage was the same grey as the mound of rock – even the door was greyish with dust – but David was astonished that he could have walked past it without noticing. He returned to the foot of the steps for Joelle. 'These builders get everywhere, don't they?'

She rested a hand on his shoulder and jumped down. 'Hello,' she called tentatively, and cupping her hands around her mouth, 'Hello?'

'There's hardly going to be anyone living in there now. Come and see if you can make out what's been growing down here.'

His shadow spilled across the patch of vegetation, and then Joelle's did, shrinking as though the growth was swallowing it when she crouched for a closer look. 'I'm sure these were grown,' she said after a while, 'but I can't imagine what for or when. Do you mind if we just walk to the end of the island and then go back across the beach?'

'It's your surprise,' David said in agreement, then lingered to squint at the knots of thin stems more grey with dust than green, the minute buds clenched around glimpses of blue and purple and red. As Joelle's shadow withdrew, the colours brightened and the labyrinth of stems defined itself more precisely, and he had the sense of being close to some revelation. He was about to stoop, though with no idea of why, when Joelle called to him in a shrill whisper that wanted to be a cry. 'David. David, quick.'

'I'm here,' he said, turning so fast that the sky blackened momentarily. 'What have you seen?'

'Oh, David, look at her.'

Joelle's voice was wavering as she gazed through the front window of the cottage, clasping her hands together as though in unconscious prayer. Two steps brought David alongside her while everything around him – the dusty smell of the baked stone underfoot, the weeds drooping from cracks in the wall of the cottage huddled under the rockfall, the hint in the air of a perfume which wasn't Joelle's and which he assumed was emanating from the undisciplined garden – grew intensely clear. As he put his arm around Joelle's waist and looked where her attention was fixed, he felt her shiver.

The room, which the thickness of the bare walls made unexpectedly small, was unfurnished except for a pallet spread with dry grass and weeds. Lying on the pallet was a woman. In the sunlight which slanted through the window her face and her hair, which hung over the end of the bed and trailed on the stone floor, were almost as white as the dress that covered her from her throat to her toes. Her eyes were closed, her long slim fingers were folded on her chest. David thought she might be the oldest person he had ever seen; yet her repose, and the aura of sunlight surrounding her, made her seem youthful and utterly innocent. He wasn't aware of holding his breath until Joelle groped for his hand. 'She's dead, isn't she?' she whispered.

'I think so.' When Joelle gripped his fingers, bruising them, he said reluctantly 'We'd better make sure.'

'Will you?'

'If you'll be all right here.'

'I've just never seen anyone dead before.'

David had – three of his grandparents at different times before he was at secondary school – but it wasn't an experience you got used to. He heard himself shuffling as he advanced to the door. The old wood gritted beneath his fingertips, and it swung away easily, ushering him into the room.

As he stepped through the low stone opening he realised that the cottage must have been hacked out of the island itself; he was still treading on the floor of the hollow. The professional side of him was admiring the workmanship, the strength of the roof which needed no beams to support it even now it was buried under rock, the cunning with which the wooden hinges of the front door and of another that led to an inner room to his right were held fast by wedges driven into holes in the rock, the eccentric shapes of the doors themselves, cut to fit the frames. All this observation was a

15

way of delaying what he had to do in the room. He glanced at Joelle, who was still at the window, and gave her a smile that felt meaningless as he took the first of three steps to the bed. Clutching his knees to steady himself, he looked the body in the face.

It was a long oval with a rounded chin and small ears delicate as porcelain. Where the hair was swept back from the forehead he thought he saw silvery glints of dust. Though the face had none of the collapsed appearance he recalled from his grandparents' faces, the pale almost colourless lips were parted. He must have been too far away to notice that before, but it was as though the woman had pronounced a silent secret word as David had entered the cottage. All he had to do was place his hand just above her mouth to feel if she was breathing, except that the notion dismayed him. He reached for her uppermost wrist instead to search for a pulse.

He was bracing himself for her flesh to be cold, but if anything her wrist was warmer than his fingers. Of course that could be the effect of the sunlight, a less than reassuring thought if she had been dead for some time. He made himself hold her thin wrist firmly, but the longer he did so the less certain he was whether it was his own pulse that he was feeling. 'I don't know,' he said aloud.

Joelle snapped her handbag open on the stone windowsill. 'Do you want to use my mirror?'

'To look for her breath, you mean.' He was relieved to replace the hand, which was light as a young child's, on top of the other, because he'd noticed how the fingernails were ground down to the quick, under which were embedded what looked like scrapings of rock. He pushed himself away from the wall, which felt scratched, and hurried to accept the mirror Joelle was holding out to him. 'This'll make sure,' he promised her and himself.

As soon as he directed it towards the supine woman's face it trailed sunlight across her eyes, and for a moment he expected them to open. He stooped to hold the glass surface an inch above her lips. He poised it there while he took his time about counting ten, his hand hardly trembling, then he turned the mirror towards himself. He could see no trace of breath – nothing except a blaze of light which blinded him.

It was broad daylight, Joelle was almost close enough to touch, but he wouldn't feel safe in the room until he was able to see. Once his vision cleared he held the mirror above the woman's lips again, this time for at least thirty seconds. He went down on his knees to keep out of the sun, but the light in the mirror attacked his eyes before the glass could show him anything. 'Can't *you* see?' he said rather sharply to Joelle.

'Not from here. Do you want me to come in?'

'That wouldn't do any good.' He handed her the mirror and strode almost furiously back to the bed. 'She's had it,' he muttered, gazing at the stilled face and feeling ashamed of wanting to have spoken the truth. 'This is the last thing I do,' he said for Joelle to hear, casting his shadow over the woman's breasts as he planted his hands on either side of her and leaned down to press one ear against her heart.

Perhaps it was unreasonable of him to assume that the mound on the front of her dress would yield, but the sensation of resting his ear against a firm breast came as a shock. No wonder he could hear a heartbeat: it was his own. He was clenching and unclenching his fists, trying to think of another way to search for a heartbeat besides placing his hand on her breast, when she moved beneath him.

He felt as if the world had. Her chest had stirred, rising a fraction and falling. At the same moment Joelle cried 'David, her hand.'

He lurched away from the pallet so violently that he would have sprawled across it if he hadn't dug his knuckles into a depression in the wall. The woman's left hand, which he'd laid on top of the other, was now lying palm uppermost on the dead grass beside her thigh. 'God love her,' he babbled, 'she isn't—'

Reeling to his feet had made him dizzy and turned his vision black. When a hand closed around his arm he gasped and jerked. 'Are you all right?' Joelle said in his ear.

'I will be.' He put his hand over hers on his arm until his eyesight seeped back. The woman on the bed was definitely breathing. Even if her chest was moving almost imperceptibly, how could he have failed to notice the movement as soon as he'd approached the bed? 'What do you suppose is wrong with her?' he wondered.

'I'm a decorator, David, not a nurse.' Joelle knelt by the bed and took hold of the woman's hands. 'Couldn't you tell she was alive when you felt these?'

'I've seen corpses, but I've never touched one except to kiss them on their makeup.'

'Sorry. I can't talk.' Joelle began to rub the woman's hands gently and leaned forward to murmur in her ear. 'Hello? Can you hear me? We're friends, we want to help you. Can you open your eyes for me?' She scrutinised the face and stroked the forehead, then went back to rubbing the woman's hands and talking soothingly to her. After some minutes she shook her head and got to her feet. 'I'm wasting time, David. I don't really know what I'm doing.'

'I thought you were doing fine.'

'We shouldn't be trying to help her when we don't know what's wrong. It could be exposure or malnutrition or some kind of sleeping sickness. She needs a doctor.'

'Do you want to try carrying her up to the car?'

'It mightn't be right to move her.'

'Then let's fetch a doctor.'

'One of us should stay with her.'

'I'll do whichever you like.'

Joelle gazed at him and produced a smile. 'You're faster.'

He felt as if he should have known that their conversation would come to this end. 'I won't be any longer than I have to be. If there isn't a doctor in Porthow'syourfather I'll ring one and meet him here.'

When he made to give Joelle an encouraging hug she pushed him away. 'Go on then, be quick.'

He thought of offering to stay while she went for the doctor, but the offer and the time it wasted would only annoy her. He ran out of the cottage and up the uneven steps, and glanced back from the edge of the hollow. Joelle had come to the doorway for a last sight of him. 'I'll be fine,' she said as if she'd heard someone say different. She waved urgently to him, and as the hollow cut off his view of her he heard her call 'Don't dawdle or we'll never get to our bedroom.'

# Three

'We'll never get to our bedroom,' Joelle called, and felt ashamed of being selfish. Suppose the woman had heard? Joelle glanced over her shoulder to reassure herself that the supine figure hadn't moved, and heard David stumble on the ridge. By holding her breath and straining her ears she managed to hear him hurrying onwards, and then there was a silence which made each of her movements sound as though it was taking place no more than an inch from her ears. She left her handbag in the doorway of the cottage and went to sit with her back against the wall of the hollow where she had an unobstructed view of the woman on the bed.

Joelle felt inadequate – incomplete. There was no point in trying to minister to the invalid when she didn't know what she was treating or even if the woman was aware of her in any way. Did anyone know that the woman lived here by herself, or had she taken refuge on the island only recently? Someone ought to be responsible for her, Joelle thought, but her growing anger was simply working on her nerves, not that she had any reason to be nervous. She inched her bottom forwards, thinking wryly that Mrs Thomas at the hotel was bound to form her own conclusions about marks on the back of Joelle's skirt, then she lay back and, turning her face up to the sun, closed her eyes.

It was easy to forget where she was and why she was there. Once the sunlight settled on her face and bare limbs she felt full of light and floating away on a dream. She wouldn't fall asleep so long as she listened for movement in the cottage and for David coming back, not that she ought to begin expecting him just yet, not for at least an hour. She consulted her watch, large and friendly as favourite toys had seemed to her as a child, and saw that it was later than she'd thought – two minutes past four. Plenty of daylight yet, far more than David would need. She tilted her head back again, closing her eyes.

Thirteen minutes past four. She oughtn't to keep glancing at her watch, but the silence was making her feel in danger of dozing off.

Whenever she peered around her, the residue of sunlight on her eyeballs gave her surroundings a pale brittle look. Perhaps she should walk up and down the island or at least around the hollow, because the need to keep opening her eyes in order to remain awake had begun to make her feel as though there was something she ought to notice when she opened them – indeed, it was beginning to make her feel watched. She turned her head slowly to survey the hollow and to rid herself of the notion, then she gazed through the doorway at the figure on the pallet until she had to close her eyes to stop their stinging. She would count to a thousand – no, ten thousand – in her head before she opened them again, or lose a bet with herself.

Two thousand one hundred and ninety-five, two thousand one hundred and ninety-six . . . This had to be the most tedious activity she had ever undertaken, and what was worse, she felt trapped in the undertaking. Two thousand one hundred and ninety-seven . . . She couldn't tell if she was slowing down, but at this rate she thought David might return before she'd finished. Then something moved between her and the sunlight, a mixture of scents closed around her, and she was all at once cold as fog.

She didn't react blindly, she didn't cry out. The first part of her which she moved was her eyelids, and then she was almost able to laugh at herself. The sun had clouded over, that was all. The sudden gloom did make the hollow feel deeper, and set the depths of the herbs glimmering. Joelle pushed herself to her feet and went into the cottage in search of warmth. 'If you don't mind, I'll stay and talk to you for a while,' she told the woman on the bed.

It was darker in the cottage than in the hollow, so that she had to bend close to the pallet to reassure herself that the woman was breathing. The lips had remained open, the upper lip delicately furred as a moth's wing, and Joelle tilted her cheek to the woman's face. The dead grass rustled, though only because Joelle was resting one hand on it, and then she was rewarded with the sensation of an unexpectedly warm breath in her ear. 'There you are,' she said with a laugh she had to force past some nervousness.

She wouldn't mind sitting, but not on the bed. Might there be a chair in the other room? Even if there was, she didn't like to pry into what, after all, she had no right to assume wasn't the woman's home. She hoisted herself onto the windowsill, above which there was just enough space for her to sit comfortably. 'My name's Joelle,' she said. 'I wish I knew yours.'

The breast of the white garment rose and fell minutely in the dimness, but that was all. 'My husband's called David,' Joelle said. 'He's gone to fetch someone to take care of you. A doctor, I mean.'

She mustn't be tempted to look over her shoulder; she would hear David when he returned. 'We improve people's homes. Home-Makers, that's our name, our business name. I expect we could even do something—' she said, and trailed off, glad that the woman couldn't see her grimacing at the bleak room.

'I'll tell you how we started, shall I? We sort of drifted into what we do. How it happened was some years ago, we hadn't long been married, some neighbours of ours were having a bad time with a builder – he kept leaving things unfinished and trying to make our neighbours feel guilty about calling him back. There were rooms they couldn't get into for days because he'd taken up so much of the floor to rewire the house and put in central heating, and he'd kept putting the job off so long that it was nearly winter.'

The thought, or the chill at her back, made her shiver. 'Do you know, once when they had to call him out because he'd left some live wires exposed he complained they'd stopped him fixing his old mother's toilet. We happened to be there when he said that, and like a fool I said to our neighbours that David could have done a better job and not made them feel anything that went wrong was their fault, to which wouldn't you know the builder said David was welcome to it and walked out of the job, and probably told his old mum how badly he'd been treated, don't you think?'

Joelle rubbed her shoulders and hugged herself. 'It's all right, you needn't answer,' she said, suddenly wondering how she would feel if the woman did. 'I should say that David had done all the work that needed doing when we bought our house, and surprised himself by how good he was at it except for decorating, which I really enjoyed, but obviously we didn't do that for a living then, we both worked in the post office in Chester. Only our neighbours had been put off trusting builders they didn't know, and because they'd only just moved to that house from the other side of the country they didn't know anyone they could ask to recommend someone, and because they'd seen what we'd done with our house they asked if we could do the same with theirs. Well, we rather felt responsible for losing them their builder, not that he was any loss, and because they'd already paid him too much money we thought we'd save them some. And David took double the care with their house he had with ours, but he still hardly slept at night in case he got anything wrong.'

She paused and listened to the silence of the hollow. David

hadn't had time to return from the village yet – it was only twenty to five – but she did wish the sun would come out to keep her company. 'So,' she said, 'this couple were so pleased with our work that they invited all the friends they'd made by now to see it, and before we knew it we had a reputation and people were ringing us up from miles away to do work for them. And by the next summer it was goodbye to the post office. There's nothing like feeling needed, is—'

A rustle of dry grass made Joelle suck in her breath, which tasted faintly like a head cold. She leaned forward and peered at the bed. The woman appeared not to have shifted; she wasn't moving perceptibly now. 'Can you hear me?' Joelle said, hearing the walls render her voice almost lifeless. 'Do you know I'm here?'

After a while she sat back, steadying herself with her hands on the cold stone that framed her. 'I hope I wasn't sounding holier than thou before,' she said with a reasonably unforced laugh. 'I mean, the job is fun, some kinds we weren't expecting. I suppose everyone has something to hide, but you'd be amazed what people don't mind us knowing about them or maybe want us to know, not that we've a problem with them inventing things to do in bed.'

There had been the policewoman who kept a pair of handcuffs by her bed, and the customs officer with a cupboard full of videocassettes whose covers alone must have been enough to get them seized, and the couple who'd provided the guest room with an album full of photographs of themselves having sex together. The photographs had given David and Joelle enough ideas that they'd spent an hour in the room while their clients were out of the house, but they'd thought better of owning up in case the couple had had plans for a foursome.

The chest of the woman on the pallet rose and fell slowly, silently. To Joelle its whiteness and quiet had begun to resemble an incarnation of peace, and she felt prompted to confess what she had just been thinking. 'Some people don't seem to mind enough,' she said instead, mostly to herself. 'Maybe they don't realise they've anything to be ashamed of, except I've got a suspicion they flaunt it because they think there's nothing we can do . . .'

She made herself stop thinking of the Pinnocks, the child whose cries went on too long, the dirty nappy in the cot, the stale neglected smell of the bedroom, but the memories left her open to the growing chill in the air. She jumped down from the window, the soles of her sandals whacking the floor. 'I'm just going for a walk to warm myself up,' she said.

She was barely out of the cottage when she halted, clearing her throat of the taste of the air. The sun was covered not by clouds but by a bank of fog.

As she scrambled to the top of the hollow, clutching at the slippery steps with both hands, the fog rose above her, then the billowing grey tent of it collapsed towards her. Her head poked over the ridge, and the sound of the sea raced to meet her. It sounded dull and very close. Another step, and she was able to distinguish the slate-coloured waves surging out of the fog. She seized the jagged ridge and heaved herself onto it, and set her feet wide apart to fend off an unsteadiness that was at least partly due to the sight that had been awaiting her. On either side of her, and as far along the island as she could see in both directions before the fog drowned it, waves were shattering against the rock.

It was impossible to judge how far they had progressed towards the coast; she couldn't even make out the end of the ridge. The island appeared to be floating out to sea, having been dislodged by the waves and swept along by the fog. If David was on his way back with a doctor then surely his companion would prevent him from risking himself on Joelle's behalf – she only had to wait until the tide retreated, after all – but suppose he was by himself? Suppose he was lost in the fog and cut off by the tide? If she called to him and got no response, that had to mean he was safe. She covered her mouth to keep as much fog out of it as she could while she took a deep breath, then she threw the longest loudest shout she could produce. 'Daaaaviiid.'

Her voice sounded even flatter than it had inside the cottage – sopped up by the fog. The only response was a thick inert silence. If David was on the beach he would have heard her, but suppose the fog had descended while he was driving back along the unsignposted lane? The end of the lane was perilous enough in broad daylight. She took a hasty breath, only to cough and clear her throat and have to breathe again before she could shout. 'Daaaaaavid.'

'Owain.'

Joelle thought she was going to fall off the ridge. As she swung round, her feet skidding in search of new footholds, the broken sea leapt at her up the dripping blackened rocks. The voice had been little more than a whisper in the midst of the hissing and thumps of the waves, but hadn't it been accompanied by a sound of movement in dry grass? Certainly it had come from behind and below her.

She set one foot on the first step and strained her eyes at the cottage. She would have to go all the way down to see inside, though could she really have heard what she'd thought she heard when the sea was so loud? The lingering impression was making her reluctant to call out again in case she provoked a response other than David's, although why should she fear that? She didn't know what, if anything, was happening below her, and so she ought to go down. She had taken one determined step when she heard her name.

It was somewhere in the fog – David's voice was. He sounded preoccupied with whatever difficulties he was in. 'Here I am, David,' she shouted, and jumped onto the ridge, flapping her arms to maintain her balance. 'Can you see me? Can you see the island?'

'Not yet. I'll find you. Keep talking.'

He wasn't as confident as he was trying to sound. 'The tide's in,' she shouted, and swallowed a cough. 'It may be round the whole island. Are you cut off?'

'Was, but I don't think I am now.'

'I'm walking up the island to see if I can see you.' Despite the fog and the waves, both of which obscured where and how distant he was, she felt practically certain that he was between the coast and the island. She made her way along the glistening ridge, watching her feet as often as she stared into the fog. 'If you see anything moving it'll be me,' she called, and raised her head to be confronted by a scrawny shape crippled by swellings and stretching out its arms to embrace her.

The tree appeared to be offering her its decaying single fruit, on which a drop of fog gathered and then fell. She climbed past the tree and perched on the highest point of the ridge, waving her hands as if that might both render her more noticeable and clear away some of the fog. As far ahead as she could see, the waves were gulping at the island. She cupped her hands around her mouth. 'David, can you hear me? Why have you stopped talking?'

A wave smashed against the foot of the slope to her left. The thud wasn't only of water against rock. Two objects floated to the surface about a foot apart, and then a larger object which looked just as lifeless bobbed up between them. That on the left snagged on a rock for a few seconds before floundering away – long enough for Joelle to be sure that it and the others were dead fish. 'David,' she called, the fog and an indefinable panic turning her voice harsh.

His shaky response drifted out of the murk. 'I'm here. I bloody fell, that's all.'

He sounded more distant, unless his fall had left him less breath to shout with. 'Are you hurt?' Joelle called.

'Not so you'd notice.'

If he intended not to worry her, the trouble was that she could tell he did. 'Stay where you are unless you have to move,' she yelled. 'I'll walk along to see if it's worth you trying to get here.'

As she trod the ridge as fast as she dared, the sea made spiky whitish grabs at her. The fog was playing with her, retreating towards the invisible limit of the ridge and then dancing back towards her, enclosing her with the relentless surges of the waves. A break in the fog let her glimpse the tip of the ridge perhaps a hundred yards ahead, though not whether the sea had reached beyond that end of the island. She stopped in order to work loose a pebble that had begun to dig into the arch of her left foot, and the fog parted again. For a moment she had a disorienting impression that the island had been transformed into the long boat which it resembled, because the prow had risen several feet higher. A silhouette had climbed onto it, that was why, and was looming ahead of her.

It was David, of course. She knew that without needing to see his face. While she made her way to him through the fog he stumbled higher on the ridge to meet her. Beyond him she saw the waves rushing past the island and rebounding against it, growing deeper as she watched. No wonder David's trousers were soaked as far up as the knees. His shirt was stained with patches of sand; there was sand in his carroty hair, which was untidier than ever, and his broad round wide-mouthed face looked weighed down, his blue eyes almost as dull as the fog. 'Sorry,' he said like a schoolboy caught at something stupid. 'I didn't even get to land. I got lost in the fog and then the sea came up behind me.'

'I expect I would have.'

'Come up behind me? I wish you had.'

'Got lost,' she said, brushing sand off his fingers. 'Well, you've had a good time at the seaside, haven't you? How bad is it out there? Are we cut off?'

'Even if the fog lifts I think we're stuck here for a while.'

'Let's hope we're off by nightfall.'

'We can hope. I don't suppose you've any kind of a snack in your bag to keep us going.'

'I may have some chocolate. Let's go and see.'

'I wouldn't mind leaning on you.'

'Have you hurt yourself? Why didn't you say?'

'Just a twisted ankle, not even a sprain. I won't be challenging you to any more races today, that's all.'

They had to walk in single file along the ridge, Joelle leading, David resting a hand on her shoulder. There was no point in trying to talk further until they reached the hollow, and so it wasn't until she was helping him down the steps that he said rather shamefacedly 'How is she?'

'She was breathing when I left her,' Joelle said, and turned to the cottage as he hobbled down the last few steps. The sight of the immobile white form on the pallet robbed her of breath until she went close enough to see the rise and fall of the draped breasts. 'She's the same,' she told David.

'All we can do is watch her until we can get off the island.'

Joelle heard him trying to reassure her, but he didn't yet know why she'd sounded uneasy. 'David,' she murmured as he came over to her, 'I thought she spoke.'

'I didn't hear anything.'

'Not now. Just about when I started calling to you.'

He squinted fiercely at the sleeper as though that might rouse her. 'Did you hear what she said?'

Joelle was beginning to regret having raised the subject while they were in the low dim tomb-like room. 'Owain,' she whispered.

He took hold of her shoulder to make her look at him. 'Owain?' he said loudly in disbelief.

She raised a finger to hush him, but her hand faltered in mid-air. She stared at him, at his expression mirroring her own wide eyes and open mouth. This time there was no question that the woman on the bed had spoken. 'That's my name,' she'd said.

# Four

It seemed to Joelle that she and David were trapped in one of their private games – that whoever looked first at the woman would lose. In reality no more than a few seconds could have passed before David turned to the bed and she followed his gaze. The woman's eyes were open.

They were so grey that the irises resembled two slate discs embedded in the marble of the whites, and they were staring at the underside of the roof. Apart from them, only her mouth had moved, drooping open as if the words had exhausted her. 'Are you feeling better?' David said uncertainly. 'Do you want to sit up?'

'Can we do anything for you?' Joelle said.

The woman expelled a long slow breath which might have been a sigh of relief. She raised her head, but she had barely focused on the Owains when it sank back onto the wad of rustling grass. 'Would you have anything to eat about you?' she managed to pronounce, and closed her eyes.

'I think I have.' Joelle grabbed her handbag and rummaged in it. Keys, address book, half a packet of Kleenex, a wad of Home-Makers business cards in a rubber band, her purse thin with banknotes, half a ticket from Paul McCartney's return to Liverpool, lipstick, a sample sachet of a perfume called Seduction which had scented her bag without even being opened – a large bar of Fruit and Nut chocolate. It had broken into several irregular pieces, but the foil was intact within the scuffed wrapper. 'Can you eat chocolate?' she said.

'Anything you offer me.' The woman blinked her eyes before fixing them on Joelle, and raised her left hand with an effort to point her fingers at her mouth. 'Could you put it in for me?'

Joelle tore off the wrapper and gave it to David to tidy into his trousers pocket while she opened the foil. Selecting a medium-sized chunk she said 'Shall I lift your head?'

'You needn't trouble. I won't choke.'

27

'There are nuts in it.'

'I still have all my teeth,' the woman said, and showed them in a momentary grin. They were very white. She opened her mouth wide and closed her eyes, and Joelle was reminded both of her own first French kiss and of taking communion when as a child she had attended church. She let the chocolate fall less than an inch onto the pale tongue, and the woman closed her mouth. Perhaps she was savouring the chocolate, because Joelle had to hold her breath for a painfully long time before the woman's jaws moved and her teeth bit through a nut with an explosive crunch. 'What an odd taste,' she mumbled.

'I hope it's all right. I hope it hasn't been in my bag too long.'

The woman closed her fists around two handfuls of dead vegetation as if that gave her the strength to raise her head and fix the Owains with a stare of friendly reproof. As her head subsided she said 'You both have some. We must share.'

Her voice was firmer, her Welsh lilt more sinuous. The snack was doing her good, Joelle thought, breaking a piece more or less in half and handing David the larger portion. The chocolate did taste faintly of Seduction. There was silence except for their crunching, which they did their best to muffle. 'That's better,' said the woman, and extended a hand. 'Let me share it out for you.'

When she raised her almost invisible eyebrows Joelle placed the rest of the chocolate in her hand. The long fingers were colder than the room now, and Joelle was overcome by a shiver. 'Is that all you have to wear?' the woman said.

'While we're here,' David admitted.

'See what you can find in the next room, I beg you. There are things people brought me.'

'I'll go,' David said, and hobbled to the inner door so quickly that Joelle thought he was anxious to put some distance between himself and the woman; then she realised that after his soaking he must be even colder than she was. The door swung shut behind him, fitting into its frame with a satisfied thump.

'So people do visit you,' Joelle said.

'Only when they have to.'

'But at least you've a family nearby.'

'Have I?' The woman gazed at her with a blankness which she seemed to expect Joelle to fill somehow. At last she said 'Not for a very long time.'

Joelle felt bound to ask the next question, but reluctant too. 'What was your name again?'

'Gwendolen. Gwen.'

'Oh, *Gwen*,' David said, sounding exasperated with himself, as he reappeared from the inner room. He was cradling an armful of three large blankets, multicoloured but faded. 'Were these what you meant, Gwen? If you don't mind me being so familiar.'

'I always like people to feel at their ease with me, especially if you're likely to be with me for a while.'

David handed her and Joelle blankets and draped the third around himself. 'Chocolate. Chocolate,' Gwendolen said, giving the Owains a generous piece each. 'You won't stand there like my guardian angels until the fog lets you go.'

'I didn't see any chairs,' David said.

'They would only remind me there was nobody to sit in them,' Gwendolen said with a shrug that rustled the grass as though wings were stirring at her shoulders. She pulled the blanket over her breasts and fed herself the last of the chocolate from the foil, which she crumpled and threw into a corner of the room. 'It isn't often I can be untidy,' she said through the mouthful and, resting one hand on the pallet, swung her feet in three jerky movements to the floor. 'Now there's room for us all.'

'Are you sure you wouldn't rather stay lying down?' Joelle protested. 'At least you'll tell us if you feel you want to.'

'I know I shan't. You two have brought me back to life. I only wish I had some food and drink to offer you.' Gwendolen dabbed at her lips with the blanket, a gesture which made her seem momentarily much older, and patted the bed on either side of her. Before the Owains could respond to the invitation she looked coy and shifted herself to the head of the pallet. 'You two will want to be together,' she said, 'David and Joelle.'

David clutched at his blanket as it almost slipped away from him. 'How do you—'

'I told her,' Joelle explained, and met Gwendolen's eyes. 'Did you hear everything I said?'

'Every word. Didn't you intend me to?'

'Of course, or I wouldn't have . . .' Joelle trailed off, unable to recall how much she had thought rather than said.

'I'm sorry if you thought I was dead to the world. I just had to get my energy back. You become used to sleeping when there's nothing else to do.'

Joelle waited until David took the middle of the pallet before she sat down. 'So you've heard a bit about us, have you?' he asked Gwendolen.

'I know you're a kind young couple who couldn't be more welcome in my house.'

David stared out at the fog which was lapping at the edge of the hollow. 'Do you have any idea how long the weather's likely to carry on like this?'

'It comes and goes.'

'Like – well, anyway.'

He'd almost said 'Like a rabbit', Joelle knew. She grinned sidelong at him, and was taken aback to see Gwendolen laying a hand on top of his and giving him a tolerant knowing smile. Joelle leaned over David and said 'Have you been living here long?'

'I used to like moving on.'

That and its wistfulness hardly seemed to constitute an answer, but surely Gwendolen's age entitled her to be vague now and then. Joelle tried again. 'People do know you're here.'

'They used to row out to me.'

'When did they stop?' David demanded.

'Time means little at my age.'

'But you can't have been living like this for long, all by yourself.'

Gwendolen patted his arm. 'When you have to live you just get on with it, I find.'

David gave up, looking so frustrated that Joelle rubbed her shoulder against his. 'What's this place called?' she asked.

'They had an old name for it.'

Joelle waited, but apparently that was all, because Gwendolen sat back and closed her eyes. David was poised to speak when Gwendolen said 'And what brought you two here?'

'We thought—' Joelle began, and decided against mentioning the figure they had thought they'd seen; it might unnerve Gwendolen and besides, it must have been the tree. 'We just wanted to see what was out here.'

'And ended up saddled with me.'

'Hardly saddled,' David said.

'I knew you'd be too kind to say so. Tell yourself it's good for the soul.' Gwendolen was gazing at the fog, which had closed over the hollow like an inverted stagnant pool. 'How shall we pass the time?'

After an awkward pause David said 'We play games.'

'I knew you did.'

'With words,' Joelle told her.

'I too. It's good to have something in your head to keep you company.' Gwendolen clapped her hands softly. 'Will you go, David?'

'Fog.'

'Grey,' Joelle said.

'Head,' Gwendolen said at once.

'Wise,' David said.

'Owl.'

'Omen.'

'Future.'

'Past.'

'Sins.'

For a moment Joelle thought David was about to query Gwendolen's response, but he said 'Forgive.'

'Forget,' said Joelle.

'Bury.'

'Goose.'

'Oh, *David*,' Joelle protested. 'Gooseberry back at you.'

'More than one word. Gwen's turn.'

'Game.'

'Hunter,' David said.

Gwendolen looked puzzled, as though she hadn't meant 'game' in that sense; maybe she'd been thinking of some bygone pastime. She rallied and said 'Hungry.'

'Eat.'

There was a longer pause before Gwendolen responded 'Swallow.'

'Summer.'

'Storm.'

'Strike.'

'Iron.'

'Ah,' David said, 'blacksmith.'

Joelle could have called for a new game on the grounds that he'd uttered more than one word, but she was happy just to listen: the pauses between responses seemed to be lengthening, the way gaps grew between the numbers you were asked to count when you'd been given an anaesthetic. 'Village,' Gwendolen said.

'Cross.'

'Churchyard.'

'Peace.'

'Eternal.'

For a moment Gwendolen sounded as though she'd forgotten the words were only a game. 'Infernal,' David countered.

'Earth.'

Hell on earth, thought Joelle, which was presumably the connection, though if she were David she would query it. She was considering raising the question herself, although David had already said 'Electricity', when she must have nodded off, because the next thing she heard was Gwendolen saying 'Fluid.' Or did that fit? Perhaps David was wondering too, because there was silence while Joelle's thoughts stumbled and bumped amiably into one another in the murk inside her head. She never knew what conclusion he reached, for when she wakened, the game had ended and David and Gwendolen were deep in conversation. 'They used to tell me I looked like her,' David was saying.

Joelle managed to hoist her eyelids. The room was darker, but she could just see that he was holding a photograph, brown and cracked and curled as a dead leaf. It showed a large family group, surrounded and partly erased by an oval iris. In the midst of them, wearing what Joelle instinctively identified as a confirmation dress, was a solemn young girl whose features were so familiar that for a dreamy instant she thought it was David in drag as a child. Joelle would have asked who she was except that going back to sleep was easier.

The next time she wakened, the room was wholly dark. She was nestling against David, who had wrapped the two blankets about them and put an arm around her waist, his hand resting on her thigh. She could hear his breathing, and the sound beyond him must be Gwendolen's, although it sounded slow and eternal as the sea.

When Joelle wakened again she was lying alone on the pallet, cocooned in the blankets. The cold gripped her face, and the shock of it snatched her eyes open. David was outside the cottage, jogging on the spot and rubbing his arms. Her call to him turned into a cough. 'That was a good sleep. We're ready when you are,' he said.

'But we can't—' she said, then saw that it wasn't fog which lay greyly in the hollow, it was the dawn. 'You said we,' she realised, contriving to sit up without relinquishing the blankets or their warmth.

A creak of the inner door alerted her to Gwendolen emerging from the other room, gripping her blanket about her with one hand and holding an almost shapeless leather bag by its neck with the other. 'I hope you don't mind, Joelle. David said you two would help me to the village.'

'It's the least we can do for my long-lost relative,' David said.

# Five

Joelle looked as though she wasn't sure she was awake, and David knew how she felt. Although it seemed that he and Gwendolen had been talking for most of the night, he could recall hardly anything they'd said. His one clear memory was of the photograph she'd shown him just before total darkness fell – the photograph of his father's mother as a child, who had apparently been a distant cousin of Gwendolen's, though close enough for Gwendolen to have been visible at the extreme left-hand edge of the image. It was at least as real to him as any of his present sensations, his eyes feeling as if a wind had been blowing sand in them, his limbs deciding between stiff and shivery, the object which felt both cumbersome and weightless in his skull and which was his brain – it was almost more real than Joelle's bemused voice. 'So your name was Owain after all,' she said.

'I don't think David quite believed it until he saw my picture.'

'I saw it too,' Joelle said slowly. 'I thought I might have been dreaming.'

'Take my word for it,' Gwendolen said, and let the inner door thud shut behind her. 'Do you mind if we go soon?'

'God, I'm sorry. I'm wasting your strength.' Joelle threw off the blankets and gasped as the early-morning chill washed over her. 'Lean on me if you need to.'

'I thought we'd give Gwen breakfast at the hotel.'

'My treat,' Gwendolen insisted, shaking the leather bag, which sounded full of coins.

'And then is there someone in the village we can take you to?' Joelle said.

It wouldn't do to patronise Gwendolen – the night had taught David that much. 'You'd think so, would you?' Gwendolen said, and stepped out of the cottage. He moved towards her, his ankle aching no more than several other parts of him, in case he could help, but she halted him with a gracious gesture while still hugging

33

the blanket to herself with the rest of her arm. 'Unless you would carry my bag,' she said.

'Certainly.' He took hold of the neck, which was throttled by a frayed cord. The bag was even heavier than it had sounded. 'You don't carry this as a rule, do you?'

'I've never been afraid of theft. My money's safe as any in the world.'

Presumably that was a negative answer, but Joelle was frowning at her back as though Gwendolen was being wilfully obscure. 'Don't you want to change into something more—'

'I'm comfortable, thank you, Joelle,' Gwendolen said, and wound the blanket more firmly about herself.

'Ladies,' David said, and stood at the foot of the steps to help them up. Gwendolen supported herself on his forearm and then climbed steadily, touching the wall of the hollow with her fingertips at each step. 'Don't you want to take a blanket?' he murmured to Joelle as she reached him.

'I'll be fine so long as we keep moving. Do *you* need a hand?'

'Not even a finger,' David said, leaning his weight on his ankle in the hope that would lance his drowsiness, and followed her up the steps.

Gwendolen was already at the tree. During the night the single fruit must have dropped, for the branch was bare. The tide had withdrawn beyond the island, having inscribed its underlying patterns on the sand. Mist hovered just beyond the margin of the sea and lingered on the mainland, where the fields beyond the cliff above the deserted village looked faded as an old photograph. David hurried after the women in case Gwendolen needed help, though she seemed the surest of any of them on the ridge.

It was only when she reached the landward end of the island that she grew uncertain how to proceed. 'I'll go first,' Joelle said, and lowered herself down the rock until she reached a foothold wide enough for two people. Gwendolen hesitated, pinching the blanket together at her throat, then waved David onwards with an impatience which he suspected was aimed at herself. 'I can manage as far as that. You two go down to the beach.'

David clambered laboriously down to Joelle and watched her find the least precarious route over the slippery rocks at the bottom of the island. Once he'd joined her on the beach he tried to clear the way further by tearing off handfuls of slimy seaweed and flinging them across the sand. Gwendolen was on the ledge about ten feet up, pressing her shoulders against the rock above it as though she was on the edge of an abyss, and David wondered if she behaved like this every time she left the island. Perhaps she was suddenly feeling old. 'Shall I come back up?' he called.

'No, don't do that.' The proposal appeared to dismay her. 'Stay there. Just tell me, tell me to—'

'Come on, Gwen,' Joelle said. 'We've got you.'

Apparently that was all Gwendolen needed. She unwound the blanket and sent it sailing like a magic carpet above the beach, and as it flopped on the sand she came down the rocks so swiftly that the Owains thought she was falling. They reached their hands up just in time for Gwendolen to use them both to support herself in her leap off the island. She felt so light that David imagined her flying, skimming over the beach towards the mainland. She made a graceful landing and ran to snatch her blanket and wrap it around herself. 'Don't stop now,' she said breathlessly. 'We mustn't have you two catching cold on my behalf.'

'I hope I have that much energy when I'm her age,' David murmured as Gwendolen strode towards the deserted village. The blanket flapped behind her, and he thought she looked like a great bird swooping across the beach. The heels of her dusty black boots dug crescents in the sand, a trail of identical fixed grins. She didn't slow down until she arrived at the foot of the path up the cliff, having skirted the village. She was glaring at the ruined cottages in what might have been dislike or triumph when the Owains reached her, but at once she gave her companions an encouraging smile. 'Take it steady,' she said.

By the time he and Joelle were halfway up the path they were having to rest at each bend while Gwendolen halted above them. If nothing else, David thought as he sat with Joelle on the least uncomfortable rock and took deep breaths with an aftertaste of fog and waited for his heartbeats to stop making his whole body throb, life on the island had toughened her up, so much so that he wondered why she had needed their help. In a moment he felt ashamed of wondering; even if she was capable of walking to the nearest village, did he begrudge her the ride? He shoved himself to his feet, bruising the heel of his hand on a spiky rock, and forced himself to climb, panting and staggering, without a pause until he was able to drag himself over the edge to the car.

He leaned against the Volvo, which gave him more support than his legs had left in them, while Joelle toiled up the last stretch of path. The fog had returned to the beach around the island, which looked abandoned by the landscape. As Joelle slapped the car roof as though it was the finishing post in a game and emitted a phew of relief, Gwendolen turned her back on the island. The fog closed around it, though to David it appeared to collapse like a trampled fungus, puffing out greyness, and he realised how little sleep he'd had. 'Maybe you could drive,' he said to Joelle.

'Don't you want another crack at that thing they call a road?'

'You must say if I'm too much trouble,' Gwendolen said.

'No trouble,' Joelle told her. 'Just a private joke.'

Before long the twisting road began to make David feel sick. Hedges lurched at him out of a mist and grew greener as they came. He closed his eyes until the Volvo turned onto the main road, whose meanderings, once he'd swallowed a couple of times, were bearable. He glanced at Gwendolen's face in the driving mirror. She seemed entranced by the passing show – mist glittering minutely on the hairs of the moss on the walls, transforming clumps of ferns into jewelled green crowns, turning distant trees into intricate cut-outs of uniform grey – and her delight renewed the spectacle for him.

The sun was clearing mist out of the fishing village. A milk float groaned uphill past a cycling postman with an empty bag under his arm, the chimney of a cottage threaded the blue sky with smoke. As Joelle steered the car alongside the pavement in front of the boarding-house, Mrs Thomas was straightening up from the doorstep with a wire basket loaded with four milk-bottles in her hand. '*Well*,' she said loudly with reference to the reappearance of her guests or the sight of Gwendolen allowing the blanket to slip onto the back seat as she stepped out of the car.

David felt absurdly guilty. 'I'm sorry, Mrs Thomas, we've been stranded all night with no way of letting anyone know.'

'I had to get our policeman out of bed.' She was staring at the stained legs of David's trousers. 'Climbing, were you?'

'Just walking. We'd have been fine except for the fog.'

'It doesn't do to go too far round here unless you're sure of what you're doing.'

'Yes, well, we weren't just wandering. We did have—' David said, indicating Gwendolen, and lost patience with justifying himself. 'We'd like to invite a guest for breakfast if that won't put you out too much.'

'Breakfast isn't until eight,' Mrs Thomas said, and in the same tone, verging on discouragement: 'Was your friend lost too?'

'No, she lives not far from here. Without a phone, unfortunately. Or very much else,' Joelle added, and seemed to regret having presumed to do so.

'She did our best for us, and now we are for her.'

'I suppose she's got a name.'

'Gwendolen,' David said. 'Owain, like us.'

When the landlady revived the scepticism with which she'd met their name Joelle said 'It's a long story. Shall we tell it to you inside?'

'I thought you were after your breakfasts.' Mrs Thomas sounded more accusing than concerned as she said 'When did you last have a proper meal?'

'Us, yesterday afternoon. Gwen?'

'It depends what you mean by proper,' Gwendolen said, and with a firmness that made David wonder if it was a failure of her memory she resented having attention drawn to: 'I really can't recall.'

'Will bacon, eggs and sausages do you?' Mrs Thomas said.

'Whatever you can spare,' Gwendolen said. 'I'm used to eating what's put in front of me.'

Mrs Thomas clearly didn't know whether to be insulted. She pointed the way to the bathroom, which when it was David's turn to use it smelled like a large cold flower. By the time he emerged, the aromas of breakfast were inviting him to the dining room.

Apart from the one where Joelle and Gwendolen were sitting, the several tables were surrounded by chairs leaning forward on their front legs as though inspecting the tablecloths. A Welsh dresser and every other available surface, including the backs of the chairs, were draped in frilly linen. Beyond a window, tall plants were tolling silent purple bells in a breeze. As David joined the women he heard the purr of a telephone dial in Mrs Thomas's office and then her saying 'Glenys? Is Elwyn there? When he comes in you can tell him the guests I had to ring about –' before the clunk of the door truncated her voice.

David gave Joelle and Gwendolen a grin which he meant to express complicity and resignation, and looked around the room. A framed map beside the dresser showed the Lleyn Peninsula, though it wasn't very detailed: it didn't include either the deserted village or Gwendolen's island. The fishing village was the nearest community to the island by a good few miles, he saw. 'So have you many friends here, Gwen?' Joelle said.

'It hasn't been easy for me to make friends, but when I do I keep them for life.'

'Us too,' David felt compelled to respond. 'I think Joelle means you do know some local people.'

'If they want to know me. They're a close lot, you may have noticed.'

'But you're from round here, aren't you?' Joelle said.

'As Welsh as the mountains, I am.'

At this point Mrs Thomas reappeared. 'Our policeman's only this minute come home,' she said, 'and now he's had to go after some dogs that are worrying the sheep, otherwise he'd be wanting a word with you two.'

'I hope you passed on our apologies,' David said.

'I'm not sure we've much to apologise for,' Joelle said. 'As a matter of fact—'

Gwendolen touched the back of Joelle's hand. 'Never mind, Joelle. I appreciated your help.'

Mrs Thomas flounced into the kitchen and let fly a barrage of Welsh, which sent forth a large red-faced girl in a skin-tight apron, bearing a tray crammed with three cups and a coffee-pot. The cups stopped chattering in their saucers once she'd placed them on the table, and most of the coffee she poured landed inside the cups. She fled into the kitchen to meet another outburst of Welsh. 'Can you understand that?' Joelle asked Gwendolen.

'Pretty much what you'd expect. Just some pettiness.'

The Welsh explosions continued at intervals, and Gwendolen looked more amused by each offstage monologue and less inclined to translate. The blushing girl brought a trayful of three plates with a sausage and a fried egg and a curl of bacon on each, and Gwendolen made an appreciative sound which mightn't, David thought, have been the joke which Mrs Thomas in the kitchen doorway took it for. Two very young children whom the smell of breakfast had tempted along the hall giggled at Gwendolen, who winked at them, then bolted upstairs to their parents. 'You haven't any children,' Gwendolen said to Joelle.

'David told you, did he?'

'He said it was his fault, as though it was something to be blamed for,' Gwendolen said, favouring David with a gentle frown. 'Just so long as you two make the most of your life together.'

'And you should make the most of yours,' David blurted.

'I intend to now.'

'Now?' said Joelle.

38

'While I can.'

Nobody had anything further to say until Gwendolen crunched her last mouthful and sat back. 'Did you want some more of anything?' Joelle said.

'Only of your company.'

'That isn't limited.'

'I'm glad for it.'

Gwendolen seemed puzzled by David's choice of words, not that they had been any great shakes as a pun. The aproned girl removed their plates and saved him from feeling bound to explain. 'You might ask Mrs Thomas if we can pay when she has a moment,' he said.

Gwendolen picked up her jangling bag. 'You mustn't think of it,' Joelle told her. 'You gave us everything you could at your house.'

'Not quite everything,' Gwendolen said as Mrs Thomas bustled out of the kitchen, wiping her hands on a Welsh souvenir towel which she hung on the door-handle. 'Off again already?' Mrs Thomas complained. 'There's some never seem to stop wandering. I'll have to charge you for your room, you know.'

'We never thought otherwise,' Joelle said. 'I take it our suitcase is up there? Come up with me, Gwen, if you want to use the mirror.'

'Don't I look all right?'

'You look perfect.' Gwendolen had sounded so anxious that David spoke more vehemently than he meant to, though indeed eating seemed to have rejuvenated her. 'Doesn't she, Jo? And so do you.'

Mrs Thomas suffered this exchange before beckoning David into her office to entrust him with the key. In the bedroom, linen dangled tassels from the bed and dressing-table and a single chair, and a framed text – 'Use hospitality one to another' – occupied the wall above the virgin pillows. He was changing his clothes at last when Joelle tapped at the door, having paid the bill. 'Not my idea of where to spend a sinful weekend,' she said, pulling her T-shirt over her head, and caught his wrist when he started to stroke her back. 'Better not while the new member of the family's waiting for us.'

'You don't mind that she is, do you?'

'Why should I mind? She's harmless and sad, and we ought to take care of her before we go home. I'm rather hoping that policeman may come back while we're here. I've got his address.

But maybe we should take her round the village in case she meets someone who knows her.'

'And ask them . . .'

'Where she lives. She couldn't have been living out there long.'

'Wouldn't it be simpler to ask her where?'

'But not very kind, David, if she has to admit she doesn't know. Maybe she'll remember while we're walking and we won't have to ask.'

'I'll keep an eye on her,' David said, and closed the door on the sight of Joelle's panties slipping down her bottom as she wriggled out of her skirt. Now he could see into the hall. He'd left Gwendolen waiting in the sunlight at the foot of the stairs, but there was no sign of her, and the front door was open.

He felt as though he and Joelle had been unforgivably careless. He ran downstairs, his ankle giving a reminiscent twinge, and saw her standing on the garden path. Seen from the stairs, she resembled a lost child. The similarity took his emotions unawares, so that when she turned to him he had to fake a sneeze in order to dab at his eyes. 'We thought we might have a wander round the village to stretch our legs.'

'That's what they used to do to witches.'

'Hah,' David gasped, turning his surprise into mirth. When she glanced at him, one eyebrow raised as if she was ready to let it and the joke drop, he burst out laughing, and so did she. He had the impression that she mightn't have laughed for quite some time, and the more she did the more girlish she sounded, which struck him as funny too. They were still giggling when Joelle brought the suitcase down and handed the key to the landlady. 'You two seem to be getting on well,' she said.

'Don't vex yourself. I'm no threat,' Gwendolen told her, 'unless he has a lust for older women.'

'*Well*,' Mrs Thomas said at the top of her voice, and rattled the key like a jailor.

Gwendolen gazed innocently at her. 'No reason to lose any sleep, Mrs Thomas. I'm sure *you're* safe.'

As soon as Joelle stepped onto the path the landlady closed the door behind her. 'Well, there wasn't much room at that inn,' Gwendolen remarked loudly enough to be heard through the door, and was rewarded with an angry jangle of the key.

Her wicked mood deserted her as swiftly as it had manifested itself. When David had unlocked the boot of the Volvo and stowed the case she said 'Would my bag be safe there, do you suppose?'

'I'm sure it would. I can't imagine there are many thieves round here.'

'Everyone has secrets,' Gwendolen reflected in a tone David couldn't quite identify, and watched him lock up her bag. 'Are we to walk anywhere particular?'

'Where would you like to go?' said Joelle.

'I'm content just to wander.'

David thought she might be trying not to acknowledge a lapse of memory. 'Nothing wrong with that,' he said.

It took longer than he was anticipating to walk through the village, largely because of the cant of the streets. Joelle led the way down to the main road, where on a curve out of sight of the few concessions to holidaymakers they found a block of shops – a fishmonger's with a stone slab like an altar in the window, a greengrocer's where the empty wooden trays big enough for someone to lie in looked darkened by soil, a chemist's displaying a giant stoppered jug of purple glass. 'Are these shops any good, Gwen?' Joelle said.

'I'm sure they must be as shops go.'

'And how's that?' David asked.

'Forgive me, I don't mean to be unhelpful.'

David couldn't help feeling wryly amused by the frustration he was sharing with Joelle. The three of them turned along the next side street, the last before the road led out towards the hills that were reclaiming all their colours from the mist, and made their way up the uncompromising slope. On the main road they had encountered only a passing car, and the side street was deserted. The colours and scents of the flowers with which the small gardens were packed were sharpened by the stark whiteness of the lines of empty houses. 'Everyone must have gone up,' Gwendolen said.

She was pointing heavenward, or at least to the top of the village, where a steep-roofed church spiked the blue sky with its grey spire. 'I wouldn't mind a closer look,' Joelle said.

Though they followed a route which managed to include all the streets below the church, Gwendolen gave no sign of recognising any of them. At one point Joelle went along a garden path and rang a doorbell, but there was no police car outside the house, and no response from within. Further up they began to hear the blare of an organ and the congregation singing in Welsh. 'Let's wait until the service is over,' Joelle said, 'and then we can see inside.'

A graveyard surrounded the church and climbed the hill above it. Along the marble avenues, angels raised their hands as though

41

directing the traffic of souls. In the silence between hymns a bird was singing in a yew tree, a sound that sunlight on ripples might have made if it could be rendered audible. David unlatched the wooden gate in the low plump wall and let Joelle into the churchyard while Gwendolen gazed at a line of boats that were rooted in the bay. 'Aren't you coming, Gwen?' Joelle said, and Gwendolen followed her at once.

A hymn which sounded joyous enough to be final commenced as David closed the gate. Gwendolen was striding past the church to the oldest graves, where moss rather than bagged bouquets decorated the headstones. David watched her stoop to a slab that was leaning backwards and begin to stroke its green fur. He was making for her when Joelle caught his arm. 'She'll be all right, David. We can have a quiet word with the minister while she's exploring.'

Gwendolen was touching the moss in order to trace the inscription beneath it, David realised now. She moved to the next stone as the hymn ended with a long deep organ note. The minister's voice echoed briefly, and was followed by a chorus of shuffling shot through with an organ voluntary. As the porch door opened and the congregation began to emerge past the minister, who shook their hands and emitted homilies, David stepped back to watch. Everyone glanced at him and Joelle and then at Gwendolen, but not a man or woman or child appeared to recognise any of them.

The minister was retreating into the porch, having seen off the last of his parishioners, when Joelle overtook him. 'Excuse me, have you a moment?'

'Always.'

He was a pudgy middle-aged man with a face pale as innocence except for purple veins which marked his cheeks like leaf-prints on paper. As with every minister David had encountered, his black uniform looked dusty. 'Welcome to St David's,' he said. 'Would you care for the tour?'

'Could we just talk?' Joelle said. 'You're English, aren't you?'

'As cricket and rain,' he responded, obviously not for the first time. 'Most Welsh people don't burn down your house just because they hear an accent from over the border.'

'Have you been here long, my wife means.'

'Five years come the first of March.'

'So you'll know most of the people round here,' Joelle said.

'There isn't a soul who's managed to hide from me so far as I know. When the man in black comes calling they know God's looking over their shoulder.' He fixed his sky-blue gaze on her and said 'Whom can I help you to find?'

Joelle pointed over her shoulder like a stone angel. 'Whoever her friends are, we hope.'

The minister blinked at Gwendolen as she moved along a line of eroded gravestones. 'What would their names be, I wonder?'

'We don't know,' Joelle said, lowering her voice, 'and we think she may not either. But don't you recognise her?'

'I'd be fibbing if I said I did. Isn't she here with you?'

'In a way she is,' David said, 'in fact she's a distant relative, too distant for me even to know. We found her living rough last night, just off the coast round there. Do you visit people outside, oh, er . . .'

He gestured impatiently at the village, but the minister pronounced the name without faltering. 'I go to the farms, of course, but I'm certain nobody is living offshore. Someone besides me would have known they were there and told me. I always make a point of finding out who the nearest neighbours are.'

David was grateful both that he didn't live in the man's parish and, more grudgingly, that the minister was so thorough. 'Can you really be sure she doesn't come from your village?'

'Not in the years I've been here, as God is my judge.' He clasped his hands over his stomach, the prayer of a contented man. 'Is there anything else I can help with?'

'Would you mind having a word with her?'

'That was understood, of course,' the minister said primly. 'May I know the lady's name?'

'Gwendolen Owain.'

'You see, we have no Owains in this parish. Is it your name and your wife's too?'

'It would have to be, wouldn't it?'

'Then I expect you'll have more idea than I where to find it.' The minister made his way between the turfy mounds to Gwendolen, who was mouthing the aged inscriptions and smiling to herself. 'Gwendolen, isn't it?' he said, rubbing his palms together so heartily that David could hear them across the churchyard. 'Interested in our traditions, are you?'

'They made me.'

She'd turned the smile on him, which increased his heartiness. 'So how are we today?'

'Better than I have been since I can remember.'

'Let's hope you continue to be blessed with a good life. Did I miss seeing you in church today?'

'It's been a long time since I was in a church.'

'You mustn't let that make you feel unwelcome.'

'That doesn't,' Gwendolen said, and stared at him.

David was restraining himself from taking charge of the conversation when the minister said 'Your family tells me you've been living – now, where did they find you?'

'Off the coast as far as I could go.'

'My dear lady, why would you want to do that?'

Gwendolen reached to pat his hand across a horizontal slab cracked by age and framed with ragged grass. 'You're too young and too holy to know.'

'I assure you, Miss Owain, I've encountered most of the worst that people are capable of. It comes with the cloth.'

'Then that makes two of us,' Gwendolen said, sounding less than convinced of his worldliness.

'It is Miss, is it, or Ms? Would you—'

'It's Miss. I don't know the other thing. What were you going to offer me?'

'I was wondering if you might like a private talk with me.'

Gwendolen gave him a coy look. 'Why, whatever can you have in mind? Do your flock know what's under your uniform?'

The purple blotches on the minister's cheeks grew alarmingly larger. 'Perhaps at least I may know where you come from.'

'May you? Oh, I see, you're asking. Far away and long ago, from a place you won't have heard of.'

'I assume it has a name.'

'Everything does for those who know it.'

If she was growing defensive, that was presumably because the minister was forcing her to acknowledge to herself that she'd forgotten, and he relented. 'Would you happen to know who your nearest relatives are?'

'David and Joelle here are the only ones I know of.'

'Then you're lucky to have them.' The minister nodded to them and made a gesture which either embraced them and Gwendolen at a distance or urged them together. 'Do excuse me now, will you? I shall be in my house if I'm required,' he said, and hurried away, blackly flapping.

He wasn't past the gate when Gwendolen said to the Owains 'If I embarrassed you I'm sorry. I've good reason not to care for priests.'

The latch of the gate clicked like a gun with an empty chamber, and David avoided glancing after the minister. 'We'll be in the church,' he told Gwendolen.

Beyond the porch with its racks of bilingual pamphlets about AIDS and drugs and famines and prayer, the long narrow nave shone with pine and white stone. A monk filled with light as the sun found his stained-glass window. He was reading a Bible while hauling a plough and treading on a wine-bottle. David and Joelle sat in his light at the end of a pew. 'At least the questions you wanted to ask got asked,' David said.

'But he didn't get the answers we wanted to hear.'

'Do you think she could have been born round here, whatever she told him? That could be why she came back.'

'It doesn't really help, does it, if she's got nobody here now and she's been wandering for however long she has. By the way, David, we shouldn't leave her out there by herself for too long in case she goes wandering off.'

'She seems happy enough reading what was said about folk. All the same, what are we going to do about her?'

Joelle sighed and turned her palms up towards the severe window. 'I wish I knew. I wish someone would come and tell us.'

'I think the least we can decently—'

David heard the inner door open behind them with a sound like a single large heartbeat. As he turned he was hoping that the minister might have returned with an idea, and so he was abashed when he saw Gwendolen. She halted just beyond the ray through the window as if it was dazzling her. 'I wonder if you know of anywhere that would put up with me? I'd pay my way,' she said.

# Six

'Herb,' Mary called, and at once he was awake, though for a
moment he thought she was in the double bed with him. He was
sprawled across most of it, straitjacketed by the quilt, which
he'd managed to wrap around himself in his sleep. When the
doorbell rang again he struggled into a sitting position, and his
left leg was instantly impaled by a cramp. He bit his tongue in
the effort not to scream as he rolled off the bed and fell to his
knees on the carpet. The cramp sprang him to his feet, and he
hurled the quilt away, draping the dressing-table as though he
wanted to conceal how bare it was now. Emptied hangers
jangled in the wardrobe as he lurched moaning to the window
and heaved at the sash.

He'd kept meaning to ask David Owain to ease it, and now it was
sticking more stubbornly than ever. At least he could see Mary,
who had retreated to the end of the garden, her garden, which it
was already apparent he had no idea how to care for. 'Can't you let
yourself in?' he shouted as loud as the pain in his tongue would
allow.

She looked up from frowning at the weeds in her flowerbeds.
She was wearing the blue dress he liked, which left her shoulders
almost bare and which he hadn't seen her in since last summer. A
breeze parted the foliage of the tree outside the garden and let the
Sunday morning sunlight illuminate her face as she turned it to
him. Her glossy black hair swayed back from her small ears as
though it was exhibiting her dark eyes, her nose whose upturned
tip he'd loved to kiss, her pale pink lips which he could almost
taste. She looked resigned to the sight of him hopping and writhing
at the window. 'I'll ow,' he shouted, biting his tongue again. 'I'll
come down, shall I?'

When she responded with the patient gaze she'd trained on him
more and more frequently that year, and perhaps earlier than that
if he had only noticed, Herb stumbled away from the window,
thumping the floor with the heel of his left foot as if that might

dislodge his problem. When at last he succeeded in turning up his toes far enough to terminate the cramp he limped out of the room and swayed downstairs like a drunken sailor, past the hooks which he'd hammered into the wall for Mary's Victorian miniatures and the holes where he hadn't quite.

A breeze lifted her summer dress as he threw the door open, a theatrical gesture prompted by his losing his balance, and she smoothed the skirt down over her long thighs with her slim fingers. He was suddenly embarrassed that she should see him in this state, his hairy stomach peeking one-eyed over the waistband of the pyjama trousers that were all he was wearing. He yanked them up, wondering if he looked so unkempt that she might take pity on him, but she shook her head and pursed those lips that tasted cool and sweet. 'Go in for heaven's sake, Herb. People will see you.'

'There's only you, and you've seen worse.'

'That's right enough,' she said with half the smile she would have given him last year. Half was a start, it surely suggested their life hadn't come to an end, and if he could just coax the whole smile once onto her face . . . 'Come in and make yourself a coffee while I have a shower and get dressed,' he said, and when she appeared less than tempted, 'or I'll make us one.'

'Neither, thanks, Herb. Just go in before those fall down. I hope you haven't been wearing them for the last fortnight.'

'Only in bed. Of course not,' he scoffed at himself, though in fact he had indeed not changed his nightwear; changing it was one of the innumerable things which her departure had rendered meaningless. He clutched at the waistband with both hands and limped into the front room, wincing as he felt the cramp considering whether to revive in his thigh. 'Come right in,' he called.

The room felt less denuded than the bedroom or bathroom or kitchen. There were the shelves and television stand he'd built from kits, bruising his palms with the handle of the Posidrive until his hands felt as though blunt nails had been driven through them, cursing the kits which always seemed to contain fewer parts than they were meant to insofar as he could understand the instructions in pidgin English. He'd built the furniture partly to show Mary that he didn't have to go running to David Owain every time a job needed doing in the house – he'd begun to feel that was how she felt he behaved, even though this view of him wasn't entirely fair – but by then it must have been too late. Perhaps the sight of the tipsy shelves and the stand from which the television constantly appeared to be about to slide might at least draw a reminiscent smile from Mary, assuming that she hadn't decided against venturing into the house. He was about to lunge out of the capacious mock-leather armchair when the front door clicked shut and Mary came into the room. 'Just stay there, Herb,' she said.

As she shrugged off her canvas shoulder-bag it pulled down a strap of her dress, exposing the slope of one freckled breast. Whereas two weeks ago – indeed, for longer than he cared to think – the glimpse of her body would have been too familiar to turn him on, now that she had become a stranger who wasn't quite at ease in the house or with him, it did. If she was aware of the effect she was having on him, she ignored it and lifted a framed picture out of her bag. 'I thought you might like to keep this.'

It was a seascape which, on the basis of the little he'd learned from the rather more she knew, he took to be Victorian. It showed a woman in an ankle-length white dress standing on a pale flat beach and gazing across the long waves at the horizon, which was featureless except for an object which might have been a lighthouse emitting faint rays or the mast of a ship or, surely least likely, a cross. 'Isn't this the one I bought you the first time we were in Cornwall?' Herb said.

'It may have been.'

He knew that she knew they both knew it was. When had they begun to talk to each other this way, as if admitting to remembering what they'd shared or what they knew about each other lost them a point in some game they hadn't even realised they were playing until they couldn't stop? If he could just remember when it had started, if he could persuade her to admit she did . . . 'It turns out not to be as early as I thought,' she said.

'Doesn't mean you have to leave yet, does it?'

Her wince as she stood the picture on the timber mantelpiece above the chunky hearth David Owain had built them last year looked less amused than heartfelt. 'I thought it might have some sentimental value for you,' she said.

'Hasn't it any for you?'

'Don't start, Herb, please. Didn't we agree to make going our ways as easy on each other as we could?'

'You did.'

She wasn't sure how to take that, and he found he didn't want her to be. 'Anyway, keep the picture or do whatever you want with it,' she said. 'There isn't really room for it where I am now.'

'You forgot to tell me where that is.'

'Herb, please.' She sat down in the armchair opposite him and leaned forward, raising her hands as though to fend him off. 'You know perfectly well that I didn't forget. If there's any mail it can be forwarded to me at work.'

At least she was sitting, and their exchanges had stopped sidling around one another. 'Why don't you want me to know where you're living?'

'Why do you want to know?'

'Suppose I needed to get in touch urgently?'

'Why would you, Herb? If you don't find someone to take my place you can always rely on David and Joelle.'

'I'm across the road the moment anything goes wrong, you mean.'

'I didn't say that.' She moved her legs aside as he stretched out one bare foot. 'None of that, please, Herb, or I'll leave.'

He had only been trying to relax his leg to head off the threat of renewed cramp. 'I still don't understand what you're afraid of, why you won't give me your address.'

'Because I know you. If you knew where I was you wouldn't be able to stay away even if you promised to.'

Was she about to relent? 'I remember when you seemed to like that,' he said.

'That was before we were married. A lot of things were.' She rubbed her mouth with her fingertips as though it was an envelope she was sealing. 'Don't make me say things like that. I apologise.'

Herb tried to accept mutely, but his words got the better of him. 'I didn't make you, you did it yourself.'

'You see, we're starting again. I knew we would.' She stood up so abruptly that the armchair fled, its castors squealing. 'When people start to make each other petty it's time to say goodbye. Here's the key I forgot to give you.'

'Why don't you hang onto it? You never know when you might want it.'

'Herb,' she said almost affectionately, placing the key with a clink against the glass of the seascape, and turned back to him once she reached the hall. 'Look after yourself. You're going to have to sooner or later. If I had my way there'd be a law against parents having an only child.'

'You're making me feel like one.' When her face stayed determinedly blank he said 'Unlike whatever his name is, I suppose.'

'Now you're sounding like one.'

'I can't help it if I think you wanted someone with a brain as good as yours, can I?'

'There's nothing wrong with your brain, Herb, if you just didn't let it idle so much.'

'See, it's brains that matter to you. It's someone at the visitors' centre, isn't it? Is it the young dark-faced bugger with the earring and the pony-tail?'

'It's nobody I work with, Herb, and I'm not being interrogated further.' She glanced at the grandmother clock in the hall. 'And please don't try to see me or phone me at work. Let's make this a goodbye neither of us will regret,' she said, and having opened the front door just wide enough to slip through, waved tersely to him as she closed it behind her.

She was hurrying to meet whoever she'd left him for, Herb thought with a clarity that felt like an imminent migraine. He'd failed in everything he'd set out to achieve since she had entered the house, but he hadn't lost her yet. He raced upstairs and wriggled into the clothes he'd dumped on the floor at the end of the bed last night. 'Don't start, I'm warning you,' he snarled at his calf, which recalled his cramp as he shoved his foot into a shoe without untying the shoelace. He ran downstairs three treads at a time, feeling grubby and sweaty and yelling 'Ow, ow, ow, ow, ow' at his calf, and dashed out of the house.

The tree at the end of the crazy-paved path scattered fragments of sunlight over him as he dragged the gate out of his way. In the open he smelled stronger than the flowers, and that made him feel primitive, a caveman limping in search of his mate. Beyond the broken ranks of newish cars sunning themselves between the trees or, in two cases, being doused in soapy water by their owners' children, he saw Mary disappearing around the curve towards the main road, her dress lighting up like a blue beacon as she emerged from a patch of shade. He closed the gate with a carefulness which felt as though it was guaranteeing his success, and followed at precisely her pace, ready to dodge out of sight if she looked like glancing behind her. 'Keep up the good work' and 'Keep up the good work,' he said to the car-washers, to convince them that he was behaving normally and that in any case it was none of their business.

Mary turned right at the sandstone cross opposite the garage on the main road, a move that led towards the centre of Chester. The road ran more or less straight for half a mile, past hotels and pubs with drinkers seated outside, until it reached the bridge over the railway, but there was plenty of cover once Herb sprinted to the opposite pavement, buses large and small taking their time as if the day was too hot or too holy for haste. Twice he had to fake tying his shoelace beside a car when he thought Mary was about to turn around, but peering through the windows of the cars showed him he was mistaken. He didn't lose sight of her until she hurried over the bridge.

At the same time as hunching itself over the bridge the road snaked before descending to an intersection where cars were jabbing their headlights at one another. There was no sign of Mary on the downward slope, and so she could only have descended the steps to the railway station. Herb peered around the wall at the top of the steps at her until the prolonged façade of the station blocked his view, then he ran down in time to see her climbing into the ticket office, a temporary cabin outside the station entrance. When she left the cabin he was behind it, fiddling with his shoelaces while he watched for her legs. As soon as she was through the booking hall he followed her, almost tripping himself up with an untied shoelace, which he knotted viciously by propping his sole against the outside of the cabin. He sidled past the bookstall, which the Sabbath had transformed into a Sunday newspaper shop, and doled the left side of his face around the corner of the refreshment counter.

Apart from two young women dressed like cyclists and puffing cigarettes above a toddler in a buggy, the platforms were deserted. Mary was on the only train, which should leave, all two carriages of it, for Hooton in three minutes. Herb dodged around the bookstall so as to sneak up on the train from the other direction, then feigned interest in a timetable on the wall lest Mary or the driver recognise him, even though both were facing forward. He watched the station clock out of the corner of his eye, and as it was about to finger the departure time he lunged for the doors furthest from Mary and the driver. Three deafening heartbeats later the rubber edges of the doors bumped together and the train moved off.

Riding on a train he wasn't driving made him feel as though he was a boy again, and so, if he was honest with himself, did knowing that Mary was just a few yards away and unaware of him. Outside Chester the colours of summer streamed past, but he was concentrating on the window at the end of the carriage, beyond which a similar window was swaying not quite in time with it. Bache station halted the train, and then Capenhurst did, keeping its nuclear secrets. That left only Hooton on the route, and Mary detrained there and crossed the platform to board the foremost of another pair of carriages.

Herb skulked behind the hut which sold newspapers, and darted round it when the doors of the train began to close, and crouched on a seat from which, if he leaned into the aisle, he could just see Mary's right shoulder. Each time he spied through the swaying windows the motion of the train seemed to have sent her blue shoulder-strap a little lower, and he felt as if he was undressing her by remote control, though each time a station brought the train to a halt she pulled up the strap. When the train slowed for Bebington he allowed himself another peek. She was rising to her feet and turning towards him.

'Ow,' Herb growled as he fell on his knees between the seats. The train whined to a stop and gasped its doors open, and he crouched lower over his shoes, poking his buttocks at the platform. He heard the heels of Mary's sandals flapping away across the flagstones, and swung round, still in his crouch, to shove a fist between the nearest pair of closing doors. They tried to fit their rubber edges to his knuckles before springing apart, exposing him to Mary as she stepped onto the ramp which led down to the street. She must be in too much of a hurry to look back. Three rapid steps carried her below the level of the platform, onto which Herb bounded just before his stoop could resuscitate the cramp.

As soon as she'd had time to reach the street he hurried down the ramp, flashing his British Rail pass at the ticket collector. Mary was heading into Port Sunlight village, past a mullioned window out of which someone was shaking a towel. When Herb came abreast of the window Mary was hurrying alongside the art gallery. He loitered on a shadow island beneath a tree until she turned the corner of the building, then he loped across the road and along the pillared façade just in time to glimpse her at the top of the wide steps.

He'd visited the gallery once, in the days when she had been trying to educate him. He remembered a maze of rooms, the kind of setting where as a child he would have loved to chase someone. He heard the chink of a coin as Mary dropped it into the donation box at the entrance. He waited and then strolled up the steps, nodding to a security guard behind a desk, who raised his eyebrows as though he thought Herb looked like a tramp. Perhaps Herb did, with his crumpled clothes and unshaven face and uncombed hair. 'Us artistic types, you know,' he muttered, dropping a coin which he hoped the guard didn't see was a penny into the box.

Beyond the entrance was a circular white room beneath a dome upheld by pillars. As Herb ventured under the dome, catching sight of a naked marble lady feeding a snake from a dish, his footsteps multiplied until he seemed to have as many feet as there were rooms off the circle. Straight ahead, through a room where a frieze of robed white figures danced the length of a mantelpiece, was the main hall. Herb was preparing to edge his face around an entrance to the hall when a security guard appeared through it. There was nothing close enough to Herb for him to fake a sudden interest, and so he had to stroll like a robot into the hall.

Though he couldn't see Mary among the visitors stooping to the inlaid tables or standing back from the Victorian paintings, one of which showed bathers posing coyly as nudists in an old film, Herb didn't feel safe until he noticed an enclosed staircase leading up to one of two balconies that overlooked the hall. He managed not to hum to show how normally he was behaving as he made for the stairs, but once he was between the walls he allowed himself a groan of relief. He wiped his forehead with the back of his hand and used the banister to drag himself up the staircase.

The balcony displayed paintings which had once been used to advertise Sunlight Soap, showing children red-cheeked with innocence. At the end a bulbous mirror drew the reflection of the balcony to a point from which Herb saw himself emerging, a figure almost too small to see. This made him feel less invisible than insignificant, a microbe under a lens, and he was turning away from it when a child said 'He's sick, isn't he, Mummy?'

She sounded close enough to be standing beside him, though she was in the middle of the hall below him, pointing at a picture which he remembered Mary telling him was by Holman somebody, 'The Scapegoat' – an animal abandoned in a poisoned landscape, its coat matted, its eyes shining with a diseased gleam. 'I expect they didn't have vets in those days,' the little girl's mother said, steering her towards a side room full of clocks. As the couple disappeared, Mary said 'There you are' in Herb's ear.

She wasn't talking to him. She was at the end of the hall furthest from the domed room. He'd had enough of hiding. He folded his arms and leaned on the edge of the balcony and watched as she walked fast to meet a bearded man wearing a shirt and grey waistcoat and pinstriped trousers and glossy black shoes. 'How was it?' the man said.

'Worse than last time, Victor. Dusty and empty as if I hadn't lived there for years, or maybe never at all.'

54

'I hope you aren't feeling responsible.'

'I always did. I used to feel if I didn't take care of him nobody would, otherwise I'd have been off sooner, you know that.'

'Was he really that bad?'

'He wasn't *bad* at all. He just had even more trouble growing up than the rest of us. Well, I've finished with being a substitute mother and father. I want the chance to be whoever I'm capable of being, and maybe I've given Herb that chance.'

They were murmuring directly beneath him. Each sibilant felt like a hiss in his ear. When he leaned over the balcony he saw the tops of their heads. Mary's hair was parted in the middle, and the pink skin put him in mind of her vagina. The man's black curly mat was parted at the side, displaying whitish skin. Two cunts, Herb thought and almost muttered as Mary said 'He can't go on living like that much longer, can he? He'll have to change.'

'Of course he will, dear. He's got a good job, and nobody can afford to let one of those go nowadays. He'll learn to look after himself.' The black scalp reached out a hand and stroked the blonde hair. 'I've my break in twenty minutes. Will you wait or go to the house?'

'Home,' Herb whispered. 'Go home. I'll see you at home.' He thought they might have heard him until Mary said 'I'll hang around. You can buy me a coffee.'

'I'll even make you one.'

The black scalp and the blonde moved together, and Herb began to ache. When they separated, having shared a kiss so brief that nobody except Herb appeared to have noticed, he found that he was bruising his elbows on the edge of the balcony. He ground them against the wood as if that might cause Mary to look up. But the scalps moved away, sprouting bodies as they went, and exited through doorways on opposite sides of the hall. There was nobody to see Herb grasping the edge of the balcony so hard that it creaked. 'Victor, eh? *Vic-tor*,' he squeaked in the most grotesque voice he could summon up, and shoved himself away from the edge, towards the mirror. He couldn't stand the sight of the microbe, and so he paced towards it, watching his forehead start to bulge, his shoulders grow broad, his biceps more muscular. When he was satisfied with his image he clattered downstairs into the hall.

He was hoping Mary would happen upon him. 'I thought I'd take another look round like you kept wanting me to,' he would say. 'You started changing me, you can't expect me to stop.' Maybe then he would leave, having sown a seed of guilt in her mind, unless she accused him of following her, in which case would he act innocent or injured or turn on her? He felt the possibilities grinding together inside his head as he stared into the yellow eyes of the scapegoat. He had the notion that the eyes might have a message for him if he could only read the gleam of the thin pointed vertical pupils, and he was gazing at them as though he had forgotten how to blink when footsteps entered the hall and halted behind him. 'It's a powerful image, isn't it?' the man said.

It was Victor. Herb felt his shoulders hunching up like the reflection – he thought he felt his forehead swelling. As he turned he was filled with an impulse to grab the man's square wiry beard or punch his broad nose flatter or poke two fingers into his intolerably friendly brown eyes, and so he shoved his hands into his trousers pockets. 'What are you admiring?' Victor said. 'The technique?'

Herb didn't say 'When did you meet my wife?' but his tone did. 'What technique?'

'The brushwork, the . . .' Victor took hold of his beard; Herb could hear it crinkle. 'I apologise if I disturbed you. It's just that I enjoy hearing our visitors' thoughts.'

'That'd be women, would it?'

'And children. Men too, of course. Anybody except anyone who prefers not to talk.'

'I'm sure some of them love it.'

'Oh, indeed,' Victor said enthusiastically, and then Herb's tone seemed to reach him. 'I'll be leaving you alone, then.'

'Don't count on it,' Herb whispered, gripping his mouth, and managed to stuff his fist back in his pocket. 'Nice to see a man enjoying what he does. Live round here, do you?'

'Not too far. Just a few stops.'

'Convenient having the station so close if you use the train.'

'It is.'

Herb was expending most of his energy on sounding pleasant rather than unduly interested, and he couldn't think how to go on, not least because his forehead was becoming an egg of pain. 'I expect I'll speak to you again sometime,' he said as lightly as he could, 'but now I'd better be buggering.' He turned before his face gave way under the strain of smiling and walked away steadily, through rooms of china behind glass, through his echoes waiting beneath the dome, into sunlight which seized his eyes and forced the long Parisian avenue, divided by glaring grass and flowerbeds and lined with cottages rather than French architecture, into them.

She mightn't have met Victor if Herb had kept visiting the

gallery with her. He felt as though he had to walk until he left that thought behind. Before long he was conscious only of the thought inside his brittle skull, and the sunlight which seemed to be thinning its shell, and his feet treading the mill of the pavements. When at last the small windows of the houses ceased to wink at him he was on the road to Chester. Cars whisked by like interruptions in the drone which the immovable thought had become, and the only plan he could conceive through it was to walk until the thought faded of its own accord.

An hour later it was too late. The road had reached open countryside, and he'd failed to realise that he should have turned off it miles back for the last railway station. The thought in his skull was less a concept any more than a dull all-embracing pain. When kicking the wild flowers of the verge as though they were his own stupidity didn't help, he began to snarl aloud and wave his arms, sending birds twittering out of the hedge he was following. 'Dusty and empty, am I? When did you meet my wife, eh? When did you *meat* my wife, more like . . .' He didn't know how loud his voice had grown when a car cruised past him and halted a few yards ahead.

It was a red French car whose roof looked like a piece of tin curled over. Herb wondered if he was about to be arrested, though surely only gendarmes drove around in cars like that and not even gendarmes if they could help it, and then it occurred to him that the driver must have taken his gestures as a desperate plea for a ride. The passenger door creaked open, and a grey-haired woman as tall and as broad as Herb's shoulders clambered out, clutching a straw hat to the level chest of her simply printed dress. 'Hop in,' she called in a voice too big for her.

He'd seen her before, and her husband, a man almost exactly in proportion with her and wearing a suit as black as his driving gloves. As Herb struggled over the recumbent seat into the back, the driver tilted his bald head so as to create the illusion of gazing down at him. 'Had enough of your Sunday stroll, old man?'

'You were at the Owains' barbecue last year,' Herb said, having recognised the booming voice. 'Don't tell me, it's – your name's on the tip – it's Archie. Archie Grey.'

'Archibald,' the driver said as though Herb had omitted the syllable out of misplaced kindness.

'Just plain Agatha's my Christian name,' his wife said.

Herb arranged himself in the back, parting his legs so that his knees didn't dig into the front seats and leaning sideways in order not to press his skull against the roof. 'I remember now,' he said as the vehicle chugged forwards, 'we saw off the Scotch between us when nearly everyone else had gone. That's right, David and Joelle had to start drinking Horlicks before we took the hint, and they couldn't get rid of us until Agatha managed to tell that joke about the nuns and the holy relic. How did it go again?'

When there was no response, not even a flicker of Agatha's eyes in the driving mirror, Herb said 'The shortest one I ever heard was two nuns in the bath, and one says "Where's the soap?" and the other one says "It certainly does".'

After a painfully prolonged silence Archibald boomed 'I'm sorry, I think that must be over my head.'

Agatha unclasped her hands, which had been squashing the hat on her square lap, and looked up at Herb in the mirror. 'How's your lovely wife?'

'She isn't just now. Not my wife, I mean. Well, she is, she certainly is, but we're having what I suppose you would call a trial separation.'

'Life is a trial,' Archibald informed him.

'It certainly feels like one at the moment,' Herb admitted, and squirmed on the seat, not only because his calf had recommenced aching. 'Not this very moment, you understand. I mean, not because of you. Either of you.'

'Are you quite comfortable?' Archibald enquired as Herb's knee poked his spine.

Herb dragged himself upright, bumping his skull loudly on the roof, and stared through the windscreen. Hedges dawdled by as if to demonstrate how slowly the car was going, and then he saw a roundabout ahead, and to the left of it a pub surrounded by parked cars. 'I know where I would be comfortable. Let me buy you both a drink.'

'It's Sunday, Herbert,' Archibald said.

'Herb. I reckon we'll be all right. That pub doesn't look shut to me.'

'My husband wasn't saying that. He means we don't really approve of drinking on the Sabbath or, to be honest, at all.'

'You did knock it back at the barbecue, but no more so than me,' Herb said, and floundered in pursuit of the implications of that. 'That's to say it must take a lot of willpower to give up so much.'

'Every one of us is given all the power he needs if he will only ask.'

'That's good to know,' Herb said, hoping Agatha would leave it at that. He grabbed his left ankle with both hands and managed to cross his left leg over his right as the car shuddered to a halt at the roundabout, though there was no other vehicle to be seen. When it had braved the intersection and was on a stretch of road virtually indistinguishable from the one it had just left except for the dwindling promise of the pub in the mirror, Archibald said 'Do you mind if I ask you a personal question, Herbert?'

'Herb. Depends what it is.'

'Have you been to church since you and hum, forgive me, became estranged?'

'Mary,' Herb said with what he hoped was sufficient reproach to make that his whole answer. When Archibald turned the left side of his face towards him while continuing to squint at the road, Herb said 'Not really. Actually, no.'

'Had you been in the habit?'

'Neither of us, no.'

'There's the problem,' Archibald declared. 'Shall I give you the best advice you've ever had in your life?'

'Ah. Well, I—'

'We've just come from the Christian Centre, but we'd like nothing better than to go to church again. Let us take you right now to the first one we come to and just you see if that isn't the most important choice you'll ever make.'

'It's very kind of you, but unfortunately, I'm rather—'

'Tell me this, Herbert. Am I not right in thinking Mary wasn't much of a drinker?'

'Herb,' Herb protested, heaving at his ankle to restore his leg to some kind of relative comfort. 'Not compared with you and me she wasn't, no.'

'Precisely. So we may say your and Mary's problems were less than ours.'

'Say what you like,' Herb said, struggling with his leg.

'So may I tell you something that should delight you as much as it delighted us?'

'Delighted,' Herb heard himself say.

'It's simply that as soon as we experienced the power of prayer we saw that all our troubles were less than nothing.'

'That much, eh? Well, that's . . . quite a lot, less than nothing. Then you wouldn't feel you had to do anything about them.'

'Do we look as if we haven't?' Agatha cried, almost deafening him. 'My husband means we knew exactly what to do.'

'So shall we?' Archibald boomed so heartily that Herb felt the roof vibrate against his own scalp. Some seconds passed before Herb realised the question was addressed to him. 'What?' he wished at once he hadn't said.

'Why, what have we been discussing, Herbert? Take you to church to pray for yourself and Mary and your new life together.'

'As I say, it's kind of you to offer, but right now I need to go straight home. Mary may be trying to get in touch.'

He thought they had seen through the lie, the silence which met his refusal was so total. For some seconds he feared that Archibald was about to stop the car and order him out of it, if feared was the word. Instead Archibald began to hum the melody of a hymn, apparently in order to announce his choice to Agatha, who joined in when he set about the words. Soon the Greys were roaring the verses and obliquely alluding to the tune, though not in unison. Once they had thoroughly dealt with that hymn Agatha fell on another. Herb suffered being sung at and fixed his eyes on the road that was oozing towards him, though he was distracted by the flickering of Archibald's key-ring, a hologram which showed Christ either robed or displaying a heart disconcertingly reminiscent of the design on a Valentine card. He was terrified that any moment one or both of the Greys would exhort him to join in the increasingly obscure hymns, and the eternity about which they kept singing seemed to pass before the car arrived at the outskirts of Chester.

'We'll leave you under the cross,' Archibald said heavily, and stopped the car by the memorial on the corner of Herb's road. Being able to stand up and walk after his sojourn in the car felt so like a miracle that Herb was only just able to resist saying so aloud. The Greys drove off, bellowing a hymn which caused pedestrians to turn and stare, and their departure was such a relief that Herb thought he was going to enjoy the rest of the day. When he came in sight of the house, blotched with the shadow of the tree at the end of the garden path, he was only starting to remember how empty it would feel when he saw the Volvo parked opposite.

'David,' he called. 'Joelle.' They were emerging from either side of the car, and waved to him. They looked slightly preoccupied; perhaps they assumed he was on his way to ask them for help. 'I just wanted to say welcome back,' he assured them. Then David opened one rear door, and Herb saw that they had brought someone home with them.

# Seven

Joelle didn't know whether to laugh or cry at the sight of Herb. His wide face bore its usual faintly surprised expression, as though he had just wakened and wasn't quite sure where he was, and his bushy eyebrows that she always wanted to comb were as unkempt as ever, but now that quality had spread to the rest of him. His collar was buttoned one hole too low, his shirt unveiled his hairy stomach with each step he took, his clothes looked as if he'd slept in them, his hair as if it hadn't been brushed for weeks. 'For heaven's sake, Herb,' she said, pushing the label of his shirt out of sight under his collar and holding her breath as she caught a whiff of him, 'what have you been up to while we were away? Sleeping rough?'

He gave her an apologetic lopsided grin that made his face even more asymmetrical. 'I just had to run out in a hurry, that's all.'

'Did you get whatever you were after?'

'Some of it,' he said, and blinked at Gwendolen, whom David was helping out of the car. 'How about you? Was your weekend all you were expecting?'

'Rather more, I'd say. Gwen, this is our friend Herb who lives across the road.'

Gwendolen let go of David's arm and took Herb's vaguely outstretched hand as though she was about to read his palm. 'Glad to meet you, Herb, even if it's only briefly.'

'It doesn't have to be.'

'I meant that it's unlikely we'll be neighbours long.'

'Gwen's a distant relative David met in Wales. She'll be staying with us while she finds somewhere to live.'

'What Joelle's too kind to say is that I'd reached a point where I couldn't take care of myself.'

It wasn't her honesty so much as the realisation that she had this insight which threw Joelle. 'I thought you were doing extremely well, Gwen, considering.'

61

'I wouldn't have made any progress without you and David. At my age you need people around you.'

'What sort of place are you looking for?' Herb said.

'Anywhere that will have an old reprobate like me.'

'The home up by the cross is meant to be good.'

'The cross at the end of the road, do you mean? Perhaps we could walk up there later, Joelle. I don't want to be more trouble to you than I can help.'

'You've been none at all,' Joelle said, feeling guilty for wishing Herb had kept his mouth shut: they needn't have found Gwendolen accommodation quite so near, not that she could think of any reason to keep her at a distance. 'I'll walk along with you in a while if you like.'

'If you wouldn't mind. In case I get confused, lose my way, that sort of thing. Don't worry that I'll start inviting myself to your house just because I live nearby. I never go anywhere unless I'm asked.'

Joelle felt her face growing hotter until Gwendolen patted her cheek with one cool hand. 'I hope you appreciate your neighbours, Herb. Joelle says she'll take me shopping for clothes when she's free.'

'You can borrow anything of mine that fits you until then,' Joelle said.

'You see what I mean, Herb. The soul of kindness.'

'I do. Well,' he said awkwardly, 'I'll be bug— I'll be off or you'll think I'm after something.'

'Whatever I have to give is yours,' Gwendolen called after him.

Joelle wondered if that was a traditional Welsh farewell. David was unlocking the house, which shrilled 'me' as he stepped across the threshold. Gwendolen's hands fluttered towards her ears. 'What's in there?' she demanded.

'Just the burglar alarm. It'll shut up in a moment. There, now he's switched it off.'

'So nobody can enter uninvited?'

'There'd be a hell of a racket if they did.'

'My bag ought to be safe, then. Can I have it now, David?' Gwendolen asked as he returned to the car.

Joelle refrained from mentioning false alarms were so common that nobody, including the police, took much notice any more. As soon as the boot was unlocked Gwendolen seized her bag and hugged it to her breasts. 'Don't think for an instant I distrust either of you, but you see how it is when you reach my age. Everything I have that's worth having is in here.'

'You hang on to what you've got,' David advised her.

If anything convinced Joelle that Gwendolen needed looking after despite her understandable attempts to persuade the Owains or herself that she was in control of her life, this behaviour did. Driving away from the Welsh village, Joelle had slowed on approaching the road to the island, but Gwendolen had shown no enthusiasm for going back. 'I'd never get up again, and you mustn't think of tiring yourselves out. There's nothing down there I want.' Which in a way had been a relief, but Joelle couldn't help wondering if Gwendolen had abandoned any clothes in the cottage or if she hadn't wanted the Owains to discover she was wearing all the clothes she had.

David lifted the suitcase and closed the boot, and used the case to hold back a thorny rose branch from the garden path so that the women could pass. 'In you come, Gwen. No need to be afraid of the alarm,' Joelle said.

The moment Gwendolen set foot in the house she halted, clasping her hands over the bag. 'Is all this your doing?'

'It's our baby all right.' Joelle always liked coming home, and Gwendolen was renewing the experience for her, admiring the wide light hall papered with a print of islands like tufts of vegetation peeking above snow, the stripped pine staircase which David had put in after they'd discovered that the creaking of the old stairs was an early symptom of dry rot. Now Gwendolen was gazing into the front room, where the sliding doors stood open beneath their white arch, displaying the dining-room and its long oval table under the chandelier, beyond which David's patio doors gave onto a lawn as extensive as the house. 'Deceptively spacious,' Joelle said.

'I beg your pardon?'

'That's how estate agents describe houses. It always sounds to us as if they're saying the houses look more spacious than they are.'

'I've never heard that before. What will they think of next?'

Joelle had a sense that the conversation had gone slightly askew, teetering on the edge of a generation gap. 'I'll show you where you can sleep.'

She opened all the doors on the upstairs landing to let out the sunlight. The bathroom breathed out scents of soap and talc, the bedrooms betrayed a faint dusty smell of their abandoned weekend until she opened the windows. She showed Gwendolen into the smaller of the front rooms, where the bed was always made up, then ushered her into the main bedroom and slid back the doors of her fitted wardrobe. 'Take your pick, Gwen.'

Gwendolen chose a long green summer dress and held it against herself. 'May I borrow this just until we've been shopping?'

'I'll give you a nightie later. Bring that dress of yours down when you've changed and I'll put it in the machine.'

'All right,' Gwendolen said, though she looked somewhat doubtful.

As she closed her door David came upstairs and dumped the suitcase by the double bed. 'Are we alone for a bit?' he murmured.

'Not enough of one to be worth having. Later, when someone's asleep.'

When she emerged from the room with an armful of washing she met Gwendolen, who looked rejuvenated by the green dress and oddly vulnerable, unsure of herself. Her own white dress was draped over her thin bare arms. 'Just add it to the pile,' Joelle said, and Gwendolen was folding it when an American voice said in the hall 'Hi. David and Joelle Owain?'

Gwendolen dropped the dress, which flapped downstairs and enshrouded the upright at the foot of the banisters. 'Who's that? Where are they?'

'On the answering machine,' Joelle said, and when that didn't seem to enlighten Gwendolen, 'The machine that takes messages when we aren't here.'

David pointed at it with the pencil he was using to scribble on a pad, and Gwendolen followed Joelle downstairs for a closer look. 'We're friends of Terry and Sarah Monk,' the voice was saying. 'They said you might be willing to check out our house for us. Jake and Henry short for Henrietta Lee with ease. We're living here in Chester. Let me give you our number, uh . . . Let me call you back.'

'Oh, with es,' Joelle realised aloud, and left David to it while she headed for the room beyond the kitchen, collecting Gwendolen's dress on the way. 'I think this is best washed by itself,' she told Gwendolen, who was shading her eyes against the dazzle of pine and spotless metal which made use of all the space in the large kitchen. As water started pouring into the drum Gwendolen looked momentarily startled. 'I expect you'll have seen these, at least in launderettes,' Joelle said.

'Not where you found me.'

'I don't suppose there was much chance of plumbing out there. What did you use, rainwater?' Joelle caught herself interrogating

Gwendolen, and tried to make up for it. 'When I was little I used to imagine washing myself in the rain. Sometimes I think we've sold our souls for all these devices.'

'I pray not,' Gwendolen said earnestly.

The American had returned to the answering machine with his telephone number, and now he had been ousted by a series of non-existent messages, merely the sounds of a party at a pub, presumably calls by a late-night clown or someone who disliked talking to machines. After three calls the perpetrator found something else to do and made way for a voice.

'Doug Singleton here. Anyone listening? Are you listening, David or Joelle? Oh, you're away for the weekend, aren't you,' he said with a hint of annoyance. 'I just wanted to make certain that David will be starting work at my aunt's tomorrow. Frankly, the sooner the house can be seen to the better.'

'That's a solicitor for you, always saying everything twice,' David complained. 'I told him I'd be there. What more does he want? All right, so I'll tell him again . . .' He was already dialling, since the machine had begun to parrot messages from last week until he switched it into its alert mode. 'Angie? No, this isn't your boyfriend, I'm sorry to say. Could I speak to your father? . . . Hello, Doug, just confirming I'll be there first thing tomorrow . . . Of course I didn't think you sounded rude. I lose sleep over people's houses myself . . .'

'I think we all deserve a cup of coffee,' Joelle said to Gwendolen, and closed the kitchen door.

'May I try?' Gwendolen said as Joelle lifted the lid of the percolator.

'Of course you can,' Joelle said, and talked her through the process. Gwendolen seemed delighted until it came to touching the switch of the electric socket, and then her hand wavered in mid-air. 'I promise it won't kill you,' Joelle said.

'I wouldn't want that to happen just yet.' Gwendolen clenched her fist except for the forefinger and stabbed at the switch with her bitten nail, and shivered so violently that Joelle made to catch hold of her, except that the spasm passed before she could. 'I'll never be afraid of that again,' Gwendolen declared, 'and now I'm going to have a proper look at your machine.'

She opened the door, letting the halting hum into the kitchen, and watched the washing machine while Joelle took down three mugs from their hooks on the wall. Eventually she said 'Ought it to be doing that?'

The hum sounded healthy enough to Joelle, and so she didn't look until she'd poured milk into the mugs; then she clapped a hand over her mouth. Most of Gwendolen's dress appeared to have gone down the drain, except for a few tatters of cloth tossing in the water. 'I don't know what to say, Gwen. It's never done that before. Was it special in some way, that dress?'

'Don't spare it another thought. It was only a worn-out old thing, like me.'

She seemed even more embarrassed than Joelle was. When they carried the mugs into the front room she hadn't said anything else. Joelle liked being quiet towards the end of a day as long as this one had been, but Gwendolen's presence altered the silence. Perhaps that was why David abruptly returned to the hall and called the Americans to promise them a visit. Gwendolen sipped her coffee daintily yet rapidly and set the mug down immediately she'd finished. 'Shall we have that stroll along the road to see if there's room for me?'

'There's room for you here, Gwen,' Joelle said, 'until you find somewhere you feel at home.'

'I'll never forget that, but you deserve to be able to put me out of your minds for a while.'

'You mustn't think for a moment that we want to,' Joelle said, feeling trapped into insincerity, and drained her mug. 'Actually, I wouldn't mind a walk after all that driving.'

'I'll see to dinner, shall I?' David said.

'Seeing's about the extent of it. What were you going to surprise us with?'

'I could open some cans if you tell me which.'

'One of worms, so don't,' Joelle said, and to Gwendolen, 'You'll appreciate this is an old-fashioned marriage.'

'It's the oldest things that won't lie down,' Gwendolen said with a wink that looked little short of salacious.

'Find something in the freezer we'll all like, David, if you want to help. Anything you particularly fancy, Gwen?'

'Something with a bit of life in it. I've had the same taste in my mouth for so long.'

'And you could give this rosebush a clip round the head,' Joelle called to David as she and Gwendolen sidled down the path.

Herb was in his front garden, tugging desultorily at weeds and peering about for somewhere else to make a false start. He waved a bouquet of dandelions at the women, and Joelle told herself not to worry about him so much. A black cat was sitting under one of the kerbside trees, gazing up at a nestful of sparrows as though they were fruit poised to fall, and Joelle clapped her hands until the cat slunk away. At first Gwendolen appeared to wonder what business Joelle had with the animal; then she said 'You're protecting the young.'

'Someone has to.'

The Shangri-La Retirement Home had only recently been opened. It was one of the two largest houses in the road, and overlooked the small green beneath the trees which towered above the First World War memorial. Two imprecisely Chinese creatures squatted on the brick gateposts, beyond which half a dozen wicker chairs were set at random on the lawn in front of the symmetrical white house. A gravel drive led around the building to a car park occupied by two cars and a minibus. As the women crossed the springy lawn a hymn came to meet them through the open French windows to the left of the tall porch. 'They've never fitted a choir and an organ in there,' Gwendolen protested.

'Just a television, I should think.'

Two paces later they could see one of several old people in armchairs waving her stick at the screen. 'Nobody wants to listen to that bawling, do they? Let's have something to cheer us up.' A panting fat man who was sunk deep in a chair tossed her the remote control, and she switched channels until she lit on a word-game show. 'That's more like it, something to keep our brains awake.'

Gwendolen was gazing through the window in such fascination that Joelle didn't like to interrupt. A contestant made sense of a jumble of letters, but Joelle was still waiting for Gwendolen to lose interest when a woman opened the porch door. 'Can I do anything for you ladies?'

To Joelle she looked vaguely familiar: hair like curls of mahogany, blue eyes enlarged by spectacles, a broad face whose plumpness seemed to slow her expressions down . . . 'You're a friend of the Greys,' Joelle said.

The woman sketched a quick cross in the air as a parody of Archibald and Agatha. 'Used to be more of one before they had their change of life. Didn't you do up their house? Joelle, isn't it? Brenda Mickling.'

Gwendolen held out her hand to shake. 'Gwen Owain. I like your home.'

'All our residents do. Was that a disinterested comment, or are you looking for a place?'

'I think I mayn't have to look any farther.'

'We still have room. Come in and look around by all means.' As Gwendolen stepped into the hall and opened the door of the television lounge, Brenda murmured 'Knows her own mind, doesn't she? I like that. Has she been living with you?'

'Just arrived.'

'Any problems? Don't be shy of telling.'

'A bit forgetful. Well, a lot sometimes.'

'Aren't we all. I bet you overlook things just like I do, and half the time you don't realise until it's too late. We all of us start getting old the moment we pop out, and it's about time more of us had the foresight to make our arrangements before we aren't able to. I'm just saying more of us ought to have your sense of responsibility, Gwen,' she said, having followed her into the lounge. 'Let me introduce you to our family.'

Joelle felt excluded and unexpectedly regretful. She stayed outside the room while Brenda made the introductions: 'Daisy, Theda, Naomi and her stick she likes to have with her in case we're burgled or she meets anyone objectionable when she goes out for a walk, Reggie, Edgar – don't worry, Edgar, we know you can get up . . .' This last was to the panting man, who subsided gratefully into his groaning chair. 'Do come with us, Joelle,' Brenda said as she emerged from the room.

She told them the cost of accommodation as she gave them the tour of the ground floor and then led the way upstairs. One room on the top floor was unoccupied, with a view of the back of the cross. The curtains and bedclothes and wallpaper shared a pattern of tiny white blossoms on a green background, and Gwendolen said 'I could live here' at once.

'Would you like to sleep on it?'

'I've done enough of that to last me, thank you, Brenda. Don't you think this is for me, Joelle?'

'I like it, but I'm not you.'

'You could be,' Gwendolen said, and turned to Brenda. 'Joelle thinks if she's too enthusiastic it will seem that she wants to be rid of me. She'll be able to see I'm well looked after, won't she? Not that she'll need to.'

'Most assuredly,' Brenda told them. 'When were you thinking of becoming one of us?'

'Could I start tomorrow?'

'I see no reason why not. Let's go down if you've seen all you want to.' At the bottom of the stairs she called into the television lounge 'We'll have a party to welcome Gwen tomorrow.'

'I could make some cakes,' Gwendolen said eagerly.

'For your own party? Not on your life.' Brenda led the way to her basement office, where filing cabinets flanked a desk the same white as the walls. She took a blank file from a cabinet and sat behind the desk. 'Gwen . . . do . . . len? Len . . . *Owain*,' she said as she wrote. 'So, Gwen. Date of birth?'

'So long ago I've forgotten, truth to tell.'

'But you'll have your birth certificate, won't you? Or the date will be in your pension book.'

Gwendolen only stared, and Joelle took pity on her. 'I expect they're in your bag at home.'

'We can fill in any details that we have to later. How about place, Gwen? Of birth, I mean.'

'Wales.'

'Could you be more, um—'

'On the border.'

'Powys, would that be? Gwent?'

'As far as you could imagine walking,' Gwendolen said to Joelle.

This seemed so obviously a disguised plea that Joelle said 'Could it wait until you have the certificate, Brenda?'

'Whatever's least trouble,' Brenda said, spidering her fingers down the page. 'Well then. Next of kin.'

'I expect you can put David and me down.'

Brenda nodded approvingly at that. 'We do like to have a month's money in advance,' she said as she laid down her pen, 'but that can wait until tomorrow.'

As the two women walked home through dabs of shadow planted under the trees by the evening light, Gwendolen said 'Joelle, I don't know how to thank you.'

'Good heavens, Gwen, for what?'

'You don't know the load you've taken off my mind. I mean to give you and David something special when I can.'

'We've plenty. You keep what you've got.'

'That's the last thing I mean to do,' Gwendolen said mostly to herself, staring at the foot of the tree where they had seen the cat. Three fledglings had fallen or been pushed out of the nest and lay dead among the knuckly roots. 'Never mind, you did your best,' she said.

David was cursing a severed branch of the rosebush before flinging it onto the lawn and sucking his finger. 'Dinner's waiting to go on the turntable,' he mumbled.

Gwendolen seemed prepared to watch the entire operation of

the microwave. David had selected cartons of Joelle's best Indian dinner. Joelle wondered if it might be too fierce for their guest, but once the aroma began to seep out of the microwave Gwendolen raised her head and sniffed the air approvingly. She greeted her first mouthful of lamb curry with even more enthusiasm than she had expressed for breakfast that morning. 'You do enjoy your food,' David said.

'Yes, for a wonder.'

He filled three glasses from a wine box of Bulgarian red. 'What shall we drink to?'

'To having somewhere to lay your head,' Gwendolen proposed at once.

They lingered over dinner, listening to birdsong piercing the foliage around the garden beyond the open patio doors. 'Is it an early night all round?' David said once he'd washed up.

'Would there be time for me to have a bath?'

'Take your time, Gwen,' Joelle said, and found herself considering for the first time how Gwendolen smelled: very faintly, almost like a home-made perfume, of dry grass. It wasn't offensive, just rather odd. She followed Gwendolen upstairs and laid a nightdress on the guest-room bed as water thundered into the tub.

David had switched on the television and was sipping one more glass of wine, apparently to help him indulge *Liverpool Loo*, a joke which had managed to prolong itself into a second six-episode series. 'You look very dutiful,' Joelle said.

'If Bill comes to the barbecue he's bound to ask if we've been watching.'

As if he'd been waiting for David to give him his cue the credits made way for Bill Messenger, sitting on his canvas stool outside the Gents near a pub in a Liverpool suburb. The title of the episode – 'The Princess and the Pee' – and the first line of Bill's monologue to the camera – 'Flushed with pride, that's me' – were enough to send Joelle into the back garden with that day's *Observer*. She was halfway through the review section when Gwendolen came downstairs, wearing the ankle-length nightdress and smelling, it seemed, of all the soaps in the bathroom. 'We won't watch this if you'd rather not,' David said. 'It's only that he's a customer of ours.'

'An actor! What is he like?'

'Difficult to say,' Joelle said, joining David on the couch. 'Superior to his material. He doesn't really have that Scouse accent

70

or wear that ghastly cap. Sometimes when we were altering his house I used to wonder what his real voice sounded like.'

Some element of what they'd told Gwendolen must have taken her fancy, because she watched the programme to its end while her hosts winced; then she gazed at the latest news without flinching, though the dismaying parade – famine, assassination, child abuse, yet another baby stolen from outside a shop which banned prams – made Joelle's innards feel like a fist. The weather forecast showed a map strewn with suns that had fallen to earth, and Gwendolen seemed prepared to watch for as long as there was any broadcast. 'Shall we leave you to it?' Joelle said.

'Will I set off your alarm?'

'You will if we put it on and you move.'

'I had to get used to keeping still,' Gwendolen said, and turned away from the screen as though it was distracting her. 'I don't want you even knowing I'm here. I'll go up.'

'Would you like a book to read?' Joelle said.

'I don't think there is anything books can teach me.'

'Upstairs isn't alarmed,' David said, 'but down here there are eyes all over the house like the one behind you that can see anything that moves, even in the dark.'

'Like God.'

Joelle glanced at her in surprise, and felt bound to explain. 'I'm sorry, Gwen, it just shows how wrong you can be about people. I had the impression you weren't religious.'

'I doubt you'll meet anyone who believes in sin more than I do.'

David had just switched off the television, leaving the three of them isolated by a silence. 'Well, I'll say goodnight,' he said and, given the silence, did.

'Night, Gwen.'

'Enjoy your night,' Gwendolen told them both.

When Joelle went into the bathroom to brush her teeth it was foggy with steam, though the mirror bore a clear patch approximately the size and shape of an adult face. She pulled the cord of the extractor fan and left it whirring as she made for the bedroom, where David was lying under the quilt, his bare arms behind his head. 'How about you?' he said.

'What about me?'

'Do *you* believe in sin?'

'Just watch me,' she said, already undressing. Once she was naked she snatched the quilt off him, and his penis rose as though it was being lifted by an invisible winch. She kissed it and followed a

71

trail of familiar kisses up to his mouth, and he had barely tongued her nipples before her body was gasping for him. Though his thrusts were as gentle as he could manage, he wasn't able to hold back for more than a few; after all, she thought in the midst of the flaring of her own sensations, he'd been waiting all weekend. They dozed for a while, comfortably entangled, and then he entered her again. Second times were often the best, at least for Joelle, though she couldn't help being aware that Gwendolen was next door. Surely she wouldn't be able to hear them for the humming of the fan.

Perhaps it was a combination of the events of the weekend and Joelle's awareness of a stranger in the house which, in the depths of the night, made her dream. She was lying on the bottom of a boat which was being rowed out to an island, and she was unable to move. Then she could, and was above the island, watching a figure stooping to an immobile body in the dusk and straightening up, its jaws working. She didn't much care for that, but it gave way to the sight of a woman dancing far out on a surface which Joelle took to be a slate floor until she realised it was an utterly still sea. The woman was crowned with a rosebush which was pressed down as low as her eyebrows. This was the image that wakened Joelle, and for a moment she was certain that someone had been watching her and David and had just withdrawn, at least as far as the darkest corner of the room. The watcher was naked, she thought. The impression was so fleeting and so unlikely that she went back to sleep at once.

# Eight

The voices of the small choir met beneath the ribs of the vaulted ceiling and flocked down into the nave of the cathedral. Their echoes soared beyond the massive arches, sounding the walls like an immense sandstone bell, and Henrie could imagine them awakening the stones. She could almost see the angels carved on the choir screen borrowing the voices and swooping through the aisles to revive the carvings that made her every step across the tiled floor a step towards a discovery – an amiable lion, a mediaeval elephant whose unlikeliness suggested it belonged to a lost species, a pelican tapping its own breast for blood. She was heading for the cloisters, since it didn't look as though Jake and Terry and the rest of the choir would be through rehearsing for a while, when a woman with an accent Henrie identified as Lancashire – each word chopped off like meat on a slab – said behind her 'What's that they're singing?'

'Perotin,' Henrie said at once.

'Never,' said the woman with what Henrie gathered was irony, which provoked her to respond further, even though it was clear that the elderly woman and her companion who could almost have been her identical twin, each of whom appeared to be propping up the other, regarded her as having robbed them of a good few minutes' leisurely conversation. 'Twelfth-century French. Steve Reich and your Sir Michael Tippett admire him.'

They stared at her as if they thought she was some wiseass American tourist who was about to start explaining their heritage to them. 'Enjoy,' she said.

The more bejewelled and funereally dressed of the women said 'We mean to, love.'

Nobody except the British, Henrie thought, could use the last word to imply something like its opposite, but as she watched the women stump away in search of enjoyment she was less offended than amused. Watching Jake and Terry singing baritone together beneath the angels continued to disconcert her, however. When

73

she felt her mouth preparing to smile at Jake in case he glanced in her direction, she turned her back on the choir. Feeling as though the stony presence of the building was poised to settle on her scalp, she walked quickly through the cloisters, past window after window full of flattened saints, and out of the cathedral.

Sightseers were reading the inscriptions on the tombstones which made up the path. Henrie glimpsed 'Here lies' beneath her feet as she passed the isolated bell-tower and climbed the steps onto the Roman city wall. A few hundred yards along it, a Victorian clock on wrought-iron arches straddled the wall. When she stood under the clock she felt like a native of Chester – would Castrian be the word? She gazed down at Eastgate Street, its timbered buildings black and white as a nun's uniform, the crowds gathering around the cross at the meeting of the main streets, where the town crier was ringing his bell. 'Oyez, oyez' was all she could distinguish of his tiny shout, but she no longer experienced the tourist's urge to go and listen. She held onto the railings, gliding her hands up and down the cool metal, until she felt happy to have left New York.

She had reasons. Just reading the ads on the sides of the buses passing under the bridge without her being advised to phone 212-COPKILL brought some of them back. Here she'd made friends who didn't even know anyone who'd been shot at or raped or mugged. Here you could ride the train all the way to Liverpool, where it turned into a subway, without anyone performing a panhandling song or a monologue – here she never felt the need to cut off her awareness until she wasn't sure if fellow passengers were talking to her or to themselves. She remembered the undernourished black woman who'd sat next to her in the waiting area at Penn Station, shouting 'Bang, bang, bang . . . I'm going to the beach . . . Anyone here going to the beach? . . . You're all fucked up . . . Bang, bang, bang . . .' That had been last July, when the heat never seemed to move except for the illusion of a breeze in the trees beyond the air conditioning in her and Jake's apartment on West 91st, and she remembered thinking she'd met that day's crazy person and so she ought to be safe until tomorrow. Maybe the thought had finally convinced her that she and Jake needed to move, but why couldn't they have moved upstate or to Connecticut? How had Chester seemed to have been waiting for them to fall out of love with New York?

They'd visited it on their only previous trip to England, because Terry and Sarah Monk had invited them to stay at their house.

They'd met the Monks at a Brahms concert in Central Park two years ago, where Jake had been able to provide a corkscrew upon overhearing Terry bewailing his lack of a tool to uncork a bottle, and from sharing the wine they'd progressed to discovering that both men sang early choral music, and the next night the four of them had met for dinner at the Southern restaurant on Duke Ellington Avenue, and now Henrie was nostalgic for New York. It wouldn't matter so much if she didn't feel there was no going back, but the moment the plane had left the ground at Kennedy her dislike of flying had turned into a panic so inexplicable and uncontrollable that she couldn't imagine ever boarding another flight. Had it related to something other than flying? She'd thought that the sense of layer on layer of history had made Chester irresistible to her and Jake, but if the place had a secret appeal for her, why couldn't it have let her into the secret sooner? The tiny shout of the crier fell silent, and all at once Henrie felt alone and exposed and out of place. She hurried to the inscribed path and through the corridor of pressed saints back into the cathedral.

She was in time to see the choir pronounce their last notes and close their mouths as though to keep the echoes from returning to them. Terry had shut his eyes the better to listen to the spaciousness. Jake looked, though she tried not to think it, a little smug, taking too much credit for the music. The echoes vanished, swallowed by the past, and the conductor said 'Same time next week.' The choir said their goodbyes, their voices suddenly much smaller, and Terry and Jake came to meet Henrie in the nave. 'Here she is,' Jake said. 'We thought you'd run away and left us, didn't we, Terry?'

'Something along those lines. Hello, Henrie. Are you well?'

'I'm pretty good, and you?'

'Oh, well, you know,' Terry said, sweeping his hair back with a gesture which she'd come to realise was only nervous, not pretentious. 'Can't complain.'

'I should say not,' Jake said, 'with a wife like Sarah.'

'Then you certainly can't, Jake,' Terry said.

'But I'm not married to Sarah. Oh, you mean this one. Just kidding, Henrie,' Jake said, putting his arm round her shoulders and squeezing, 'as if you didn't know.'

'So where did you think I'd have run away to?'

She was looking at Terry, who shrugged hard and held his hands out palms upward. 'Nowhere, I guess,' Jake said.

'Then I couldn't have, could I?' She gazed at Terry with all the force she felt like turning on Jake. 'Did you persuade Sarah to meet us for a walk?'

'She'll be at an antiques fair in Preston until late.'

'In that case do you guys mind if I take a rain check on the walk?' Jake said. 'There's a few things I'd like to fix at the shop before we open. You guys go ahead, though.'

'Are you certain you don't need me?' Henrie said.

'Only to make dinner.'

'It's my turn again, huh?'

'Henrie, you know I can't cook for shit. Pardon *me*,' he added to a glass saint in the cloisters through which they were walking. 'You know one of the reasons I had to marry you was you made the best meals I ever ate. It's the same with you and Sarah, Terry, am I right?'

'I believe so.'

'And you tell her, don't you?'

'Maybe not as often as I should.'

'Fuck,' Jake muttered, and found himself facing a nun as he opened the outer door. Her wrinkled lips formed a silent O of disapproval as she brushed past him. '*Fuck*,' he said with feeling once the door shut behind him. 'Listen, I'm sorry, I just don't like being made to feel I can't pay you a compliment without checking first that it's politically correct. I'm sorry, okay?'

'You always are, Jake.'

'All right, so I'm sorry now.' He began to sing 'Who's Sorry Now?' and dance backwards on the grass in the spiky shadow of the cathedral.

'Stop it, Jake.'

He shook his head and extended both hands to her as he continued singing. When she ran to him she had to catch hold of his face before she could shut his mouth with a kiss. She pressed her lips against his until she was convinced he wouldn't burst into song once she let go. When she did he said 'Hey, Terry, you can look now. No need to be embarrassed.'

'I assure you I'm not.'

'God, I love this country. "Assure you"! I thought even the Brits didn't talk like that except in old movies. Hey, no offence, Terry.' He swung towards the other man and stretched his arms out, and Henrie thought Terry looked exactly as though he was bracing himself for the onslaught of some hound larger than himself that was about to jump up and lick his face. As Jake hugged him and slapped his back, his stricken eyes were visible over Jake's shoulder. After a few seconds even Jake must have sensed his reserve, and flung his arms wide. 'Listen, I'd better be getting to work before people start wondering what's with you and the loudmouthed American.'

'Jake,' Henrie said, 'are you absolutely sure you don't want me to come with you?'

'I've had my fun today, now you have yours. Just leave yourself time to fix dinner.'

They were crossing a cobbled yard of Georgian houses that overlooked the cathedral. The Abbey Gateway, an arch so thick it was inhabited by a uniformed man in a window, led them onto Northgate Street, where the remains of several Roman columns suggested that the street had been arranged as a display of architecture through mediaeval to modern. An infuriating reluctance to leave Jake led Henrie down St Werburgh Street, past the front of the cathedral, to the Choral Store on Eastgate. It was in a crypt below the Rows, stone-flagged arcades which ran parallel to the streets, through the fronts of the buildings above them. As he opened the door, pushing back a wad of business mail, a man wearing a checked cap and a sad moustache hurried out of the crowd. 'Excuse me, are you open?'

'Soon,' Henric said, indicating the notice in the window full of Requiems.

Jake gave her one of his goggling double-takes. 'Take a look around,' he told the customer, 'and if you see anything you need I'll hold it for you.'

This time she genuinely felt that he was telling her to walk, and she did so under the clock on the bridge, so fast that Terry had to trot in order to keep up. As she turned along a side street he said 'What was I supposed to make of all that?'

'He's always hyped up after he's been singing, and he's going to be nervous about the shop until he sees how it works out.'

'But did I get the impression he was trying to tell me something?'

'I don't know, did you?' Terry was extending a hand as if he wanted to hold her still, and she halted because she felt too edgy to want to be touched. 'About the shop, do you mean?'

His generously rounded face took on an expression of reserved pain that seemed quintessentially English. 'Before the shop.'

'Like what?'

'I can't say,' Terry said, sweeping his hair back. 'You know him better than me. Than I do.'

'Too well,' Henrie said, and tried to control her words, which were getting her no place. 'Well enough to promise you don't need to worry so much about him. How about that walk? I really wouldn't mind one.'

Terry's face turned several shades of pink. 'Oh, I'm sorry. I—'

'Don't say what you were thinking and I won't either. Wishes aren't meant to come true if you tell them.'

She flashed him a smile so fleeting he could make what he liked of it and set out for the riverside, feeling light on her feet, suddenly capable of dancing, though she could imagine that embarrassing him horribly here in public. Beyond a partially excavated Roman amphitheatre where gladiators must have clashed and there was a shrine to Nemesis, the road led past a pinkish Norman church to a stone-walled path down to the river. The sound of wind in the singing trees above the walls gave way to the shouts of rowers playing pirates in hired boats. Henrie walked up the ramp from the promenade onto the wide suspension bridge, and as she caught sight of her cottage along the river bank the movements of the crowd of sightseers caused the bridge to stagger. When she grabbed Terry's arm he looked both amused and relieved. 'It's been standing for a long time,' he assured her.

'You sound like one of your *Carry On* movies.' She disengaged herself gently from him and headed for the far bank, where she waited as he followed her down the iron steps, looking flustered again. They were silent as they walked as far as the shrine to Minerva, a quarry which appeared to retain the ghost of a carving on the stone, and then they crossed the old bridge above the slanting weir and returned along the Groves, the promenade. Children were wrestling at the water's edge, a bearded old lady was being wheeled through the strolling crowd, a boatman shouted to a colleague 'Have you seen my number three?' From above the promenade the Old Orleans restaurant faced a paddle-boat called the *Mark Twain* beyond a Victorian bandstand. 'Watch out, you're being colonised,' Henrie said.

'I'm no chauvinist.'

'I'll say you're not.' The undertow of their words made her continue 'Well, I guess I'd better head for home. This walk is meant to end with me in the kitchen, right?'

'I'll say goodbye here, shall I?'

'Only if you want to.'

'I don't.'

'Then don't.'

Two motorboats collided in the middle of the river with a creaking thud and separated, surrounding themselves with a web of ripples, the edge of which splashed onto the grassy footpath as Henrie opened her gate. Whenever she stepped into the small garden packed with flowers on either side of the winding cobbled path, she felt as though she was stepping into the photograph of this row of cottages beyond the promenade, which Terry had found at the real estate agent's and sent her and Jake. Once they'd realised that selling the Upper West Side apartment would buy the cottage that was for sale and leave them as much in change, they hadn't even seemed to need to make a choice. 'Thanks, Terry,' she said, unhooking her keys from a belt loop of her jeans.

'For what?'

She hadn't really intended to be heard. 'For bringing me here,' she said.

That kept him at the gate as though he wasn't sure if she was dismissing him. 'To live, I mean,' she said, and stood in the open doorway until he ventured up the path.

The ground floor was a single large square room. A stout oak staircase without a banister climbed the wall beside the front door. Most of the room was furnished with the contents of the apartment: sofas, a rocker which her grandmother in Rhode Island used to own, a spindly graceful dining suite designed by an old girlfriend of Jake's who had later exhibited sculptures at the Museum of Modern Art, rugs scattered on the wide stone flags of the floor. As soon as she reached the built-in aluminium kitchen Henrie switched on the radio, only to be met by the voices of two men discussing a naked woman who was running across a cricket pitch. 'I thought this was your all-day music channel,' she said.

'This is Blighty, remember. Every summer we replace Bach with balls.'

'Well, I guess I've had my fix of music for today.' She hunkered down to sort out vegetables from the plastic rack to make a salad. She felt her jeans stretch tight over her bottom and between her legs, and sensed Terry's eyes on her. Abruptly she stood up and turned to face him. 'The hell with being told to make dinner. Just for that he can buy me dinner at the Orleans. As long as we're here, can you use a coffee?'

'I wouldn't say no.'

'Hand me the grounds then, would you?'

He took some seconds to look away from her in order to find the glass-topped jar. He closed his hands around it and brought it to her. As he made to place it on the aluminium surface where the grinder stood she put out a hand for it, and their fingers touched.

He would have dropped the jar if she hadn't slipped her free hand beneath it. Somehow they managed together to convey the jar to the nearest horizontal surface, and then their fingers intertwined as their bodies drew together. One touch had been enough to erase all the words and doubts which had hindered them, and she felt as though nothing had existed before this moment except their first time. When his tongue began to play with hers as he pulled her T-shirt out of her jeans she raised her face from his long enough to murmur 'Not downstairs'.

His mouth found hers again as he lifted her, one arm around her shoulders and the other behind her knees. As he carried her past the front door she pushed the bolt home. The stairs creaked beneath them like a bed. She was unbuttoning his shirt, but as she yanked it out of his trousers a thread snapped, and she heard a button go rattling downstairs. She clasped her arms around his bare torso to indicate that she would find the button later. A slight pressure of her hand on his left shoulder as they arrived at the top of the stairs was enough to direct him into the guest room. He heeled the door shut and deposited her on the bed as if she was an armful of some kind of treasure, and then he was unzipping her jeans and easing them and her panties down her legs while she unbuckled his belt. A shrug of his buttocks helped his trousers on their way, then she and Terry flung their remaining clothes onto the unadorned floorboards and he knelt between her legs. His penis was reaching for her, but he only gazed at her. 'What?' she said.

'I can't help saying it again. You're the most beautiful woman I've ever seen.'

She couldn't help saying what she'd only thought last time. 'Not Sarah?'

'I love her, I want you to realise that, but not in that way any more.'

'And I want you to know Jake and I agreed at the start we wouldn't put a barbed-wire fence around each other. Is that enough dialogue for now?'

The moment he set about kissing her all over she didn't need to be told how beautiful he thought she was: his touch was renewing her sense of herself. When he turned her over and ran his tongue up her spine from the cleft of her bottom she stretched out her arms and dug her fingernails into the sides of the mattress, her nipples tingling against the cool quilt. When his tongue reached the nape of her neck a shiver raced down her and parted her. She twisted onto her back and raised her hips and closed one hand around his penis to feed it into her, and after that she could hardly distinguish his limbs or his thrusting from her own. She was riding waves of sensation that blotted out everything else until at last they crested and exploded and left her and Terry gasping on the dishevelled bed.

For a while his breathing was so loud she could have taken it for her own. They laid their heads on the crumpled pillows, and sounds outside the house began to come into focus: a baby crying in the distance, children shouting, a man calling over and over 'Come in number three.' Several ducks began to quack, and the sound had brought a drowsy smile to Henrie's lips when she heard the click of the latch of a garden gate.

It needn't be hers just because it sounded like hers, but Terry had raised his head like an animal scenting danger. She touched a forefinger to his lips and held herself very still. She heard footsteps on a path, coming closer until there was no question that it led to the door under the bedroom, halting at the door as Jake rested three fingers on the outside of his trousers pocket while he used thumb and forefinger to probe for his keys – and then the doorbell rang.

So it couldn't be Jake. She didn't care who else it was, but all the same, she wanted to know. She hurried to the window, where she crouched so that the tops of her breasts were level with the sill. Suppose, she thought just too late, that Jake had left his keys somewhere? Then the visitor stepped back, and she saw the top of a head of untidy red hair, which certainly wasn't Jake's. The man raised his broad round face and saw her before she could retreat, and his wide mouth seemed uncertain whether to smile. 'Ah, hello?' he called. 'Mrs Henrietta Lee?'

Terry jerked upright and almost slid off the quilt. 'Good God,' he said, 'it's David Owain.'

# Nine

'Never Terry Monk,' Joelle protested.

'If we know another Terry, tell me,' David said.

'You don't really mean to say they were—'

'I think if it hadn't been for the coffee they might have left me believing it was just my evil mind.'

She kicked off her shoes and drew her legs under her on the couch. 'Don't be infuriating. What coffee?'

'The coffee that never was,' he said, and grinned between his hands, which he'd raised as if she might be about to fling some missile at him. 'I'm getting ahead of the story. As I say, I saw this bust in both senses of the word at the window, and she called to Terry would he mind letting me in while she got dressed? So I waited, and I mightn't even have thought anything about how long if it hadn't been for him. Only as soon as he opened the door he told me Mrs Lee was just getting dressed from having a shower, and he was so anxious for me to believe it I almost kidded him about it because I thought it was true, you see. I mean, he didn't look what you'd call dressed, but that was no surprise in that heat. So he came out with this steaming mug in his hand and went and leaned on the gate, and I wouldn't have thought there was anything odd about that, he just wanted us to wait until she was dressed enough to let us in. Then he starts telling me how he'd met her and her husband that summer he and Sarah went to the States, and how he sings in the choir with her husband, and all the time he's drinking out of the mug and trying to look as if he's enjoying it. Then all of a sudden he says "I can't make this kind of coffee" and chucks what's left in the mug on the flowerbed.'

'What sort of coffee?' Joelle demanded, wriggling her feet under her.

'The sort you have to grind yourself, I was supposed to think. At least that's the kind she had in the house.'

'So what's so sinister about that?'

'I'll tell you. He must have been hoping he'd be too quick for me to see what was in the mug, but some of it landed on a bit of marble in the rockery. It wasn't coffee, it was just hot water. He must have filled the mug from the hot tap.'

Joelle poked out her tongue in disgust, scraping it with her teeth. 'Did he realise you'd noticed?'

'I didn't let him. He'd only just done it when she opened the door. If he'd waited another couple of seconds I wouldn't have seen.'

'Go on, then. What's she like?'

'Red hair and freckles. Big grey eyes and a mouth you could imagine standing on end, if you know what I mean. Legs I bet gave Terry a few bruised ribs – long like yours. Pretty sexy, especially when I was thinking what she and Terry must have just been up to.'

'I'm glad she met with your approval.'

'Don't be like that. I'm not envying him.'

'I should bloody well hope not.'

'So don't start thinking they gave me ideas for anyone else but you. It was like most of the secrets we've found out – a bit sexy and a bit pathetic.'

David sat beside her and stroked her legs. Sometimes their discoveries ended up as fantasies they acted out together, but this one didn't turn her on – not while she had to wonder 'Does Sarah know?'

'Christ, I hope not. How do you think she could?'

'I can't imagine Terry telling her, and she won't find out from us.' Joelle squeezed his hand and trapped it on her knee. 'Won't it be a strain, working for this couple and knowing what may still be going on?'

'The Lees, you mean? That's the joke of it. There's nothing wrong with their cottage that an hour or two with a hammer and nails won't put right. A few loose floorboards, but no rot. They needn't have called me in at all.'

He patted her under one thigh and stood up. 'In a way that's all to the good. Want a beer?'

'I think I'll walk off dinner and maybe see how Gwen's settling in.'

'I suppose I should.'

'You needn't if you want to watch that film. To the good in what way?'

'Oh,' he called on his way to the refrigerator, 'just that Doug Singleton's aunt's place is going to see off a few weeks of our life.'

'Problems?'

'Wherever I went, it began to seem like, and you know how big those houses are.' A can of lager hissed as he pulled the tag, and after a thorough gulp he said 'I'm afraid the aunt may be one.'

Joelle met him in the hall and took a mouthful of his drink. 'Doug did say she had her off days, didn't he?'

'I hope this was one of them. The first thing she did when she opened the door was wipe her feet on the mat, presumably to show me how to do it.'

'Tell Doug to hire someone else if you're not happy with the job.'

'You know I'd be worried they would rip him off or not do everything that needs doing. He wouldn't have called us if he hadn't liked the work we did for him.' David tapped the rim of the can against his front teeth. 'Tell Gwen I'll see her soon. Arnie can show Cuthbert how to trash the house.'

'I'll leave you three to be men together,' Joelle said, and kissed him quickly so that he wouldn't notice she was on edge.

She more or less knew why she was, though it seemed to have crept up on her. At least she didn't have to worry about Herb just now, she thought as she emerged into the evening light: she could see his television flickering, keeping him the next best thing to occupied. Someone, or perhaps a cat, had cleared away the dead birds from beneath the tree on the pavement. Beyond the open windows of the Shangri-La Retirement Home she heard thuds and grunts as the Schwarzenegger film began. Gwendolen might be watching it, might well be fascinated, and Brenda Mickling had insisted she had more time than Joelle to take her shopping, but these weren't the only reasons why Joelle walked past the home.

As she crossed the main road near the sandstone cross a sports car crammed with youths waving bottles, all of whom looked too young to drive, raced through a red light towards the motorway. A ragged cheer and a few protests were raised by drinkers at tables outside the pubs, then the street went back to dozing. Joelle passed the Ba Ba Guest House and turned along a side street into Hoole, the suburb which was mostly on this side of the main road. Here the streets were narrower and straighter, the houses packed together. Two middle-aged women with shopping bags were cycling abreast up the street while a driver who made his Mini look even more dwarfish fumed behind them. He overtook with a roar of himself and the engine as Joelle approached the row of houses where the Pinnocks lived.

Theirs was near the middle of about a dozen houses which appeared to have been squashed thin and white. Velvet curtains were gathered aside from the single downstairs window, framing plastic models on the inner windowsill: a monster with bolts poking out of his neck, a spaceship which at first Joelle thought was called the Enterprise in reference to some employment scheme, a man whose head was masked by a black helmet, a bald man with pins studding his face. As Joelle loitered, listening for sounds she didn't want to hear, the window above the front door slid up, clattering its sash-weights. 'Never seen monsters before? We're not a shop, you know,' Hayley Pinnock shouted, dropping cigarette ash which Joelle had to step back to avoid. 'Oh, it's Joelle, isn't it. Wait there, I'll be down.'

Nineteen-month-old Rutger appeared beside her, to be snatched back at once with a thud and a howl. 'Don't start,' Hayley yelled as the window slammed. 'You know to stay away from windows. And how many times did I tell you to go downstairs? Can't your mam and the baby have a moment to themselves?'

The baby was news to Joelle, and not good news. She waited while a considerable amount of thumping descended the stairs. Apparently most of that was Hayley, who proved to be wearing her pregnancy overalls again. Her jowly face looked heavier and far too old, while her excessively blonde hair and several areas of makeup only conspired to render her appearance unreal. Behind her Rutger was clambering downstairs backwards below the safety gate, which wasn't shut. Hayley saw Joelle notice that, and turned on him. 'You stay down where you're told. Say hello to Mrs Owain and then go play in the playroom Mr and Mrs Owain made so nice for you. That's right, get down and say hello. He can say it when he wants to. Say hello.'

'Hello, Rutger,' Joelle called. 'How are you today?'

The sound he emitted as he bumped onto each stair combined a reminiscence of the howls caused by his fall in the bedroom with the beginnings of a cough. 'Mrs Owain's speaking to you,' Hayley warned him. 'You're champion, aren't you? That's kids for you, make a row till you could strangle them, not really, then when you want to hear from them they clam up.'

Rutger lowered himself onto the hall floor and staggered round, holding onto the lowest post of the banisters, to gaze at Joelle. His blue eyes were the liveliest part of his unformed doughy face. 'Look at you,' Hayley said in a conversational shout, as if she had only just observed the food encrusting the front of his rompers.

'What do you think Mrs Owain thinks of you? You can just stay like that till you learn how to eat nicely.'

'Actually,' Joelle said, 'I think—'

Rutger stumbled towards her. She thought he'd lost his balance, having let go of the post, but Hayley grabbed his arm and yanked him backwards. 'What have you been told about not running out of the house? How many times do you need to be told?' she yelled, still jerking his arm. 'Don't start that row or I'll give you a reason to make it. And I'll tell your dad when he comes home.'

'I shouldn't pull his arm like that,' Joelle said as calmly as she could. 'You might hurt his shoulder.'

'I don't suppose you would, but you aren't a mother, are you? We can't all take the day off from him like his dad who's playing Dungeons and Dragons with his mates.' Hayley gave Rutger's arm a final yank and stooped to him before recoiling in disgust. 'Poo,' she cried. 'Have you messed yourself again? You can stay like that for a while and see how you like it. Your dad can change you if he ever decides to come home.'

Joelle could smell only the cigarette smoke in which the house always seemed to be steeped. She clenched her fists behind her back. 'I'll change him if you like.'

'You're not having one after all, are you?'

'One what?'

'A brat. A kid. I mean, you aren't trying to get into practice for when it comes.'

'I thought I told you when we were here David can't.'

'You must have if you say so. Don't be miffed if I turn you down, will you? He gets disturbed if anyone but me or Scott undresses him. I just hope he grows out of it by the time he's old enough for us to get him to a playgroup.'

'Then shouldn't you—'

'I may change him once you're gone. He doesn't like other people seeing him undressed. And,' she roared into Rutger's face, 'if he stops his row and goes in the playroom we had made specially for him. The sight would put you off your food, Joelle, if you saw what he'll be like now.'

'Even if it did I wouldn't blame him.'

Hayley focused her attention on the pack of cigarettes she'd taken from her pocket. 'I used to think the job would come with as much patience as you needed, but if you want the truth, I reckon you and David have a lot to be grateful for. Ask any parent and I bet they'll tell you the same, sometimes they could choke them or drown them, not really. Yes, you know I'm talking about you, don't you,' she yelled at Rutger. 'He can understand when he wants to. Get in the playroom this minute or I'll give all your toys to some poor child who'll appreciate them. And don't you dare make a mess for your mother to clear up. One toy at a time and then put it back where it belongs.'

Rutger's face had begun to crumple, but he thought better of crying as she continued to glare at him. He lurched away, rubbing his shoulder, and made lopsidedly for the small back room that was the playroom. 'You see, that's what it takes,' Hayley told Joelle. 'Too much of the time, it does. You'd get tired of it before long. Was there something you wanted?'

'I was just passing, and I thought . . .'

What she'd thought was feeble compared to what she was thinking now, but there didn't seem to be anything more she could reasonably say or do. Unreasonably, on the other hand . . . 'Don't be miffed if I don't invite you in, will you?' Hayley said. 'I've got a million things to do. Us mothers always have.' She lit another cigarette from the stub which she shied into the gutter, then stepped back and shut the door.

Joelle listened, rubbing her palms dry on her culottes. When she heard no sound from Rutger she made herself walk away. At least, she thought and hoped, Hayley must have realised she was suspicious. If she treated Rutger like that in front of Joelle, what might she do to him when there were no witnesses? Surely he'd been walking awkwardly because he was still learning, but if Joelle even suspected that he'd been limping . . . She shook her fists and almost turned back. She ought to talk to David first, she decided, and hurried to the main road, where an early streetlamp was making the sandstone cross glow like a dying coal. As she waited for a rush of motorcycles to pass, a woman came out of Joelle's road. It was Sarah Monk, Terry's wife.

Her capacious kaftan billowed as she waved to Joelle and halted by the cross. Joelle was yearning for more traffic to give her time to think, but she'd had little success when a gap too extensive to ignore appeared. The best she could manage as she stepped onto the opposite pavement was 'What brings you here, Sarah?'

'I just wanted to check you got the message from our American friends. I never trust those machines.'

'Oh yes, we did,' Joelle said, wishing that Sarah had mentioned anything other than the American couple. 'As a matter of fact

David's been, that's to say he went to their house. Didn't anyone tell you?'

She heard what she'd just asked, and had to struggle not to squeeze her eyes shut or clap a hand over her mouth. Sarah cocked her head, which was cropped too short for her large wide high-browed face, and looked concerned. 'Joelle, what's the matter?'

She was the last person Joelle could inform and the only person she should. Joelle thought of a response that would sound like the truth, though it made her feel more desperate than inspired. 'I was just thinking how unfair it is that people like you who want children can't have them when people who don't deserve to have them do.'

Sarah shaded her eyes with one broad hand; her wedding ring glittered under the streetlamp. 'What started you thinking along those lines?'

'One of our customers you *won't* be seeing at the barbecue. She's got one toddler and another on the way, and you wouldn't treat a dog the way she treats the one she's got. If I could just be sure she's doing something she isn't allowed to do to him . . .'

'Sounds to me as if you need to sit and talk. Come on, I'll buy you a drink and we can sit outside and watch the world go by.'

Joelle felt she'd said most of what she could risk saying to Sarah just now, but she had barely hesitated when Sarah said 'Don't if you want to get home. I can imagine you might rather talk to David.'

She was being considerate, and Joelle was shocked to find herself blaming Sarah for it – thinking that if Sarah didn't always care more for others than for herself Terry might not have strayed. Joelle had seen friends of hers turned gradually more shapeless by motherhood, their bodies and their personalities losing definition, but since Sarah was infertile she lacked that excuse. Joelle didn't feel safe in talking to her while she was beset by such thoughts. 'I think you're right, Sarah,' she said, and sensed the disappointment behind Sarah's instantly agreeable expression. She kissed Sarah on both too-plump cheeks, glimpsing the grey roots of her black hair. 'We'll get together soon, I promise, and have a good talk.'

She watched Sarah cross the road, her kaftan outlining her thick legs, and waved to her in a way that she hoped was encouraging; then she headed home. The windows of the Shangri-La were still open, and the Schwarzenegger film was being urged on by a shrill orchestra. She didn't want to talk to Gwendolen just now after all. As she passed the gates, however, Brenda Mickling hurried out of the porch and across the lawn, calling 'Mrs Owain?'

Joelle rested a hand on the prickly stone wall. 'Gwen's all right, isn't she?'

'Gwen's fine.' The proprietor stopped on the other side of the wall to catch her breath. 'I just want to talk to you about the money she tried to pay with.'

# Ten

When Bill heard the couple begin to complain about the painting he moved to stand behind them. The man was tugging at the right handlebar of his moustache, clearly a favourite gesture of his, since that side was longer than the other. His wife was peering over the narrow gilded rectangles of her glasses and scratching her steely hair, which made a sound like a hamster in a nest. 'What's that supposed to be when it's at home?' she said.

'A waste of whatever they paid for it, which I hope wasn't much.'

'Looks like my old raincoat when we'd finished painting the conservatory.'

'You oughtn't to have thrown it out. You could have sold it to whoever they pay to chuck money about, and then we could have gone to the Cape twice this year.' The man's face grew even purpler as he twisted his moustache. 'It's an insult to us and every other pensioner, squandering our taxes on piffle like this while they dole us out as little as they think they can get away with.'

The woman was patting her disarranged perm into shape. 'And if our taxes aren't supporting stuff like this they're being used to buy needles for addicts. There's a connection, if you ask me.'

'Excuse me,' Bill said, 'would you like any help?'

Both heads turned slowly and examined him. 'Do you work here at the Tate?' the woman said.

'No, but I couldn't help noticing you were discussing my work.'

The man let go of his moustache so as to jab a stubby black-gloved finger at the plaque beside the painting. 'You're the creator, are you?'

'Are you saying it like that because I don't look like an artist or it doesn't look like art to you?'

'You look like someone who would paint that.'

'Well, thank you very much. Most kind of you to say so.'

The woman's lips crinkled as if she couldn't judge how innocent his response was, and her husband returned to the attack. 'Maybe you can explain your painting to us in language ordinary folk like us will understand.'

'My pleasure. It's about what you don't see.'

The couple each gave it a hostile glance. 'There's plenty of that,' the man said.

'Yes, but that's the point. It's about the conflict between the surface and the hidden meaning, to put it in layperson's language.'

'Layman's,' the woman corrected him. 'You've certainly hidden it well.'

'But if I've got it right, by the time I'm, if you'll excuse me, your age the surface will have begun to wear and the viewer will be able to form an impression of what's underneath.'

The man expelled two fierce breaths before concluding that they weren't sufficiently unambiguous. 'I suppose one of us will have to ask. What's underneath?'

'A Victorian landscape. School of Constable.'

The woman stepped back with a gasp as if Bill had trodden on her foot. 'You're telling us you vandalised – they let you vandalise—'

'I'd rather call it preservation. You do understand I owned the painting – found it in an attic. It was up to me what I did with it, wouldn't you agree? Don't you like the idea of it coming to light when the world has forgotten there was any such thing? Look,' he said as the couple breathed furiously in unison, 'and you'll see what I mean. I left just one place uncovered so people can spot there's a landscape underneath. See if you can find the tree.'

The man was tugging both ends of his moustache, widening the fleshy groove which divided it. 'Do the curators of the gallery know about this?'

'I haven't told them what I've told you, no.'

'Are you going to show us where the tree is?'

'I wouldn't want to rob you of the pleasure of the hunt.'

'As you wish,' the man rumbled, and poked his face at the picture, gripping his hands together behind his back. As his wife took up exactly the same position beside him, Bill said 'Will you excuse me if I head off back to work? I just like to be incognito sometimes so I can meet my audience.'

He was hoping that might jog their memories, but perhaps they genuinely had no basis for recognising him, or they were too bent on finding evidence with which to confront the gallery staff. Bill walked through the lobby, where about a dozen young people in wheelchairs were admiring a massively muscular Epstein statue, and out through the revolving doors, which two fat schoolboys were using as a merry-go-round, onto the Albert Dock.

Sightseers in groups of no fewer than three were strolling abreast along the colonnades of the warehouses which had been reclaimed by apartments and shops. A boat loaded with children and their parents, all wearing pirate hats or eyepatches, was setting off for a tour of the docks, past the floating map of Britain from which a television weather-prophet broadcast. Lunchtime sunlight rested on the tamed water and glanced from the windows of cars speeding along the dock road as though a succession of cameras was flashing at Bill – at least, so it seemed for a moment to him. The sunlight brightened his face as he emerged from the colonnade and headed for the studio, but the heat must be slowing people's minds down, because nobody appeared to know him, even when he stood on the warehouse steps and surveyed the passing crowd. 'See you at home,' he told them, not that any of them was listening, and stepped through the thick doorway with its brass-handled Georgian door.

'Arnoon, Mr Messenger.'

'Arnoon, Fred.' Sometimes Bill found himself echoing people with an exactness they understandably resented, and he seemed compelled to reproduce Fred's greeting whenever he encountered the guard penned behind his desk. 'Everyone back from lunch?' he said hastily.

'Just.'

'Had yours?'

'Having it now.'

Bill had asked without wanting to know, and he felt even less enthusiastic when the guard held up a sandwich composed of one slice of white bread and one brown with a bite taken out of it like a section in a diagram. 'End of one loaf and the start of another,' the guard said. 'But here, look at this. I warrant you've never seen the like. Ham and banana, would you credit it? She's got my belly so it doesn't know if it's coming or going. Let's see what other surprises she's got for me . . . Sausage and pineapple, I shouldn't wonder . . . prawns and custard, I'll swear she gave me once . . .'

Bill left him rummaging in his lunchbox and dodged into the corridor beyond the desk, telling himself that he mustn't even consider using Fred's complaint as material when Fred's wife would be sure to realise that Bill had. He lingered in the plasterboard corridor that was open to the high stone ceiling of the warehouse and combed his hair without needing a mirror, then he let himself into the production office.

It felt like an outsize lidless carton with one side of bare bricks. Several of the production team were sitting at some of the desks strewn with papers. Paddy and Tremaine were crouched over their scripts, chewed pencils at the ready as if to ward off anyone who ventured near their work. Indira, the director, had the glazed expression which meant she was taking a last mental look at a shot which the budget of *Liverpool Loo* couldn't afford. Jonty, the producer, lit his S-bend pipe with a match he struck on the brick wall, leaving yet another prisoner's mark. 'Here's our missing ingredient,' he announced, and puffed repeatedly like an old train attempting to start. 'Have you been strutting anywhere useful, Bill?'

'Just meeting some of our public. I spun them a yarn until they twigged who I was.'

'So tell us, was the break productive? Got anything topical and funny for us?'

'Not this week.'

'Don't be bashful, now. Always like to have some input from every member of the team. Let's all think topical and funny until we've wrapped the series, eh? That's what we told the company you'd give them, Bill, or there may not be another.'

'I thought I had been.'

'You're a marvel, Bill, we all think so. Indira does, don't you, love? Your scenes are the ones we look forward to most. Nothing like an old pro to make life easy. One take and we can go home early for once. Stick you on the front and the end and it's umpteen times the show it would have been. Tell you what, Bill, we'll give you the topics so long as you give us the fun.'

'You want me to be funnier, is that what you're saying?'

'No pies in your face, cross my heart. Nothing that'll harm your reputation as a thespian. We don't want you falling backwards off your stool or anything like that. Wry Scouse comments on the world, that's what you're about on this show. I was just saying while you were out, though, I happened to see us on the box last week in a bar, and I could have done with hearing a few roars among the grunts of appreciation, understand what I mean? Get them in the belly, Bill, that's the secret. You're with me, you've been live in your time. On the stage,' he explained to nobody in particular.

'I am again this Christmas.'

'So you've something to thank us for, haven't you? Star of *Liverpool Loo*, it'll say on the posters. We'll be giving you the ideal opportunity to brush up your technique.' Jonty stuck his pipe between his teeth and turned to his colleagues, rubbing his hands. 'What have we got for Bill to sparkle with?'

Paddy shoved his pencil behind one large blushing ear and handed Bill the pages. 'There's some material we came up with in the pub.'

'Scrap anything you can improve on,' Tremaine said, kneading his plumply ridged forehead.

Apart from tinkering with the language of the gags based on that week's news they had Bill suggesting that the toilet should be renamed Bide-a-wee. 'I can make this work,' he said.

'There speaks a pro,' Jonty declared, digging in the bowl of his pipe with a spent match.

'Shall you type this or I?' Tremaine asked his partner.

'Shall you,' Paddy said as though he was quoting.

'Keep the language simple in the script, boys,' Jonty warned them, leaning back in his swivel chair and dumping his feet on his desk.

As Tremaine set to work on his portable typewriter Indira sat forwards, her back to her desk. 'What about the lady with the money who lives somewhere near you, Bill?'

He knew that her way of making people have to question her was intended to give her some hold on the conversation – her way of concealing shyness – but this was one of the times he found it irritating. 'Which lady's that?'

'I thought someone else might have read about her this morning,' Indira said, but everyone looked blank. 'She's in a retirement home in Chester. She tried to pay cash for her room and board with coins that are so old they aren't even legal tender.'

'I don't see any gag in that,' Paddy said.

'Well, that isn't the end of the story. One of the residents has a son who deals in coins, and it turns out some of hers are worth enough to pay her way for the rest of her life.'

'My granny gave me an old sovereign once,' Tremaine said, his fingers racing.

'My granny gave me a kick up the arse,' Paddy said.

'These weren't sovereigns, they were silver pennies. Some of them hundreds of years old, and a few the coin dealer says aren't even catalogued.'

'So,' Jonty asked the ceiling, 'what's the joke?'

'I didn't say there was one. I just thought Bill might be interested.'

'I am,' Bill assured her. 'You'd wonder how she came by all that money.'

'So long as she earned it,' Paddy growled.

That was hardly likely if the coins were so old, Bill thought, and realised that Paddy was teasing Tremaine into one of their political disagreements, the kind of conflict they used to give their scripts more life. By the time Tremaine wound the last page out of the machine and fed it to the photocopier they were blaming each other for a generous selection of the ills of the world. No doubt as usual they would end up cursing each other over drinks in the nearest pub before they arrived at the hand-shaking back-slapping stage. 'I'll see you in the morning then, shall I?' Bill said.

'Wake up hilarious,' Jonty told him. 'It's a sin not to use all the talent you've got. See if you can't make these two glumps laugh at their own jokes for once.'

Bill stuffed his pages into the pocket of his summer jacket as he left the office. Fred was arguing with someone on the phone about a studio booking and gesturing a crash-helmeted courier to wait, but managed to call after Bill 'See you mow.'

'Mow,' Bill agreed, and stepped into the spotlight of the sun. Two teenage schoolgirls whose leggings made their skinny legs look wallpapered were sharing a cigarette outside the warehouse. 'Are you on telly, mister?' one demanded.

'I cannot tell a lie. I'm the man who sits outside the loo.'

She made a face which he would have expected to shatter her elaborate makeup. 'He says he shits outside the loo.'

'Dirty ould git.'

'No, I mean *Liverpool Loo*. The comedy show. Every Sunday night at nine pee em. I'm the first and the last thing you see.'

'The last thing I'd want to, an' all.'

'Stick yourself down it and pull the chain,' the first girl advised him in a tone which sounded almost compassionate.

'Do yourselves a favour and watch something else besides antipodean droppings. It's local, it's funny, it's—'

'Shit,' the girls said in unison, and ran off giggling.

'Ignore me while you can.' Bill strode away from the warehouse, into a blaze of sunlight from the water as though another spotlight had been directed at him. 'You'll have heard of me before you're much older,' he said, no longer caring who overheard.

# Eleven

'Morning, Miss Singleton. How are you today?'

'Who's there?'

'David. David Owain.'

'What are you mumbling about? Can't you speak up?'

'It's David Owain.'

'The postman, is it? I'm not expecting any parcels, and I won't have firms sending me goods I haven't asked for, so if that's what it is you can just put it back in your van.'

David crouched and poked at the letter-flap with his thumbs. Rust gritted under his nails, paint cracked and sprinkled the mossy doorstep. With some effort he managed to push the flap inwards, making it screech. 'Miss—'

'If it's one of those cards to say you've been unable to deliver, save yourself the trouble. I won't be collecting any parcels from your sorting office. If the merchandise was any good they wouldn't need to force it on people who never wanted it in the first place.'

'It's David Owain the builder, Miss Singleton.'

'What's that you say?' The cardiganed stomach which had been haranguing David lowered itself until, with a groan and a thud of hands against the inside of the door, it produced a wrinkled face with a mouth almost the shape of the letter-slot. A further groan brought two faded eyes level with his. 'Aren't you my nephew's builder? Why have you had me thinking you were the postman?'

'Well, I've been trying—'

She straightened up with a grunt that sounded like agreement. 'Wait there,' she muttered, and kept up a monologue behind the noises of a bolt being dragged out of its socket, a chain, another bolt. Then activity ceased for quite a few seconds, so that David was wondering if she'd collapsed, and considering another rattle of the dangling doorbell, when the lock emitted a mousy squeak and the door juddered open. 'I'll fix those hinges for you,' he said.

'Douglas says all they need is a squirt of oil.'

97

'We'll give that a try by all means. I don't want to cost you any more than I have to.'

'I understood that was to be agreed between you and Douglas.'

'That's what we said, and you can rely on a solicitor to drive a hard bargain.'

'It's my money,' she retorted, 'and my choice to use some of it to put the house in order for when it passes to him.'

'I'm all for keeping things in the family. Shall I come in?'

She stepped back grudgingly, wiping her feet on the doormat. 'I suppose you'll want a cup of tea.'

'Only if you're having one.'

'I'm not.'

'Well then, let me get to work,' David said, earning himself a glare as if he'd accused her of preventing him. 'Did you have a chance to clear some space in those rooms upstairs?'

'I said I would when I found the time. We can't all be big strong men who can cart furniture around as soon as look at it.'

'Would you like me to do it?'

'Can't it wait?'

David felt as though the musty dimness of the hall was seeping into his mind, as though the damp which underlay the grubby wallpaper whose vague patterns reminded him of fungus was gathering on him. 'I do like to have an idea of all the work that needs doing before I start. That way I can do whatever's best for the house.'

She tugged her shaggy bluish cardigan down, hiding the large safety-pin which held her trousers together above the zip. 'Shall we go up?' he said. 'Or I can find my own way if you like.'

'I don't,' she said without glancing at him, and set about climbing the wide stairs with one hand on the banisters and the other on the small of her back.

Each stair creaked when stepped upon. David felt some of them give beneath a carpet which had all the qualities of an old sponge. The broad two-storey house, one of a streetful near a playing-field above the river, was reaching its centenary, and problems were to be expected in any building of that age, but it looked to David as if it had ceased to be cared for some considerable time ago. As Miss Singleton conquered the summit of the stairs, the banister wavered in her grasp. 'Careful,' he protested, running up to her.

'I believe I know my own house.'

'You'd be surprised what you can find once you start looking.'

98

'Well, naturally. That's your job,' she said, and clicked her tongue as loudly as a mousetrap when he shook the banister. 'No need to make it worse.'

'I'll glue these uprights in before I go.' He crossed the shifty floorboards to the nearest of several spare rooms. 'May I?'

As he lifted the door clear of the arc it had scraped in the carpet and pushed it open, the smell of the gloomy room spilled out – a smell of sunlight trapped in the dusty net curtains sagging on their wire, of the cartons of letters and stale bills and books with dislocated bindings that turned the piebald carpet into a maze, a smell made mustier by damp and, he was almost certain, worse. Miss Singleton wrinkled the long nostrils of her pointed nose and pursed her faded lips. 'It needs the window opening.'

'That wouldn't do any harm. Can I move some of these boxes?'

'Must you?'

'So I can see what work needs doing.'

'I know exactly where everything is.'

David wasn't sure if that was a complaint or a warning. He left his toolbox on the landing and picked his way between the cartons, in most of which the contents were stacked higher than his knees, to the outermost corner of the room. From outside he'd observed that at some time that corner of the exterior wall had been patched up. A pile of photograph albums was lolling against the obscurely repetitive wallpaper. He must remember to ask Gwendolen for another look at her photograph, he thought as he hugged the carton and rose to his feet, having gathered the topmost albums to his chest. The carton was by no means equal to its burden, which was heavier than he'd expected, and he had barely enough time to stagger to the nearest sufficiently large space before the container gave up. As he dumped the albums on the carpet through the bomb-doors of the carton, there came a rush of debris behind him and an outraged cry from Miss Singleton. The pile of albums had been supporting the plaster above them behind the wallpaper.

David was starting to peel away the paper when Miss Singleton cried 'What do you think you're doing?'

'Finding out the worst. I'll fix it, don't worry, whatever it is.'

'I want Douglas here.'

David thought she was ordering him to bring her nephew until she marched out of the room. Her side of the conversation was loud enough to be heard all the way up the stairs. 'Mr Singleton, please . . . Yes, I'm a client, and I'm also his aunt, so I advise you to put me through at once . . . I don't care what he said, you aren't asking me to believe you can't make an exception in an emergency . . . The wall of my house has collapsed, will that satisfy you, young lady? Just you tell him I need him the moment he's finished with this client who's supposed to be so important, and I'd like to know who that is . . . I'll have *your* name before you cut me off, at any rate . . .'

Sometimes the glimpses of domestic life that came with David's job dispirited him: were people's lives really that banal? He busied himself with moving the cartons away from the walls, and was leaning in the doorway for a short rest, having covered himself with dust and grime and sweat, when the bell emitted a muffled clatter. He wondered how long she might interrogate the visitor, but having ascertained only once that it was her nephew, she admitted him. 'Are you all right?' he heard Doug say. 'I came as soon as I could, and my secretary is calling David Owain.'

'Your friend is here,' Miss Singleton said in a tone she might have used to disapprove of a girlfriend.

'My? David, do you mean?'

'He's your friend, isn't he?'

'None better, but if he's here I don't see why I'm needed. I'm sure he can handle whatever the crisis is.'

'I want you to be the judge, if it's not too much trouble. If your clients take precedence over your family you must say so.'

'You know perfectly well that's not true, Auntie,' Doug pleaded, and glanced up as a creak betrayed David's arrival at the top of the stairs. The solicitor's high pinkish forehead, which together with his overhanging eyebrows rather dwarfed the rest of his face, winced and grew smooth. 'What's this I hear about you knocking down my aunt's wall?'

'I don't think it's quite that bad. Come and have a look.'

Doug sprinted upstairs, lifting the knees of his long legs high and unbuttoning the jacket of his discreetly patterned suit. 'You'll understand if I look and run, won't you? Complications with a will. They seem to take a delight in leaving trouble behind them, some of these old—' He punched a cough with his fist. 'We'll have plenty of time for a chinwag at your barbecue on Saturday.'

'Try not to be late for once.'

'Easier said than done with two women in the house, now the daughter's practising to be one.'

'Shall I show you too, Miss Singleton? As you say, it's your house.'

'Nobody said any different,' Doug assured her, tugging at his right ear as though he was encouraging her to reply rather than simply impatient with her slow progress up the stairs. 'Really, I do think David can be left to deal with this. Even I can see that all it needs is replastering.'

'I don't know if it's going to be quite that simple,' David said, scooping the debris and a wad of cobwebs away from the corner with his hands. As he pulled back the dog-eared carpet he felt floorboards yield under his knuckles. He uprooted a rusty bent nail with the claw of his hammer, then he levered up the board, which gave a sound like all the creaks of the house put together.

'Heaven help us,' Miss Singleton cried, 'is the man a vandal?'

'I'm afraid this is what I was afraid of.' David reached into the gap he'd made and grasped the joist nearest the corner of the room. Despite years of encountering it, this was still a sensation which dismayed him – feeling the wood that supported a floor flaking like chocolate between his fingers. He pulled out a chunk as large as his hand to show the Singletons the tendrils of fungus eating the wood. 'Dry rot,' he said. 'Years old.'

Doug kneaded his cheeks as though he was trying to sculpt an appropriate expression. 'What will it entail?'

'I won't know exactly until I've taken up the floor.'

'*What* does he want to do?'

'It can't be helped, Auntie. It's hardly his fault.'

'I hope you aren't saying it's mine.'

'I wouldn't dare,' Doug said, and turned to David. 'It's just in this room, isn't it?'

'I can't say until I've been through the house.'

'I'll leave you to it then, shall I? I'll see you on Saturday, David, and you, Auntie, very soon.'

She pursed her lips and glared so furiously at him that at first it was no more apparent to him than to David that she was awaiting a kiss. David rubbed his hands above the hole in the floor and made for the bathroom, where a rack which stood in the somewhat enamelled bath was spread with ageing underwear. He washed his hands in the capacious marble sink with cold water and a sliver of soap like a primitive knife, and dried himself on a corner of a threadbare whitish towel. By this time the hollow dripping of one bath tap was insufferable, but as he reached for it the floor yawed alarmingly beneath him. 'Miss Singleton—'

Doug followed her into the bathroom, and David felt the boards sag further. 'If I were you—'

'You aren't.'

'I was going to say I wouldn't come in until I've checked this floor.'

'What nonsense,' she said, and strode into the room, only to stumble against the bath. As she leaned all her weight on the side, the end nearest the window sank at least an inch, sending the rack of underwear skittering over the enamel. She recoiled, grabbing the pin at her belt as though she felt exposed. 'It's never done that before,' she said accusingly.

'Do whatever you have to,' Doug told David, and retreated out of the house.

David pulled out a handful of rotten joist from under the bathroom floor to show Miss Singleton, but she was barely speaking to him, though she had plenty to say to herself: 'So I'm to be told what to do in my own house . . . Not even allowed to bathe . . .' David promised to start work on the bathroom tomorrow and phoned the joiner he would be employing, then called the timber yard with the measurements and went through the rest of the house. There were rotten window-frames, loose slates on the roof, addled plaster in all the downstairs rooms, rising damp in the kitchen, but no more dry rot, thank God. 'I'll be here first thing. You'll have a bathroom by the weekend,' he promised Miss Singleton, and wiped his feet on the mat without thinking as he stepped out of the house.

He'd had worse jobs and more difficult customers, and he could put up with her as long as she had to put up with him. It couldn't be easy for her to learn that so much was amiss with her house and to have to live through the upheaval, he reflected as he drove the Volvo down to the narrow bridge over the weir. When the traffic lights let him cross he made for home. The one-way system within the city walls was further complicated by tourists who had lost their way, and it took him almost twenty minutes to crawl as far as the railway station, and another five to move up a queue of traffic to the cross. Once he was past it he celebrated by reaching the speed limit, but as the car rounded the curve into his road he tramped on the brake. Someone was lying in the road outside the Shangri-La Retirement Home.

David parked so hastily that he scraped the kerb with one nearside tyre and mounted the pavement with the other. Several people were standing or crouching between him and the woman who was lying on the tarmac, and all he could see of her face was a glimpse of bright red. Beyond her a car with a dent in the bonnet had been driven haphazardly onto the verge. He felt laden with guilt, the more heavily because he couldn't define why: if he and Joelle had insisted that Gwendolen stay with them for a while – if they had at least taken into account that she wasn't always as competent as she liked to think— His hands had grown clumsy, and he dropped his keys as he struggled out of the car.

The slam of the door made two of the women by the body glance at him. One was Brenda Mickling; the other was Gwendolen. David experienced such a flood of relief that he felt ashamed of dismissing whoever the victim was. 'What happened?' he said. 'Can I help?'

A wide-eyed man whose face looked uncertain whether to blush or grow pale turned to him. 'She ran straight in front of my car. Neither of us had a chance.'

'Straight downstairs and out of the house without even taking her stick,' Brenda told him. 'I wonder if she thought she saw someone she knew. Did she say anything to you, Gwen? Gwen's room is next to hers.'

'I can't tell you what made Naomi do what she did.'

The woman on the tarmac didn't look as bad as David's first glimpse had suggested. The bright red was lipstick like a slash of crayon on the tissue paper of her face. Her eyes were shut, and she was breathing so regularly she appeared to be asleep. Nevertheless David was uneasy about talking as if she either wasn't present or was unaware of anyone around her. 'So what have you been up to, Gwen?' he murmured, stepping back from the supine body so that Gwendolen would follow. 'I mean, how are you doing?'

The next moment he forgot her and his questions, because Naomi had opened her eyes and was gazing at him. Her eyelids faltered shut, then they widened and her lips parted, showing reddened teeth. David thought she was revealing evidence of some worse injury until he saw that they too were crimson with lipstick. With an effort that made him wince she managed to tilt her head to one side, still gazing at him, and raise her pointed chin. 'I'm sorry, do you want me?' he said, feeling awkward and foolish.

'Didn't you say we oughtn't to disturb her, Brenda, until the physician arrives?' Gwendolen said.

'The ambulance, you mean. Lie still, Naomi. The ambulance is on its way.'

As David went down on his knees beside Naomi, his knuckles hitting the tarmac, her right hand groped towards his and clutched it with unexpected vigour. Perhaps she had put too much of her strength into the action, because her eyelids fell shut and her lips moved silently. She drew a breath, digging her fingernails into the back of David's hand, and succeeded in pronouncing what might have been a word. 'Th—'

David leaned closer, keeping his hand in hers, though her grip was bringing tears to his eyes. 'I can hear you. The what, Naomi?'

Her eyelids wavered open, but she appeared not to see him. Her mouth worked, and her purplish tongue poked at her lips as though she was trying to locate them or to define them to herself. This time she took only a shallow breath, and her words barely emerged from her mouth. 'Dirty people,' David thought she said loosely before emitting what might have been a gasp or a syllable. Two further syllables, and she let go of his hand.

'Save who, Naomi? Save her, is that what you said?'

A frown flickered and vanished before it could gain much of a hold on her face. David had the unhappy impression that he'd failed her. He closed his hand around hers to reassure her that he hadn't gone away, and lowered his head towards her mouth. A hollow shriek seemed to rise from her lips, growing louder and higher, though it could have taken him only a few moments to realise he was hearing the ambulance as it swung into the road. As though the approach of help had relieved her of having to cling to consciousness, Naomi's feeble grasp on his hand slackened, and David stood up. 'What did she say?' Gwendolen asked at once.

'Nothing that made any sense to me.'

'Was she rambling?'

'I think she must have been.'

'Poor thing, no wonder after what she's been through.' Gwendolen linked arms with him and led him onto the pavement as the ambulance drew up. 'I've been meaning to ask you or Joelle how many people will be coming to your barbecue.'

'Not so many you'll be overwhelmed. Why do you ask?'

'Because I want to contribute.'

'Just contribute yourself, Gwen.'

She squeezed his arm with her free hand. 'No, I must bring this. It's important to me.'

'Don't go spending much. Money doesn't last for ever, however much you've got that you didn't even know you had.'

'It'll last long enough. I'll just be buying some ingredients.'

'Can I let Joelle know what you'll be making?'

'Something to round off the day. Wait and see.' Gwendolen watched as Naomi was lifted into the ambulance. The doors were locked, the vehicle sped away, and Gwendolen relinquished his arm. 'An old recipe,' she said.

# Twelve

That Saturday afternoon Joelle was buying supplies for the barbecue when she saw Hayley Pinnock. Hayley was squinting at the display in the supermarket window through the smoke of the cigarette in her mouth as Joelle paid for an armful of hamburger rolls. She caught sight of Joelle and pretended not to have done so, and pushed the buggy onwards, reaching the shop doorway as Joelle did. 'Quiet for a change,' Joelle remarked, though saying so made her feel like more of an accomplice than she cared to be – and then she saw that the silent object in the buggy was a flesh-coloured plastic bag of potatoes. 'I wasn't meaning to be rude about Rutger,' she said.

'He wouldn't know it if you were, or much else either.'

'So where is he today? Somewhere sunny with his dad?'

'Home where they ought to be,' Hayley said, which dislodged a crumbling stub of ash that she brushed from the front of her denim overalls.

'You've managed to involve Scott a bit more, then.'

'It's his mates who put him off being a father. Too busy fighting their dragons and God knows what monsters to help look after the kids they were happy enough to stick in us. Do you know what he had the cheek to tell me? That him and his mates are only acting out the way things ought to have stayed.'

'Isn't there anyone who could have a word with him? Someone in your family?'

'Don't talk to me about families. They've steered well clear since we had to get married, not that you can blame them for steering clear of Rutger. Half the time I think all kids do is bring diseases in the house,' Hayley said, and demonstrated with a hacking cough between drags at her cigarette. 'It's all very well you looking like that, you don't know what it's like. Nobody does.'

'I'm sure there are people who do, Hayley, and mightn't it help if you talked to some of them? If you like I could try—'

'Don't bother.'

'I was only going to suggest—'

'Don't.'

Hayley was blinking rapidly, though it might be the smoke that was stinging her eyes. Joelle took a deep breath and said 'In case you were wondering why I look as if I'm going to feed the five thousand, we're having a barbecue tonight. Would you and Scott and Rutger like to come?'

'That's nice of you. I appreciate it.' Hayley produced another cigarette from behind one ear like a magician and substituted it in her mouth. 'Don't be miffed, but since you're not a mother I don't think you realise what you'd be inviting. Rutger would be on top of your barbecue before you knew where he was.'

'Well, you'll both have to keep an eye on him, won't you? And whoever's attending to the barbecue will.'

Hayley dropped the butt, and the edge of the kerb knocked a shower of sparks out of it. 'I don't know if Scott would be able to come. I've no idea what time he'll be home.'

'I thought he was home now, looking after Rutger.'

'That's what you wanted to think. *I* never said so,' Hayley said, looking more reproving than defensive. 'Rutger won't come to any harm in his cot. He started screaming, so I locked him in his room.'

There was so much that Joelle wanted to but couldn't say that her mouth felt glued shut from within. 'Try to come with Rutger even if Scott can't,' she virtually pleaded. 'There'll be plenty to eat and drink, but bring extra if you like. I'm sure you can use the break.'

'I'll see how I feel and how he behaves. Thanks for asking us,' Hayley said, and with even less enthusiasm 'Now I reckon you think I'd better be rushing off home in case he feels neglected.'

Joelle watched her trudge away along the narrow street and heard the cellophane in which the hamburger rolls were wrapped crackling like a broken eggshell as she crushed the carrier bag. Rather than succumb to the impulse to follow Hayley, she marched herself towards the main road. She hoped Hayley would accept her invitation, but only – if she was honest with herself – so that somebody besides David with whom she could discuss the situation would see how Hayley treated Rutger. Just now David would do if he was home from Miss Singleton's house.

He was in the shower. Joelle unloaded the rolls onto the kitchen table and went up to him. 'Been home long?'

'Just this minute back.'

His voice beyond the curtain and the downpour sounded somewhat fed up. 'More problems?' she said.

'Well, only that she didn't seem to be expecting me to put in a new window. Seemed to think all it needed was some putty sticking round the glass to stop it falling out on someone's head. I showed her the frame was rotten, but according to her if you can't poke your finger right through it it can't be all that bad.'

'Did she call Doug?'

'Tried, but she got Maureen. Seemed convinced Maureen was hiding him from her, only pretending he'd had to go and see a client, especially when Maureen wouldn't let her have the client's number.'

'Sounds like a charmer.'

'Oh, she's all right. Just feeling vulnerable and won't admit it. I put in the new window and left the old one round the back for Doug to see the next time he visits.' David turned off the shower and stepped out of the bath, shaking his wet hair at Joelle like a dog. 'I feel better for that,' he said.

'What, for making me wet?' She dabbed her face with a bath towel and towelled his face roughly, then she set about drying the rest of him. When she reached his penis it rose to greet her, and she couldn't resist such a naked approach. She closed her hand around it and led David into their bedroom. Being just a couple on their own had its advantages, she thought, and experienced a twinge of guilt. It lasted no longer than it took her to pull off her T-shirt and kick off her sandals and wriggle out of her shorts and panties, and then for quite a while there was no need to think.

'I feel better for that,' she said most of half an hour later. Indeed, she felt like staying in David's arms and falling asleep. There would be time later to talk about Hayley, especially if some Pinnocks turned up at the barbecue. Joelle dozed for a few minutes, or thought she did, but found she'd been drifting for longer when David kissed her awake. 'We ought to start getting things ready for people,' he said.

The barbecue was a permanent structure built against the far wall of the back garden, with a cast-iron tray which fitted into different slots in the waist-high brick box. David heaped charcoal under the tray and unfolded chairs on the quarter of an acre of lawn while Joelle set out salads and paper cups and plates in the kitchen, then the Owains gave themselves the first cupfuls from a bottle of Chardonnay and went into the garden.

Shadows were returning to their nests in the sycamore which

overhung the far wall. The soft light turned the reds and yellows of Joelle's roses pastel and seemed to hush the murmur of traffic on the main road until it sounded like waves seeking a beach. Joelle felt as if she could sense the glow settling on her, as though the air was being transformed into light. She was sipping her drink, feeling emptied of thoughts and letting everything around her be what it wanted to be, when the doorbell rang.

'I'll get it,' she said, and opened the front door before she'd had time to decide who she hoped was there. 'Doug and Maureen and is this really Angela? You look—'

'She looks older than is good for her, if you ask me.'

'Doug,' Maureen murmured. 'Not here.'

'If she won't listen at home perhaps she'll listen when there's an audience.'

Joelle intervened gently before the evening could get off to more of that kind of a start. 'I think you all look just fine, and I'm sure Angie's going to be perfectly safe.'

If she had been at all taken aback on opening the door it hadn't been because Angie looked years older than fourteen in her black mini-dress and leggings; it was that Joelle had never seen her look so like a refinement of her parents – Doug's lankiness rendered slim and graceful, Maureen's delicately pretty features transferred from her short thick-legged breast-heavy form, which appeared even dumpier now that Maureen's hair was cropped. 'If I were you, Doug, I'd be proud of her,' Joelle said, and called 'Come over whenever you're ready, Herb.'

Herb had been peering shyly around his front door, behind which he now ducked and reappeared with a skittle-shaped bottle of wine. 'We aren't the first, are we?' Maureen protested.

'Someone had to be, and you'll do.'

'You see, you needn't have rushed me, Doug. You know I didn't mean to wear this dress.'

'I'm sure nobody will realise,' Joelle said, though it did give Maureen a certain resemblance to an occasional table draped in a long flowered tablecloth and decorated with her head. 'Come in, you too, Herb, and I'll point you in the direction of the drink.'

David was opening bottles in the kitchen. 'Oh great, lots of salads,' Angie said.

'They're for everyone, not just you,' Doug told her.

'I never said they were. I can have just salad, can't I, Joelle?'

'You can have whatever you like. Why, have you taken the pledge?'

'I'm afraid she and some of her friends have swallowed animal rights,' Doug said. 'We're still swallowing animals, so she gets whatever the rest of the meal is. It can't be good for her at her age. Herb, isn't it? I don't know if you remember our daughter. I'm thinking of calling her Leopard.'

'Why's that?'

'Because she can't change her spots, of course.'

Herb responded with a token laugh which he seemed to regret as much as having asked. 'I think I know more about nutrition than you, Doug,' Maureen said.

'I'd better change the subject, then. How are you this year, Herb? Is your charming wife lingering over her toilet?'

Angie covered a snort at his choice of phrase with her hand. He was staring at her, his jutting eyebrows high, when Herb stammered 'Actually, I'm afraid we aren't living together just now.'

'So long as it's only just now,' Doug said, and must have read doubt or pain in Herb's eyes. 'Then again, if you need any professional help . . .'

'I thought we agreed to leave business at home tonight, Doug.'

'Well,' David intervened, 'who wants what to drink?'

'Red for me and Maureen, and anything but alcohol for her.'

'Dad, when Linzi or Ramona or Carmen who's almost six months younger than me go out for dinner—'

'If I'd wanted to hear from you I'd have hired a ventriloquist.'

Herb emitted a stutter of mirth, the bit he had failed to suppress. 'Thank you, Herb. It's good to be appreciated,' Doug said, and turned to David with a swiftness Joelle hoped he showed on behalf of his clients. 'How's progress at my aunt's? Maureen said she called this afternoon while I was out, but I'm assuming you took care of the matter.'

'You might just want to look in and reassure her.'

'I'll trust your judgment and you do the same. I'll give her a bell, maybe tomorrow. Cheers,' Doug said, and half emptied his paper cup.

'What would you like, Angie?' Joelle said.

'Could I just have a Coke?'

'No just about it,' Doug said as the doorbell rang. 'Perfectly decent drink.'

'I'll see who it is, shall I?' Herb offered, and fled to admit too much of a hubbub of greetings for Joelle to be able to identify the speakers. He reappeared following Terry and Sarah Monk, Terry

111

sweeping his hair back from his round face as he saw there were more people than the Owains in the kitchen, Sarah letting her large hands dangle on either side of her ambitiously low-cut white dress as though she was resisting an urge to yank it up over the tops of her pale freckled breasts. 'You all know one another, don't you?' David said, lifting two cups off the stack. 'You met here last year.'

'And these are our friends from America,' Sarah said, 'Henrie and Jake.'

They'd been waiting in the hall until Herb sidled past the Monks. Both of them were tall and slim, the man's long-nosed high-boned face made to look humorous rather than superior by its rounded dimpled chin, the woman with the red hair and large grey eyes and sensual mouth and sprinkling of freckles which David had reported after Terry Monk had let him into her house. 'Oh,' David said distractedly, 'I didn't realise you all came together.'

Joelle busied herself with pouring Angie's drink – anything rather than meet his eyes while that was the last phrase in the air. 'Americans, eh?' Doug said. 'You must have smelled Joelle opening the Coke. Are you on the history trail? Is Terry putting you up?'

'We've bought a place down by the river,' Jake said in an accent which struck Joelle as barely American. 'We've just opened a music store in town. If you like choral music at all, come visit.'

'And you can hear these guys sing in the cathedral if you want a free sample,' Henrie added.

'Well, if I ever go in there that'll be why,' Doug said. 'I hope you holy folk aren't going to make me feel sinful.'

This time it was Joelle who dashed to answer the doorbell. 'Archie and Agatha,' she said with enthusiasm which owed something to her having temporarily escaped the conversational minefield in the kitchen. 'Come in, do.'

The Greys looked even more polite than they already had. 'Thank you for the invitation,' Archie said in his booming voice which she thought it must take most of his squat barrel torso to produce. 'We won't stay very long.'

'It was kind of you to ask us,' Agatha said in almost as much of a boom, and presented Joelle with two litres of mineral water. 'Please pass this out to your guests.'

The Greys advanced on the kitchen in almost identical postures, trotting doggedly forwards as if trying to catch up with something which, to judge by their expressions, they couldn't quite bring into focus but which they already knew they weren't going to like. As soon as Archie caught sight of Herb he ignored everyone else. 'Herbert, isn't it? Has your marriage mended itself yet? We've been praying that it will.'

'Herb. Not yet. Maybe you've got, I don't know, a crossed line.'

'No prayer goes unheard,' Agatha boomed at him.

Doug drained his cup and reached for the open bottle. 'You two are having us on, aren't you? As I remember, last time we were all here—'

'That made us see the error of our ways,' Archie proclaimed.

'I see the error of mine every morning after.'

David managed to head off Archibald's response by performing the introductions. 'Henry! Is that a girl's name in America?' Agatha enquired.

'Henrietta is,' Henrie said.

'We don't believe in mutilating names, you see. I suppose it matters less when it isn't a saint's,' Archibald said. 'Shall we take our drinks into the garden? We'll each have a small orange juice if we may.'

'Don't feel obliged to follow our example,' Agatha told everyone. 'It's just that we prefer not to be in an enclosed space where alcohol is being drunk.'

The doorbell ended an awkward silence, and David went to answer it while Joelle opened more bottles. The Greys bore their juices outside as David returned with Bill Messenger. 'Here are some people who won't know you,' David said. 'Henrie—'

'That's all right,' Bill said, 'I'll introduce myself.'

His wide flat snub-nosed deceptively open face wore the innocent look which told Joelle he was about to invent a role for himself, and she thought the party could do with some mischief. 'Henry,' he said effusively, extending a hand to Jake.

Jake shook it and his head. 'I'm Jake.'

'I'm Henrie short for Henrietta,' Henrie said.

'Bill Messenger. Bill that used to be short for Wilhelmina.' He took her hand and met her eyes. 'I like that about Americans, the way you take such things in your stride.'

'I knew a footballer at high school who became a woman when he grew up.'

'The hardest part, not that I've any very hard part, is keeping my voice this low.'

'You needn't if it's just on our behalf,' Jake said.

'Well, that's most agreeable of you,' Bill said, raising his voice

113

an octave and modulating it so that Joelle would have sworn it was a woman's. 'I suppose you've the advantage of not having met me as a woman last year.'

Everyone was listening in different kinds of fascination, except for Angie, who had hurried into the garden to stifle her giggles, and the Greys, who were just outside the patio doors and scowling vigorously at Bill. 'You see,' he said before Joelle could stop him, 'my appearance has taken our friends Archie and Agatha aback.'

'There's nothing wrong with your appearance.'

'It's sweet of you to say so, Archie,' Bill said, fluttering the collar of his flowered shirt with his fingertips.

'It's your words we find objectionable. And it's Archibald, if you don't mind.'

'Bald and proud of it, that's the way to be. I'll do my best to live up to your example if the good Lord pinches my hair.'

'I hope nobody could accuse myself or Agatha of lacking a sense of humour, but we'd be grateful if you wouldn't take the name of Our Lord in vain.'

'Mea cupcake,' Bill said, intersecting his fingers prayerfully, and then he stared hard at the Greys. 'Christ on a croissant, you aren't serious, are you? I thought you were going along with the joke.'

'We've heard no joke,' Agatha informed him, 'only falsehoods on a subject hardly suitable for discussion in front of the impressionable young.'

Angie stopped giggling behind her hand and glared at Agatha. 'Well, that's me thoroughly put in my place,' Bill said. 'Sorry, Henrie. Just an old mummer trying to be funny. I was going to tell you if you didn't guess.'

'Of course we did. Bill short for Wilhelmina? Come *on*,' Henrie said, slapping his arm.

'Don't let us spoil the party. I'm sure nobody owes us an apology,' Archibald said.

'Bill, you haven't got a drink,' Joelle said, which seemed to be the signal for the party to rearrange itself. Bill emptied his paper cup of vaguely Germanic hock at a gulp and having received a refill, went to expand on his apologies to the Greys, though he looked too sincere for Joelle not to suspect him of having at least some fun. The Lees and the Monks drifted to the far end of the garden, where Henrie seemed glad to sit down, while Angie came in to protest about having been patronised by Agatha and Herb consulted David about a problem with his house. That left Joelle to answer the door, and she found herself hoping it wouldn't be

114

Hayley Pinnock who had rung the bell; there were enough undercurrents to be going on with.

'Rich and Jude and Olga and Simon. We weren't sure if you were coming.'

'We'll go away again if you like,' Richard Vale said.

'You will not.' His face always made Joelle smile at the way he talked, by dropping his jaw as if to display how little he moved the fat slice of ham that was his tongue. His eyebrows and moustache resembled patches of a greyish carpet which moving more of the upper half of his face might dislodge. 'Come and help restore my sanity,' Joelle said.

'It wouldn't be a party if everything went as planned,' Judith said, shaking back her straight hair from her broad sleepy-eyed permanently amused face and stuffing a bag of hamburgers and rolls more snugly under her arm before urging the children forwards, her hands on their shoulders. 'What can I do?'

'Is Angie here yet?' Olga demanded.

'Where is she?' Simon asked as eagerly, and they raced along the hall as though they'd forgotten they were thirteen years old.

Angie was sitting alone in the garden, but gave up looking rejected once Simon showed her a pocket computer game and Olga started gossiping to her. 'Rich and Jude,' David was saying meanwhile. 'Grab yourself drinks and join the fray.'

'As in nerves, do you mean?' Richard suggested.

'I'll say nothing except promise you an interesting evening,' David said under his breath.

Doug caught sight of the newcomers and came in from the garden. 'Hi there,' he said with a heartiness which drew attention to his having forgotten their names. 'How's business?'

'Never better for the customer. Everything's in our summer sale till the end of the month, so if your daughter's got a birthday or even if she hasn't and is looking for computer games or programs or maybe a computer . . .'

'That's what I like to see, a positive attitude,' Doug told him. 'Maureen, you remember the computer expert and, don't tell me, and his wife, don't you? Another man who isn't shy of trying to drum up business when he meets people. You wouldn't want to stop him, would you, it's on the tip of my tongue?'

'Jude,' Richard said.

'Is that your name, Jude?' Agatha asked him, she and Archibald having swooped to greet the late arrivals. 'It has a special meaning for us. Perhaps you can guess.'

Joelle would have intervened, but Richard said 'Do I get a clue?'

'Don't you know your twelve disciples?'

'I didn't realise I had any,' Richard said and blinked at her, the second blink more of a frown. 'I'm awfully sorry if I was rude or blasphemous or whatever. Only last time we were here you were, that's to say, you weren't . . .'

'It was after that,' Agatha said, gazing forgivingly up at him, 'we had occasion to thank St Jude.'

'Well, that's Joelle for you. I can't imagine her letting anyone go short.'

He must have meant that as a gentle defence in case Joelle felt her catering was under attack, but he clearly hadn't foreseen that it could be construed as a reference to Agatha's stature. There were several kinds of silence, which Terry broke by introducing the Lees to the newcomers. 'We've been friends of the Monks ever since we met in Central Park,' Jake explained.

'Just good friends, obviously,' Judith said to Henrie.

'I guess. Sure. How do you mean?' Henrie said, and seemed to want to prop herself up.

'Just that friends of monks would have to be. Celibate, I mean.'

'It would do the rest of us no harm,' Archibald resonated.

Henrie produced a belated laugh at Judith's comment. 'I'm entirely serious, I assure you,' Archibald said, reddening.

'Sorry,' Judith said, mostly to Henrie. 'My jokes improve as the evening progresses. I wasn't meaning to imply any—'

'Are those for everyone or just for the family, Jude?' Joelle said, grabbing the hamburgers and rolls. 'Apologies for interrupting, but we may as well get started since nearly everyone's here.'

As though she had cued it, the doorbell rang. If only it had saved her from having to interrupt Judith! At least it allowed everyone to be amused by its timing and, Joelle observed thankfully, to regroup. She rather hoped it was announcing Hayley Pinnock now that Judith had arrived; Hayley couldn't accuse her or Maureen of not being a mother. Joelle grasped the latch and swung the door open.

The late arrival wasn't Hayley. It was Gwendolen, dressed from head to foot in a black dress and wearing a bright pale mask. When Gwendolen smiled, etching more lines in and around her lips, Joelle thought the mask was about to crack or tear or fall off. Then she saw that a ray of low sunlight between the houses had caught

116

Gwendolen's face, emphasising her makeup against the background of the street full of shadows that were growing darker and clearer. Gwendolen held up the bag which was her constant companion and then clasped it to herself. 'Are you ready for me?' she said.

# Thirteen

The party had settled down by the time it began to grow dark. Almost everyone was moderately drunk, not least because the younger Vales had elected themselves wine waiters. Richard was doing his best to persuade Jake Lee that the Choral Store needed a computer. Having discovered that the Vales were nudists, Sarah was questioning Judith about the Yugoslavian resort where they took their holidays and seeming not quite able to believe that nudists didn't care what shape they were. Herb was singing popular operatic melodies more or less in tune while Terry Monk wove harmonies around them and Angie listened with a mixture of amusement and superiority to the way grownups behaved. Joelle and Maureen were deep in a discussion of the Pinnocks and their toddler Rutger, though Joelle appeared less than satisfied with what she was having to hear. Every time the Greys showed signs of preparing to leave, Bill Messenger detained them with a long and detailed anecdote about yet another of his relatives who had become a nun or had a vision or spoken in tongues. Henrie was listening to him with an expression at least as innocent as his – so innocent that David knew exactly what Joelle thought of her as she kept glancing past Maureen. He was still at the barbecue, turning the last of the hamburgers. 'Anybody besides the kids want one?' he called, to a general shaking of heads. 'Not even you, Gwen? They must be feeding you well up the road.'

Gwendolen came out of the kitchen, where she had been drinking a cupful of water. For over an hour she'd been moving from group to group, meeting everyone and lingering to listen, and David thought she must have put on so much makeup in preparation for meeting so many strangers all at once. In the glare of the lamp above the patio doors, which turned itself on at night whenever it sensed an intruder in the garden, her face looked clearer than the rest of her. 'I'll never owe them as much as I owe you and Joelle,' she said.

119

'I'd say they ought to thank you for the publicity,' Joelle said, 'especially since you let Brenda do all the talking to reporters.'

'And there should be quite a few coin collectors and museum curators remembering you in their prayers,' David added.

Bill stopped short of demonstrating how a relative of his spoke in tongues. 'Are you the lady with the trove of coins? I didn't realise we had a celebrity at the feast.'

'Why, we heard about that on your local news,' Henrie told Gwendolen. 'Did you truly not know how much they were worth?'

'Blame it on my years.'

'Don't think me inquisitive,' Doug said in a tone which David thought rather too professional, 'but do you happen to know where they came from?'

Gwendolen held out one empty hand to him. 'Services rendered.'

'I suppose so, but surely not by you. I was meaning, just out of interest, how *you* acquired them.'

'Trust a lawyer to think like one,' Maureen said.

Doug turned his reproachful back on her. 'It's as well to establish ownership, Gwen, in case anyone should try to claim title.'

'Don't fret yourself on my behalf. There's nobody alive who could.'

Doug looked dissatisfied, but Angie spoke before he had a chance to respond. 'Have you got any of those coins in your bag?'

Olga and Simon gazed eagerly at Gwendolen, and most of the adults were intrigued, though David heard Archibald mutter not quite inaudibly about avarice. 'I only want to see what one looks like,' Angie protested.

'Manners,' Doug warned her.

'I'm sorry, I had to get rid of all the coins. I have brought something, but I didn't realise there would be so many people here.'

'What?' Olga and Simon said in chorus, and Angie might have joined in if she hadn't remembered she was almost two years older.

'Perhaps you won't think it's anything very exciting.' Gwendolen pivoted slowly to survey all the guests, and then she loosened the drawstrings of her bag and reached in.

David stayed at the barbecue to scoop the last hamburgers onto a paper plate, and saw Gwendolen lift out a shapeless bundle about the size of her head. In the glare which the growing darkness intensified, the wrapping seemed more like skin than her face did.

120

He stepped forward as she unfolded it, but she held up one palm to stop him. 'Perhaps I should make something extra special for you and Joelle, otherwise there won't be anything like enough.'

Simon edged close enough to peek into the bundle. 'Oh,' he said.

'Oh,' Olga agreed, equally failing not to sound disappointed, 'cakes.'

'There won't be any for either of you unless you eat your burgers,' Judith said.

'It's all right, someone else can have mine,' Olga said.

Simon nodded in agreement and headed for the barbecue, and Archibald advanced on Gwendolen with his leaning gait which made him and Agatha appear drunker than anyone else. 'Please give ours to anyone who would like them. We're neither of us much of a sweet person.'

'Please at least share one or I'll feel as though you want to cast me out.'

Archibald sent a loud breath out of his nose. 'I shouldn't like anyone to think us unchristian.'

'Follow me, then.' Gwendolen let her bag fall on the grass, where it lay like a collapsed lung, and went to the kitchen table, the hem of her black dress flapping about her ankles. As she pushed salad bowls out of the way and spread the cakes on their wrapping across the table, David was put in mind of a priest about to celebrate a ritual. She took a paper plate from the depleted stack and a pair of tongs from the dishwasher, and after a hesitation so brief that David thought he had imagined it, selected a cake which she dropped on the plate. 'This is yours, Archibald,' she said, holding out the plate to him.

He ducked his face towards it as though it might be the goal to which his dogged gait had been leading him. 'May we ask what's in it?'

'My secret. Perhaps you'll be able to guess.' Gwendolen returned to the table, dismissing him, and put another cake on a plate. 'This must be for Bill.'

'Has it got my name on it?'

When she only gazed at him he hastened to the doorway and accepted the plate. He picked up the cake and bit it in half. 'Ah. Mmm. Ah *hah*,' he said.

David wasn't sure how much of this enthusiasm was simulated, particularly since the Greys weren't trying to hide how dutifully they were chewing. In any case, Bill's performance was wasted on

Gwendolen, who appeared to have lost interest in him as soon as he'd taken the plate. Now she was back at the kitchen door with another. The light on the wall burdened her face with the shadow of the doorway and made her look abruptly sombre. 'Herb,' she called.

Next came Richard. Maybe this was how her generation served dessert in her part of the world, David thought, or maybe it was just the way her age was causing her mind to work. He suspected that the guests were assuming the latter and indulging her because of it, going to the house as their names were called, their shadows shrinking into them and then growing bigger and blacker, staining the lawn as they returned to it. Doug was summoned to the threshold, then Terry, and David saw that only one cake remained. He thought the silence which the ritual had imposed wouldn't be broken until Gwendolen called the last name, and so when Angie spoke his heart jumped. 'Can I have that one?'

'Sure, you go ahead.'

Henrie had spoken, David gathered, because Gwendolen's gaze had fastened on her. 'Here,' Terry said, breaking his cake in half, 'try this.'

There was a general murmur for Angie to have the last cake, though David wondered if they were covering embarrassment at the sight of Terry sharing his with Jake's wife. Gwendolen hesitated before offering the plate to Angie. 'If you find it doesn't appeal to you . . .' she said, and seemed not to know what to suggest. She retreated into the kitchen, the shadow of the entrance slipping from her face.

Doug moved close to Angie. 'You asked for it, young lady, you finish it,' he muttered.

Having sniffed at it, she refrained from making a face and bit off a small piece. 'Where's my orange drink?' she said at once.

'Wherever you left it.'

'Here you are, Angie,' David said, retrieving the paper cup from its pillar of shadow on the grass.

As she turned to him she took the opportunity to grimace. 'Will you taste it for me? It tastes a bit . . .'

'The least I can do as your host.' It was a kind of rock cake, he saw; indeed, in the lurid vigilant light it very much resembled a rounded stone. A faint trace of Angie's saliva glistened in the bite. He bit into the other side of the cake.

It tasted odd. The texture was surprisingly light – the pastry seemed almost to vanish the moment he chewed it – but he couldn't decide if he liked the flavour or even whether it was sweet or bitter or both. Perhaps his straining to grasp the elusive taste was heightening all his senses, because he was intensely aware of Angie's slim pink tongue parting her lips and licking a crumb from the corner of her mouth. 'I know,' she confided to him, 'it tastes old, like my dad's aunt's cakes.'

'Remember your manners, young lady,' Doug growled behind her. 'You're not too old to be taught the way you used to learn.'

Angie squeezed her eyes shut and kept her back to him. She must be struggling not to retort or betray her embarrassment, but to David she looked as though she was suppressing cries of pain. The impression was so disconcerting that he touched her hand, which was slim and cool and trembling slightly. 'Don't eat the rest if you don't want to,' he murmured.

'Thanks, David.' She opened her eyes and met his with a directness which made the moment feel considerably longer. He swayed and told himself he shouldn't have drunk so much. Then she dodged around him, chasing her shadow down the garden towards the other children, and he saw Gwendolen.

She had crumpled the wrapping of the cakes and was throwing it into the kitchen bin. As soon as she'd done that she lowered herself onto a chair, her face so slack that it looked exhausted of character. David hardly noticed the remains of the cake falling from his hand as he ran to the house. 'Gwen, what's wrong? What do you need?'

'Nothing now. I didn't realise this would take so much out of me.' She raised her head with her fingertips beneath her eyes. 'I'll be fine. You enjoy yourselves while you can.'

'I'll drink to that,' Richard said, lurching into the kitchen. 'Can I get you one?'

'I may as well celebrate,' she said, and gazed through the doorway. 'So long as everyone eats their cake.'

If she spotted the cake David had dropped he would feel obliged to pick it up – his moment of closeness to Angie had left him feeling guilty for no reason he could grasp. At least the remains of the cake appeared to have fallen too low in the grass to cast a shadow. As Gwendolen took a paper cup from Richard, David saw Joelle nibbling the last of a cake. He hurried to her, treading the last of the one on the lawn into the grass. 'Whose was that?'

'Rich gave it me to taste.'

'What's in it, do you think?'

'None of us can tell. Why, do you want me to get the recipe?'

'I wouldn't say I was overwhelmed.'

Joelle popped the morsel into her mouth and sent it down with a gulp of wine. 'At least now they're over and done with and they made Gwen feel good.'

'I don't know if they did,' David said, but when he glanced into the kitchen Gwendolen had risen to her feet and was holding out the cup of wine across the table towards everyone before taking a sizeable drink. Richard drained his cup and refilled it and swayed onto the lawn. 'Come on, you gloomy sods, you heard what Gwen said. This is supposed to be a party, not a wake.'

When the Greys stared at him he misinterpreted their disapproval. 'I don't just mean you two. Who's got a party trick for us?' he shouted, waggling his fingers as though to conjure up something out of the ground. 'Who's going to show us what they can do?'

'So long as you don't show us what you showed me that night at your house, Rich,' David said.

'What might that have been?' Agatha demanded.

'It *might* have been all sorts of things,' Richard said, 'but what it was—'

'Is best left to the imagination,' David overrode him, remembering the drunken meal and drunker aftermath which the Vales had given him and Joelle to thank them for working on the house. As the Owains had stumbled into the night air Richard had brandished his penis at David from the stairs, presumably a nudist's farewell rather than an unsubtle attempt at seduction. 'Let's not be too excessive, Rich,' he said.

'Me? Soul of moderation.' Richard indicated himself with the cup, flinging wine into his face in the process. 'Who'll give us a song at least? You wouldn't want me to, I'll warn you.'

Few things killed a party faster, David thought, than someone determined to be its life and soul. He was groping for some question about computers with which to distract Richard when Bill began to hum the 'Ode to Joy'. After a few bars Terry started singing – '*Freude, schöner Götterfunken*' – and at the next line Henrie set about singing a translation – 'Daughter from Elysium.' Not to be outdone, Jake began to harmonise in German, and after clearing her throat shyly twice Sarah joined in Henrie's translation. To David they sounded close enough to soloists he'd heard, but the relentless light isolated the spectacle of Terry and Henrie performing in unison while Jake looped sounds around them as if he was displaying how he hardly needed them and Sarah tried to be like Henrie. He was glad when Bill and Richard took up the basic

124

melody, even though they didn't know the words. 'Bum bum bum bum . . .' Bill settled for, and Richard translated it: 'Diddle diddle diddle dum . . .' Someone commenced a muffled lowing, and someone else a noise like the flight of a dangerously somnolent wasp, and David thought he heard another voice, putting words to the melody that were both unfamiliar and disconcerting:

'Cockalorum peccatorum,
We shall age as all things must,
First we'll mumble, then we'll fumble,
Then we'll crumble into dust . . .'

The voice was gone before he could locate or identify it, but its words kept repeating themselves over the repetition of the melody. Perhaps it had always been in his head, though where had the words come from? He wasn't sure if he wanted to think he'd made them up himself. The quartet fell silent, and Richard and Bill relented after a final dum and bum. 'That was fun,' Richard said. 'What next?'

'Nothing to drink for a while?' Judith suggested.

'Less to drink's not the point, more to eat is.' Richard bowed towards Joelle, either to express deference or the better to focus on her. 'Don't think for a moment, I mean, your catering's perfect, only I usually have a bit of cheese at the end of a meal. I don't want to be a nuisance. I'll go and buy some now if anywhere's open.'

'Of course you won't. I should have remembered you with your chunk of cheese. Who else is for some while I'm putting it out?'

Richard attacked the Cheddar on the cheeseboard with such single-mindedness that the other guests left him to it. Gwendolen wandered into the garden and came up to David to smile at him. He read gratitude in her eyes, but for a moment he thought she was examining his face – for what? Perhaps her memory was faltering, he thought as she ambled from person to person, smiling with a vagueness that suggested their identities escaped her. 'Feeling better for that drink, Gwen?' Sarah blurted as Gwendolen's attention lit on her.

'Feeling better, yes. Much better.'

'What was wrong?' Joelle said.

'Nothing that can touch me any more. Nothing you'd want to know about, Joelle.'

'We'll have to be leaving soon,' said Terry. 'Can we give you a lift, Gwen?'

'You've never room for another woman in your car.' She turned her unreadable smile on Terry, and David felt suffocated, desperate for somewhere to look. 'I'll walk, thanks all the same,' she said. 'I haven't far to go now, thanks to David and Joelle.'

'I'll walk with you when you go if you like,' Joelle said.

'No need to trouble yourself, Joelle. I like feeling the night by myself.'

'How's the lady who was on your floor, Gwen?' David said.

'Naomi? She's in whatever you call it, intensive care. I'm visiting her, don't worry. You can put her out of your mind.'

David would have if Gwendolen hadn't told him to, but part of his mind grew annoyingly stubborn at once. 'Dirty people . . . Save her . . .' Or had Naomi said 'savour'? That seemed to make even less sense. He was struggling to grasp what he might actually have heard when Richard stepped carefully out of the kitchen, elevating another drink. 'Here's to our hosts,' he proposed, omitting a few consonants, 'and all we owe to them.'

'David and Joelle,' Gwendolen cried.

Perhaps it was her tone, which sounded almost regretful, that dissatisfied him. Cups were raised, but Richard stared at his before taking a swig as if that might clarify his language. 'Everyone here owes the Owains,' he declared. 'You'll give me that, won't you, Archie, Archib, Arsybald? They were the answer to your prayers.'

'I'd prefer not to put it like that, but of course we appreciate what they've done for us.'

'Here's to them, then. Here's to them,' Richard repeated, squinting ferociously at Archibald's immobile cup.

'Don't toast us any more,' Joelle said, 'or we'll be overdone.'

'Thank you, Joelle,' Agatha said briskly. 'I agree that's entirely enough.'

David was afraid she had provoked a further outburst until Richard gave a shrug that hoisted his cup of wine to his mouth. 'Anybody for another drink?' David said, intending to lift the pall the Greys had cast, but he was too late. Without warning, Sarah rounded on Archibald. 'What exactly have you two got against people enjoying themselves?'

'Nothing so long as they do it acceptably.'

'Acceptably to whom?'

'Acceptably in front of the young, apart from anything else.'

'If we had children,' Agatha said, 'we would never take them anywhere there was alcohol.'

'Well, you haven't, so it's hardly up to you to criticise people who have.'

'The world is so rotten that we chose not to bring children into it.'

'Sarah doesn't have a choice,' Terry said. 'Since you're into praying, why don't you pray for a doctor who can give her one.'

'There's no hope to be found in the things of this world,' Archibald informed him. 'If it's God's will that you have no children then you should make that your choice.'

Terry swung towards Sarah but didn't meet her eyes. 'You sanctimonious prat,' he muttered. 'Shag off.'

Agatha was booming, and so the Greys either didn't hear him or ignored him. 'Nothing man achieves without God's help is worth achieving,' she said.

Richard pointed at the Greys with his cup, baptising them with a few drops of wine. 'Not even what David and Joelle did to your house?'

'I don't think we need insult our hosts,' Agatha said with a look that might have been accusing him of doing so. When he swayed as though her gaze had pushed him she said to her husband 'I believe we really ought to be on our way now.'

'I trust we haven't outstayed our welcome.'

'Oh, er,' David assured them with an enthusiasm which he managed to keep noncommittal, and Joelle said 'Ah' in so nearly the same tone that he avoided looking at her for fear that they might start to laugh. 'I'll see you out,' he said.

The Greys had begun their downcast advance towards the house when Archibald veered at Richard. 'Permit me to say one more word to you. I hope that in the morning you'll remember your behaviour and resolve never to give yourself occasion to repeat it. Shame is God's way of bringing us closer to Him.'

Richard flung his arms wide in a gesture of helpless amazement so vigorous that he had to sit down in the nearest folding chair. David felt close to being as intoxicated, and unable to move towards the Greys, who turned to look back as they entered the kitchen. 'May God help you all,' Agatha boomed.

When the front door slammed behind them Maureen Singleton gasped 'Well.'

'Jesus,' said Jake.

Joelle slackened her grip on her paper cup, which had started to creak. 'I wouldn't want you or Henrie to think they're typically English.'

'Gee, Joelle, we already knew that,' Henrie said.

That was the cue for another awkward silence, which David was about to break with yet another offer of drinks all round when Richard levered himself carefully to his feet. 'This feels like the end of the party to me.'

'It isn't unless you want it to be,' David felt bound to protest.

'It better had be, then. You and the kids stay if you like, Jude, and I'll walk.'

'Don't you at least want some coffee?' Joelle said.

Richard shook his head and winced. 'It'd only keep me awake.'

'We'll go as well,' Judith said. 'Come on, you two, say goodbye to Angie before you fall asleep.'

Before David quite realised it everyone was making for the front door. Gwendolen was the last to go, and lingered at the gate, shadows of leaves fluttering over her face like a swarm of moths at a pale flame. 'Are you sure you wouldn't like one of us to walk with you?' Joelle said.

'Quite sure, thank you. I'm only sorry that your party turned out as it did.'

'Don't be silly,' David said at once. 'It wasn't your fault, for heaven's sake.'

They watched Gwendolen gliding away through the tunnel of shadows beneath the trees. Several birds flew out of a tree as she passed under it, then the shadows made her into one of themselves and the Owains turned away. 'Well, that was some evening,' David said.

'The barbecue to end all barbecues.'

'Until we're mad enough to hold the next one.'

'With a slightly altered guest list.'

'Who knows what they'll all be like by next year.'

'So long as you're the same, David.'

'You know me, so reliable it's boring.'

'Reliable and boring sounds just perfect to me right now. Why don't you reliably and boringly tidy up the garden while I clear up in here.'

They were in the kitchen. David headed for the door, not too fast while his skull felt light and unfamiliar. 'To hear is to ob—' he said, and faltered. Where he'd dropped the remains of Angie's cake, a black glistening shape as large as his head was writhing on the lawn.

As he staggered out to peer at it the shape screeched and disintegrated and rose into the air, shedding black shards that floated towards the lawn. They were feathers – the feathers of half a dozen birds which soared squabbling over the roof. As they flew over him, one or more of them spattered the back of his left hand. He was about to let Joelle know what they'd presented him with when he saw they had left more than feathers on the grass.

He tore off several lengths of kitchen towel and hurried across the lawn. Falling clumsily to his knees, he wiped his hand on the grass and wrapped the objects in the towels before running to the dustbin, then he busied himself with collecting the abandoned plates and cups. The stain on his hand, almost black in the lurid light, had been not droppings but blood. The objects on the lawn, separated by a splash wider than the body they no longer possessed, had been two bird's wings.

# Fourteen

About lunchtime Richard decided it must be the worst hangover he'd ever had. Even when he stood in the shop doorway his mind seemed unable to grasp his surroundings. Cars and larger vehicles stampeded past on the ring road, some of their hubcaps appearing to wag. A flash of light as tall as a man drew his attention to a Roman soldier in armour who was conducting sightseers around the city wall. Tourists and office workers were strolling to the artfully aged pubs in the side streets, but nobody so much as glanced at Richard or at his window. 'Everything half price,' he thought of calling, if only to prove that he and the shop were really there, 'or make me an offer.' Instead he retreated into the shop.

Beneath the exposed timbers of the ceiling the plaster had started to flake away from the massive old stones of the walls. Whereas during his first year of renting it the shop had felt companionably snug, now it seemed to be invoking its seniority, suggesting that his business was no more than a passing fad. He couldn't afford to hire Joelle Owain just now, and he wasn't about to ask her to wait to be paid, though he knew she would offer her services on that basis if she even suspected he needed them. He perched behind the rampart of the counter to open the noon mail.

Three envelopes were of that drab brown colour which it occurred to him bailiffs might wear. 'Bill, meet Bill,' he muttered, clawing the envelopes open. 'Bill, this is little Bill and, Jesus wept, big Bill.' The white envelope framed the name and address of the shop in a window like the mouth of a tragic mask. 'Be nice,' he pleaded, poking a finger under the flap so hard that he sliced his skin. He tore open the bloodstained envelope and sucked his finger while he shook the letter open on the counter with his free hand. It was an invitation to quote his price for providing a school with twelve computers.

'God bless you, Mrs Squiggle,' Richard said, squinting at the jagged line of ink which presumably was the signature of A. Saint

131

(Mrs), Headmistress. He pulled the telephone to him and typed the number of the school, then stuck his stinging finger in his mouth as a voice so efficient it sounded like a rebuke announced 'Hoole School.'

Perhaps she used that tone so that nobody would be tempted to make a joke. 'Is that A. Saint?' Richard said.

'I beg your pardon?'

Richard gave his finger a last comforting suck that tasted of iron and took it out of his mouth. 'A. Saint?'

'Mrs Saint, I assume you mean,' she said like even more of a warning against levity. 'What was it concerning?'

'She—'

'Are you some kind of popular music shop?'

'Popular? Wish we were. Not music, computers. Computer Explosion, to be precise.'

'Indeed,' she said as if she thought he was being the reverse.

'Your headmistress wrote to me about putting computers in. For a costing, I mean. An estimate. Can I speak to her?'

'She's dealing with a situation at the present.'

'Aren't we all?' he managed only to think, and said 'When won't she be? I don't suppose you can say. Can you ask her to call me back?'

'If the headmistress wrote to you I'm sure she expects you to respond by letter.'

'I will, but wouldn't it be fairer all round if I—'

He wanted the headmistress to know as soon as possible how low his prices for installation and maintenance were, but the secretary seemed determined to prevent this. 'I'm afraid I can't hear you for all the noise.'

'Then can't you tell whoever it is to pipe down?'

'Well, I never did.'

'I didn't say you—' Richard began, and realised at last why she had accused him of being a music shop: because of the electronic jingles which the computers were emitting while they demonstrated themselves over and over as they waited for someone to play with them. He lunged at the three monitors and turned the sound off. 'Sorry about that. You get so used to it that you don't notice.'

'Heaven forbid.'

'Anyway, as I was saying, I think your headmistress would like to know as soon as possible what I can offer. I think she wants to discuss the options with me before I write to her.'

132

An ageing blue Vauxhall patched with white paint sped by on the ring road, one flattish tyre thumping like a heart, and for several seconds that was all Richard heard. Then the secretary said 'I assume you want to make an appointment.'

'Whatever's quickest for her.'

'Very well, I'll inform her that you called.'

'I'll give you my number, shall I?'

He wouldn't have been surprised if the secretary had responded 'If you must.' Instead she snapped 'Please do.'

He did, then replaced the handset in its cradle and slapped the counter with both hands. He thought of calling Judith with the good news, but telling the family would be something to look forward to. He switched on the sound of the Amiga monitor and played *Kidnapper* to celebrate, making his way up and down a building with so many floors it would have touched the sky if it had been real. Whenever he shot kidnappers they expired with a satisfying spurt of cartoon blood, and whenever he was shot he sprouted wings and sailed up to an offscreen heaven. He had one life left, and a chance still to rescue the women and children, when two schoolboys in their early teens wandered into the shop.

Neither seemed impressed. The taller and more long-haired of them poked at the bridge of his spectacles with an inky finger while he glanced at the screens and then at the games locked in the glass-fronted cupboards. 'Got it, got it, got it,' he kept saying.

His slow fat friend snorted and giggled and looked sidelong at Richard, who lost his life to a gunman skulking behind a door. 'You were wasted, sucker,' the computer announced in a mechanically triumphant voice in case he couldn't read the writing on the screen, and Richard twirled on his chair to face the boys. 'Anything I can show you gentlemen?'

The taller boy removed his spectacles and set about bending the arms. 'If you've got anything new,' he said without glancing at Richard.

'Won't good do? I don't know if you noticed everything's half price.'

'It'd have to be.'

'He's got everything,' the fat boy told Richard as though sharing a joke with him.

'I'll stake my life that he hasn't got these,' Richard said, stooping to lift onto the counter the parcel which the arrival of the letter and the bills had hindered him from opening. As he straightened up he saw that a thin pinstriped man with a briefcase had entered the shop. 'Do you mind if I see to the whiz kids first?' Richard asked him.

'By all means do.'

He angled himself at the display cupboards while Richard split the adhesive tape on the carton with a razor-blade and peeled back the flaps of the lid. The fat boy was looking ready to be amused, his friend was blinking bare-eyed at Richard as though he was considering whether it was worth donning his spectacles. 'I expect you'll have seen how well these were reviewed,' Richard said, spreading a dozen multicoloured boxes along the counter. 'New out this month.'

The boy hooked the spectacles over his ears and stabbed the bridge with a forefinger. It took him three blinks to identify the games. 'Got them,' he said.

'Not officially, you can't have.'

'He's in a club,' the fat boy said, hardly able to contain his mirth.

'What are you, his straight man?' Richard demanded, shoving games aside to lean across the counter at the bespectacled boy. 'Look, son, if you've got pirate copies you ought to know they may have viruses. They could corrupt everything you've got that's legitimate.'

The pinstriped man jerked his head so that his left ear faced Richard. 'What's that about corruption?'

'Could you bear with me a minute? What I'm trying to say, son—'

'He thinks you gave me a virus, Dad.'

The man's ears flared red, and he shook his face, which was over-generously provided with teeth, at Richard. 'What the devil business is it of yours what I give my son?'

'Well, I think it's some of my business.' When Richard's mildness and his gesture at the contents of the shop only provoked the man to protrude his lower lip, Richard said 'And the law comes into it too, you know.'

'The law? You've got the gall to talk about the law? The law,' the man repeated with more of a whinny each time, 'might have something to say about you putting that violence up there on the screen for any age of child to see if they look in your window.'

'It might, but I don't think it would. Whereas, excuse me, but if you're doing what this lad seemed to imply you're doing, that certainly is against the law.'

The boys were observing with scientific detachment how

everything Richard said caused the man's characteristics to become further exaggerated. 'What are you accusing my son of?' the man whinnied, and had to wipe his mouth.

Richard saw he'd lost himself a customer – and by God, he thought with a sudden raw anger, he'd make sure this one stayed lost. 'What sort of corruption do you think we've been talking about? Child abuse?'

For an unsettling moment, as the man's ears virtually glowed red, Richard thought he'd stumbled on some truth. The man swung towards the boys, but only to say 'Come along. This isn't for your ears.'

'Nor yours,' Richard couldn't resist murmuring, 'by the look of them.'

The man shook the briefcase at him. 'Have you any idea to whom you're talking?'

'Not till you let me into the secret.'

'Tell him, Dad.'

'I'm with the planning office. What have you to say now?'

'What would you like me to say?'

The man grinned widely with his lips pinched shut as though Richard had rebuffed a last chance, and steered the boys out of the shop. 'When I get back to the office,' he said over his shoulder, 'I shall be taking a long hard look at the conditions of your lease.'

'Look until your eyes drop out,' Richard muttered, and was tempted to shout it. It seemed not to matter what he did, because he was experiencing a panic which made him feel hollow until he succeeded in reminding himself that it was only a feeling and that feelings always came to an end. Perhaps it was a symptom of the hangover which had lingered through Sunday and into today, even though on Sunday he'd drunk only soft drinks. He found it so hard to shake off his regret at having drunk so much on Saturday that he felt as if Archibald Grey's words had taken root in his mind.

The man from the planning office couldn't know that the lease of the shop was due for renewal. Though Richard couldn't recall the exact terms of the lease, surely it contained nothing which could be used against him now. His copy was at home, and he might have phoned Judith except that by this time she would have begun her shift at the off-licence. He ejected the discs from the computers and inserted three of the new arrivals for anyone to see who looked into the shop, and set about playing *Amazed*, which the reviews had described as 'addictive' and 'compulsive'. He was a comical gnome with a bobble hat drooping on his big head, who had to penetrate a series of mazes which grew more extensive and more complicated each time he conquered one. Whenever he stood still for more than ten seconds his hat turned into a dunce's cap and he started running uncontrollably into the maze. Several passers-by came singly into the shop during the afternoon to watch, and one woman whose necklace kept clacking like an executive toy said she would consider it as a birthday present for her nephew. Richard gave her his latest price list and a brochure describing most of the new games, and returned to his joystick. He was back on the route which led to the lair of a black blob which sent a tentacle to char him if he ventured within half a screen's width towards it – he was almost sure he knew which alternative route he had to follow – when the phone trilled.

'Just let me – just hold—' he protested, and glanced at his watch. It was after four o'clock. No wonder the traffic on the ring road was so loud now that he was aware of it. He scanned the instruction leaflet to determine which key might pause the game, but he was already racing through the labyrinth, dunce's cap on head. He turned his back on his plight and grabbed the phone. 'Computer Explosion. Richard Vale speaking.'

'Mr Vale?'

It was going to be one of those calls, Richard thought, which most calls seemed to be – calls that made him say who he was at least twice. 'Richard Vale here.'

'Ah, Mr Vale. Arabella Saint.'

He recognised her once he was past the hurdle of her first name. 'You're the headmistress.'

'Of Hoole School, yes.'

Richard thought she sounded capable of taking a joke about it, but he hadn't thought of one by the time he'd gagged the computers. 'I'm sorry I couldn't get back to you sooner,' the headmistress said.

'Why, your secretary—'

'I'm sorry?'

'I was only going to say your secretary, well, maybe I got the wrong impression, but I kind of thought, she sort of implied you wouldn't call me back.'

'Was there some problem you wish me to know about?'

'I don't want to get anyone in trouble,' Richard told her, and saw at once that if he didn't that was the last thing he ought to have said. 'I expect she deals with parents a lot, does she?'

'In what way?'

136

'Well, if they ring up with, you know, a complaint or anything.' It seemed to Richard that the conversation was spiralling into meaninglessness and that he was being carried helplessly with it. 'You mustn't think I'm trying to imply they've any reason to complain about your school, but you know parents. Not that I can talk, I'm one myself. Twice,' he amplified, and managed to stop.

'Indeed.'

'Two children, I mean. Boy and a girl. I expect they'd be at your school if we lived nearer. You've a reputation, haven't you? Your school has. I'll look forward to seeing it for myself.'

'Yes. I'm sorry, Mr Vale, that's why I'm calling.'

'Sorry for what now? Sorry, I mean, why are you apologising?'

'Because I'm afraid that the letter was sent by mistake.'

'You've got to be – I mean, you mean you didn't mean to write to me?'

'Of course I did. I hope you don't think anybody here is quite that inefficient.' She paused long enough for the rebuke to make itself felt, but not long enough for him to apologise. 'It's simply that between my drafting the letter and its reaching you we've received an estimate which it would be uneconomic for you to match.'

'But you can't say that. I mean, you can, you have, but I don't see how. If whoever it is can do it that cheap for you, how do you know I can't?'

'Mr Vale, to help us with our budgetary problems which we're suffering in common with all schools at present he'll provide computers at cost and waive his labour charge.'

'But that's ridi—' Richard slapped himself across the face and struggled to be calmer. 'What is he, a saint, you know, a martyr? How can anyone make a living acting like that?'

'Obviously he sees this as a special case. He's related to one of our governors, and he assures me the cash flow of his company is sufficient to absorb the gesture.'

'What company's that? I mean, I don't mean to worry you, but I don't know of any round here that could afford to write all that off just now, and I think I would.'

'It isn't local.'

'Well, if it's not, don't you think you ought—'

'I'm sorry, Mr Vale, I've taken my decision. It was only out of courtesy to you that I telephoned rather than write.'

'Couldn't we at least—' Richard pleaded, but he was talking to a mechanical drone that sounded as hollow as himself. 'At least what? At least let me put in a few computers at a loss?' His voice seemed as meaningless as the aching of his face, and the sight of the dunce in the maze filled him with a loathing he could almost taste. As he switched off the monitor, his mind grew as blank. Everything was meaningless – everything except Judith and Olga and Simon, and how could his life be when he had them? He tried to think how many computers or games he would need to sell, and how soon, in order to pay the bills on time and not be dreading the next flock. How many days had it been since he'd made a sale? The number loomed over his mind, growing heavier and more immovable, until he wondered if he was looking at the situation from the wrong angle: mustn't each day that failed to bring sales make it more likely that the next would bring some? He imagined each day as a coin he was tossing – he considered tossing one to test the principle, but panic was threatening to erupt from the depths of him. He replaced *Amazed* in the machine with *Kidnapper* and did his best to revel in the cartoon deaths until the parade of home-going workers persuaded him that he could go home.

He switched off the computers and on the alarm and locked the shop, and ran across the pedestrian crossing, where a paralysed green man bleeped like a stuck computer, to the car park. He'd left the little Nissan on the top storey, descending from which involved driving down five minutes' worth of ramps that seemed barely wide enough to let the car turn into them. At each corner he winced in anticipation of the screech of metal against concrete. Eventually he reached the pay booth, which raised its insect leg and released him into the homeward race.

The ring road was interrupted by several three-lane round-abouts. Perhaps it was his hangover, but they had never looked so dangerous to him, cars rushing after one another like dogs, nose to tail. As he hesitated in the middle lane on the edge of the largest roundabout a car blared its horn behind him and the driver shouted wide-mouthed but inaudibly at him. The Nissan gave a nervous lurch and almost stalled, and then was veering around the roundabout. A Land-Rover swerved into its path from the left just as a Ford estate came up fast behind it and a Toyota on its right signalled a left turn. Richard was all at once aware how flimsy the car was – as flimsy as his skull – yet he was suddenly no longer experiencing panic. Then the Land-Rover accelerated, and there was enough room for them all to take the second exit from the intersection.

Once past the archipelago of roundabouts the Whitchurch road grew narrower. In some of the windows of the blocks of small shops the displays looked faded, and the hems of the buildings were grey with dried mud. Beyond the adopted church which he always thought of as the Chapel of the Antique Furniture, the road led towards open countryside, past large houses with gardens extensive enough for caravans to gather in some of them, but Richard's route home took him into a maze of streets so narrow that they crowded the front gardens against the terraced red-brick blocks, leaving space for only a few tall thin plants behind each gap-toothed fence. Some of the junctions managed to find room for patches of weedy waste ground that nobody mowed. It was the insides of houses that mattered, Judith always said, and since the Owains had redesigned the interior of the Vales' house it was roomier than Richard could have dreamed of. He was on his way to recapturing that sense of satisfied amazement he'd experienced on wakening in what was virtually a new house when he turned along the street and saw his family standing on the pavement outside the house.

Panic seized him. They each had a key to the front door. He backed into the space outside the gate, braking just in time as the windscreen of a parked car rushed into the mirror, and struggled free of his safety belt, trapping it in the door as he shoved himself away from the Nissan. By then the children had converged on him while Judith tried to explain over their heads. 'Simon's—'

'Simon got his key stuck in the door,' Olga said in the lofty tones of a sister older by two minutes.

'Don't interrupt, Olga. I've left a message on the Owains' machine.'

'It wasn't my fault,' Simon complained. 'It broke.'

'You're always breaking things. That's boys, isn't it, Mummy?'

'Shut your face like she told you. I said last night it was getting bendy, but nobody listens to me.'

'That's because you talk so much crap.'

'Olga, that's quite enough. I'm sure they don't allow you to use words like that at school.'

'Miss Hendle did when she trod in some outside the gates.'

'Well, that doesn't mean you have to. You've been too ready with it lately.'

'Never mind smirking like that, Simon. It's all right for him, he hasn't got as much homework as I have, and I could be doing it now if he hadn't insisted on sticking his stupid key in the door instead of letting me use mine when I said.'

'So? It's you who always wants to have a stupid race to the house.'

Judith clapped her hands. 'Both of you. All this rivalry about keys sounds deeply Freudian to me, Rich.'

Perhaps she was wondering why he hadn't yet said a word. Surely his panic ought to have faded by now, and he was afraid to understand why it hadn't done so. 'How bad is it?' he blurted, making for the house before anyone could answer. 'Let me have a look.'

The shaft of Simon's key had snapped, protruding about half an inch from the lock. Either the boy had tried to turn the key before it was fully inserted or he'd twisted it too hard while trying to extract it, and Richard had to suppress an urge to demand which, because what did it matter? 'Did you try to move it before you called David?' he asked Judith.

'I would have if I'd been able to borrow some pliers,' she said, and grimaced as he pinched the metal stub between his thumb and injured finger. 'Be careful of your nails.'

'There isn't enough left of them to take care of,' Richard muttered, wondering when he had started to chew them and why. As he grasped the remains of the key he felt as though the sting of the metal was seeping into his bloodstream. Surely the pain had to mean something if he made it do so. He closed his eyes and twisted the stump of the key as hard as he could. He smelled dusty soil and dead weeds, and his exertion or the stagnant heat or his hangover seemed to turn his skull into a balloon, and he wasn't sure if it was only that which gave him the impression that the key had shifted in the lock. He exerted a last despairing twist and tug, and the shaft of the key slipped out of the slot like one of the metal puzzles he'd battled with as a child. He staggered back with the unexpectedness of it and flung the shaft away as if that would rid him of the pain, and heard it clink in the distance like a thrown-away coin. He leaned against the wall of the house and sucked his finger, which felt as though it had been poisoned by a coin. 'Well done, but are you all right?' Judith said.

'I'll be fine once we're inside.'

'Here, let me open up.'

Richard listened to her unlocking the door and waited for his panic to subside. He heard Simon and Olga hurry in, squabbling about who should go first and who had pushed whom, and realised that he'd just lied to Judith and himself. He opened his eyes and did his best to smile into her broad sleepy-eyed face, whose

permanently amused look was squashed beneath a frown of
concern, but she and everything around them appeared darkened,
as if he'd been drinking too much. It was only the hangover, he told
himself; eventually it would leave him alone. 'I'll be fine,' he
repeated, and followed her into the house.

# Fifteen

By the end of that week David was convinced that Miss Singleton's house was as secretive as its owner. He had barely started drilling the kitchen wall in preparation for injecting a silicon damp course when he blew the fuse that controlled all the sockets in the building. He replaced the wire in the china fuse in the cobwebbed fuse-box under the stairs, but as soon as he switched on the drill the fuse blew again. The least the house needed was an up-to-date fuse-box, and there was no point in providing one without first rewiring the entire place. He set about tracing the cables, and the more he exposed, the worse they looked: ancient wires wrapped in cloth gone rotten, some of them squashed against the bricks behind the skirting-boards, some trailing behind the wallpaper and not even stapled to the walls. 'I don't know who the cowboy was who rewired your house last time,' he said eventually, 'but I don't wonder he rode off into the sunset.'

She pressed her lips together, and they and her long nostrils turned almost as pale as her eyes. 'I'm sorry if he was a friend of yours,' David said, 'but all the same, he'd no right to leave you in this state.'

She yanked up her pinned trousers, a gesture which somehow managed to express hauteur, and folded her arms. 'He was my father.'

'Ah, well. Well. Ah . . .' For some seconds 'even so' were the only other words David could think of. 'Did he do it all himself?' he asked with what he hoped might seem a willingness to be impressed.

'I should hope so, since it was his trade.'

'Doug never told me that, the bastard,' David admitted, leaving the last two words unsaid. 'I wonder if I might have heard of him. What would his name have been?'

'What do you imagine my father's name would be?'

'His trade name, I was meaning.'

'He had no reason to conceal his name.'

'Traded as Singleton, did he? Before my time, I'm afraid.'

'No doubt you would recognise his workmanship.'

All the responses David could bring to mind seemed at the very least unfortunate, and no doubt Miss Singleton took his silence as one of them. 'I won't leave you in the dark tonight,' he said, 'but for heaven's sake don't plug anything in.'

On Thursday she took even longer than usual to unbolt and unchain the front door, and met Joelle with a blink of what looked like unpleasant surprise, although David had told her yesterday that Joelle would be accompanying him. He had to remember that her memory might let her down sometimes, just like Gwendolen's. 'This is my wife Joelle,' he said. 'She's the creative side of the partnership.'

'Today I'm just the electrician's mate.'

Miss Singleton turned to scrape her feet on the doormat, a gesture that increasingly reminded David of a cat in a litter-box, then swung round as if to catch Joelle unawares. 'I thought your husband said you were a decorator.'

'That's what I mainly am. If you'd like me to bring my sample books—'

'Then how can you be qualified to deal with electrical matters?'

'I'm just here to help him feed the new wires through.'

'Of course if Mr Owain feels that's necessary.'

He thought she was both scoring a point against Joelle and implying that her father had been more self-sufficient than David. 'Best mate an electrician ever had,' he murmured to Joelle, giving her a wink.

'We'll be replacing the lights, won't we?' she said as they stepped into the musty gloom. 'Do you have an idea of what you'd like, Miss Singleton?'

'I wasn't aware that any such change was proposed.'

'It's never advisable to put old fittings on new cables. Would you like me to drive you to the wholesalers so you can see what's on offer?'

'That won't be necessary, thank you.'

'You can trust us to brighten up the place for you,' Joelle said with more confidence than David sensed she felt.

'I can see everything I need to see.'

'That must be a blessing, but you don't want to strain your eyes unnecessarily, do you?' Taking her silence as more agreeable than David thought it was, Joelle said 'I was going to ask, would you like me to redecorate?'

'I seem to have been left no choice.'

'Well, of course you have. It's entirely up to you,' Joelle said in a voice which sounded beaten flat. When Miss Singleton didn't respond she said 'I'd better be getting on with what I was asked to do, then' so coldly that David felt some of the chill was directed at him.

For much of the day walls or floors separated them, except when they needed to move the contents of rooms or roll carpets back. She wrinkled her nose at the feel of the perished rubber underlays, and gave a cry when several withered spiders fell into her hair as she took down a lampshade. As he threaded wires through to her he heard her trying vainly to make conversation with Miss Singleton, until he could sense her awaiting the sight of wire with an eagerness that was almost pitiful.

By the time the electricity was ready to be restored it was almost as dark outside as it had been all day in the house. Usually the act of pulling the main switch after a rewiring job made David feel festive, as though he was turning on illuminations at Christmas; but the renewed light of these bare bulbs was pitiless, revealing the shabbiness of the furniture and the starkness of the cluttered rooms, throwing shadows like indelible spilled ink. 'Will that do for tonight?' David asked Miss Singleton.

'It will have to. Thank you,' she said, unexpectedly subdued.

'I'll be back in the morning with our book of shades.'

He loaded the tools into the boot of the car while Joelle patrolled the pavement, flexing her muscles. When she started the car Miss Singleton was still in the doorway, gazing at the twilight as though reluctant to confront the revelations of her house. 'Someone else for us to worry about,' David commented as the car turned out of the road.

'She's old enough to be responsible for herself.'

Joelle's tone threw him. He couldn't blame her for having had enough of the old woman – that was why he'd said he would come back alone tomorrow – but she seemed less angry than preoccupied to the point of indifference to anything else. Ever since the barbecue he'd been experiencing something like preoccupation himself, some thought or feeling that stayed just beyond the light of his mind. During dinner he had a sense that the unspoken had intervened between them, and making love afterwards felt like a substitute for talking. Once Joelle was asleep he lay awake, straining his mind to grasp some impression that was darker than the dark.

In the morning Miss Singleton chose the cheapest lampshades from the catalogue, those which would do least to tone down the glare of the bulbs. When he returned with what she'd ordered she convinced herself it wasn't quite, but wouldn't be persuaded to compare the lampshades with the illustrations in the catalogue. Most of the shades did go some way towards assuaging the bleakness of the house, so that when he'd finished and was wiping sweat that felt dusty off his forehead with the back of his hand, he risked saying 'What do you think? Is that an improvement?'

'For whom?'

'Miss Singleton, if there's anything you don't like you should tell me. You're the boss.'

'Do you think so?' she said with such bitterness that he didn't answer. Whatever might be between her and her relatives had nothing to do with him. 'I'll be here first thing on Monday,' he said, meaning it to sound more like a promise than an imposition, and released himself into the late afternoon.

He wouldn't blame Joelle if she decided against redecorating that house. It was a matter of pride for the Owains never to abandon a job, but as he arrived home the prospect of discussing it felt like a kind of relief. When he let himself in, however, he was greeted by the sight of a letter protruding from an envelope on the stairs. 'Who's this from?' he called.

'From someone you don't know, to me,' Joelle said at the top of the stairs. 'Read it if you like.'

David unfolded the nondescript sheet of white paper, which at some point had been crumpled up and then smoothed out. Apart from the illegible signature, the letter was typed. It bore no address.

Dear Joely,
I don't know if you'll remember, but I've been thinking how much we both wanted children at school that you must have some by now. I've got one at last, and I need to talk to someone but frankly don't know who I can. Would you be willing to help? Don't bother to reply, I'm not even sure why I'm troubling you after so long, but if I can sort my ideas out a bit perhaps we'll be in touch again.
Hoping we're still close—

David squinted at the jagged line of ink, which looked as though the pen or its wielder had been trying to squirm off the page. 'Who does this say?'

'The signature?' Joelle leaned over the banister, her hair curtaining her face. 'Ellie. Ellen. It used to be Joely and Ellie at school.'

'What kind of person was she?'

'We used to be pretty alike.'

'Well, I hope you aren't still. It doesn't sound as if you are. When did this come?'

Joelle pushed her hair back, then let it fall across her eyes again. 'While you were out.'

That needn't mean today, and he suspected it didn't, given how obviously the letter explained her preoccupation of the last few days. At some point she must have screwed up the letter and then decided not to throw it away, at least not until he'd read it. He sensed that she found it as disturbing as he did, and he thought he saw one reason why. 'What does she mean by saying she's got a child? Had one, does she mean?'

'What else could she?'

'You might wonder. You'll notice she doesn't mention a man.'

'If there is one, maybe he's part of her problem.'

'And if there isn't?'

'Maybe there was and they've split up.' Joelle came halfway down the stairs and gazed at David as though he was forcing her to consider implications she hadn't thought of. 'What are you getting at, David, if anything?'

'Suppose the child doesn't belong to her?'

'I don't think anyone who got that desperate would write letters about it, do you?'

'They might if they made sure nobody could read their name or find out their address except the person they were writing to. Do you know where she lives?'

'It looks as if she thinks I do, but I can't remember.'

'You're not just saying that?'

'Why would I?' Joelle sat on the stairs, pressing her legs together. 'Even if I did remember, it wouldn't be much use. She moved away years ago.'

'Sorry, Jo. I'm not blaming you.' When Joelle's stare didn't soften he glanced away, feeling abashed, until his attention focused on the envelope. 'Maybe she wasn't so clever,' he said, and turned it over. But the postmark was blurred beyond recognition, even the date.

'You won't say she did that on purpose too,' Joelle said. 'Unless you think I did it, of course.'

'Look, I've said I'm sorry,' David told her, not quite certain why he was apologising. 'I think if the letter has got to you that much you ought to show it to the police.'

'And have them give her even more problems than it sounds like she already has? I'd have expected better of you, David.' Joelle held out her hand for the letter. When he stuffed it into the envelope and gave it to her she said 'Let's wait and see if she gets in touch.'

Her tone ended any argument, and David tried to be satisfied to let the matter lie. Maybe it explained his preoccupation as well, that he'd been preoccupied with not knowing what hers was. They had both been less aware recently of things that would ordinarily have concerned them. That much he realised while they were getting ready for bed, when Joelle remarked as she drew the curtains 'Do you think Herb's found someone else?'

'I wouldn't blame him. What makes you ask?'

'He doesn't seem to be at home tonight.'

'Good for him, if that's what it is,' David said, and dozed off with a vision of Herb driving a train with a young woman in black lacy underwear and sheer black stockings perched on his lap. 'A bit too young for you, you old lecher,' he thought he mouthed as he fell asleep.

Later he seemed to awaken, though remaining so nearly asleep that he couldn't judge whether it was the sheet or the stagnant summer darkness that clung to him. He was descending steps of half-formed thoughts when he heard a faint thin voice outside the window. It was singing in little more than a whisper, and he couldn't tell if it was expressing joy or grief or both. He raised himself from the bed, meeting no resistance, and went to the gap which Joelle always liked to leave between the curtains. Resting his hands on his bare thighs, he stooped to peer through the gap.

Mops of shadow stretched away from the trees beside the streetlamps. In the yellowish glow, which seemed muffled by the weight of the darkest part of the night, the street resembled an old photograph. Only the wavering distant voice gave it anything like life. The sound drew his gaze across the road to Herb's house.

A figure was standing in the doorway of the unlit house. At first David thought it was facing him, its long hair blotting out its face, and stretching its arms wide to him. Then he saw that it was pressing the palms of its hands against the walls on either side of the door as if it had been crucified in that position or was seeking sanctuary in the house. That was as much as he could distinguish within the shadow of a tree – not even what the figure was wearing, if anything at all. At that distance it looked like an insect pinned to the building, and he rather hoped it was the distance which made it appear thinner than it had any right to be while retaining the ability to move, let alone sing. He felt as though he had to watch until it moved, which meant he might see its face, and then he found himself hoping that it never would.

Either he returned to bed at some point or had never left it, because that was where birdsong and sunlight wakened him. 'That,' he said to himself, 'was one hell of a dream.' It must have grown out of his thinking about Herb last night, he decided. He tried to piece it together in his mind so as to describe it to Joelle, but the sound of her running into the house and almost falling on the stairs drove it out of his head – he hadn't even realised she was outside – and he forgot it entirely once he learned what had happened to Herb.

# Sixteen

Herb spent most of the afternoon following the Owains' barbecue in his front garden, grubbing at parched weeds with the help of a fork and a trowel until his fingertips felt stuffed with earth. Every time he thought he'd finished he would catch sight of yet another stubborn growth, taunting or rebuking him. At last he allowed himself to take a shower and scrub his fingers with a nailbrush. He microwaved a container of more or less Italian lasagne and ate it out of the plastic, then he went into the front room to see what he could do about the furniture.

The television seemed to nod forwards to greet him. Last week he'd discovered that the stand had become so warped he couldn't move the drawer at its base. Though he had never found a use for the drawer, he was determined that if he made it work he would think of one – or Mary would. Deep within himself he felt that if he managed to repair the stand she might come back to him.

As soon as he lifted the television, the stand gave a creak so grateful that he didn't dare replace the set on it, even though he'd forgotten to disconnect the leads. He hugged the television with one arm, the twenty-four-inch screen nuzzling his chest, and struggled to pull out the connections at the back. Aerial lead, vision in, audio in – none of the leads was long enough to let him rest the television on the floor while he withdrew them, or rather they'd composed themselves into such a knot behind the stand that they each might as well be half their length. As he strained to yank out the audio jack, which seemed to be jammed in the socket, the television slid down his chest until the edge of its base located a protrusion on which to rest its weight – Herb's crotch. 'Ah,' he told it on a rising note, 'oh, ag, ee,' and succeeded in wrenching the jack loose just as the lead began to winch up the videorecorder and drag the stand towards him. The recorder subsided with a thud, as did Herb, on the carpet with the television rocking forward on its bulbous screen onto his chin. For a moment he thought his jaws had snipped off the end of his tongue. 'Yag,' he commented with feeling, and managed to refrain from slinging the television off himself until he was capable of sitting up and lowering it onto the carpet; then he massaged his tongue between one thumb and forefinger, though it felt enormous and barely under his control, more like the tip of a giant worm. When he'd assured himself that it was intact he lifted the videorecorder out of the stand and disentangled the leads and laid them out side by side on the floor. 'You've had your fun, now let's get serious,' he told everything around him, and set out the materials for rescuing the stand.

Last week he'd measured the ends and designed two pieces that should just fit against their insides, supporting the top of the stand. David Owain had ordered them from his joiner and brought them to Herb the day before the barbecue and offered to fit them, but that was a labour Herb had set himself. Now he spread pages of the local newspaper on the carpet, glimpsing a headline which said PENSIONER'S HOARD OF FORTUNE and wondering if Gwendolen could in fact receive a pension when she had so little of herself to give officialdom. He laid the two pieces of wood on the paper and tussled with the screw top of the tube of superglue until his fingertips felt as though its ridges were embedded in them. When it came loose he squirted a snotty blob onto one piece of wood and scribbled it into a resemblance to the track of a crazed snail, and inserted the wood under the top of the stand.

It nearly fitted. It lodged between the left side and the top like a crutch beneath an arm, but there was an angle of perhaps thirty degrees between it and the side. He'd more or less expected that, since the stand had warped, and now he had only to force the stand back into shape. He stood it on its left side, which he ought to have done in the first place, and stamped on the middle of the new piece.

There was a creak so sharp he thought the stand had come apart. When he forced himself to look, however, the new piece was flush against the side. The new legs were wider than the originals, but they had to be in order to fit over the shelf for the videorecorder, and their obtrusiveness might make them a conversation piece. He balanced the stand on its other side, which was more warped, and scrawled glue over the inner surface of the second piece before edging it into place. Its angle was at least forty degrees, which he'd anticipated, he told himself. He wagged a finger at it to show it who was in charge and tramped hard on it. It didn't budge.

More force was called for, that was clear. He aimed his heel at the centre of the piece, feeling like an apprentice martial artist, and brought it down with all his strength. Something moved with a screech of wood on wood. One more good tromp should do it. He slammed his heel down and heard wood splinter.

Sweat sprouted on his forehead and prickled in his armpits. The new piece was wedged at an angle of twenty degrees or so, its front leg trapping the drawer beneath the shelf. At first he was afraid to touch the stand, then he became so furious that he tipped it onto its legs with a crash. Since it didn't collapse he risked placing the television on it and replugged the leads, and rested the video-recorder askew on its shelf in order to connect it to the television. It wasn't until he tried to push the videorecorder into its old position that he realised the new piece was in the way; if he manoeuvred the recorder into position the piece would block one end of the cassette slot. His armpits were crawling as if someone's beard had been thrust into them. He left the videorecorder protruding at an angle from the stand and dashed out of the house to hire a film to watch.

He felt like something violent. The video library across the main road was about to close for the night, and he grabbed the first cassette which looked as though it might be savage enough to take away his rage – *Blood Slash*, its cover depicting a face chopped into so many pieces he couldn't tell whether it belonged to a man or a woman. The mottled faintly moustached youth who had been too lethargic to exclude Herb seemed about to comment, until Herb's expression made it plain that his choice of film was nobody's business except his own. He hurried home, the plastic box growing warm and sweaty in his hand. Though the stand hadn't collapsed, he experienced a surge of fury as he shoved the cassette into the machine.

At the outset the film seemed much as he understood most horror films to be, the kind Mary would never have allowed into the house. He didn't recognise a single name in the slothful parade of credits, and he suspected that the parents of the performers and technicians mightn't either. A director's name which looked as though it must have been inaccurately transcribed oozed by, and the camera began to prowl through a graveyard and out into a street and at length around a corner, ducking back as it saw a policeman, until Herb started willing it to get wherever it was bound for, or rather whoever. Ultimately it caught sight of a young woman who seemed far too skimpily dressed for so late at night, and rushed at her, reaching her just as she turned and – Herb assumed she was about to scream, but the most she achieved was a split second's squeak before it was broad daylight and police were

153

draping tarpaulins over what, if it was her, had been generously distributed about the street. The narrative blackout disconcerted Herb almost as much as though he himself had forgotten what had happened, and when the police began discussing the murder to the accompaniment of subtitles summarising their conversation he found it hard to grasp whether he was hearing or reading their words. This was unsettling enough, but when the less ugly of the policemen met his stripper girlfriend and the image of them fell back in order to accommodate a bearded man who stood beside the screen and gesticulated in time with their dialogue, Herb shrieked through his teeth and dragged the film out of the machine. The grubby label informed him that the cassette had been subtitled and signed for the deaf.

No doubt the youth haunted by a moustache had been going to warn him. Herb watched as much as he could stand, but whenever the camera wandered off in search of victims it never did more than make them jump, until it became clear that all the slashing had been committed by the censor, leaving very little blood. The subtitles included the sounds of a police siren and footsteps and a door opening. When the stripper's boyfriend was left groaning from a beating by a gang which seemed to have nothing to do with the plot, and a subtitle said 'Ooh', Herb arrested the film and stormed off to bed.

He thought he had only just managed to fall asleep, having wriggled and writhed beneath the single hot sheet until he was aware of every wrinkle in it, when he was awakened by a crash downstairs. He sprang out of bed, stubbing one big toe on the footboard, and did his best to hop and scream quietly on his way to the door. Rather than burglars, could it be Mary, who'd tried to return without wakening him? He sat rapidly from stair to stair all the way to the hall, where he threw open the door of the front room and slapped the light-switch. The top of the stand had given way, dumping the television on the videorecorder. One corner of the television had smashed through the cassette tray, crushing *Blood Slash*.

Herb sprawled in an armchair and drummed his heels in fury, then he surged out of the chair and heaved the television onto the carpet before stumping out of the room. He had to get up before dawn, and when he did his eyes and his brain felt prickly, invaded by something like hair. The shower was too fierce, needles of water jabbing at his skin, and then too weak; too cold and then too hot, and then he was unable to judge which. He struggled into his uniform and gulped half a pint of milk out of the bottle, the bland taste mixing with the flavour of toothpaste. The sight of the damage in the front room rekindled his fury, aggravating the sensation of prickly growth in his eyes and his brain, and he flung himself out of the house.

The dark before dawn had settled like a fall of soot on the houses and trees and streetlamps, and he felt as if he was breathing it in. Above the cross on the main road, branches cawed and flapped their black wings. A milk float was groaning through the side streets, but otherwise Herb was alone with his rage. When he crossed the bridge and trudged down the steps to the station he encountered three of his colleagues sipping coffee from paper cups. 'See you later,' he told them, which was as much conversation as he felt he could sustain, and hurried past the wall-chart which boasted how many trains had been on time and how many not more than five minutes late.

He found his train and let himself into the cabin, where holidays meant that the guard's seat would be unoccupied all week. He dug his key into the slot and almost managed to switch off the alarm before it began to squawk and flash red, then he lowered himself onto the small barely padded chair and switched on the lights and trod on the dead man's pedal and gripped the knobs of the control levers, brake in his left hand, throttle in his right. He eased the train out of the station and saw the night coming to meet him, and felt as dark inside himself.

Apart from the occasional station, distant chalky scratches that grew into long deserted slabs which rushed past him with a hollow roar, he saw only the lines being reeled in beneath him, their clatter threatening to form words. At last the pylons above Hooton appeared, their power cables glinting like slashes on the black metal of the air, and Herb slowed the train for its first stop. Three women whom he took to be cleaners were already waiting. He opened the doors to them and held the train still until it was time for it to move, then sent it along the glimmering track.

The route led through docklands into the centre of Birkenhead before tunnelling under the river and following a loop beneath Liverpool. When the train came into the open again, the world was growing brighter, but Herb felt as though the night had buried a hairball between his brain and his eyes. Back to Hooton to pick up more women, back to the loop, back to Hooton, back to the loop . . . The world was continuing to waken, the first briefcase-carriers running for the train. Whenever he used the intercom to advise passengers where to change for other lines, he wasn't sure if he could hear his voice grow tinny and minute behind him. Back to Hooton, and then the first station was Bromborough, where passengers raced down the steps from the bridge as they heard the train. One of them had a briefcase and a beard, and Herb's fists clenched on the knobs. 'Victor,' he cried in a voice so delighted he startled himself.

Victor's small flat broad-nosed face was red from exertion. His baggy white shirt bulged and deflated, his spotted bow tie jerked like a butterfly just out of the cocoon. Herb's surroundings were all at once brighter and clearer. 'Good to see you again, Vic,' he said almost into the man's face, which passed so close to him that he could see hairs stirring around the panting mouth.

As soon as the platform was deserted Herb shut the doors tight. A lanky man with shocked grey hair appeared on the steps from the bridge, running extravagantly and throwing out one arm as though he could catch hold of the train, but the only passenger Herb wanted to take care of was on board. Victor's station was Bebington, heralded by the sight of the twin domes of the art gallery, which struck Herb as very much resembling greenish breasts. He eased the train into position by the platform with a carefulness so precise it felt ecstatic. 'See you later, cunt curator,' he said as the man's black curly scalp bobbed down the steps beyond the ticket barrier.

Now that he knew in which district Victor lived, anything seemed possible. Whenever he followed the loop of darkness beyond the river it seemed to trace a noose he would be able to draw tight, and he hadn't been so excited by driving a train since his first days in the job. The last journey of his shift returned him to Hooton at last, and he withdrew his keys and hurried past the ticket office to the Beefeater.

This was a large pub surrounded by dozens of expensive cars. 'I'm not a violent person,' a young woman was saying as she nibbled peanuts from a dish on the bar, 'but I wish I'd had a hammer to smash in their heads.' Herb had memorised the number of the art gallery, the Lady Lever, days ago, and at last he knew how to proceed. He fed a coin into the slot of the phone beyond the bar and dialled, and after a pair of rings a voice which he took to be female announced 'Lady Lever.'

'I'm just checking that someone still works for you. Victor . . . Victor . . .'

156

Perhaps this wouldn't be as easy as Herb had anticipated, because the woman seemed content to let him repeat the name like the refrain of a song. 'Victor, Victor, lead me to the lictor,' a voice commenced singing in his skull until he said sharply 'I've forgotten his last name.'

'Would you be thinking of Victor Harper?'

'That'll be the man I'm after,' Herb said, then saw the trap he'd almost fallen into. 'If he's your only Victor.'

'I hope we all are in our way.'

Herb was tearing through the phone directory while he gripped the receiver between his ear and shoulder. Grubb, Guy, Hardman, Harper . . . There was only one Harper, Victor, and he lived in Bromborough. Herb's fingernail left a dent in the page where the listing was. 'I think you're right,' he said.

'But yes, we just have Mr Harper here. Would you like to speak to him?'

'That won't be necessary, thank you,' Herb said, and played a lie. 'I only want to write to him.'

'Because if you want a word, I'm looking straight at him.'

So was Herb, at the face which his mind was squashing even smaller, turning it an anguished crimson as though its beard was a gag. 'I'd like to sort my ideas out first,' he said.

'May I at least give him a name?'

'Dusty and empty.'

'Justin who, sorry?' Her voice dwindled as the receiver slithered from Herb's grip and swung upside down while the directory sprawled on the floor. 'I didn't quite catch it,' he heard her apologising as he retrieved the directory and hooked the receiver into place. 'He will,' he muttered, striding out of the pub.

He raised one hand to wipe his forehead, which the phone conversation had left streaming with sweat, and the sleeve of his uniform appeared in front of his eyes. Did he really want to risk being seen in uniform by Victor's neighbours? The delay infuriated him, but he ought to have time. He sprinted over the bridge and sprang between the doors onto the Chester train.

He couldn't help urging it faster, snarling through his teeth. Walking, when the train had dawdled into Chester, was at least something to do with his rage, though he was itching with sweat before he'd dealt with half the half-mile between the station and the cross. He rushed into his house and upstairs, cursing the video-cassette which would have to wait until he came back, and exchanged his uniform for the topmost pair of trousers that hadn't fallen off the pile at the end of the bed. Snatching his keys from the stairs where he'd dropped them, he slammed the front door and ran, stopping and starting like a train he wasn't in control of, back to the station.

Someone who recognised him waved him through the barrier just in time for him to stagger onto the next train for Hooton. At Hooton, where his heart and lungs had ceased to feel like a single failing organ, he dashed onto the Bromborough train, only to have to wait for five minutes before the doors bumped shut. At least there was nobody at the Bromborough barrier to see and perhaps recognise him, and he stalked up the steps to the main road.

A woman towed by a Yorkshire terrier pointed Herb towards the street he asked for. Nearly all the buildings in the side road it branched from were bungalows, even a school. The low roofs made the sky seem wider and Herb taller, his skull absorbing the heat of the sun it almost touched. He rubbed his scalp to soothe the itching that was apparently less in it than beneath it as he approached the cul-de-sac where Victor lived.

Though Herb could hear the repetitive murmur of a lawn-mower, and a dog which kept emitting three yaps, the stubby road looked deserted. He veered into it, trying to decide what pace would be neither too fast nor too slow, trying to convince anyone who noticed him that he might have mistaken the road. Victor's bungalow was in the midst of the left-hand row, and at first sight it appeared to have little to distinguish it from its neighbours, so that Herb was unprepared for the loathing which surged into his brain as he came abreast of the house. The first things he saw beyond the picture window were the miniatures on the walls, paintings displayed not so much like exhibits in a gallery, he thought, as like trophies from Victor's triumph over him. He stared hairy-eyed at the antique furniture the colour of turds, at the brass knocker that must be several times as old as the front door. He imagined Victor's face on the plate of the knocker, imagined himself smashing it with the brass knob until it caved in, and then he blundered out of the cul-de-sac, his burning head held low for fear that someone might glimpse whatever expression was on his face.

He managed to stop punching the air as he passed the school, though not before at least one child in the playground had pointed at him. He strolled to the station and back to the side road and past Victory Road, which wasn't its name yet, back to the station . . . The more he walked, the less able he was to rehearse what he would say. Once he became convinced that Victor had been given a lift home, but when he strode to the bungalow there was no sign of anyone inside. He would have stayed nearby except that cars were beginning to return to their driveways, families were regathering themselves. He saw Victor's face on every distant figure that came up from the station, and smashed the face in his mind when he'd established that nobody in sight was Victor. Eventually the stream of commuters became just a few drips, but it took Herb several more patrols to convince himself that Victor wasn't coming home for dinner.

He was with Mary. At this very moment they were in a restaurant, clinking glasses of wine, their bodies touching under the table, Mary's hand falling lightly on Victor's knee as it used to fall on Herb's whenever she laughed as they sat close . . . When had she stopped doing that? The day she'd met Victor? Trying to remember when she had last touched him that way filled his skull with prickles, and he hadn't succeeded when he arrived at the station. He dug his hand into his hip pocket, his thoughts scraping together, and found only emptiness. His British Rail pass was in his uniform, and he hadn't a penny on him.

At the foot of the steps a uniformed man turned to confront him with an alert impersonal gaze and a thin replica of a smile, and Herb felt as if an image of a face had been held up to meet him. 'Staff,' Herb said.

'May I see some identification?'

'You could, except it's at home,' Herb said with a laugh at his own expense, and turned his pockets inside out. 'I'm from Chester. Herb Crantry. As you see, I'm miles from home without a pittance to my name.'

'I'm sorry, sir, I can't allow you through without a ticket or a pass.'

'I know you can't normally, and you're only doing your job, but as one railwayman to another . . .' The youthful efficient face seemed to have less behind it than ever, and Herb began to plead, because otherwise he was afraid his rage would surface. 'Look, are you here tomorrow? I'll be bringing up the train from Hooton on the early shift, and you can check then that I'm who I say I am. Herb Crantry. If you aren't on in the morning you can ask whoever is to check.'

'I'm sorry, sir, I'm not authorised to admit anyone without a valid ticket or a pass.'

'I know, but can't you look the other way for once?' Herb's hands and feet were starting to prickle as much as his skull. 'Or all right, don't look the other way, look at me. Do I look like a liar to you? Who's going to come in here pretending to be me just to get to Hooton?'

'I'm sorry, sir, I've told you—'

'Yes, you keep telling me. What are you, a recording? Haven't you any feelings at all?'

'I'm afraid that attitude will get you nowhere, sir.'

'You're right. Of course you've got feelings just like the rest of us. If you don't do your job properly you might find them pulling the chain on you, pulling the plug, I mean.' When that provoked a total absence of visible response Herb blurted 'Listen, here's the solution. Give me a bit of paper and a pen and I'll write an IOU. I'll pay for the journey as soon as I get here tomorrow.'

'I'm sorry, sir, I'm not authorised to accept anything—'

'Except tickets and passes, I know that, but for God's sake, I've told you I'm staff.' As an argument that no longer had much weight, Herb saw, and he tried to delay the ticket collector while he thought of one which had. 'Look, look, look—'

He heard himself clucking like a demented hen. The ticket collector was no longer looking at him. 'Will you stand aside, please, sir? These people have a train to catch.'

'Fuck them and you, then,' Herb screamed, feeling his rage bursting out of his control, knowing that he had to damage something, he didn't much care what. As he swung away from the ticket collector, whose lips had formed into a thin almost colourless line, he was certain that he would come face to face with Mary and Victor. When he saw two old ladies with shocked round mouths and postures that challenged him to make them flinch, he sidled wildly past them, scraping one elbow on the wood that enclosed the bridge. Halfway up he drove his fist into the wood, hearing it splinter and feeling the bridge shake. That, and outraged cries from the old ladies, made him fractionally less enraged. He lurched off the steps onto the pavement, rubbing his bruised knuckles, and stalked towards the Chester road.

By the time he reached it ten minutes later, his shirt was sticking to his spiky armpits. As he turned towards Chester, he saw two children outside a fish-and-chip shop giggling at him, and realised that the pockets he'd pulled out were still flapping like used condoms about his hips. He stuffed them back into his trousers and felt a scream of fury building up inside him as he focused on a distant signboard showing ten miles to Chester.

If any of the drivers of the increasingly less frequent vehicles bound for Chester assumed that his uncontrollable gestures were pleading for a lift, they didn't stop for him; indeed, at least one car speeded up. It took him as long to trudge the last couple of miles as walking the rest of the unlit road had, and he felt as if the night was gathering on his shoulders. When he gained the edge of Chester, the grudging light seemed to drag at him. He was aware of every aching footstep he took to arrive at the next streetlamp, the next building, the next flagstone . . . Half an hour later he passed the cross that glowed like a huge brand beneath the lamp. He had trouble letting himself into the house, because the trembling of his legs had extended to his hands. He needed to hold his wrist with his other hand before he was able to admit himself to the dark.

He clawed at the light-switches and floundered upstairs to the toilet, where for some seconds he thought he was going to be sick, and eventually downstairs to fall into a chair in front of the ruins of the television stand and videorecorder. It was far too late for him to return the cassette. He gripped the arms of the chair until his fingers felt steady enough to dial, then he fumbled the telephone onto his lap. Either Victor and Mary weren't at the bungalow yet or they were too busy to answer.

'I know what you're doing, you bastard, you bitch,' he said in a whisper which the receiver pressed against his ear, making him feel hooked up to his rage on a closed circuit. He slammed the phone together and waited as long as he could before dialling again, but there was still no response. Did they know it was Herb? 'You can't keep it up for ever, you'll have to come sooner or later,' he snarled, and ground the edge of the mouthpiece against his teeth.

When the phone fell apart in his lap as he dozed he hustled himself upstairs to bed. Lying at the vague cluttered edge of sleep, he felt as though he was trudging the lightless road, and whenever sleep engulfed him he thought he was falling face down on the tarmac. He seemed hardly to have slept when the bedside clock began clanging at his ear.

His rage wakened with him, filling his eyes and his skull. It saw him into the spiky shower and into uniform and marched him to the station. It placed his hands on the levers and moved the train to Hooton. It sent the train with its few early travellers to Liverpool and brought it back, and set out again for the buried noose. It was waiting for the sight of Victor running for the train. But when Victor sailed into view he was already on the platform.

He was at the far end of the chorus line of commuters, his beard glinting like wire in the sunlight, his briefcase snug beneath his pinstriped arm. As the train snaked under the bridge he leaned out from the platform. Herb saw him lose his balance and sprawl on the tracks, and prepared to let go of the brake. Then Victor flinched back as though sensing Herb's temptation, and glanced into the cabin. His eyes met Herb's, drifted disinterestedly away, returned sharply, stared at him. Perhaps because of whatever expression Herb was unable to dismiss from his face, Victor had recognised him.

He raised his head slightly, aiming his beard at Herb, his moist brown eyes scrutinising him. Just as the cabin came abreast of him he turned his gaze towards the carriages. Herb saw a hint of guilt in his eyes, although by no means enough, and Victor seemed to think better of feeling even that, because he took longer than anyone else to board, as if to prove he wasn't nervous of Herb. He took as much time to quit the train at Bebington, and crossed the platform so slowly that Herb knew Victor must be sensing his glare like a gun at his back.

When at last he reached the end of the line for the final time that day, there was nothing in his head except dull rage. It accompanied him home beneath the screeching trees, and hovered like an observer while he struggled to extract the videocassette. When he managed to drag the cassette out of the narrow rectangular mouth which had begun to remind him of a mask in some kind of play, the tape snagged on a shard of plastic. Two feet or more of celluloid unspooled in front of him and maddened him. He seized both ends where they emerged from the cassette and ripped the tape out of the machine, creasing and tearing it. 'Serve you right,' he grated, then screwed his finger into the socket of a spool until he'd wound most of the tape back into the cassette. He crammed the splintered cassette into its plastic box and stamped out of the house.

The rattling of a fragment of plastic inside the box enraged him, and so did the sight of a black sports car parked on the pavement outside the video library. He was preparing to sidle past the vehicle when a wiry youth in tattered jeans and singlet with a name-tag dangling from his corded neck strutted out of the library and vaulted over the car door into the driver's seat. The exhaust roared fumes at Herb, and before he knew what to do he'd done it. As the car veered off the pavement with a squeal of tyres he dropped the videocassette, and the right-hand rear wheel crushed it with a satisfying crunch.

If the driver heard it, he didn't look back. The owner of the shop gaped unfavourably through the window at Herb. When Herb took him the cassette and the box in his cupped hands, he gaped at the remains and rubbed the ridges of his plump frown so hard that his whole face shook. 'What did you do to my film?'

His voice was as blurred as his face, and Herb had to pause for the sense of the words to catch up with him. 'I didn't do it,' he said then. 'Your other member did.'

'Who?'

'Mr Stringy in the car.' When this provoked only a ripple in the man's forehead, Herb said 'The young bugger who just came out of your shop. I was trying to get past his car that was parked where it shouldn't have been when he ran over your video.'

'He's no member of mine.'

'He was in your shop,' Herb protested.

'So are you.'

'Yes, well, I am one. You know me.' The owner's expression admitted no such thing, and Herb's skull began to prickle. 'I've been borrowing since you opened,' he said. 'You've never had any trouble with me.'

'I hope I won't now. Let's have a gander at the damage.' The owner leaned his forehead at the ruin on the counter, and having poked at the remains with his short thick fingers, emitted a tight-lipped groan which Herb thought was the best impression of a cow he'd ever heard. 'I wish you'd wrecked almost anything except one of these. They're the pride of my shop. People come from miles around.'

Herb was unable to keep quiet long enough to think. 'What on earth for?'

The owner stared reproachfully at him. 'Don't you care what it's like to be differently advantaged?'

'To be which?'

'I'm saying,' the owner said, and began to separate each syllable as though hyphenating on behalf of a slow reader, 'you're not prejudiced against the aurally challenged, are you?'

'No, just against this bloody awful film. I'm facially challenged myself,' Herb said, and cleared his throat before returning to the issue at hand. 'You'd think the deaf and dumb would have enough to put up with without having to watch stuff like that.'

'We don't use that term for the hearing impaired. Nobody uses it about my daughter.' As though to ensure Herb had no chance to apologise, the owner at once said 'I notice you thought this was worth borrowing.'

'Yes. Well, that was because . . .' The owner was nodding

triumphantly, wobbling his face, and Herb was too infuriated to continue, even when he thought of inventing a deaf relative for himself. 'Anyway,' he said, 'now I've brought it back.'

'You might as well have said you'd lost it and have done with it. It'll cost you the same.'

'Not me, the chap you let park where he shouldn't have parked.'

'I didn't get his name and address,' the owner said, lowering his head until his chin rested on a bag of fat. 'But I've got yours.'

'Much good may it do you. Just out of interest, what sort of price did you have in mind?'

'The film's hardly been out, and I don't know if I can replace it. Sixty pounds.'

'Sick—' Herb began, and felt a grin tugging at his mouth. 'Hang on, if it's hardly been out then even the dea— the differently how's your father can't think much of it.'

'They've had no chance to judge. I'd only just acquired it.'

'Then they should think themselves lucky. That they've been saved from wasting their time, I mean.'

'My daughter thought it was quite good,' the owner said, and raised his face to glower at Herb, his chins deflating. 'Do you intend to pay for the damage or not?'

'Not sixty pounds' worth or anything like.'

'If you won't pay, I know someone who will.'

'Just what I've been saying,' Herb said, but the man's smug look put paid to his sense of relief. 'Who are we talking about?'

'Someone I know better than you, I think. Your wife.'

Herb planted his hands on the counter, feeling his nails dig into the wood. 'What are you trying to say about my wife?'

'What were you trying to imply about my daughter?'

'Fuck your daughter, which you may for all I know.' As the man rocked his chair forward and made to seize the front of Herb's shirt, Herb wrenched the cassette apart with both hands and grasped a pointed sliver of black plastic. 'I want to hear what you know about my wife.'

The owner looked as though he wanted to back out of reach but had forgotten how. 'I know she'd do her best for people less fortunate than herself.'

'That's what you call it, is it? Less fucking—' Then Herb realised that the man wasn't talking about Victor, he was referring to the deaf. 'And what else?' he demanded, unable to relinquish the weapon in his hand.

'I've not a word to say against her. Against her, not a syllable.'

Herb felt his fury slip into another gear. 'Is that a fact? Well, let me tell you—' No, he didn't want to do that. He threw down the blade, which skittered across the counter and over the edge. 'Fine, you try making up to her. See where it gets you,' he said, and marched out of the shop.

'Don't think I won't,' the owner shouted after him, dabbing his forehead with a handkerchief so large it put Herb in mind of a window-cleaner's cloth.

The sight of the man's sweat went a little way towards satisfying Herb's rage. At home he sprawled on the bed and closed his aching eyes, seeing Victor's face on the gross body rocking away from him, unable to escape his reach. When he awoke it was dark. He located his bedside glass of water and took a gulp, then ground his teeth so as not to spit out the mouthful. The water must be days old. He spat it into the toilet and brushed his teeth to get rid of the taste, wondering belatedly if it had been in his mouth before he'd drunk the water. Hadn't he been tasting it faintly for days? He microwaved a carton of chili con carne to blot it out and took the container into the front room. But nothing was on the television except sound.

Shoving the aerial lead directly into the set made no difference. Herb poked buttons and turned knobs and jiggled loose bits at the back, but the fall must have jarred some internal component loose. Listening to the news without being able to see the subjects under discussion made him feel robbed of a sense. He scraped out the carton and sucked the spoon clean and dropped the container in the kitchen bin. When the sight of the dull screen met him again he wrenched the plug out of the wall-socket and sent himself for a walk.

He was opening the front door when he noticed a woman moving away from his gate in the direction of the cross. It was Gwendolen, who must have been passing – he hardly thought she had been standing still outside his house. He went down the path, intending to call out to her, but as he pulled the gate open she darted across the road. Perhaps walking by herself at night was troubling her nerves. 'Gwen,' Herb called over the parked cars daubed with the shadows of trees. 'It's Herb. I was at the barbecue.'

She was some way ahead when she stopped and looked back. Shadows of leaves swarmed over her face as though darkness was hatching from it. Though he couldn't make out her expression, he sensed that she recognised him. He took a step towards her, and she fled into the garishly illuminated garden of the Shangri-La Retirement Home. Herb was lifting his hands in a plea which he was unable to articulate when she let herself into the building with as little noise as she'd made on the road and closed the door against him.

Herb ran along the pavement and halted opposite the Shangri-La, hoping that Gwendolen would bring someone to the door so that he could explain what had happened and who he was. The security lights of the building glared at him, and he felt helplessly guilty, as if Gwendolen knew something about him which he didn't know. When the house beyond the lawn that was frosted with light stayed shut he veered away and almost ran to the nearest pub on the main road. He tossed several Scotches into himself and thought of approaching a long-legged young woman sitting alone on the wall outside until she was claimed by a pony-tailed motorcyclist noisy with leather, leaving a space on the wall which looked so empty to Herb that he could only stare at it and gulp his Scotch and blunder home in a rage which the drink had enlarged.

He seemed barely to have slept when his late dinner wakened him. 'Bleg,' he said, which tasted like all the alcohol in the Scotches mixed with all the chilies in the chili, 'blerp.' He sprinted to the bathroom, swallowing the oily fire and then swallowing it again, and found that Mary had left some indigestion tablets in the bathroom, thank God. He chewed two and stared at himself in the mirror, and saw himself drawing back his fist at the sight of his exhausted face on which the nearest thing to an expression was the cobwebby darkness under the eyes. In the bedroom he lay gripping the plastic bottle, trying to clog his throat with the stale chalky taste of the tablets.

'Blug,' he felt compelled to say on the way to the station, 'blump.' At Hooton he threw a handful of tablets into his mouth, earning himself a suspicious scrutiny from a commuter. He felt as though he had less control than usual while driving – certainly he wished the cabin wouldn't rock so much. The eventual sunlight made the platforms sprout passengers, and he felt as if he couldn't waken properly until he saw Victor. He was returning from yet another tour of the concealed noose when he caught sight of his rival on the opposite platform at Bromborough.

The man was unaware that Herb was creeping up on him, and there was nothing Herb could do to take advantage of the situation. The darkness of the bridge clenched on his skull as he left the station behind, and clenched again as he returned from

Hooton. When Victor barely glanced at him, blinking instead at the train as though it was late, Herb experienced a gush of rage that seemed to be all the proof he had that he existed. Victor had seen him, or he wouldn't have taken so long to board and alight from the train.

As the greenish breasts of the art gallery sank beyond the houses Herb felt the heat solidify inside him. He had to stop the train and vomit harshly between the lines. It took several journeys before the taste faded enough to be ignored, but he'd never missed a day's work in his life, and he was damned if Victor and Mary would make him call in sick. Each time he passed that stretch of line he saw himself returning to his own vomit like a dog. At the end of his shift the train to Chester threw him about on a musty seat, and on his walk home he needed to take steps small enough to ensure that he wouldn't lose his balance. At last the front door fell away from him. A letter was waiting in the hall.

It was addressed to Mary in handwriting that seemed vaguely familiar. His rage lessened somewhat when he realised it could scarcely be from Victor. He crossed out the address on the envelope and substituted Victor's from the phone book, and managed to walk more or less steadily to the post-box on the main road. In the sunlight the red tube looked flayed. Herb dropped the letter through the slot and told more than one neighbour on his way home 'Don't worry, I'm not drunk.'

When he'd succeeded in drawing the bedroom curtains without overbalancing and tearing them off the rail he fell back on the bed. Now Victor and Mary would know that he knew where to find them, and perhaps Mary would get in touch to find out how he knew; perhaps Victor would try to dissuade her – perhaps the disagreement would put an end to their relationship and send her back to Herb. The idea calmed him and the unsteadiness which had narrowed itself down to his skull. But he awoke in a twilight which was no longer only in the room, and lunged for his jacket so violently that his head reeled. When he found his membership card for the video library he punched himself on the forehead. The handwriting on the card was indeed the same as that on the envelope he'd forwarded to his wife.

Had it just contained a bill for the cassette, or had the owner written to her about Herb? The idea of her discussing with Victor whatever the man might have written sent Herb downstairs in a fury. He dialled Victor's number and stared at the wreckage in the front room. Ring ring, ri— 'Harper?' Victor said.

167

At once Herb's throat felt thick with threats and insults, and he couldn't say a word. 'Hello, Harper?' said the voice nuzzling his ear.

The swine was talking to himself, Herb thought. A spurt of savage laughter rose like bile into his throat, and he clapped his hand over the mouthpiece. 'Is someone there?' Victor said.

'I'm someone all right. You'll find out I'm someone.'

'If anyone's there, would they like to speak up?'

'Why, are your ears challenged? Need subtitles, do you?' Herb was beginning to enjoy himself – he was about to let go of the mouthpiece – when Victor said 'It's nobody' and cut him off.

'Don't you tell my wife I'm nobody, you cuntfaced fuck. I'll show you who I am.' Herb was scrabbling at the dial to call Victor back when a light across the road drew his attention to Joelle Owain in her front room. The notion of her glimpsing him haranguing Victor made Herb feel absurd, and angrier because of it. 'I'll be seeing you,' he promised Victor through his teeth, and ground the receiver into its cradle.

He microwaved the mildest dinner that was left in the refrigerator and tried to listen to the television, but hearing faceless voices made him feel as if someone unseen was talking about him. He went out for a stroll, heading away from the Shangri-La for fear of coming face to face with Gwendolen, only to lose his way in a maze of unfamiliar streets whose houses lit up whenever they sensed his approach. Hours later he found his way home, and stared at the phone for too long before suffering a night that was jagged with unfinished dreams. When he trudged to the station he felt as though the night would never end.

It did in time to show him Victor jutting his beard at the train and gazing straight at him. He looked smug in the knowledge that Herb couldn't touch him, Herb could do nothing but his job. 'Tomorrow,' Herb snarled as Victor stepped down towards the art gallery, and heard his shrunken voice tell that to the passengers through the intercom which he'd forgotten to switch off.

He was bringing the train into Bromborough for almost the last time that day when he caught sight of the ticket collector. Herb stopped the train with his cabin as near to the foot of the bridge as was feasible and lowered the window. 'Remember me?'

The collector was scanning the carriages as though to catch Victor's eye, but of course Victor wasn't on the train. 'You in the uniform,' Herb shouted. 'I'm driving the train. Recognise me now?'

The image of a face turned its disinterested gaze to him. 'Have we met?'

'Damn right we have. Remember stopping someone catching a train the other day?'

'There's been quite a haul of those.'

'Yes, but they weren't colleagues of yours, were they, or were they?' Herb couldn't judge where his fury was leading him. 'Herb Crantry. Remember Herb Crantry?'

'Why do you think I should do so?'

'Because here he is. He's me. I'm him. You made me walk to bloody Chester, and now you can see your mistake.'

'You'll forgive me, but what point are you trying to make? If I refused you access to the trains I must have been doing my job.'

'I know all about your job and how you do it. The point I'm making is maybe you owe me an apology.'

'I hardly think so.' The collector's face had become impersonal as a poster. 'I think if one of those is owed it should be to the elderly couple you terrorised.'

'So you do remember, you young—' Herb shouted, and heard himself admit the accusation. 'Terrorised my arse. You know I wasn't talking to them. You got me mad and they happened to be there.'

'No good comes of blaming others for what you do yourself, Mr Crantry. Thank you for reminding me of your name. If those ladies wish to lay a complaint as they seemed inclined to I shall have to identify you.'

'And come in your pants while you're at it, I shouldn't wonder,' Herb roared, shoving himself to his feet. 'Want some more identification? I'll give you—'

'If you do that, Mr Crantry, I shall have to report you for abandoning your vehicle.'

'I'll show you what you have to do, you dried-up—' Herb said, but then he subsided. All at once the collector seemed to resemble nothing so much as a life-size cut-out figure propped at the foot of the bridge. It wasn't worth wasting rage on him that Herb could save for Victor. Herb contented himself with sending the train onwards and tightening the dark beneath the bridge around the man. When the train returned he avoided Herb's eyes, which made their prickling feel like a kind of power.

On the way to Chester he kept punching his thighs to ensure that the train didn't rock him to sleep. As he limped home he winced and grunted and glared at anyone who looked at him. The garden was green with new weeds. He went through the house, where even the doormat was empty, to fetch tools from the shed.

He was still gardening, digging at the thirsty earth as though in search of something he'd lost, as twilight fell. He couldn't have said what brought the change, but suddenly the fork and trowel standing upright in the gloom became grotesque, the utensils of a madman who'd been trying to make a meal of the soil. He retreated into the house and dialled Victor's number, willing Mary to answer. After five minutes a mechanical voice interrupted the pulse of the machine to tell him there was no reply.

Mary ought to be there by now, and Victor. Perhaps she was cooking his dinner while he grinned at the phone, wagging his beard at it. Or perhaps the two of them were naked and grunting and clutching sweatily at each other. Herb placed the receiver in its cradle with a daintiness which was all that could prevent him from smashing it, then he lifted it and dialled again. He waited until the voice redundant as the subtitles on the cassette he'd destroyed told him there was no reply, planted the receiver and dialled . . . He had no idea how many times he'd done so, nor why he was continuing except that his mounting fury gave him no choice, when Victor snapped 'Harper. Harper? Yes?'

'Don't harp on it. Stick your beard in your gob and give me my wife.' Herb heard himself gabble this and worse; the trouble was that he couldn't open his mouth. He shoved his tongue against his locked teeth and managed to poke the tip beneath the edge of the upper set, but that only allowed him to produce a snort through his nose. Then Victor said in his ear 'What's the hindrance? Are you dumb?'

Herb sucked in a breath through his teeth. Even the pain of that couldn't separate them. 'Differently articulate, that's what we call it,' he didn't hear himself say so much as imagine himself saying, because suddenly he couldn't remember what his voice sounded like. If he could just pronounce his retort he would be able to speak, but the effort set his entire body prickling. Before he'd emitted more than a gurgle in his throat he heard Mary in the background. 'Who is it?'

'It's . . .' That was the whole of Victor's spoken response, but Herb knew he was gesturing, caricaturing him. 'Let me speak to him,' Mary said.

She had already sounded as though she knew it was Herb. No other prospect could have weighed down her voice with such a mixture of weariness and determination. Herb felt his lips writhe back from his teeth. He was fighting to speak, but he must look as if he'd done with speaking. He'd always been able to talk to her; what was stopping him now? Perhaps having overheard her tone wishing him away before she even spoke to him. He felt her breath on his cheek as she took the receiver, and then she said 'Is that you, Herb? What's got into you, for heaven's sake?'

If anything had, he was glad of it. He ought to be able to say so if he put his mind to it, or his rage – except that each second he remained speechless added to the hurdle, until he found he couldn't breathe. 'We know it's you, Herb, so don't try that game,' Mary said. 'You'll have to give up sooner or later. Be a good loser and leave us alone, all right? Do that one last thing for me so I'll have something nice to remember.'

Herb thought she was about to cut him off, but he was too quick for her. He snatched the receiver away from his face and began to smash the earpiece against the dial. One blow splintered it, the next shattered it into black fragments of his rage. He hurled the telephone at the television screen and watched the blackness fly apart. Perhaps he had never really believed he could repair the damage in the room or that Mary would come back. Damage was what he was good at, and he'd hardly begun.

It was dark enough for him not to be observed as he pulled up all the flowers in the front garden, although he was past caring if anyone saw him. When roses pricked him he felt as if the prickling of his fury had become the world. He leaned on the gate, his shadow lost in the shadow of the tree beside the streetlamp, and surveyed the ruin of the garden before launching himself at the house. He shoved the miniature which Mary had returned to him off the hook and watched it fall downstairs, then he kicked it out of the front door and tramped on it and sowed the garden with shards of glass, some of which nicked his fingers. Having trodden the painting into the soil, he stumbled upstairs to fall instantly asleep.

He awoke five minutes before the alarm would have roused him. He took a cold shower to ensure he was fully awake, shivering and punching the water and gulping mouthfuls of it for a drink, ignoring the way it reopened the cuts on his hands. By the time he'd finished the bathroom was drenched, and as he went downstairs he heard water dripping into the kitchen. He saluted the debris in the front room and the garden, and trampled his house keys into the earth.

The day felt cold and clear and absolutely black, or the inside of his skull did. The streetlamps and the lights of Chester station couldn't touch him. The wheels of the train he drove to Hooton whined as if they were sharpening the blades of the lines. The darkness under the bridge at Bromborough closed around him, growing darker each time as the platform grew less dark. The only function of the sunlight was to show him Victor, and at the appointed time it did.

Victor was standing at the far end of the platform from the bridge. Herb thought he was making certain he was noticed, though he gave Herb no more than a disparaging blink. If he'd looked closer he might have seen Herb's blood on the controls. He waited until everyone else had boarded and then did Herb the favour of climbing aboard, thrusting his beard before him. Herb watched Victor's trouser leg and polished gleaming black shoe vanish into the carriage, and closed the doors. He gripped the knobs of the controls with both hands, which felt as though splinters were embedded in them, and inhaled a lingering breath; then he reached out and opened the doors. 'All change,' he said into the intercom. 'This train is now out of service.'

A murmur of dissatisfaction emerged from the two carriages ahead of the commuters. He'd counted them as they'd boarded at Hooton and this station, where one had alighted. He craned his neck to watch the platform. Eighteen people, nineteen – just one more, and it mustn't be Victor. Nor was it: it was a mother with twins in a buggy, and she'd taken time to unwrap them a sweet each. Either because he'd boarded last or to show Herb that he wasn't to be ordered about, Victor had waited for all the other passengers to disembark. 'Not you, Victor Harper,' Herb said into the microphone, shutting the doors tight and sending the train forwards.

At first there was silence except for the wind rushing past the cabin and the sleepers clicking busily as knitting needles beneath the carriages, until Herb began to fear that Victor had somehow managed to quit the train. Then he heard the man clear his throat and clear it again more peremptorily, and he grinned savagely at the Englishness of it and increased the speed of the train, blaring the horn to keep commuters back from the edge of the platform of the approaching station. 'Bromborough Rake,' he announced over the intercom. 'Soon there'll be one less of those.'

'What's going on?' The door of the cabin muted Victor's question, as though he was asking it of himself or hoping he wasn't the sole passenger, then his voice rose. 'Is this supposed to be some kind of joke?'

Herb sounded the horn again and watched commuters retreat across the platform flashing by. 'I'm dead serious. You in bed with my wife, now *that's* a joke.'

The train was speeding along the embankment above Dibbinsdale, where trees pirouetted and shed birds into the empty sky, when the door behind Herb began to rattle, and then a fist thumped it. 'I'll report you for this,' Victor yelled. 'Let me off at once.'

'Not till we get where we're going. Don't you like having your very own train? Just sit back and enjoy the ride.' Herb sounded the horn and saw commuters recoil. 'Spital,' he announced, and spat loudly on the floor.

'Stop this train immediately. If you don't stop this train—' Victor's shouting faltered as the station raced by. All he had to do was pull the emergency lever to apply the brakes, but he must think the lever only sounded an alarm in the cabin. Herb gripped the knobs harder, imagining them as Victor's testicles, that the pain was in them rather than in his hands. Factories fed by pipes big enough to stuff a body into began to crowd beside the lines which the distant platforms of Port Sunlight had trapped. 'All right,' Victor said, 'you've made your point. I'll stand down. I'll send your wife back to you if that's what you want.'

He was speaking more quietly. His beard must be crushed against the door for Herb to be able to hear him. Herb imagined the man's chin prickling as though Herb had transferred the sensation to him. Herb leaned on the horn as the platforms appeared to part to let him through. 'What kind of curator are you?' he demanded, the blare still ringing in his ears. 'You're never offering me damaged goods.'

The station fell behind, the art gallery came in sight beyond Tudor-style houses, and he heard Victor stumbling away from the cabin. The rotting breasts were crawling with white which it took Herb some moments to identify as birds. A film of a view from the front of a train raced towards him as he sensed Victor digging his fingertips into the rubber between the carriage doors, trying vainly to wrench them apart. Herb sounded the horn and watched the breasts squash together. Then he heard Victor thumping on the window of the carriage and yelling 'Help!'

He wished he could see Victor starting to panic. Nobody on the platform appeared to have noticed, and even if they had—He felt as if the lines were drawing the train like a magnet; he felt as helpless as Victor must feel, but in Herb's case that was indistinguishable

from calm. 'You should have helped yourself while you had the
chance,' he said into the microphone. 'You shouldn't have helped
yourself to my wife.'

He sounded the horn all the way through Rock Ferry station to
blot out Victor's appeals for help. He could hear a pleading voice,
reduced almost to nothing by the horn, and a muffled thumping
which put him in mind of someone who'd been buried alive.
'Nearly there,' he said. 'Nearly the end of the line.'

So far he'd met only one train. At Birkenhead Central the routes
to Liverpool converged, but he didn't mean to let that be a
problem. Having run virtually straight so far, the line was
beginning to curve through a housing estate near the riverside
docks. 'Not here,' Herb said, mostly to himself. 'Too many
people.' When he blared the horn between the massive lichened
walls of Green Lane station it sounded huge, the last roar of a
dinosaur. 'Report me for that,' he muttered as he saw commuters
covering their ears.

The train raced into sunlight, but not for long. The line was
curving downwards to the tunnel which led into Birkenhead
Central. Herb saw a speed restriction sign ahead, and put on
speed. As the sign flew by it seemed to be swallowed by his skull. 'I
hope you said goodbye to Mary,' he said into the microphone. 'I
never did.'

He hadn't realised so much anger was still inside him until he
spoke. The darkness into which the train was about to plunge was
indistinguishable from the darkness that filled his head. Victor
began to thump the door of the cabin. 'You don't frighten me,' he
shouted in a voice which contradicted him.

Up to that instant Herb thought he might have been content with
terrifying Victor, but no longer. 'This will,' he said conversation-
ally, and as the train screeched around the curve into the tunnel he
shoved the throttle all the way forward.

The train left the rails at once. For a second which felt capable of
lasting forever, during which Herb's heart stopped and he couldn't
breathe, it seemed to hang suspended in the air. 'Come fly with
me,' he gasped, and as if that had released it, the train smashed
into the tunnel wall.

The wall and the cabin exploded. Bricks crunched like broken
teeth, the windscreen clanged and shattered, and Herb found
himself hurtling across the control panel into utter darkness. He
had time to smell exposed earth before it and the glass and the
pulverised bricks met him. He felt he was falling into a pit full of

knives and rubble, he felt as though it was his skull that had given way and was grinding together around him. All he had time to conceive was that he would be taking Victor with him, and he thought he grinned before his face caved in like a clay pot thrown at a wall.

# Seventeen

Joelle was still asleep when David was ready to leave. She needed it, he thought: she hadn't slept much these last few nights. Her face on the pillow looked heavy and slack, her lips were slightly parted as if she had been talking in her sleep, sharing a secret with the night but not with him. He kissed her clammy forehead, which wrinkled momentarily but seemed determined to grow smooth, then he eased the bedroom door shut and let himself out of the house.

Life went on. Today the builders were due to scaffold Miss Singleton's house, and he'd made such an issue on her behalf of their doing so as soon as practicable that he couldn't very well put them off. As he unlocked the car he saw the For Sale sign across the road, a flag as motionless as the July air. He put it out of his mind once he'd swerved the car in a U-turn that mounted the pavement, and headed for the main road.

The trees above the cross sang as sunlight descended their branches. It took him five minutes to spot a gap worth risking in the race towards the motorway. In the centre of Chester the daylight was fading the lights of the shops. He drove across the river, beside which an assortment of dogs was being exercised while a lone wet-suited woman rowed a boat like a straightened banana away from the weir, and into the suburb where all the Singletons lived.

Redundant streetlamps stood in gardens, sunflowers nodded regally at him. More than one house among the large pairs was ringing as though someone was leaning on a giant doorbell. Car alarms yapped to greet their owners, and he saw almost nobody on foot who wasn't heading for a car. He was well on the way to Miss Singleton's when he caught sight of a schoolgirl slinking behind a tree for a quick drag at a cigarette.

Moments like this made him glad he and Joelle had no offspring except Cuthbert, though he wouldn't say so while Joelle was in her present mood. He drove past the tree, sparing the girl's long bare legs and dangerously short skirt a glance, and couldn't resist

177

peering in the mirror to see what her face was like. He heard his lips part as his jaw dropped. She was Angie Singleton.

Though she'd noticed the car, she didn't appear to have recognised him. He honked the horn, as much to warn her that he'd seen the cigarette she was concealing behind the tree as to identify himself. At once he had to brake for a Mercedes that backed fast out of a driveway. He glanced over his shoulder at Angie, and she shaded her eyes with her non-smoking hand and then waved it at him and ran to the car.

David lowered the window of the front passenger door. As Angie stooped to gaze at him, her glossy black hair swaying to cup her face, he imagined her skirt riding higher on her thighs, and was ambushed by the notion that to anyone who might be watching it must look as though either he or Angie was about to proposition the other. A smoky odour spicier than he expected cigarettes to be drifted into his nostrils and troubled him further. 'What is it, Angie?' he demanded.

'Are you going to my aunt's? I'm walking to my friend's who lives near her.'

The tip of her pink tongue flickered for an instant between her pinker lips, and he couldn't judge from the expression in her oddly sleepy eyes whether she was playing with him or hadn't realised he was enquiring about the cigarette. 'Are you asking me for a lift?' he found himself saying.

'Yes please.' Angie slung her shoulder-bag into the car and climbed in after it, stretching out her legs to heel it under them. She let her head fall back against the headrest of the front seat before turning her face towards David. 'Belt,' he said.

'Oh, right. Dad always makes me sit in the back.'

She pulled the seatbelt across her until it clicked into the slot, then gave the front of her skirt, which was more than halfway up her long bare downy thighs, a cursory tug. As David sent the car lurching forward she dangled her left hand out of the window as though she was trailing her fingers in the water beside a boat. David coughed and stared at the secluded street. 'I hope I didn't see what I thought I just saw.'

Her right hand darted to her lap and spread its fingers. 'What?'

'Not—' Best to pretend he hadn't noticed her protective gesture, since to say he hadn't meant to say what she was thinking would only embarrass her further. 'What were you up to behind the tree?'

'Oh, that. This, you mean,' she said and brought her other hand into the car. She opened her fist, displaying the stub of a scrawny hand-rolled cigarette and releasing a hint of the spicy odour that was on her breath, and blinked her heavy eyelids at him as though she'd grasped why he sounded reproving. 'We aren't going to school today, only to the zoo for our science project.'

'I don't care where you're going. You're teasing me, aren't you? Tobacco's bad enough, especially at your age, but you aren't telling me – that isn't really—' When Angie gave him a slow conspiratorial smile David trod on the brake, stalling the car. 'Get rid of it for heaven's sake, before you get both of us arrested.'

She regarded him for what seemed a considerable few moments, then she licked her lips and opened her mouth. She put out her tongue and placed the stub of cigarette on it, and he remembered sharing the cake with her at the barbecue, remembered the glint of her saliva in the bite. He felt as if the memory was holding time still. Then her tongue disappeared into her mouth with a faint moist sound and she swallowed daintily. 'Gone,' she said.

As David started the car she smoothed her striped tie down the front of her white blouse, emphasising her by no means insignificant breasts, a gesture whose artlessness made it all the more unsettling. 'Where on earth did you get that from?' he demanded.

'My friend at school, not the friend I'm going to now, gets it from her dad.' When David recoiled Angie began to smile, then her expression faltered and her eyes widened. 'You wouldn't tell my dad about just now, would you? You aren't like him.'

'You'd be surprised. Some things I can't look away from.'

'Please, David, you wouldn't really tell, would you?' Angie sat forward, hugging herself, her forehead almost touching the dashboard. 'I don't know what he'd do if he found out. You don't know what he's like.'

'Sit up now before you hurt yourself,' David told her, braking gently well in advance of a crossroads. He was hearing Doug say to her at the barbecue 'You're not too old to learn the way you used to be taught.' He waited at the deserted crossroads until she straightened up. 'Just suppose I were to keep this to myself,' he said. 'Will you promise me not to touch that stuff or anything like it again?'

'Oh yes, I will, I mean I promise.' She squirmed around to face him, and he heard the seat of her skirt rubbing against the leather of the upholstery. 'Only please don't tell on me.'

'How do I know I can trust you?'

'Because I couldn't unless you could.'

That made sense – indeed, its sophistication left him feeling outmanoeuvred. 'All I can say,' he told her as he drove across the junction, 'is be glad you're not my daughter.'

'Why?'

Her slow blink at him seemed disconcertingly coquettish. 'Because if any daughter of mine got mixed up with drugs at your age,' David said without thinking, 'I'd—'

'What would you do to her, David?'

All at once his senses were so heightened that he heard her bare thighs brushing together. The only response he could find in his mind was 'I don't think you need to ask.'

'She might like it. You never know.'

Angie was gazing ahead with a dreamy expression, her lips slightly parted. At least she wasn't looking at him, thank God. He rested his hand on the gear lever in order to conceal his anguished erection, only to realise that his hand was an inch from her thigh. 'Is it far to your friend's now?' he asked wildly.

'Not very. Why?'

'Because I need to finish at your aunt's before the funeral.'

'Mr Crantry's, you mean. I wish I could be there, except my dad will be.'

'Never mind, Angie, it's the thought that counts.'

At the moment David's were still counting for a good deal. He felt bad enough about using Herb's funeral as a distraction, but worse since it had failed to shrink his problem. 'Try to understand your father,' he babbled. 'I'm sure he loves you. I expect all fathers have trouble with their daughters growing up, parents do with children, I mean.'

'Here it comes.'

It seemed safest to assume she was disparaging his lecture, until he saw she was referring to her aunt's house. 'You can let me out here,' she said. 'I haven't far to walk.'

She was already releasing her seatbelt and reaching for her bag. As soon as the car came abreast of the house she opened the door and swung her legs onto the grass verge and ducked out of the vehicle. Her pleated skirt rose momentarily, displaying an inch of her bottom encased in crescents of white cotton, dazzling in the sunlight. She swung round at once and having slammed the door, stooped to the window. 'Thanks, David,' she said and gave him a wink so brief he wasn't certain he'd seen it at all.

She couldn't know she was keeping a secret on his behalf just as he was keeping one for her, but he felt as if she did, especially when

180

she glanced back and saw he was still in the car. He eased his feet onto the tarmac and hobbled in as little of a crouch as he could manage to the boot, and straightened up with a toolbox once he felt capable of walking normally. Watching the scaffolders frame the house ought to help him shift his encounter with Angie out of his head.

Two hours later, however, the scaffolders hadn't arrived. He called the builder's number seven times before he was able to rouse anything except an engaged tone, and then it was an answering machine. As he left a sharp message Miss Singleton watched him with a look that said her father would never have let such a situation develop. 'Will you excuse me if I head off now?' David said. 'If the scaffolders turn up give me a ring.'

'Someone will be in, will they?'

'We won't until late this afternoon, but the machine will be.'

'I hate those soulless things.'

'Wait until there's a soul at my place then if you like.' He couldn't resist adding 'If anyone comes I expect you'll keep an eye on them,' and at once was ashamed of his slyness. It would have to take its place in line, a long way after his guilt over Herb and now Angie. Maybe he'd feel easier about Angie once he discussed her with Joelle, though he had to admit he didn't mind postponing that when he found Gwendolen was already at their house.

She met him as he stepped into the hall. She was dressed from head to foot in black, and more thoroughly made up than ever. Her hair was pinned up, which gave her face the appearance of some kind of ceremonial mask. 'Come in,' she said as though it was her house, 'and tell your wife not to take so many troubles on herself.'

'We've both been doing a bit of that lately. Someone has to, after all.'

'As long as there've been people on the earth.'

'We're teaing if you want a cup before you set off,' Joelle told him on her way from the front room to the kitchen. 'Did you manage to get it up this morning?' she called.

To David's horror, his immediate response was a nervous giggle. 'What do you mean?'

'Nothing like that where Doug's aunt is concerned, I hope,' Joelle said as if they were alone. 'Did everything go smoothly, or did she get in the way?'

Her questions wouldn't have thrown him if Gwendolen hadn't been scrutinising him. Surely his face wasn't revealing his secret, and how could she know that he had one? 'The scaffolders never

181

turned up,' he shouted loudly enough that Gwendolen should have felt too close to him. 'I take it nobody rang.'

'Only Bill Messenger to check it's at the crematorium.'

'Is he coming? I didn't think he knew Herb.'

'Only from our barbecues. No reason why he shouldn't come, is there?'

'None that I know of, him or anyone else. The more the – let's hope the merrier.' He was relieved that Gwendolen had withdrawn into the front room until he realised why she might have. 'And there's certainly no reason why you shouldn't, Gwen.'

'I feel I should if you're sure nobody will mind.'

'Good heavens, all Mary or Herb's parents need to know is you're a relative of mine.'

'That's true,' Gwendolen said, so much as if she'd had to be reminded that only the arrival of his cup of tea prevented David from reassuring her. 'Let me take that,' he said before Joelle could shake any more of it into the saucer.

'God forgive me, but I don't think Mary has much right to object to anything just now.'

'We were still here, and I should have noticed there was something wrong. I keep wondering if I didn't realise I'd seen what he'd done to the garden, because I'm sure I dreamed something about it before we heard what had happened to him, not that dreaming's any use.'

'You might have realised if we hadn't been so busy arguing. If I'd known the kind of state he was in . . .'

Joelle meant their argument about the letter that was propped up on the mantelpiece, from her friend who was having problems with a toddler. 'You didn't get a chance to know,' David assured her. 'If anyone's to blame it's what's her name, Ellie, not you.'

That produced such an awkward silence he felt compelled to break it. 'At least nobody can hold you responsible for any of this, Gwen.'

She bowed her head, presumably to indicate gratitude, and he gulped his tea. 'We ought to be off if we want to be sure of getting there ahead of Mary,' he said.

'You wouldn't be taking her but for me, would you?'

'I'm very sorry, but I wouldn't want her in our car,' Joelle said, and more gently 'We wouldn't be taking her anyway, Gwen. The family go in the official car.'

'Forgive me if some things are still unfamiliar. It's been some time since I was last at a funeral.'

'Was it so different where you were?'

'They liked to keep the old ways alive.'

'Nothing wrong with that,' David said, though Gwendolen's tone made him add 'Is there?'

'Perhaps you'll have the opportunity to make up your own minds.'

David couldn't tell if she was wishing that or the reverse. While Joelle switched on the alarm he went out to the car. The curtains of the house across the road were open, and he saw several people in the front room, Mary among them. His hand jerked up in a vague inadvertent salute. He let Gwendolen into the car before ducking in, and as soon as he was seated he thumbed the buttons which slid the windows down. 'It was hellish in here,' he told Joelle as she climbed in beside him. 'Hot, I mean.'

'That doesn't surprise me.'

There was no reason why it should have – no reason for him to have explained. He started the car, and Gwendolen said 'Excuse me, what's that smell?'

His feet grew clumsy on the pedals until he succeeded in manufacturing an answer. 'The house I was at this morning, I expect.'

'It was in your car when I got in. Something burning, I thought. I only asked in case there was something wrong with the engine.'

'Now you mention it, I noticed it too. What have you been up to, David?'

'Me? Me, nothing.' He was able to leave it at that while he manoeuvred the car onto the main road, but once he was past the cross he couldn't ignore Joelle's patient look. 'Not me, as I say. Just some, summer, some old hippy who flagged me down for directions as I was coming back.'

'You mean he was smoking what I think you mean? Did you let him in the car?'

'Her. At least I think it was her. When I was Angie's age, Gwen, you know, Doug and Maureen's daughter, the Singletons who you met at the barbecue, that's to say when I was at secondary school, half the time you couldn't tell for the hair. Not that we were allowed to have it like that at school, you understand, the boys, that's to say, but the ones who'd left school did.'

'Did you let her in the car?'

'I was coming to that, Jo. No, just her head and whatever she was smoking.'

'Where did she want to go?'

'Ah, she didn't seem very certain. Along the road of life, man, I expect, you know how they are.'

'But where did she ask you to direct her to?'

'The er, ah, oh, the cathedral. Can I concentrate on driving now? You'll have us ending up at the cathedral if we're not careful.'

'I could have driven if you didn't want to.'

David was tempted to let her do so if that would distract her, except that there was nowhere to stop the car while they changed places. They were at a three-lane roundabout beyond the railway station, and at least he had an excuse to fall silent while he sped the car into the appropriate lane. He turned off the ring road at Chester College, where some of the students looked little older than Angie, and Joelle gave his hand on the wheel a squeeze. Only staring straight ahead allowed him to smile in response.

Five minutes later the road hunched itself over a greenish canal, beyond which he steered the car into the grounds of the crematorium. Notices saying PLEASE DO NOT PUT FLOWERS ON GRASSED AREAS stood on the verge of an expanse of grass, absolutely flat and empty apart from a few ranks of headstones at the edges and a yellow mechanical digger gouging out a fresh grave. Trees harsh with crows marked out a grid of paths. David found a space for the Volvo in the small car park and followed the women into the crematorium, a long low concrete wedge that poked its highest corner at the unadorned blue sky and put him in mind of a jawbone whitened by the sun. A man in black opened the glass doors of the wide pale foyer and murmured 'Crantry' like a password, unfolding his free hand towards a wooden inner door and then gliding to that door to open it for them.

Beyond it was a chapel which seemed designed for unobtrusiveness: walls of no particular colour, slim pine pews, organ music so soft and so difficult to locate that David couldn't help thinking of it as muzak for the bereaved. Apart from the front row to the right of the coffin, the chapel was almost full. Among the crowd, many of whom David gathered were railway employees, he saw Archibald and Agatha Grey, and further forward the Singletons had kept a space for several people in the middle of a row. 'Anything I should know?' Doug asked as David sidled in front of him.

David felt as if Angie's father had grabbed him by the scruff of the neck. 'Such as what?' he made himself whisper.

'Everything all right?'

'Why wouldn't it be? Except for why we're here.'

184

'That goes without saying,' Doug murmured. 'Everything's in order at my aunt's house.'

It sounded so unlike a question that David was inclined to let it lie, until Doug glanced sideways at him. 'We're making progress,' David whispered. 'There was a bit of a misunderstanding today. Nothing to lose any sleep over.'

'With whom?'

David found his gaze seizing on the coffin as an excuse for silence, but for the moment his mind was unable to grasp that it was anything more than a large closed box with handles. 'With whom what?' he heard himself whisper.

'A misunderstanding with whom?'

'Oh. Wither, with the scaffolders. They were meant to come early so I could give them an idea, but they never showed.'

'I trust they won't expect to be paid.'

'Well, not until they've put their stuff up.'

Maureen nudged her husband. 'This is hardly the place to talk business, Doug.'

'It isn't just business, it's family,' he muttered, then pursed his lips and trained his gaze ahead.

Now that was over, David noticed Terry and Sarah Monk along the row in front of him, Sarah looking even bulkier in black. Terry nodded to the Owains and told Sarah 'I think everyone's here now. I don't expect Jake and Henrie will be coming, they only met Herb once.'

'Why on earth would you expect them to come?'

'That's what I say. I don't,' Terry persisted, and David willed him to shut up before his guilty conscience became as apparent to Sarah as it was to David. Sarah gave a shrug which rustled her black bag of a dress, and he could only hope she hadn't heard the grunt of disapproval which Joelle had failed to smother. He patted Joelle's hand, a gesture that made her send a sharp look at Terry's back before she composed her face, as Gwendolen murmured 'This isn't a church.'

Could it be relief that David heard in her voice? 'How do you mean?'

'It's simply a place where you should feel at peace.'

'Well, I'm trying,' he said, feeling instead that she knew more about him than he would like. 'I mean, I more or less do, considering.'

'You as well,' she said and stretched one empty hand towards the coffin. 'I was speaking of the dead. I do hope he can be at peace.'

David still found it hard to imagine that the box contained what was left of Herb. On its bare stage which curtains had been drawn back to reveal, it looked like an absence rendered solid, a prop left behind by a play. The sight of Gwendolen's face at the edge of his vision didn't help, since a trick of his senses turned it into a vague mask hanging unsupported in the air. The subdued creak of the door from the foyer, and the shuffling of the party everyone was waiting for, came as a relief.

Perhaps it was their loss that made Herb's parents appear even older than David was expecting – slow and stooped and wasted and, he thought, almost colourless with grief. By contrast Mary, who was following them at a discreet distance as they supported each other up the aisle, seemed defiantly young, her head held so high that she might have been refusing to acknowledge the coffin or the mourners, her pale pink lips set in a determined line below the pertly upturned nose. As she waited for Herb's parents to drag themselves along the front row she faced the coffin and planted her hands on her hips. Someone behind David sucked in a shocked breath. When Mary edged along the front pew and sat without ceremony on the bench, David found he couldn't take his eyes off her. Only the arrival of a priest allowed him even to begin to relax.

The murmur of the taped organ ceased as the priest ascended the all-purpose pulpit, more like a sketch of one in wood than the real thing. His plump scrubbed cherubic face struck David as rather youthful for the occasion, especially when he let his hands drop on the pulpit and leaned forward over them as though gazing at the mourners from beneath his unimpressive eyebrows would lend him an acceptably weighty look. When Herb's mother sobbed he inclined his head towards her and interweaved his fingers before surveying the congregation. 'Herbert Homer Crantry,' he said.

This reminded David of a judge instructing a defendant to rise. The priest cleared his throat twice as though to test the acoustics of the chapel, and subdued his voice a little. 'We are here to present our last respects to Herbert. I can see by looking in front of me how much he was loved.'

He must be referring to the size of the congregation, but to Mary it might well sound like a rebuke. Herb's mother sobbed again and leaned against her husband, and David wanted to be tactful but couldn't unglue his attention from Mary, who had stiffened and was gripping the front of the pew and tossing her head back as if to force the priest to meet her eyes.

'I shall not dwell on the events which took Herbert from us, but I hope that when this saddest time is past he will be remembered for his heroism. Some of us are passengers in this life, and some have the courage to grasp the controls. I think everyone here, from his family to his colleagues and friends, will agree with me when I place Herbert among this latter breed. There can be heroism in the workplace as much as on the battlefield, in our own homes as much as in the uncivilised places of the world, and no man or woman knows if he or she is a hero or heroine until he or she is put to the test. Perhaps we shall never know the precise nature of the test which Herbert faced, but I think I can presume to say he faced it bravely, having first ensured that as far as he knew all the passengers for whom he had responsibility were safe although, alas, through no fault that we can apportion one was overlooked. Then Herbert undertook to drive his vehicle to a place where it would cause no danger to the traffic on the railway and where whatever problem had developed could be attended to . . .'

David had succeeded in focusing his attention on the coffin when a muffled commotion snatched his gaze to the front row. He thought Herb's mother had struck Mary, who'd emitted a stifled outraged shriek, but then he realised Herb's mother had made the sound on seeing Mary thump the pew with her fist. When Herb's father touched Mary's arm, whether to soothe her or to persuade her to contain herself David couldn't tell, Mary freed herself with a furious shrug and retreated towards the aisle. The priest lowered his head to give her a sympathetic frown, then his head drifted up like a balloon.

'I promised not to harp on Herbert's passing. I am sure that each one of you here could speak a tribute to him beside which mine might seem inadequate. Let us take heart from knowing that Herbert will live in the memories of each of you while we hope to meet him in a better place. May I ask now that we bow our heads and think of Herbert and say a silent prayer or make a wish for him . . .'

The priest's head sank, and most of the congregation nodded in response, though David wondered how many of them besides Joelle and himself were unable to stop watching Mary, whose face was still turned squarely to the coffin. He managed to drop his gaze before the priest stepped down from the pulpit, and when he glanced up he saw that the curtains had closed with a final unobtrusiveness.

By the time the Owains reached the exit beside the curtains there seemed to be nothing to say to the priest that hadn't already been said. Several railwaymen preceded them, mumbling 'Good sermon' and 'Thanks for that' and 'Nice one' as they filed past him. Gwendolen took his hand as though she was testing its weight or its substance and then, smiling faintly, let it drop. Joelle and David thanked him and emerged onto a patio laden with wreaths, beyond which Herb's father was helping his wife into the limousine. Mary stood staring expressionlessly at the wreaths while various of the mourners lingered nearby. David was about to tell her that he and the women would see her at Herb's parents' house when the Greys finished booming their appreciation at the priest and swooped on her. 'May we be of use?' Agatha enquired in a subdued boom.

'You've done your bit, thanks, Agatha. You came.'

'Of course you must tell us if we're intruding,' Archibald said. 'We understand if you'd like time to grieve in private. In due course you may find you'll welcome counselling by people who were friends of Herbert's, and then you must feel free to call on us. Perhaps we can just give you our address and telephone number.'

'You can do what you want.'

'Well, no, Mary, none of us can do that. To believe you can is to turn your back on God, which I don't think you have, seeing that you had a priest here today.'

'His parents wanted one, and it didn't matter either way to me.'

'I'm sure in time you'll find it will, Mary,' Agatha said. 'Even a good soul such as Herbert's needs our prayers.'

'A what?'

'A goo—'

'If you feel you have to see the best in everyone I'm saying nothing, except don't try doing that with him.'

Agatha's mouth stayed open, and Archibald opened his, but it was Richard Vale who intervened. 'Go ahead, Mary, say whatever you feel you have to. You're among friends. We know how you must feel. We all miss Herb.'

'What are you trying – what do you think I was talking about? Do you seriously believe I miss him?'

Richard looked bewildered and unable to retreat. 'I know you had your differences recently, but I mean, you're here.'

'I shouldn't be.'

'This isn't the place to blame yourself,' Archibald told her. 'Later, when you've had time to reflect—'

'Blame *myself*?' Mary gaped at him with half her mouth twisted into a grin. 'I think you must have drunk so much last year at David and Joelle's that it's affected your brain ever since.'

'Say what you like to me,' Archibald offered, drawing himself up to all the height he had. 'I can bear your grief.'

'Then you'd better have your ears seen to,' Mary cried. 'Don't you really understand I only came so his parents wouldn't be upset and now I wish I hadn't? Someone tell them I won't be going back to their house, because if I do I'll only start letting them know what their son was like. He never grew up, which maybe was their fault. He ended up mad and probably worse, and don't you dare think that was mine. The reason I shouldn't be here, and if this upsets anyone I'm sorry, is that I loathe and despise him. Tomorrow I'll be at the funeral I should be at, of the man I left him for.'

Her speech seemed to have exhausted her. Richard turned away, pressing the fingertips of one hand against his mouth. Terry Monk cleared his throat, then looked as if he wished he hadn't drawn attention to himself. It was Bill Messenger who broke the frozen silence. 'I don't know if you should do that,' he said.

Mary knuckled the corners of her eyes. 'Why not?' she demanded.

'Because of what I dreamed last night. I dreamed Herb told me that if you went to another man's funeral he'd haunt you for the rest of your life.'

# Eighteen

In fact Bill had dreamed nothing of the kind, nor could he have explained the impulse which made him say he had. Mary stared unseeingly at him and rubbed the left side of her face, where a nerve must have sprung to life, then she spun round and walked stiffly past the wreaths. When she reached the limousine she made a gesture of pushing the vehicle away from herself for the driver to see and walked faster towards the gates, and Bill felt as if all this was the continuation of a story he was telling. The rest of the mourners appeared to be playing a game where the loser was whoever first moved or spoke. 'I'll see if she wants a lift anywhere,' Richard eventually said, and strode after her.

'Rich, I should just leave—' Judith said, and having failed to detain him, ran to catch him up.

The limousine cruised away, and there was a general expulsion of breaths and embarrassed coughs and a rearrangement of expressions. 'We'd better go and pay our respects, Gwen,' David said. 'If you'd rather not come I can drop you on the way.'

'Won't I be welcome?'

'I can't imagine why not. Come by all means,' David said, visibly bemused by how much it seemed to mean to her.

'You wouldn't have room in the car for an old fibber, would you?' Bill said.

'I expect we can squeeze you in. We could do with a bit of entertainment if you've any up your sleeve.'

Bill hoped the request wasn't serious, because at the moment he had the impression that he wouldn't be in control of any story he might tell or performance he might give. As David and Joelle led the way to the car park, Gwendolen took his arm. Her touch was so light it suggested that she'd been relieved of some burden. 'You're the one who sounded as though he was enjoying the cake I made,' she said.

'Then I must have, and I'm sure everyone else did. They just weren't as noisy.'

Her thin chill fingers slid down to his wrist as if she was taking his pulse. 'I was right about you. You've a way with words.'

'They aren't all mine, you know,' Bill said, flattered none the less. 'I've a team that writes them for me.'

'That's when they put you in your little box.'

'And when I'm on stage, which I am again this Christmas. Would you like a free ticket when I am? It's an old-fashioned production, demon king and all. Might bring back your past.'

David had unlocked the car, and Bill opened the rear door for her. Beyond the gates he saw a taxi carrying Mary away while the Vales wandered back. Gwendolen lowered herself into the car. 'I've had my fill of the past,' she murmured, 'and I wouldn't plan too far ahead.'

Bill must have ducked too quickly as he followed her. His vision blackened, the roof pressed down on him, and he was crawling into a cramped dark enclosure where all he could see was Gwendolen's glimmering face. No room for two in a coffin, he thought before he could stop himself, and blamed the occasion and the setting. The car began to shift before he was out of his darkness, and he had to speak so as to reestablish contact with the reality around him. 'What did Herb's wife mean about another man?'

'Another victim,' Gwendolen said.

'You know she'd left Herb for someone else,' said Joelle, 'but Herb never told us anything about him, and I'm afraid I'm not interested.'

'Only apparently whoever it was has died too.'

'I won't say it serves her right, David, but I can't work up much sympathy either. Maybe if she'd stayed with Herb he wouldn't have tried to be a hero, he'd have had more reason to take care of himself.'

'He must have done what he thought had to be done. I did get a bit tired of all that hero stuff from the pulpit just now.'

'People have always done that,' Gwendolen said, 'made others into symbols of what they'd like to be or want to get rid of.'

Bill shut his eyes to rid himself of the closeness of her face and watched the darkness fade as though his eyelids were absorbing it. When at last he opened them the car was skirting the middle of Chester. It crossed the bridge above the railway station and, leaving behind the afternoon drinkers outside the hotels of Hoole, passed beneath the motorway and came to Mickle Trafford, a village which had grown into a suburb. Here all the roads curved and split into crescents, concrete vines overgrowing the fields of which patches survived in front of the piebald orange bungalows and semis. Some roofs were steep and Swiss, some flat as books lying face down. There was no mistaking which bungalow belonged to Herb's parents, since the crescent was packed with vehicles and the front window under the flattened roof showed a room so stuffed with people they looked incapable of movement. Bill released himself from the car and hoped Gwendolen didn't think him rude for making straight for the house.

He didn't stay inside for long. He gave each of Herb's parents, who were struggling to keep their faces presentable, a handshake that was meant to be firm and not too terse, then he sidled past them into the front room. He didn't know many of the crowd, which was beginning to sound more like a railway workers' union meeting than a wake. He inched his way to a table that had spread its wings to bear oval plates occupied by white sandwiches, shrinkwrapped columns of paper plates, bottles of sherry surrounded by glasses like pawns guarding their queens. He loaded a paper plate with a handful of sandwiches too discreet to reveal their contents, poured himself a glass of sherry and edged towards the hall, where Herb's father was mumbling comfort to his wife. Bill took a nip of sherry to fortify himself, only to discover that it was so sweet he could almost feel his teeth begin to rot. He swallowed as little as possible on his way outside in search of somewhere he could rid himself of the mouthful and the contents of the glass.

The small unfenced front lawn and paved path were almost as crowded as the room. David caught his eye and said 'Stocking up for the winter?' and Bill had to nod and produce a chuckle which threatened to suck some of the mouthful up his nose. He went to the edge of the lawn and feigned a sneeze which sprayed a neighbour's dwarfish rose-bush and sent a sunbathing black cat fleeing into the adjacent house. He turned away from the bush and held the glass behind his back, and came face to face with three railwaymen watching him through the window. He felt the hand that was holding the glass begin an automatic toast to them, but managed to tip it instead, just as someone emerged from the next house and coughed reprovingly. When Bill swung round, spattering Sarah Monk with the last drops from the glass and catching his wrist on the rose-bush, whoever it was had already gone back into the house. At least Sarah hadn't noticed the drops like tar on the bulges of her dress. Bill left the glass on the windowsill and looked for a conversation to join, but before he could reach the Singletons Judith Vale backed towards him, trapping him against the corner of the sill. 'I shouldn't have let her go off by herself,' Richard was insisting to her. 'She shouldn't be alone at a time like this.'

'Maybe she needs to be, Rich, or maybe she isn't. It isn't as if we know her that well.'

'I should have done more. I should have done *something*, for God's sake.'

The Greys had been loitering within earshot, and Archibald said 'Excuse me, Richard, but I don't think you need worry on that score.'

'What makes you say that?' said Judith.

'Pardon me for saying so, but you wouldn't have been in a position to offer Mrs Crantry much hope.'

Richard drained his glass of sherry and shuddered at the taste. 'You may be right,' he said.

'Who says we wouldn't?'

Agatha gave Judith a pitying look. 'I trust you'll forgive my pointing this out as a friend, but I think we need only look at Richard's drinking. Excess is a substitute for hope.'

'We pray that you will sicken yourself as we did, Richard, that seeing how empty your life is will make you turn to God.'

'How is your business, by the way?' Agatha said.

'My business is my business,' Richard snapped, tilting a last sweet drop into his mouth.

'Forgive *me* for saying *this*, but I think you two are possessed. You're worse than ever.'

'That's perfectly all right, Judith,' Agatha said. 'Let out your feelings, don't bottle them up. Words can't hurt us.'

'You too, Richard. Say whatever you need to say, within the bounds of decency, of course. We can promise you a sympathetic ear.'

'No good comes of keeping your own counsel. God already knows the worst about each one of us, but all He can do is grieve over it until you admit to it.'

'Otherwise all you can be, and I believe you will feel this if you only let yourself, is a void in the shape of a man yearning to be filled.'

'Christ, if that's the gift of tongues I'd pull mine out. I don't know about you, Rich, but that's as much as I'm standing still for. I could do with another drink, even of this.'

As she towed Richard away the Greys converged on Bill, who

felt more trapped than ever. 'A vacuum has to be shown it's a vacuum,' Archibald told him, and Bill couldn't think of a single truth with which to refute him. He shrugged as vaguely as he could and stuffed half a sandwich into his mouth, and saw Gwendolen watching him through the window. She was eating as though the occasion was a feast she'd been looking forward to all her life. The slanting sunlight lay like a coating of dust on the pane, transforming her face into an image on a screen or something ancient preserved under glass. Bill had the impression that she knew what he was thinking, or rather that he was unable to think, and it was this more than the closeness of the Greys which made him squirm past them. 'I must be on my way,' he mumbled. 'I didn't realise it was so late.'

He braced himself in case either of them said it, and Archibald did: 'Later than you think.' By then Bill was retreating into the hall, where he used a phone on an askew shelf surrounded by trial drilling in the plaster to call a taxi and then went in search of Herb's parents. He hadn't found them in the kitchen or the minutely tidy back garden when the driver honked outside the bungalow. As Bill excused his way towards the door he saw Gwendolen approaching across the front room, railwaymen making a path for her so that for a moment Bill thought they were shrinking back from her as he was inexplicably inclined to do. She met him before he passed the doorway of the room, and he said 'Could you tell Mr and Mrs Crantry—'

The directness of her gaze suggested that she knew what he would say before he was aware of it. 'Yes?' she prompted.

'Tell them goodbye from me.' On his way to the taxi he thought she was watching him to see what he might say next, unless the impression was his own sense of not knowing. He was on the path when he heard Sarah Monk say 'If Herb and Mary had only had children that would have kept them together.' She was talking about herself, he realised, and found himself opening his mouth to speak to her, but succeeded instead in rushing himself onto the back seat of the small hot faded dusty car crowned with a ridge displaying a name and phone number. 'Where to, pop?' the raggedly long-haired driver said, turning his head just enough to give Bill a better view of the remains of a cigarette nesting behind one ear.

'Chester,' Bill said, feeling that he needed to be as firm with himself as with the driver. 'Across the old bridge.'

The car performed a screeching three-point turn and roared

asthmatically towards the main road, casting a cloud over the wake. Gwendolen was at the kerb, but he couldn't judge if she was waving away the fumes or bidding him farewell; the heat and the exhaust blurred the sight as though she was losing some shape. All the way into Chester and across the river the rear seat poked Bill with an assortment of springs and kept sticking out a tongue of yellowish sponge around the insulation tape which had failed to mend a rip in the mock leather. 'Left here,' Bill said on the far side of the bridge. 'Right here. No, this is it, I mean. Wait here, could you? I'll be five minutes.'

His flat was on the upper floor of a block which, except for the intervention of several of its siblings, would have overlooked the river. He admitted himself through the glass doors beside the lockers set into the façade and jogged up the concrete stairs between the concrete walls. As he unlocked his door opposite its equally featureless twin, Blotch ran along the inner corridor to mew at him, her collar jingling like a jester's cap.

'Later, Blotch,' he said, clapping his hands to chase her to the kitchen, where he shook a cylinder of cat food out of its tin into her bowl to keep her occupied while he changed into something less sombre. He glanced into the main room, where sunlight was scooping at a patch of shaggy moss-green carpet beneath the trumpet of the wind-up gramophone between the desk strewn with pages of the drama he was trying to write and the table bearing a single wineglass and set of cutlery and ringed napkin, then he elbowed the bedroom door open and dropped his jacket on the quilt that always smelled like his childhood visits to the old aunt who'd let him help her stitch it. He withdrew the monogrammed cufflinks which his parents had given him on his twenty-first birthday and let his shirt fall beside the jacket, where it spread its arms and bowed its empty neck. He opened the wardrobe, sliding himself out of the full-length mirror, and having selected a riotously seasonable short-sleeved shirt, was wondering what else to change into when the bedside clock slipped a digit. His five minutes were more than up. The thought of not having told the driver the truth was unexpectedly dismaying, and so he shoved the jacket under his arm as he buttoned the shirt over his trousers and used his other hand to lock his door behind him.

The driver appeared not to have moved, unless that was a new stub behind his ear. 'Where to now, pop? Got a date?'

'Yes, with—' Abruptly Bill didn't want to know what he might have said. 'To the station, thank you,' he finished.

The driver overtook anywhere there was even a promise of room, either in case Bill was late for a train or because he wanted to be rid of him. At the station he accepted a ten-pound note and claimed to have no change. Since Bill had left all his coins on the bedside table so as not to spoil the hang of his suit, there was little he could do. 'Nothing like the truth. I'll recommend you to my friends,' he said. 'You can let them off the tip.'

A train was about to leave for Hooton, taking nobody but him. Everyone lied sometimes, he reflected as the two carriages whined along the line, so why should doing so bother him? Because as soon as he'd spoken to Herb's widow there had been no taking it back. Once he changed trains at Hooton he had company: a teenager boasting the hope of a beard who, having asked Bill if this was the Liverpool train, stuck a cigarette in his mouth and headphones over his ears, and his boots on the seat opposite himself. His personal stereo – less a Walkman, Bill thought, than a Lollman – wasn't nearly personal enough; it sounded as though a gnome was drumming on his head. As the train idled into stations and out again Bill felt increasingly wicked. 'Excuse me,' he said as the train halted at Green Lane, and more loudly 'Excuse me.'

The youth deigned to raise one headphone. 'Wha sup?'

'Someone wants you in the other carriage, some friend of yours.'

The youth peered vacantly at him and then equally so over his own shoulder. 'Can't see nobody.'

'A difficult feat, I admit. She was trying to get you to look. Maybe she got off.'

The youth craned his head back further but couldn't see the whole platform. With an even greater effort he swung his boots off the seat and slouched to the doors as they began to close. As soon as he was through them they met and the train cruised away. He sprinted to peer into the front carriage, then turned his glare from the deserted platform to Bill, who saw no reason to suppress a grin. 'Eh,' the youth shouted, pointing at him, and added more loudly 'Oy!' Even that failed to halt the train, which wormed into the sunlight as Bill started laughing. The train was almost at the next station when the sight of the cutting where Herb had crashed silenced him.

The gouge in the wall had been stoppered with concrete. The unadorned white surface in roughly the shape of an arch put Bill in mind of an enormous gravestone awaiting a name, but another resemblance troubled him as the train burrowed underground: something about the mass of whiteness veined with flaws made him think of Gwendolen. At least the train was growing more popular, and he watched the passengers in case they gave him ideas for jokes, but when the train arrived at Liverpool he was still barren of ideas. He would have to rely on his instincts at the *Liverpool Loo* meeting, and surely he'd developed those sufficiently in forty years of treading the boards and upstaging upstarts and discovering something new to say in the same words night after night and coping with petty directors and flimsy sets and fearsome landladies and audiences who might as well have been wearing bags over their heads. Surely there was material in all that for him to draw upon, even if for the moment his memory was blank.

He climbed into the sunlight at Moorfields and walked down to the Pier Head, past newsvendors emitting mangled cries, businessmen returning from late lunches, secretaries legging it on errands. Gulls seesawed out of the sky above the river as if the low white clouds were screeching into pieces. Bill arrived panting at the warehouse studios, having barely judged a gap in the three-lane race of traffic on the dock road, and heaved himself up the steps to the Georgian door. 'Arnoon, Mr Messenger,' said Fred from behind his desk.

'Afternoon, Fred,' Bill said, determined to prove that he wasn't compelled to imitate the guard's delivery, though it sounded more as though Bill was correcting him. 'Everyone here?'

'Since lunchtime.'

'What was in your sandwiches today?'

'Salad by itself. Could be worse.' Fred produced his lunchbox from beneath the counter and opened it in front of Bill. 'Could be she's learning. Better finish them off or it'll be lonely in bed for the rest of the week.'

As he took out the last sandwich and stowed his lunchbox under the counter, a soggy scrap of lettuce dropped on the floor outside the desk. Bill watched him bite into the drooping sandwich and urged himself to move on before the temptation became too much for him, but he couldn't resist it. 'What's that?' he cried.

Fred choked and sprayed crumbs. 'What?' he spluttered.

Before the guard could crane over the desk to look where Bill was pointing, Bill stepped forward and trampled on the scrap of lettuce, leaving a green stain on the linoleum. 'I don't know what it was, but it just crawled out of your sandwich.'

Fred clutched his mouth and stared about wildly in search of a receptacle, then ducked beneath the counter. Bill heard an anguished cough and a resounding spatter in the metal waste-bin before the guard rose into view again, paler-faced, and swept the rest of the sandwich off the counter into the bin. 'Insects for lunch, is it now? I'll be having a few words with her tonight, and she'd better keep her trap shut or I'll shut it for her.'

'It was only a leaf, Fred. I was trying out a scene to see if it was worth putting in the show.' A twitch of the lips which felt like the threat of a smile was as close as Bill managed to come to speaking. It didn't matter, he told himself – it had only been a joke. He left the guard glaring into the bin and made for the production office.

His colleagues were waiting, for him or for inspiration. Paddy and Tremaine were leafing through their scripts as if they were sorting indifferent hands in a card game. Indira was supporting her thoughtful face with her fingertips under the chin. Jonty seemed to be on the point of scratching his head with the stem of his pipe, but aimed the mouthpiece at Bill instead. 'Here's our missing element. Been somewhere fun?'

'A wake.'

'Awake, for morning is a bowl of shite,' Paddy said.

'So much for grace and style,' said Tremaine. 'I wince, therefore I am.'

'I remember Grace, but which was the other? She must have been the one you were trying to get your leg over after we'd all had a few.'

Tremaine let out a submissive groan, and Indira said 'You didn't mean a funeral, did you, Bill?'

'Exactly, of the chap who crashed his train the other week.'

'Sorry if he was a buddy of yours,' said Jonty. 'I didn't cotton on to where you'd been with you looking so festive.'

'He wouldn't have wanted us to be glum. He was that sort, never satisfied until he made you laugh.' That was harmless enough, even if untrue, but Bill found he had to continue. 'The lady with the coins was there, Indira. First funeral she'd ever been to.'

He didn't know what made him say that, nor why he was sure it was untrue, but what did it matter? 'Do they still put coins on their eyes?' Indira said.

'Who, corpses?'

'It'd be a lively corpse that could do that,' Tremaine said. 'I don't think you see coins on the dead in these civilised times.'

'Because all the cash ends up in the undertakers' pockets,' Paddy said with little humour.

Indira stood up. 'I think we all deserve a coffee. How about you, Bill?'

'I think you all deserve—' Bill produced a cough which was a lie in itself. When everyone stared at him he managed to respond 'Me too, thanks.'

Indira went out of the lidless carton of an office with a tray under her arm, and then there was a pause too restless to be called a silence. Jonty filled his pipe and reached for his matches. 'So, Bill, in your absence we've been disagreeing about the direction we should take. Any input for us, or do you want me to run through our thinking so far?'

Bill tried to call a joke to mind, and thought he was telling one until he heard what he'd said. 'People were talking about this last series at the wake.'

'That's what I like to hear,' said Paddy. 'They're the folk we have to please, the ones who pay to watch.'

'To tell you the truth, Paddy . . .' For a moment Bill thought he would be able to, but immediately the idea seemed meaningless. Besides, he'd said too much to backtrack now. 'They said a lot of it was too crude to be funny.'

'Precisely what some of us were saying earlier,' Jonty said.

'I only said we could risk a little more sophistication,' said Tremaine.

'So we can give some Chester prat sipping his cocktails in front of the telly a giggle?'

'Now, Paddy, remember Bill's from that part of the world.'

'He ought to know I don't mean him. I'm talking about all these prats who've made so much dough at the expense of the working class they think they've bought the right to dictate what the rest of us watch. Real people don't decide what they're allowed to laugh at, they just laugh.'

'That's a somewhat confused analysis, if you don't mind my saying so.'

'Yeah, well, maybe you're so hung up on words because you're afraid of feelings.'

This sounded ominously unlike the kind of furious yet jovial argument which the scriptwriters frequently had, and Jonty rapped his desk with his pipe as though it was a gavel. 'Before you arrived, Bill, we were saying we needed to look at enlarging our target audience.'

'Were we?' Paddy objected, and stared at Tremaine, who shrugged.

'My thought was, and I think I can say this met with general approval, we could give you an opposite number, Bill. A Ladies' next to your loo so that the attendant could express the female view of life. Plenty of scope for witty dialogue between you two, I think we all agreed. Of course whoever plays her will have second billing. You'll always be the star. Yes, Paddy, we didn't quite catch that?'

'I said that's for the viewers to decide.'

'Well, whoever said otherwise? We know Bill has a loyal following. I hope you aren't going to give me an argument about that. Bill's big enough to help develop a new talent we can all be proud to have put on the map. I'm thinking, now, I'm thinking,' Jonty said, and struck a match and applied it to his pipe. 'How about a black girl? That would reach out to an even bigger audience. Or better yet, a Muslim now there are so many of them, a whole potential audience who aren't hearing their voices on our screens.'

'You might want to see what Indira thinks.'

'I was planning to, Bill, obviously,' the producer said, then devoted himself to puffing at his pipe as Indira entered the room. She set down the tray on her desk for her colleagues to select polystyrene cups of coffee from and said 'Did I interrupt something?'

'Jonty was wondering if you could be a lavatory attendant.'

'I wouldn't put it quite like that, Bill,' Jonty said with a laugh that was determined not to be embarrassed. 'I was just having a creative rush, Indira, and wondering if there was anything in Islam that would prevent someone like you doing that job.'

'I wasn't brought up as a Muslim.'

'No reason to suppose you would have been just because, ah, yes. So you could, someone like you could, wait now, I'm thinking, they could be Bill's neighbour in the next loo who becomes his girlfriend as we develop her character. Scope there to get them away from the setting that must be part of what Bill's friends who he was telling us about object to, and for talking about racial misunderstandings, wouldn't you agree, Indira?'

'There are plenty of those around.'

'That's precisely what I was saying, wasn't it?' Jonty said, and when she only raised her eyebrows: 'Don't let me do all the talking, team. What does someone else think?'

All of Bill's thoughts were so temptingly wicked that he was afraid to open his mouth, though increasingly less afraid, because where was the truth in this room? 'It needs more thought,' Tremaine said.

'Well, that's what this conference is for.'

'I'd prefer to sleep on it, Jonty.'

'And when you wake up,' Paddy said, 'better give me a call.'

Jonty knocked his upturned pipe on his glass ashtray and shoved himself to his feet. 'I'm receiving the impression this conference has outlived its usefulness. Break until tomorrow, same time here. That won't be a problem for anyone, will it?' He was already lifting his creaky leather jacket from the line of hooks on the brick wall and turning to the door. 'Let's all have some ideas worth having.'

'I've a few right now,' Paddy muttered as soon as the producer was out of the room. When Tremaine made a noise suggestive of scepticism, Paddy stalked out too. Bill felt he'd said all he had to say to Paddy, while Indira seemed loath to go next in case she appeared to be taking sides, and so it was Tremaine who followed him.

Indira dropped her polystyrene cup into a waste-bin, where it landed on its base with a thin flat clunk. 'Was anything else said while I was out of the room that I should know about?'

Bill was heading for the door, but answering was irresistible. 'Jonty – well, I think he feels the next series ought to be directed by someone, how shall I put it, more local.'

'I know exactly what you mean.'

'Only he may not be with us for very much longer. I can't tell you who told me, but the word is he's looking to move on. Seems as though he's had enough of us.'

'He may find he has tomorrow,' Indira said with delicate grimness.

Bill attempted to open his mouth, but before he could contradict anything he'd said he was walking out of the room. It occurred to him that all the lies he'd told in it might be true of him. Fred was still penned in by the reception desk, and scowling at his lunchbox. 'See you morn,' he said without glancing at Bill.

'True enough,' Bill said, and knew at once that it was nothing of the kind. How could he face his colleagues and the distrust of one another which he'd sown in them? He'd had a bellyfull of the programme, of being professional about it, of putting so much effort into making jokes sound better than they were. If anything else was wrong with him, surely it was temporary; perhaps breaking with *Liverpool Loo* was the cure. A more immediate remedy might be a drink or several, somewhere nobody would recognise him.

He walked upriver along the dock road until he'd left the last sightseer behind and, it appeared, just about everyone else. Gaps between warehouses showed him cranes like fossils stripped of their stone above the dully glinting crumpled cellophane of the water. Across the road, houses with the pavement for their doorsteps were bunched into blocks chopped apart by side streets of the same breed of house, and Bill didn't know which looked more secretive, the dingy curtained windows or the openings no larger than embrasures in the warehouse walls. A few cars sped by, raising dust from the tarmac, but otherwise he was alone with a dwindling sense of himself and his motives. How much of himself had he made up in retrospect over the years? He was beginning to wish he'd gone home, where at least there were scrapbooks of his career that he could leaf through to prove he wasn't all fake, but he'd walked too far to turn back without dealing with his thirst. When he saw a pub on a street corner guarded by a smashed streetlamp that had been almost uprooted from the concrete, he went in.

There was only one room, reduced to two-thirds of its area and rendered L-shaped by the bar. Half a dozen round tables, each bearing a few scruffy beermats and a tin ashtray grey with use, stood on the bare floorboards. Apart from two old men playing dominoes and a youth swearing monotonously at the racing pages of a tabloid, the only other person in the room was a shirt-sleeved barman with a red face which someone, perhaps more than one, had done their best to flatten. At least his manner didn't invite conversation, and Bill was able to order a pint of bitter, rather too much of which consisted of foam, and carry it to a table by the window, where he sat on the least torn of a gathering of stools. Even here the twilight of the room wasn't much relieved, the name of the pub and a good deal of foliage having been etched on the pane, accumulating grime. If the gloom meant Bill was less noticeable, that was all to the good.

He drained the chipped tankard and had it refilled. By the time he'd downed the second pint his struggles with the truth seemed less of a problem. He bought himself another pint and set himself the task of deciphering the name of the pub, which he hadn't read on his way in, but couldn't read the letters in the window backwards or piece together their reflection in the spectacularly cracked mirror behind the bar. He promised himself he would look for the name when he left, and watched the pub beginning to fill up.

Suddenly it was crowded, though he couldn't recall most of the process. Someone was singing an old pub ballad while her friends helped her search for the melody. The clatter of dominoes was lost in the roar of conversation, and he could no longer see the old men for people standing close enough to wrestle one another. The sun had sunk behind the warehouses, adding to the blackness of the window, and the cigarettes which practically everyone was smoking made the room even darker despite the pairs of bleary lamps that sprouted from the walls. Bill listened to the women who had joined him at the table, some time ago on the evidence of the lipsticked stubs piled in the ashtray. 'So the next night our Tommy and the boys were waiting for them,' the more aggressively coiffured of the women was saying.

'I hope they gave them plenty to remember,' her bullet-headed shorn friend said.

'Took them in the alley and kicked the crap out of both of them while their friends were watching.'

'I wish I'd been there to see,' her friend said, sipping what appeared to be a champagne cocktail in a wineglass. 'Only mightn't they have identified your Tommy and the others?'

'Wouldn't matter if they did, would it? Nobody believes niggers except niggers if they know what's good for them. What are you looking at?'

This last was demanded of Bill, whose gaze had strayed towards her. 'I don't know,' he said, less an admission than an insult. 'What am I looking at?'

'Don't be so clever or you'll trip yourself up. And I wouldn't be listening if I was you.'

'What's he doing here at all? He's never from down here.'

'That's a fact.' The woman fixed her heavily underlined eyes on him. 'What do you want in here?'

Both women had raised their voices as though to attract attention, but for the moment they went unnoticed in the general uproar. Bill had only to inch his way to the door and hope they didn't shout after him. Instead he heard himself saying 'I'm the police.'

'You don't say,' the bullet-headed woman sneered. 'Better keep your trap shut, then.'

That sounded like extremely good advice – a lone policeman in here might learn to his cost how unpopular his job was – yet Bill was unable to move or to refrain from saying, 'I don't see how you can expect me to pretend I didn't hear what this lady said.'

'Do what the shit you like,' said the lady referred to.

'Don't be so sure you know what she was talking about.'

Her friend seemed less than grateful for this comment, and surely that was Bill's cue to leave – but as though compelled to enact a script he hadn't even seen he said 'Then you'd better tell me.'

'People just like you. Maybe friends of yours. Her Tommy's a policeman, get it? So what are you going to do about that?'

Bill pinched his upper arms with his fingers and thumbs as hard as he could, and didn't let go until he'd controlled himself enough to say 'What do you think I should do?'

'Sod all, if you've any loyalty to your job and the country you were born in.'

'Then I'll have to have,' Bill said, which seemed sufficiently unrelated to the truth to release him. He was wobbling to his feet and wincing at the twin aches in his arms when the coiffured woman said 'We still don't know what he was hanging round here for.'

'I'm off duty. Just came in for a drink. You ought to know we get thirsty like everyone else.'

'What division are you from?'

Bill felt the crowd and the heat and the noise closing in behind him. 'Eh?' he said.

'A Division?' The policeman's relative stared hard enough at Bill to stop him dead. 'A, did you say?'

Agreeing would take least effort and let him go soonest, and he barely managed to resist. Wouldn't that division cover the city centre, including where he was? He had no reason to assume that her Tommy worked in that division or even in Liverpool, but suppose the man did and she knew all his colleagues? Her stare was holding onto Bill, forcing him to open his mouth, to say – 'You know I'm not from round here,' he stammered. 'I'm with the police across the water.'

He didn't think he had ever delivered a line with so little conviction. No wonder the women looked less than convinced. Was he going to wait for them to stop him with another question? As they put their heads together to mutter about him he turned away, bumping into a clump of drinkers who thrust their faces over their tankards at him, and he was afraid he was going to be accused of having spilled someone's drink. He struggled and sidled and sidled and struggled closer to the door, expecting every moment that the women, whom he could no longer see for the crowd, would shout after him. Now he was within reach of the door, which opened inwards, or would have if an old man in a shabby black blazer at least one size too large for him hadn't been leaning against it. 'Excuse me,' Bill said.

The old man's right eye took longer than his left to swivel towards Bill, and then he peered at him. 'Excuse me, can I get out?' Bill said twice as loud.

The old man executed a hop, thumping the door with his shoulder, and Bill saw what he'd failed to notice for the crush – that the man had only one leg. The right leg of his trousers was pinned up above the knee, and a metal crutch was wedged beneath his armpit. 'Where do I know you from?' he said in the remains of a voice.

Bill merely had to tell him – the women couldn't hear – but what he said was 'Nowhere.'

'Don't give me that, son. I've seen you before. Hang about, it'll come to me.' The old man located his mouth with his tankard and supped, lending himself a moustache of bubbles the same size as the pores of his cheeks, then he gave another hop as though in celebration. 'The telly, that's where. You sit outside the pisshouse.'

'Not me.'

'Bill, that's your name, Bill some bloody thing. You're the star of the show, for God's sake, what's your name? The wife always watches you. She'll have my other leg if I don't get your autograph.'

'I know who you mean. I forget his name myself. I keep being mistaken for him.' Bill took hold of the old man's shoulders, feeling the pads of the blazer yield more than an inch, and steered him gently away from the door as far as the nearest wall. 'I hope your wife has the chance to meet him somewhere. I believe he's in a pantomime this Christmas,' he said and squirmed through the gap that was all the door had room to afford him.

The black sky appeared to be resting on top of the warehouses. Very few streetlamps were working for at least a mile ahead, and no cars were passing along the road. The night was relatively cool, which – together with the emptiness – came as a relief. It felt like that until he had taken half a dozen paces away from the pub, when a man shouted 'Hey, you!' behind him.

How had the police arrived so soon? Could he tell them he'd been rehearsing a part, not really posing as a policeman? He stopped beside a line of houses little wider than one-car garages, their windows dark as a coal-face, and half turned to see who was calling him. The two men who'd emerged from the pub, cigarettes in their faces, hands in the pockets of their jeans, no more resembled policemen than he did. Perhaps whoever had spoken hadn't been addressing him, Bill thought – and then they strutted quickly forward, jerking their bony hips and raising their reddening cigarettes like electronic sights at him without taking their hands out of their pockets. 'Right, you, that's who I'm talking to,' said the taller man, whose mouth was so disproportionately small it seemed to concentrate the threat which was his face. 'Having some fun with my dad, were you?'

'Should I know him?'

The man yanked the cigarette from his mouth and ground it out on the front window of the nearest house, leaving what looked like a smouldering hole in the glass. 'He wants to know if he knows my dad,' he said, treating Bill to a faceful of breath thickened by smoke and alcohol.

'Everybody knows Dean's dad,' said his companion, whose stubbled cheeks appeared to be compensating for his smooth grey scalp. 'Lost his leg in the war, he did, fighting for scallies like you.'

'I appreciate it,' Bill said, a lie which might at least help him out of his predicament. 'Good for him.'

The son shoved his hand back in his pocket and twisted his small mouth. 'I asked you what you did to him.'

'Pushed him about, he did,' his companion prompted.

'No, I just had to get out. I helped him away from the door, that was all.'

'Had to get out?' the stubbly man repeated as if he was chewing the words, and sidled alongside Bill. 'Couldn't stand the company? We don't like people who don't like us.'

'You call that helping my dad, do you, making him nearly lose his crutch and his drink? And he says you called him a liar.'

'Not a bit of it.'

'You're calling him one now.'

Bill felt as though his compulsion to lie had taken on flesh and was thrusting its face into his. 'If you put it like that I can't say anything, can I? I'm sorry if I offended your father. My mistake.'

'No use saying you're sorry to me. You go back in there and apologise to him in front of everyone and tell him you're who he says you are.'

'I can't do that.' Bill thought he sensed his own mouth shrinking, becoming someone else's mouth over which he had no control. 'I'm sorry, but he's wrong.'

The son pulled his hand, which was no longer empty, out of his pocket, and suddenly his companion was behind Bill. 'Are you calling my dad a liar again?' the son enquired.

'It's you who keeps using that word. He's getting on and he's had a bit to drink. We can all make mistakes.'

'You just made one,' the son said, bringing his face even closer to Bill's. There was a click, and a glint in his hand. 'Now are you going to tell my dad and his friends that he knows who you are?'

Bill looked down. The man was holding a Stanley knife, the sharp point and two inches of razor-sharp blade protruding from the handle. 'No. He doesn't know me,' Bill said.

It wasn't the presence of the other man behind him that was preventing him from attempting to escape, it was his conviction that nothing was about to happen – that the threat of the knife was as much of a lie as his own words, that the man was only enacting some kind of street ritual, a routine to satisfy the family honour. Surely nothing more could happen within earshot of so many people; the muffled uproar from the pub made everyday life seem close enough for him to reach out and touch it. He couldn't believe what was happening when the blade flashed into his face and sliced his cheek open, letting in the night and pain and releasing blood that seemed to push his flesh wider – not until he felt the point of the blade scrape the length of his cheekbone.

# Nineteen

The night after the funeral Joelle was so quiet that David felt he should be too. He hadn't realised Herb's death had affected her so deeply. They picked at their dinner in silence until David put on some music, spinning the dial until he settled on a radio broadcast of a Welsh folk-rock group. The lead singer had a thin high almost ghostly voice, and David wondered what old traditions she might be singing about. No doubt Gwendolen could have told him.

By the time Joelle served coffee the night was consolidating itself. The house across the road lit up, showing that Mary was home, and he watched Joelle stop herself from drawing the curtains to keep out the sight. As he made to follow her into the back garden she said 'Do we have to listen to that dirge?'

'Not if you don't want to. I only put it on because—' He wondered abruptly whether it had been an excuse to avoid telling her about his encounter with Angie Singleton that morning. 'There. Gone. We'll never know,' he said, cutting off the refrain of an old song before strolling out of the house.

He sat near Joelle on a garden chair and watched her flowers turn sad as wreaths, their colours beginning to smoulder with the last of the light, their stems transforming into ash which miraculously continued to support them without crumbling. Perhaps all this summed up a mood which Joelle needed to go through, but David felt on edge, particularly since he thought he could distinguish a blotch on the lawn where the birds had fought over the remains of the cake he'd shared with Angie Singleton. If Joelle could see it, it wouldn't mean anything to her, but suppose she wanted to know why he was staring at it? He couldn't answer the question to his own satisfaction, never mind hers. When he began to feel as though the blotch was within him rather than outside him he retreated to the kitchen sink.

He'd finished washing up when Joelle brought him her mug. 'Shall we go to bed soon?' he suggested.

'Let me have a shower and then we'll see.'

209

While she showered, David went to peer at the lawn. He was even less sure whether he was seeing a stain on the grass, though trying to distinguish it seemed to recall the taste of the cake to his mouth. When he heard the shower cease he returned to the house and locked the windows and climbed the stairs.

Joelle lay naked under the duvet, her eyes closed, her red hair gleaming on the pillow. David undressed and flung some of his things into the washing basket outside the bathroom and slipped under the duvet onto his cool side of the bed. Almost as soon as he slid his arm around her waist she turned her face to him and opened her eyes drowsily. That was an invitation he knew and loved, but now he was dismayed to find it recalling the way Angie had looked at him when he'd been severe with her. Wasn't that his cue to let Joelle know what had happened? It could be the basis of a sexy game, and hesitating made him feel guilty, because what was there in the incident for Joelle to be jealous of? Only that it involved someone less than half her age, and perhaps this wasn't a good time to tell her, not when she needed cheering up. Instead he lifted the duvet and gazed at her.

He knew her body better than his own: her long neck, the greenish flecks in her eyes, her generous mouth that had been all over him, her pale nipples, her firm breasts, the left one so slightly larger than the other that he thought even she didn't know, the blind pinkish eye of her almost flat stomach, the sharpness of her hipbones, the bushy reddish plot where her long legs met. She was beautiful, she was sexy, he heard himself telling her, but saying so at the moment seemed to be a substitute for feeling it: not daring to tell her about Angie had cut him off from her. He hugged her and began to knead her breasts and tongue them in the way she liked.

His mime of passion worked too well. Far too soon for him she responded, her thighs working so eagerly the mattress creaked, her sex loudly kissing the air. She reached for his penis with the hand that wasn't digging its nails into his back, and squeezed the flaccid sausage and ran her fingers up and down it, but none of this did anything for him, nor her squirming round to take it in her mouth. He had to tell her about Angie before she wondered if something worse was wrong.

At the thought of the schoolgirl his penis stirred and widened Joelle's mouth. As she gripped it more firmly with her soft lips he felt as though she was renewing her claim on him. She needn't feel she had to do that, he told himself, but equally he mustn't let her think she had. However disloyal he felt, surely it was more important not to let her suspect he had any reason to, not when he'd only just coaxed her out of her previous mood. He withdrew himself from her mouth and was moving down her body when his penis flopped against his thigh.

It was Angie's fault, he thought fiercely, and at once his penis stiffened. He saw Angie draping herself slowly and gracefully face down across his lap, her skirt rising to offer him her round pert bottom wrapped in white cotton. Joelle took hold of his penis and raising her hips, thrust him into herself. Her body's soft slick grasp ensured that he wouldn't let her down. He hugged her shoulders as she clawed at his, her body gaped and clutched at his penis, and when she came a second time he couldn't hold back. Her cry was enough reason for him not to brood; she was happy, never mind how he'd achieved it. 'Love you,' she murmured, and gave him a slow sleepy kiss.

'You know I do.'

'What, love yourself?'

'No, you.'

'I don't mind you loving yourself as well,' she said, so drowsily that he reassured himself she couldn't have noticed what had sounded to him like defensiveness. Before he could reply, she was asleep. He eased the duvet over both of them and put one arm around her, and pulled down the dark with the cord above the bed, and breathed in her toothpasty breaths until she was the only thought in his mind.

Next morning they didn't see much of each other. Joelle had to price a decorating job for a woman who had been so disconcerted by the answering machine that she'd shouted at it in a tone she might have used to address a wicked child, while David was to meet the scaffolders, one of whom had left a promise but no apology on the tape. As he drove to Miss Singleton's he passed dozens of schoolgirls, and found himself looking for Angie to see if she'd kept her word. When breezes began to play with their skirts, however, he concentrated on the road lest someone catch him looking, though he didn't know why he should feel guilty if they did.

Miss Singleton raised her eyebrows at him to express dissatisfaction with his being by himself. 'They'll be here soon,' he said, and had to repeat it when she came to the door again half an hour later. There was still plenty of work to be done in the house, but nothing that he'd want to interrupt in order to keep an eye on the scaffolders. 'Maybe I'd better call them.'

'I should think so,' she said, practically trampling on the last word, and hitched up today's elasticated pair of bright blue trousers so as to wipe her feet before letting him in.

After five tries he got past the engaged signal, but only as far as the answering machine. 'If anyone's listening, would they like to pick up the phone?' he said to no avail. 'They must be on their way,' he told Miss Singleton. 'They've got to come from Ince.'

'My father would have employed someone local.'

'I thought you said he did it all himself.'

'He had no head for heights. As a matter of fact, he died in a fall.'

'I didn't mean to criticise him. We all need people for something or other,' David said, and wondered for a fleeting moment what Gwendolen might have been needed for, and by whom. 'Ince isn't so far. I meant they might be held up on the road.'

'My father would have hired someone he knew he could rely on.'

'They'd be a bit past it by now, wouldn't they?'

'Some of them must have had sons,' she said as if the possibility had just occurred to her.

'Some of us can't,' David said, and was seized by an unexpected sense of loss. He went to the Volvo and tried to find fault with the engine, but when he'd finished there was still no sign of the scaffolders. Only the machine was answering the phone; it sounded fuzzier than ever. 'This is David Owain,' he warned it. 'I'm coming to see what's the problem.'

He drove back through Hoole towards the motorway and then between fields where the distant road shivered more than the grass. Ince was a village outflanked by a suburb near the Manchester Ship Canal, on which there wasn't a ship to be seen. A signboard promising MADDENS FOR ALL YOUR BUILDERS NEEDS pointed him down a side street to a high wall on top of which barbed wire coiled in the sunlight. The wooden gates crowned with barbs were open, and he drove into the yard.

As he parked beside a stack of ten-foot planks, the screech of a circular saw was cut off and a face tilted into the window of a long brick shed. David was stretching his limbs outside the car when the door of the shed staggered open to produce a large hairy man in a small oily T-shirt and trousers old enough, David thought, to be a family heirloom. 'Nobody here just now,' the man shouted, dragging a rag out of his pocket so vigorously that for a moment David assumed he'd torn the pocket itself. 'You can leave an order or I can take a message.'

'You're the machine,' David said, having recognised the voice. 'Mr Madden, isn't it.'

The man rubbed his frown, discolouring it further, and stared at the rag before stuffing it back into his pocket. 'Depends which of us you mean.'

'I didn't know I had a choice.'

'Me or my brother.'

'Whichever of you was supposed to fix me up with scaffolding in Chester.'

'Ah, that'll be Jimmy. I told him you rang. Don't tell me he never got back to you.'

'Yes, to say he'd be there first thing this morning.'

'You mean he wasn't? You're never telling me he didn't let you know.'

'I was at home until after he ought to have left for the site.'

'Ah, but will he have the number where you're working?'

'He would have if someone round here picked up the phone occasionally.'

'We can't be in two places at once. We've got to grab all the work we can get while it's there. You know work won't wait, you're in the trade.'

'Mine's been waiting for two whole days.'

'What do you want me to do? I'd put your scaffolding up myself if I had it except the quack doesn't want me climbing. I'd lend you our ladders if they weren't out on a job. I wouldn't care, it's supposed to be Jimmy who deals with this side of it. He hasn't been the same since the old man went into hospital. On top of which his judy looks like leaving and taking the kiddies with her because she thinks it's a bit on the side that keeps him out so late.'

'Thanks for the information,' David said to forestall what threatened to be a good deal more of the same, 'but I don't see—'

'I'll tell you what I'll do,' Madden said, and fell silent as if the promise itself was the favour. Apparently his silence indicated that the van which was approaching down the street belonged to the firm. It jerked to a halt behind the Volvo, almost nudging the bumper. 'That isn't him,' Madden said.

A youth with his rat's tail of hair in a rubber band that seemed to pull his blotchy face taut swung himself out of the van, releasing even more of the thumping of a ghetto blaster as long as David's arm. 'Go and see Jimmy at the bakery,' Madden shouted, 'and see if he's nearly got the scaffolding down. Mister, Mister Here should have had it by now.'

The youth shied his folded newspaper onto the dashboard, and was vaulting into the driver's seat when David called 'Wait a minute, hold on.'

'Ron can't help you,' Madden said. 'He just works here.'

'I want to look at his paper.'

'What paper?' Madden said with some nervousness.

David poked his head through the window of the van. 'Can I glance at the front page?' he said, and had to mime the request before the youth thrust the newspaper at him. As David unfolded it he moved away from the battering of the drums, but the noise drove itself into his skull as he reread the headline. 'My God, I know him.'

'Is he saying he knows you, Ron?'

'Not him, him,' David said, prodding the headline with a finger. LIVERPOOL LOO STAR IN KNIFE ATTACK, the thick black letters said. He retreated from the van until the demonic shrieking of singers and guitars was just about distant enough not to intervene between him and the paper.

Police are seeking witnesses to an unprovoked attack on local actor and comedian Bill Messenger.

Mr Messenger, best known as Sam Stool in the popular television comedy series *Liverpool Loo*, was walking on Liverpool's dock road on Tuesday evening when he was attacked by a man who slashed his face with a knife. Police are anxious to trace the driver of a white Mazda who drove Mr Messenger to the Royal Hospital, where the actor needed fifty stitches. He is said to be comfortable.

Mr Messenger describes his assailant as totally bald, between forty and fifty years old, heavily tattooed and over six feet tall, wearing football boots and a track suit under a duffel coat.

Police have so far been unable to suggest a motive for the attack, but a spokesperson for the Merseyside force warned that unprovoked attacks are on the increase. Anyone with information should call the incident room at

'You know Sam Stool?' the van driver said. 'What's he like?'

'Pretty subdued at the moment, I should think,' David said in a kind of undirected rage that made him stay where he was until Ron came to retrieve the newspaper.

'He's his mate, Ron. Don't go pestering him when he's just this moment heard what happened. You can ask him when you're at his job,' Madden said, and to David 'Listen, let me tell you what I'm going to do. How long will it take you to get back to your site?'

'Say twenty minutes.'

'Give Ron your number there and he'll have Jimmy call you as soon as you get back, how's that?' Madden said, and returned to the workshop to add the screech of a circular saw to the clangour from the van.

Ron shoved the newspaper at David, who thought he was being given it to keep; then the youth offered him what David took to be a well-chewed sweet before identifying it as a stump of pencil almost as truncated as its point. David was about to yell at him to turn the radio down when he managed to recall Miss Singleton's phone number. The pencil forced him to scrawl it above the headline about Bill in digits so large they made him feel childish. He hurried to the Volvo and waited while Ron reversed at speed out of the gate and executed a U-turn as loud as the radio. A succession of cars on the main road held up the van, and David was tempted to follow it to wherever the scaffolding was. Then the van braved a gap too cramped for David to risk following, and was out of sight before he gained the road.

Trying to ensure he arrived at the house ahead of the phone call gave him little chance to think about Bill, but his mind was a dull lump of emotions. The attack on Bill was bad enough, yet the banality of it seemed somehow worse, and how had guilt entered his feelings? He forgot the question as Miss Singleton opened her door. 'Someone has been looking for you,' she said.

'Wonderful. How long ago?'

'No more than . . .' She paused almost long enough to render the answer inaccurate. 'Two or three minutes.'

'Silly— Couldn't they have waited?' David protested, and realised she might take all that, including the word he'd censored, as being aimed at her. 'Which way did they go?'

'I haven't the least idea. It was a caller from a public telephone who claimed he was short of money.'

'I don't suppose you got a name.'

'Some person by the name of Madden.'

'You wouldn't happen to know which one?'

'I wasn't aware that you knew more than one such person.' After a pause which seemed to sum up an extensive range of unspoken comments she added 'I believe he said something about getting a message to you. A course of elocution would do him no harm, and you may tell him I said so.'

215

'Perhaps you'll have a chance to tell him to his face. Is the message coming here, did he say?'

'He may have grunted something to that effect.'

'Then I'd better wait. I'll be moving your stuff for you. If I can come in,' he had to append before she would step back.

He was bearing cartons of photographs into the room with the new floor, and reflecting that he kept forgetting to ask for another look at Gwendolen's photograph, when Miss Singleton came tramping upstairs, her face red and pinched as an old cherry. 'A person is asking for you.'

David had heard the doorbell and shortly afterwards the slam of the front door, and now he discovered she was keeping out not only Ron but also the sound of a band indistinguishable from the one he'd been sharing with anyone in earshot at the builders' yard. 'Jimmy says he'll see you here first thing tomorrow,' Ron told David, and was off as though he had fallen behind in a race.

David turned to find Miss Singleton stumping downstairs. 'He says the scaffolders—'

'I heard what he said. I take it he's deaf. If the law requires his employer to make allowances for him I suppose the rest of us are forbidden to comment, but there must be none of that cacophony as long as he works here. I have to live with my neighbours.'

'More young than deaf, I'd say. I'll tell him.'

By the time David had finished lugging the cartons he felt in need of a bath and a massage, otherwise he might have visited Gwendolen while the photograph was uppermost in his mind. He glanced at her window as he drove by, and saw her gazing out, her hands invisible beyond the frame. It must have been the motion of the car which made her seem to lean through the glass to watch him. The glimpse disconcerted him, and so did the sight of a woman ringing his doorbell. It was Brenda Mickling, who ran the retirement home.

'Brenda?' he called, and struggled out of his seatbelt as she came to his gate. 'Is it Gwen? Is she all right?'

'Thriving. Did she give you Naomi's message?'

'Naomi. Remind me.'

'The lady who was run over outside the Shangri.'

'I remember. No, I didn't get any message.'

'She wanted you visit her in hospital. She was quite anxious for you to.'

'Let me just see if I've had any calls and then maybe I can go and see her later. Did she want anything special, do you know?'

216

'To tell you something she wouldn't tell us,' Brenda said, opening the gate for him. 'I should have let you know, David. It wasn't fair to expect Gwen to remember. Don't blame her, but Naomi passed away this morning.'

# Twenty

After half an hour Richard Vale still hadn't managed to pack the computer. When he dragged the upper half of the moulded polystyrene out of the carton it gave a screech which made his teeth feel as if a drill had touched them all at once. He lifted the keyboard out of its polystyrene niche and replaced it the other way round, but the top half of the packing wouldn't let him close the carton properly, nor when he tried placing the keyboard face down. Maybe the problem was the flex of the keyboard. He tugged it out of its slot in the squealing polystyrene and dug a fingernail under the rubber band that imprisoned its coils, only for the band to snap, stinging his fingers and uncoiling the flex across the counter like a snake which had bitten him. 'Get in,' he told it in a voice which sounded as though he was imitating the polystyrene, and stuffed the folded cord into the slot, digging his fingers into the packing to make room for the electric plug. Now he remembered he'd had to buy the plug separately, and so it was the problem, but who cared? He gouged an extra hole in the upper half of the polystyrene to accommodate it, trying to ignore the sensation like a tangible screech beneath his fingernails, and shoved the packing into the carton, whose lid he was nearly able to close. That would have to do, at least until he got rid of the sensation under his nails. He picked at them with a molar but desisted once he felt them beginning to pull away from the quick, then he shook his hand as he might have shaken off a glove, in the hope that would dislodge or blot out the sensation. When it achieved neither he shoved all the fingers of that hand into his mouth and sucked them, hardly conscious of emitting a mumble that was growing closer to a scream. Then someone glanced through the doorway and dodged back.

'Wll dnn,' Richard snarled at himself around his fingers. He'd driven away a potential customer by seeming drunk or worse. He pulled his fingers, which felt as though they'd been drowning for

219

hours, out of his mouth and hurried to the doorway, ready to chase whoever it was. It was only Sarah Monk.

She was loitering in front of the antique shop next door, looking unsure either of the leaves which appeared to have been reincarnated in oak around a full-length oval mirror or of her own reflection. Since Herb's funeral her black hair had turned a prematurely autumnal red. Today's kaftan was green and viny and even more voluminous than most, and she was wearing an extravagant amount of sweet perfume. She swung round in a flurry of scent and blinked apologetically at Richard. 'I was going to come in, but you looked busy.'

Richard pressed his hypersensitive fingertips against his brisket and wondered if it could be possible that she wasn't joking. 'Are you all right?' she said.

'Up to a point. What makes you ask?'

'Your heart.'

'Oh, that,' Richard said, taking his hand away. 'That hasn't let me down yet. So what's the occasion?'

'Is there one?'

'I mean, what brings you to the cutting edge of the technological revolution?'

'That's to say your shop.'

Richard's hadn't been the kind of joke which expected a laugh, but it seemed not so much to have fallen flat as hung itself around his neck. 'Well computed,' he said.

'I just thought I'd look in to see how you were doing.'

'Look all you like,' Richard said, not caring whether or not it sounded like an invitation, and retreated behind the counter in search of adhesive tape. 'I'm still open for business. Can't afford to turn away a customer.'

Sarah wandered a couple of paces into the shop and peered at the screens above the counter, the cartoon figures limbering up to the rhythms of their loops of computer music. 'That looks good,' she said, 'especially if you have children.'

'There's always hope.'

That was cruelty posing as kindness, and he ripped the tape off the reel as though the noise might blot out what he'd said. Sarah smiled not even wryly, however. 'That's what I was going to say to you, would you believe? Except now I see there was no need.'

'If you know something I don't, tell me about it,' Richard said, baring his teeth to gnaw at the tape.

'Haven't you just made a sale?'

'To you, you mean? You mean when you mentioned children—'

She shook her head quickly, her cheeks wobbling her smile. 'I'm talking about your parcel. Isn't that for a customer?'

'What, this? I'm packing it off to the manufacturers for them to fix or replace.'

Sarah covered her mouth as if that was the only means of changing her expression. 'Otherwise has it been a good week for you?'

'It's been a nothing week for me, and worse for Jude. They've told her they can't afford to take on any more teachers, so there's no point in her trying to get back into the profession.'

'Can't she try somewhere else?'

'That was somewhere else. The last somewhere else within reach.'

'Oh heavens. Tell her I'm sorry,' Sarah said in the tone of a culprit caught red-handed. 'At least you'll have a new computer to help you carry on.'

'You think that'll make all the difference, do you?' He felt ashamed at once, not least because his sarcasm seemed pointless. So did any other response, however, and he went on: 'Is that it? Have you done what you came to do?'

'I was going to buy a game. What's the best one?'

'*Black Hole*, maybe. Or *Insanity Squared* or *Monkey in the Maze*. Who's it for?'

'It would be for a child.'

'How old?'

'Getting older every day, and very bright.'

'What system are we talking about?'

Sarah covered her mouth again and gazed pleadingly at him. 'I don't understand.'

'What computer have they got?'

'Which is the best?'

'For games, I'd say the Amiga.'

'Then that must be it. Yes, that's it, I remember, now, Amiga. I'll have, what was the last one you said, a Madness in the Maze.'

'Monkey,' Richard said, and felt bound to take pity on her, though he wasn't sure for what. 'It's only just out, I should tell you. The others I mentioned are cheaper.'

'I don't mind paying for the best. I'll feel better if I do.'

Richard fetched a boxed copy of the game from the storage room, crunching a squeaky chunk of polystyrene underfoot on the way. 'If you find it isn't right you can always bring it back.'

'I know I won't need to.' She was already signing a cheque above her and Terry's names roped together by an ampersand, and now she squinted at the price on the box. 'That's fine,' she said with such determination that Richard would have dropped the price for her if she hadn't immediately filled in the amount on the cheque. She shoved chequebook and game into her large floral canvas handbag. 'I've interrupted you enough for one day,' she said, and less distinctly 'I just wanted to say—'

'So say.'

He thought he'd silenced her, but then she snatched her hand away from her mouth. 'Just that I hope you didn't let Archibald and Agatha get to you at the funeral. If you ask me, they're jealous.'

'Then I feel sorry for them. Jealous of what?'

'Of the life you and Jude have made together. Of your children, which are the most important thing of all.'

She wasn't really talking about the Greys, he thought, and he was having difficulty grasping that she meant him either. 'Only I hope, and I know we can hardly talk about these things in public any more,' Sarah said, and ground to a halt. She fixed her gaze on the Black Hole, which was sucking in a hero who appeared to be composed almost entirely of weapons, and mumbled 'I was just going to say I hope they haven't put you off praying, if you ever do.'

'Who, the family?'

'Archibald and Agatha, of course. Because I don't think there's anything at all wrong with praying for what you need in this world, and I've been remembering you in my prayers ever since they were so unfair to you.'

'Well,' Richard said, and had to make himself add 'Thanks.'

'Prayers cost nothing. So if you ever go in for them at all you might think of what Terry and I most want.'

'I'll do my best, Sarah.'

'That's all any of us should be expected to do.' Sarah lurched towards the door, clearly the only way she could deal with the growing awkwardness of their conversation. She was on the pavement when she craned her head back and gave him a smile so radiant and grateful he felt unworthy of it, then she was gone.

'You might try praying for Bill Messenger,' Richard said, not loud enough for her to hear. If she hadn't heard what had befallen the actor, he didn't want to be the bearer of the news. Even thinking about the incident made his brain darker and emptier, though if the Greys had been the sole source of his mood, shouldn't knowing that relieve it? He was trying to remind himself that emotions never lasted when he heard someone approaching, whistling a hymn.

It was the postman, though his whistling was usually more secular. The opening line of the hymn – 'He who would valiant be' – lodged in Richard's skull, and he couldn't help feeling that the postman was here in response to Sarah's prayer. If he brought the letter Richard was expecting— He walked straight past, shading his eyes as the windscreen of a passing car flung a soundless bomb of light into the shop, and then he reappeared outside the doorway. 'Nearly missed you. That won't do,' he said as he came forward and handed Richard an envelope.

Richard turned it over and over until the shrill hymn was lost in the drone of traffic. It was indeed from the city council, and giving away no secrets through its narrow window. Suddenly he felt that he'd delayed too long, that he should have opened it while the hymn which evoked Sarah's prayers for him was audible, though what sense did that make? He thrust a finger beneath the dun flap, reawakening the wincing sensitivity of his fingertip, and shied the envelope across the counter in his haste to unfold the single sheet of official notepaper.

For some moments he couldn't grasp what it said. He was scanning the letter so fast in search of the point that the words swam away from his understanding, conveying as little to him as the bunch of digits and initials that was the reference number. Then a sentence steadied and grew black as if the words were burning their way up through the paper. 'It is regretted that owing to incompatibility of the current use of your premises with proposed future development the decision has been taken not to renew the lease.'

He stared at the words until his eyes felt capable of reducing them to ash, until the page lying on the counter seemed to be turning to stone, a weight that was gathering behind his eyes as well. 'What kind of language is that?' he muttered. 'Who wrote this, a computer?' The idea was no more meaningless than any other – just meaningless enough to hold him crouched over the sentence as if his life had frozen at that moment. An ache had rooted itself between his shoulders and was sprouting up his neck, but even when it unfolded its spikes inside the back of his skull he felt all he could do was suffer. Then the blackness of the words engulfed the page, and he closed his eyes and shoved himself to his feet, wrenching his neck. He was already grabbing the phone, and as soon as he could see again he gouged at the dial. He wasn't sure if he had dialled correctly until a voice said 'Council?'

She and her friends on the switchboard must have been sharing a joke – he told himself that they couldn't be laughing at him. 'Planners,' he cursed.

'Yes, sir,' the operator said as though his tone had sobered her. 'Who is it you wish to speak to?'

Richard hadn't thought to look, and was momentarily unable to pronounce what he read at the foot of the letter. 'Arse Impkin.'

'Mr Simpkin. Connecting you now.' She added a syllable which made it clear she couldn't wait to tell another joke, then her voice was swallowed by a void empty even of static. Richard was beginning to suspect she'd cut him off, perhaps intentionally, when almost the same voice said 'Planning.'

'That isn't R,' Richard said, 'Simpkin, is it?'

'Mr Simpkin is on site this afternoon. Do you have a reference?'

'Are you his boss?'

'I'm afraid not,' the woman said with a laugh which Richard told himself wasn't meant to be malicious, 'but I'll see if I can help. Would you like to give me the reference?'

'Is this it?' He read out the clump of digits and letters, and was repeating it for fear that he'd misread it when she said 'I have it now. What was Mr Simpkin in touch with you over?'

'He wants to close my business.'

'Ah, then you'd need to speak to him personally.'

'He's your man for wrecking people's lives for no reason, is he?'

The woman cleared her throat, an octave higher than her voice. 'I'm sure he must have given you his reason.'

'Apparently I'm in the way of your future,' Richard said, and battled not to let his mood do all the talking. 'I don't mean that personally. I know it's not your fault. Tell me one thing. Does Arse, does Mr Simpkin have a boy?'

'I beg your pardon?'

'A son. A long-haired streak with glasses and a brain too big for him, twelve or maybe thirteen. He does, doesn't he?'

'I'm afraid I'm unable to give out that information.'

'Which means he does. I'm not threatening the boy, in case that's what you think,' Richard said, and felt the idea flare up to be extinguished at once by the dark of his mind. 'I just happen to believe he's a customer of mine.'

'What is the name of your business, may I ask?'

'Computer Explosion.'

'Ah, yes.' She was silent for a moment. 'Then I'm afraid you're mistaken.'

'So he does have a son, and how do you know the young snot never came to my shop?'

This time he all but heard her deciding that silence wasn't enough of an answer. 'Because Mr Simpkin's son has been in hospital since he was knocked down by a drunken driver eighteen months ago.'

'I didn't say when he used to shop here, did I?' Richard said in an attempt to fend off some of her disapproval. 'All right, I'm sorry if I got the wrong man, but who's the one with the red ears and the big mouth?'

'I've no idea whom you mean.'

'Don't give me that. He's in your department. So thin you could stick him and his son together and make one person like the rest of us, and he'll have had a word with your boss about me. Who's that?'

'I assure you there's nobody—'

'Teeth like a horse and talks like one, and spits in your face if you're close enough while he's doing it, I shouldn't wonder. Come on, you know him. I've just forgotten his name for the moment. I need to let his son know the game he was desperate to get is in.'

'I assure you I know everyone in this department, and there's nobody of that description here.'

'So you won't mind if I tell the police that somebody's been claiming to be one of you.'

'You must do whatever you think fit, Mr—'

'Or if I come to your office personally.'

'Did you wish to make an appointment?'

Richard thought she was just a little too eager to sound efficient. 'Mr Whinny wouldn't be a friend of yours, by any chance?'

'I'm not aware of anyone called any such thing.'

'Mr Neigh. Mr Dentures, Mr Teeth, whatever he gets called behind his back. Don't tell me you'd have said ah, yes unless you know him.'

'What are you saying I said?'

'Ah, yes,' Richard said, as much in appreciation of her change of tone as answering her. 'You said ah, yes when I told you who I was. Nobody says that unless they know more than you want me to think.'

'You didn't give me your name. I've absolutely no idea who you are.'

'Pull the other one.' When he felt her hand closing oppressively over his ear, or at least over the mouthpiece of her telephone, he went on 'It's round and hairy and it's full of—'

'Who is this speaking, please?'

The appearance of a new voice was so sudden that Richard felt as though he'd been seized by its owner. 'Horseface?' he demanded.

'You're Mr . . . ?'

'Not me, you,' Richard said, not quite certain that he was enjoying himself but unable to stop. 'That's you with the big ears, isn't it, and the little snot who's got everything. I've just been telling your friend about how you break the law.'

'If you have anything to say I advise you to put it in writing.'

'You think I won't? You bet your, your Arse Impkin I will,' Richard shouted, and slammed the phone down. He'd only meant to scare the other with his parting shot, but hadn't he told himself what to do? He hauled the telephone directory off the shelf beside his knees and flung it on the counter, and tore through it until he found Doug Singleton's office number. 'Yes,' he interrupted the receptionist. 'Can I speak to him?'

'To?'

'You just said, Singleton. Doug Singleton.'

'May I ask who's calling?'

'Of course you can. A friend, Richard Vale.'

'He's on the other line. Will you hold?'

'I'll have to, won't I,' Richard said, and was immediately treated to a gaping silence that emitted the occasional click as the receptionist checked he was still there. The silence gave him time to wonder how much he'd said to the planners that he shouldn't have and to realise that he'd done so because it no longer seemed to matter what he said. In that case he might as well say nothing, and he was about to dispense with the burden of the phone in his fist when it spoke. 'Richard. How odd. What a surprise.'

'Am I?'

'Only because I was just thinking of you,' Doug said. 'We were saying it was time we looked at upgrading our computers. What can I do for you?'

'Let me handle that, by all means.'

'We're in the process of deciding. Look in next time you're

passing if you like. Is this a social call? If it's about Bill Messenger, I've heard.'

'Horrible business. You'd wonder what makes people do such things.'

'That's people for you. Can't predict them. Jude and the brood all right? I expect we'll see you all at the school play.'

'That'll be something to look forward to. Anyway, no, this isn't a social call. I wanted to ask your advice.'

'That's what we're here for.'

'I heard this morning I've been knocked back on my lease.'

'They've been doing some of that recently. Must be a blow.'

'I can appeal, though, can't I?'

'Appeal away. It's always worth trying. Are you asking me to handle it?'

'Or at least look at it and see if I have a case.'

'That would be the first step, obviously. When can you let me see the papers?'

'Tomorrow?'

'Not tomorrow. Let's see, let's say a week tomorrow. In the afternoon, before the play.'

'Haven't you anything earlier? How long have I got?'

'Only God knows that,' Doug said, and emitted a dry sound which made Richard think he'd been cut off until he realised it expressed mirth. 'Seriously, though, if there's anything that can be done we'll do it. A week's nothing in this game.'

'And you want me to have a look at your computers while I'm there, do you?'

'Makes sense to me. I expect we can work something out. Excuse me now, there's a client on the other line. Shall we say two o'clock? Two o'clock.'

When the receiver commenced droning Richard held on to it as though it was his confirmation that Doug had promised him both advice and business. Before long an officious female voice began to repeat 'Please replace the handset and try again.' He dealt the receiver rest a karate chop and dialled his own home number. The phone had started to ring when he saw that far too much had happened which he didn't want to tell Judith, certainly not over the phone when she already had enough to contend with. Best not to speak to her, he thought, and was taking the receiver away from his face when she said 'Hello?'

She sounded small and brave and hopeful, perhaps hoping it was Richard. He gazed at the receiver in case that might let him understand why he felt nothing at all. When she said 'Hello' less hopefully he jammed the receiver against his cheek. 'It's me,' he told her.

'I thought it might be. Any good news?'

He couldn't give her that without telling her the other kind, and he was beginning to think he wouldn't be able to admit what he'd said to the planners at all. 'I just wanted to see how you were,' he said.

'Still alive. How about you?'

'I must be, or I wouldn't be making this call.' At once, and without warning, he found himself trying to compute how much all this phoning had cost. 'I'll see you tonight, then, unless there's anything . . .'

'Look forward to it.'

He wasn't sure if she was saying that she would or telling him to do so, but either way the phrase conveyed little to him, especially when he echoed it. 'Bye,' he added, then thought he should have said 'Love you', only by then the connection was broken. He made a further call, a counter in his head costing the several minutes it took, to arrange for the faulty computer to be collected, and then he did his best to keep his mind as empty as the shop until it was time to go home.

# Twenty-one

As David rested from hacking at the rendering outside Miss Singleton's bedroom window he heard her coming upstairs beyond the partly open door. When the door began to swing inwards he sidled along the scaffolding until he was out of sight from the room, because the look she had given him earlier during a visit to the bedroom had made him feel so like a peeping tom that the impression had clung to him ever since. He hoped she didn't think he'd dodged back from staring into the room with its dusty dressing-table mirror, its wardrobe that smelled of mothballs and old clothes, its narrow bed with primly tucked-in sheets, especially since he had. He was renewing his assault on the outer wall when the sash of the window staggered up, its weights jangling like slow irregular pendulums inside the frame, and a long slim bare leg stretched over the sill to plant its sandalled foot on the plank that was supporting him.

He thought the old woman had finally been overtaken by senility, had removed her clothes and was about to display herself to him. Then the rest of the thigh emerged, a thin white tennis skirt rising even higher on it, and he recognised that it belonged to Angie Singleton. She swung her other leg out with a gymnast's gracefulness and ducking under the sash, perched on the sill, the back of her skirt draping itself over it and stirring in a draught through the house. 'You look hot, David. I bet that's hard.'

'Work often is,' he told her, lowering the hammer and the heavy chisel to the planks and wiping his forehead, which was plastered with a mixture of dust and sweat. Rubbing grit into his brow helped make the sight of her a little less distracting. 'I'd have thought it was too hot for tennis.'

'I'm fresh now. I've just had a shower.' She reached up to hold onto the sash, pulling her blouse out of the waistband of her skirt and exposing an inch of flat stomach, and stretched her legs out straight. 'Are you busy for a moment?'

David had glanced at his tools in order to ignore how her blouse

229

was outlining her breasts. 'Depends,' he said, and told himself he wasn't going to say what he was thinking, but did. 'Have you been behaving yourself?'

'Oh, you mean . . .' If there was a flicker of guilt in her eyes, it was immediately ousted by a wide-eyed look that seemed both innocent and knowing and therefore doubly provocative. 'I promised,' she said.

'I hope you kept it,' David told her, feeling trapped in a relationship which they were conspiring to create. 'So was that what you wanted to tell me?'

'No, I wanted to ask you—' She let go of the sash with one hand and put a finger to her lips, because Doug's aunt was calling to her outside the bedroom. 'Where are you, Angela?'

'Aren't you going to tell her?'

Angie frowned at him, then shrugged. 'I'm out here, Auntie,' she responded, and jumped down onto the planks, the windowsill momentarily lifting her skirt to show David that her knickers were as tight and white as he'd imagined them to be when she'd invaded his and Joelle's bed. Perhaps that glimpse also greeted Miss Singleton, since her outraged cry of 'Angela!' came from inside the room.

'I'm all right, Auntie. David will look after me. I'm safe with you, aren't I, David?'

Before he could disentangle an appropriate reply from his feelings, Miss Singleton craned out of the window and grabbing its frame, closed her eyes. 'I'm sure Mr Owain doesn't want you distracting him from his work.'

'Better do as she says, Angie.'

'She hasn't said yet.' Angie leaned one hand against the bare bricks of the outer wall and poked at the crumbling mortar with a fingernail. 'Anyway, I haven't told you what I came to ask you.'

'It can't be that urgent, can it?'

Angie winced and sucked her finger. 'Don't you like me either?'

'Of course I do. That's why I want to be sure you don't come to any harm.'

'You see,' Miss Singleton cried, and risked opening her eyes a slit, which made her resemble a wizened Oriental. 'Even Mr Owain has had enough of your antics.'

'We don't want to upset my employer, do we, Angie? Surely whatever you want can wait until you're inside.'

'If you say so, David,' Angie said, pushing herself away from the wall and looking down.

The platform of the scaffolding was three planks wide, and about fifteen feet above the rubble which had fallen onto the lawn. When she gasped and swayed and grabbed at her eyes David thought she was feigning dizziness for Miss Singleton's benefit. 'You're all right,' he said sharply, and watched her take a wavering step towards him. He was starting to raise an arm to catch her when she stumbled aside to the edge of the platform.

He never knew if she lost her balance as he lunged for her. She gave a little shriek of panic which sounded not unmixed with delight and fell backwards into his arms, one of which supported her shoulders while the other caught her behind the knees and swept her up. The backs of her knees were warm and soft against his forearm, and she seemed almost weightless. As he carried her to the window to deposit her in the house he remembered carrying Joelle across the threshold of their first house. Miss Singleton stepped back, patting her heart as though to reassure herself it was still there and fanning her glare with her other hand, and Angie glanced up at David, looking as much conspiratorial as grateful. As he lifted her feet towards the open window a draught pushed her skirt higher until she clapped a hand to it, and he thought how easy it would be for him to sit on the windowsill and turn her over instead of placing her inside the room. He was almost certain that Miss Singleton would approve, and as he hesitated Angie met his eyes again, hers so wide that he was convinced she knew what he was thinking. She ran the tip of her pink tongue along her lips, a gesture that seemed even more provocative if it was nervous, and David heard himself growling 'Well now, young lady . . .' The next moment she was over the sill, which favoured him with another unavoidable glimpse of her bottom, and David propped himself against the wall and expelled a shaky breath, praying that the Singletons would interpret these actions as expressing only relief. 'So what was the point of all that?' he said before anyone else could speak.

'I was giving my dad's aunt her ticket for our play at school and I thought you and Joelle might like to come. It's for charity.'

'When is it?'

'A week tonight.'

'I'll have to see if Joelle has made any plans. I'll give your dad a call when I get home, shall I?'

'Or you can call me. Would the other old lady like to come?'

'Which other, which old lady?'

'The one who was at your barbecue, who nobody knew what relative of yours she was.'

'Oh, Gwen. I'll ask her on the way home,' David said, and sidled along the platform, sensing that Miss Singleton was impatient to utter an extended rebuke. It was quite a few minutes later when he saw Angie heading for the gate. Though he was making enough noise with the hammer and chisel to fill the street with flattened echoes like slow immense applause, she didn't glance up at him. Then Miss Singleton reappeared at the bedroom window, and having ensured that he'd seen her expression, went out of the room.

Perhaps she was furious because he'd failed to prevent Angie from climbing out of the window, or because he'd had the gall to imply she was old, but hadn't she also looked suspicious? Good God, he hadn't touched Angie, had hardly touched her, not what you'd call *touched*. He attacked the wall with the chisel, refusing to let himself rest until his head and arms were aching so much he had to stop.

He felt hot and grubby, yet less than anxious to go straight home. As he drove across the bridge a clean cool breeze seemed to rise from the weir, at once transferring its attentions to the line of tourists leaning on the parapet. The city centre felt stuffed with heat and sightseers and cars that fumed as they queued to park. Near the Roman amphitheatre he ran over an already squashed bird, and found himself reflecting that it was heat such as this which brought the dead to life, or rather brought life to the dead.

Once past the cross at the end of his road he parked near the Shangri-La home. Several residents were sitting beneath large umbrellas on the lawn, two old ladies playing chess with pieces whose shapes appeared to refer to some legend David couldn't identify, a man reading a bound magazine that looked even older and more wrinkled than himself, another crouching forwards as though weighed down by his headphones which proved, when David passed close to him, to contain what sounded like an imp declaiming Shakespeare. 'The evils that men do live after them,' it squeaked as Brenda came out of the house.

'Looking for Gwen? She's in her room. I'm sure she won't mind if you go up. First on the left when you get to the top.' As she stood aside to let him into the porch she added 'You might want to knock first. We always do.'

She was advising him on the etiquette of the house, of course. Old ladies' scents lingered outside their rooms as he climbed the wide firm stairs, sunshine through a skylight over the stairwell waited for him on the flowered wall at the top. As he climbed through the light and crossed the landing to Gwendolen's door he was taken unawares by a shiver. He ought to have gone home for a shower instead of simply removing his overalls and scrubbing his hands at Miss Singleton's; he didn't feel nearly presentable enough. If Gwendolen failed to respond to his first knock he would assume she was asleep. But he was only raising his hand to the gleaming white door when she said 'Come in, David.'

He took hold of the wizened metal apple of the doorknob and pushed the door open, and stepped into a blaze of light so intense he was unable to perceive the room. All he could see at first was a mountain on the horizon, the sole object that seemed massive enough to remain solid under the onslaught of light, and then he managed to focus on the seated figure gazing at the mountain through the window. So much of the light was streaming around Gwendolen that her arms, which were outstretched on either side of her, appeared to consist of less than bones, while her head was a blaze of silver which looked about to consume its core. David covered his eyes and edged forward until he was out of the path of sunlight and could see the room.

Though Brenda Mickling had taken pains to make the rooms bright and cheerful – Gwendolen's had a pine wardrobe and dressing-table, and the bed was draped with a counterpane seeded by the floral wallpaper – the room put David in mind of a hermit's cell. He assumed that was because there was nothing of Gwendolen's to be seen in it, and he was wondering whether to mention this when she turned to him, her long white dress rustling. For a moment he thought she had lost weight and aged all at once, and then he realised he was seeing something else entirely. Could it be the light which the room was reflecting that made her face glow like marble transformed into flesh? She looked less aged than ageless, as if she'd been relieved of a burden. He remembered her seeming almost to fly away from the island across the beach, but now he had the impression that she would weigh virtually nothing. As these ideas jumbled together in his head he saw that she was waiting for him to speak. When her expression, which combined regret and resignation so faintly that David wasn't certain he was even seeing them, gave him no clue what to say, he tried 'Did you see me coming?'

'A long time ago, David.'

She must have seen him from the window just now, although the distant shining mountain dominated the view almost to the extent of rendering the rest of it imperceptible, even the stone cross hemmed in by trees. The mountain was the only subject that suggested itself to him. 'Were you looking where you've been?'

'Not yet.'

'I could drive you out there sometime if you like, to Wales or wherever.'

'That's the last thing I'd ask of you.'

The conversation was beginning to feel like quicksand from which he had to extricate himself. 'Brenda takes you on coach trips, doesn't she?'

'Oh yes, she likes to get the old folk out.'

Perhaps that wasn't meant as a rebuke, but he felt guilty none the less. 'Whenever you want to go somewhere for a change, just let me know.'

'Soon.'

He could only presume that her mind was elsewhere for her to give the word such otherwise inexplicable weight. 'So how have you been?' he said.

'As you see me?'

'Pretty good, then.'

'May as well keep up appearances. Don't stand there like a judge, David. No need for ceremony here. Sit down and tell me what you came to ask.'

Since the only space was on the bed he sat there in the sunlight. 'Could I have another look at your picture?'

She stood up and turned the chair to face him. 'What picture was that?'

'The one you showed me on the island, of our family.'

'Dear me.' She touched her forehead and then her lips as if to reassure herself that her features hadn't been consumed by the white-hot nimbus of her hair. 'I must have neglected to bring it with me. I didn't realise it meant so much to you.'

'It's just that I'd have liked . . .' David felt that in some obscure way he'd been put in the wrong, and couldn't help reacting. 'What else did you leave back there?'

'Nothing of any significance. Everything I had to bring came with me.'

'Actually,' David said to avoid further awkwardness, 'I was going to ask you if you'd like to see a play.'

'Play.'

'You know, live theatre. Actors on a stage.'

She glanced down at her fingers, which were forming a vault in her lap. 'I was sorry to hear about your actor friend.'

'That's life too often these days, I'm afraid.'

'It always was,' Gwendolen said, and let the vault collapse. 'Do they know what he was doing by himself in such a place at night?'

'He tells one story and a few minutes later he's telling another, Joelle says. She's been to visit him in hospital but couldn't get any sense out of him. It must be the shock. Were you thinking he might have brought what happened on himself?'

'It might seem that way.' She clasped her hands as though she was about to start praying, but the plea was directed to him. 'You don't think I should visit him, do you?'

'It would probably confuse him. After all, he only met you once. It's not as if you need to feel in any way responsible.'

'I take it that he won't be in your play.'

'He may not be in any for quite some time, poor old sod. The one we've been invited to is a school one. Proceeds to charity.'

'Would that there were more of it.'

'Sure enough. Anyway, you'd see the children you met at our barbecue, Simon and Olga and I expect Angie.'

'I'd forgotten there were children.'

David hardly knew how to respond, because her expressionlessly calm face gave no hint why she sounded regretful. When it became clear that she wasn't about to break the silence he said 'So shall I put you down for a ticket?'

'I'll go if you think I should.'

'Don't feel compelled. I just thought you might like to see the play and some of the people you met before.'

'True enough, I don't often see people again. Very well,' she said as though accepting a challenge, 'must I pay now?'

'I don't know what the price will be. Not much,' David said, and belatedly realised that she'd driven Joelle out of his mind. 'I'd better make sure first that Jo and I aren't up to anything that night.'

'In any case I'll see you soon.'

'You bet your life,' David said, getting up. He'd taken her words as a gentle indication that she wanted to be alone with her thoughts, but hadn't there been an undertone to them, almost a prayer? 'Anything you need, you know where we are,' he said as she turned to the blaze of light beside which the stone cross was an overgrown reddish mass. The mountain seemed to inch towards her as he withdrew from the room.

Brenda Mickling met him in the hall. 'How is she today?'

'She seems pretty content, but you'd know that, wouldn't you?'

'Of course. I wouldn't want you to think we aren't keeping an eye on her. Only we don't believe in forcing people to join in if they don't want to.'

'I didn't expect to see her dancing on the lawn, but what are you saying she does?'

'She spends a lot of time in her room, remembering her life, she says.' Brenda glanced upwards before murmuring 'I think she may be missing Naomi. She used to be up there with her for hours, telling Gwen her secrets.'

'Did Gwen tell her any of hers?'

'We'll never know, will we? Here's something you may like to hear, though – quite a few of the residents like telling Gwen theirs. Nothing seems to shock her. Someone said it's the next best thing to having a priest in the house.'

'Do you think that might have been the kind of work she used to do?'

'I was going to ask you the same question. All I got out of her when I asked was a smile.'

David considered asking what kind of smile, but didn't see how that would help. 'I've said I'll take her out for a drive soon.'

'I'm glad to hear it. Getting out more may be what she needs to give her a new lease of life.'

How could he know what Gwendolen needed when he knew almost nothing about her? Perhaps Brenda was implying he should visit her more often, and even if she wasn't he felt that he should. It occurred to him that he might be secretly afraid of Gwendolen, in which case the reason was concealing itself from him. 'If there's anything you think I should be doing,' he said to Brenda, 'don't be shy of saying.'

'As far as Gwen's concerned you couldn't have done more for her.'

All he and Joelle had done which he was able to recall was help her off the island and invite her to the barbecue, and it didn't seem nearly enough. 'She would say that, wouldn't she?' he reflected, and went out to the car. As he inserted the key in the door he looked up at Gwendolen's window.

The panes were full of sunlight, but beyond it he could just make out the tenant of the room. Above a white blotch that must be her dress was a blur which at first appeared to be the colour of bone or ash and to be streaming upwards like a flame whiter than the dress.

He felt as if the world was wavering around him. He planted one hand on the hot roof of the Volvo to support himself as he stumbled backwards a pace. His movement cleared the panes, so that he saw Gwendolen seated in her chair and gazing at or past the horizon. He had the impression that she was aware of everything around her – that she was seeing deeper into him than he would like. He felt she had reached into him in some way, and the smell of her room – a dry ancient smell, he thought now – returned as a faint fleeting taste in his mouth. He didn't realise how long he'd been gazing at her utterly still face until she raised a hand that might have been acknowledging him or sending him on his way. He returned the gesture, which felt like a parody of a benediction, before letting himself into the car.

In less than a minute he was home. As he went along the garden path the immobile sunlight made him feel as if her gaze was lingering on him, though the faceless green heads of the trees were between him and her window. Through the house he saw Joelle mowing the back lawn, her blouse knotted under her breasts, her denim shorts barely covering her bottom. The instant tingling of his penis wiped out his thoughts. He eased the front door open, anticipating how her bare waist would feel as he slid his hands around it, and saw the letter on the stairs.

The nondescript white envelope was addressed to Joelle, who had torn it open so roughly that she'd ripped her typed name in half. It bothered David that he was unable to read the postmark which stained one corner of the severely askew stamp, and he couldn't help wondering if the letter was about him, to have seized Joelle with such apparent emotion. When he unfolded the page, the message wasn't much of a relief.

Dear Joely,

I'm thinking of coming to see you because maybe if you see me with the baby, not that he's such a baby any more, you'll be able to see why I can't cope and give me some advice if that's what I need since nobody else seems able to see anything wrong. Maybe I'll call you or maybe I'll just come, though if you're out I don't know what I'll do, you can see I'm just writing what I'm thinking. I really need someone who knows me before things get any worse.

Till soon, as we used to say—

Though the signature was even more jagged and cursory than

last time, he knew it said 'Ellie'. There was no address on this letter either. His penis had drooped as soon as he'd seen the envelope, and now, as he stepped through the patio doors, the sight of Joelle wearing so little struck him as somehow sad or at least distanced from him. She didn't see him until she turned the mower at the far end of the lawn. 'You've read it,' she said as she walked towards him behind the whirring blades.

'Regretfully. Have you still got the other one?'

'I threw it away. Why?'

'I don't think this is the same typewriter. See, this type is square, but I don't think the other lot was.'

'You may be right. Does it matter?'

'It could. Do you mind turning that thing off so I can think?'

Joelle pushed the mower forwards from the patch of grass it was champing, which might have been the patch where the birds had fought over the cake, and switched it off, then leaned on the handle and gazed at him with an expression which he thought she intended to look challenging. 'So think.'

'I certainly think this time we should take it to the police.'

'And tell them what? We can't tell them where she lives or even her married name.'

'I thought you didn't know if she was married.'

'She must be. She wasn't the kind of girl to have a baby otherwise.'

'People change, and besides, we still don't know if it's her child. There's obviously a lot she doesn't want you to know yet, and if you ask me, that's part of it.'

'Strange that you think you know her so well.'

'Maybe I can see her clearer because you're too close to her, even if I can't understand how you could be. We won't get anywhere by arguing about her, will we? We need to stick together over this. What was her name when you knew her?'

'By sticking together you mean doing what you decide we ought to do.'

'I don't mean that at all. Don't argue just for the sake of it, Jo. You still haven't told me her maiden name.'

'Look, David, she's my friend whatever she may have done, and I've already told you I'm sure she's changed her name, got married, I mean.'

'In which case the police can trace her maiden name to wherever she got married and find out what she's calling herself now.'

'Oh, I see. I suppose so.' Joelle squatted beside the lawnmower. 'Hale... her name was Hale.'

'Ellen Hale. That's aitch eh ell ee?' David glanced into the dining-room for a pen or pencil with which to scribble the name at the foot of the letter, and then back at Joelle. 'Christ, Jo, don't do that. You might hurt yourself. Let me pull the plug first.'

She sat back on her heels, her knotted blouse tightening over her otherwise bare breasts, while he jerked the plug of the mower out of the socket on the outside of the house, then she returned to unwinding grass from the blades. When she got to her feet he put his arm around her waist. 'Don't feel you gave in to me. If you like I'll stay out of it so long as you tell the police. You have to see that's for the best. She needs more help than you can give her, surely you can see that. If I'm any judge she's more than a bit mad.'

'If she's mad perhaps all women are.'

'Half the population would agree with you.' When she raised her eyebrows and looked away from him he added 'Some of the time' and then 'All women except you.' Even that earned him no more than a twitch of her eyebrows. He let go of her and handed her the letter. 'You keep it. You do what you know is right. I'm going to clean up.'

'Don't be long. I want to as well.'

'There's room for two in the shower,' David said, but when she plugged in the lawnmower he trudged into the house. He felt grubbier for having invited her, or perhaps for pretending that nothing between them had changed. He dragged his clothes off and dumped them in the laundry basket and stepped beneath the snake's head of the shower. Once he'd scoured his body he raised his face into the onslaught of water, gasping, until it swept away the lingering notion that somebody knew everything about him.

# Twenty-two

Sarah Monk was leafing through an auction catalogue when she heard a child scream. She dropped the glossy brochure on the chaise longue and ran to the patio doors. The suburb appeared to be committed to persuading her that she hadn't heard the sound. On the gentle slope above her garden the pairs of houses were baking like pale loaves in the early afternoon sunlight. Next door's Siamese cat lay elongated on top of the neighbour's garden shed as if it was trying to measure the roof with its front and back paws while a chorus of lawnmowers purred on its behalf. Sarah shoved at the patio doors, their metal squealing on the runners, until they were open wide enough for her to squeeze her bulk through. She was standing on the flagstones, which continued to annoy her by not being quite the same width as the mown stripes of the lawn, and blinking at as much of the suburb as she could see beneath the silver hieroglyphs of television aerials against the painfully blue sky, when the child screamed again. His naked body flew up in the midst of a glitter of water above the hedge at the end of her garden, and Sarah felt as if the sight had seized her by the heart. Before she knew it she was pacing over the dry lawn to watch.

She knew the young mother slightly. Her name was Caroline, not pronounced Carolin, and they'd exchanged smiles and a few shy scraps of chat over the hedge. Now Caroline was wearing a token bikini and dancing seventeen-month-old Jethro in his first paddling pool. As she lifted him above her head again and sailed him down for a splash he gave another scream of excitement and delight. He sat down and waved his legs once Caroline had dunked him, and Sarah was put in mind of a baptism with the baby playing in the font. She was turning away and trying to be unobtrusive when Caroline noticed her. 'We aren't disturbing you, are we, Sarah?'

'I should say not. You ought to know you don't need to ask.'

Caroline looked so conspiratorial that Sarah leaned over the hedge, and even then the other woman glanced over her shoulder and brushed a wet strand of hair away from her face, which always seemed undecided whether to smile or to blush, before confiding 'It's just that the lady next door to me came out to suggest I might want to put some trunks on him.'

'Well, God bless us all. If I were you I'd tell her God made everything about your little object and didn't mean it to be hidden away so soon, even your little object's little object, isn't that right, Jethro?'

Jethro gave Sarah a three-toothed grin and returned to attempting to dislodge his mother's bikini top. 'I thought of saying something of the sort to her,' Caroline said, 'but Harold hates any trouble with the neighbours. It gets him so tense he can't sleep.'

'Don't you need your sleep as much as he does?'

'I've got used to going without since Jethro came along.'

'If your husband's lying awake anyway he could pick up Jethro for a change and let you have the occasional snooze. You can say I said so if you like.'

'He won't talk to me if he thinks I've been discussing him.'

'Then let him think it's what you thought, if it is.'

'Oh, it is.'

'Have you told him?'

'I try not to bother him too much at the end of a hard day at work.'

'His or yours? Looking after Jethro must be at least as hard as looking after people's stocks and shares, and you don't get days off.'

'Harold brings home quite a lot of work at night and at the weekends.'

'Then it sounds as if you could both do with a break. I'm sorry, Caroline, I'm preaching. It's easy enough to tell other people what to do when I don't have to do it myself.'

'I didn't think you were preaching. I look forward to talking to you. Too many of the neighbours seem to think this ought to be a childless zone. I'm lucky if they give me the time of day.'

'I've got as much time as you want,' Sarah said, feeling clumsy and insufficiently useful. 'I mean, if you wanted me to – if you and Harold . . .'

'You're right, we ought to talk more. Only half the time when I want to he seems to be doing calculations in his head.'

'You'll have to distract him then, won't you?'

'I know a few ways to do that,' Caroline admitted, blushing and smiling.

'Then I should use them, you should, rather,' Sarah said, her own face growing warmer. 'That's when men are most amenable.'

'Harold is when we've been out for a good dinner.'

'Well, that's what I was trying to say before. If you need a sitter you've only to shout over the hedge.'

'That's really kind of you, Sarah, really, but we've got Harold's parents up the hill. They get offended if they're not involved, and Harold likes to keep things in the family.'

'So long as you do as well.'

'I do feel sometimes we're living in their pockets. You're right.' Caroline gave Jethro, who was still tugging at her bikini top, a special smile. 'You're right, I really must have a long talk with Harold. Why, I don't think we've been out to a restaurant since this one was born. Excuse me now if I go in before Jethro has his way with me here in the garden and the neighbours start accusing me of paedophilia.'

'I'll be your witness if you want to stay outside,' Sarah offered, but Caroline was already retreating into her house. All the same, she seemed stronger for their talk, and that made Sarah feel strengthened too, suddenly able to see her way clear. As she stepped off the patio the shadow of the room settled on her, and she smelled upholstery and furniture polish, the smell of decades of antique sales which she'd begun attending on behalf of clients but which had ended up furnishing not only her home but also too much of her mind. It was a middle-aged smell, she thought, a smell of resigning herself to habits of behaviour that would shape the rest of her life, and it had nothing to do with the sight which was brightest in her mind, the toddler's body dancing in the spray of sunlit water. That image, and the way it stayed with her, felt more like a promise which she hadn't dared admit she was making to herself.

She stooped to her handbag where it sprawled against one leg of the escritoire, and shook up the contents. Her purse came to the top, then her grandmother's rosary beads, and then *Monkey in the Maze*, the game she'd bought from Richard Vale. She'd thought she had purchased it to help him, with the vague idea of keeping it until one of the Vale children had a birthday, but now she wondered if she could have secretly intended to keep it until she had someone of her own to play with it. The agencies said that she and Terry were too old to adopt a child, but who could say they were too old to have one except God? She'd fallen into the habit of believing in God because there seemed to be nothing else to believe in, but perhaps she also needed to believe in herself, and now she did. Archibald's and Agatha's God could surely never have created the child in the sunlight and water, and it occurred to her that each person got the God they deserved. That thought, and much else, made her grip the cross on the rosary and breathe the most heartfelt prayer she had ever uttered.

It felt different: stronger, clearer – she might almost dare to think of it as irresistible. It seemed to shine in the barren room, showing her how she'd allowed herself to take that state for granted. If she wasn't careful she would revert to doing so, and suddenly she was afraid to. She went to find Terry, to talk to him or just to be with him, to convey to him that they shouldn't lose hope.

He was in his workshop, which he'd turned the left-hand front room into after managing to persuade the neighbours that it wasn't really a shop. It was silent in there now, not even the murmur of a string quartet on the compact disc player. Silence almost always meant he'd reached some especially delicate stage of repairing an instrument. Sarah tiptoed forward until she could see into the room.

Its eloquence took her unawares – the skeletons of violins exposed on the walls, a battered cello slouching in a corner as though it was substituting for its teenage owner, the intestines waiting to be strung across instruments, the sight of Terry bent like a surgeon on healing objects that weren't even alive so as to give them back their voices. She felt a little unfair to him, and considered withdrawing unobtrusively from the room, since whatever he was doing at his workbench in the bay window was so demanding that he hadn't noticed her. She took a pace backwards, willing the boards not to creak. Then his shoulders writhed, and she heard him sob.

Sarah ran to him, not caring how heavy and awkward she sounded. 'Terry, what's—'

'Jesus!' He swung his chair around, banging his elbow on the edge of the bench. 'Never do that, Sarah. I could have, I could have been – Never do it, that's all.'

On the way to sweeping his hair back from his forehead he'd dabbed at his cheek. 'I didn't mean to give you a fright,' Sarah said, 'but what's wrong?'

'How do you mean?'

'You were upset. You still are.'

'I've just told you why.'

'No, crying, I mean.'

'I should damn well think so with the crack I've given my elbow.'

'There, there.' She took hold of his arm and succeeded in raising it to her lips despite its stiffness. 'Better now? But I thought you were already upset. In fact, I'm sure you were.'

'Now what was I going to be howling about?'

'Well, that's what I'm trying to find out. Surely not that,' Sarah said, peering at the violin to which he had been gluing a new bridge.

'This job can get on your nerves sometimes, you know,' Terry said, and turned back to it.

'I do know, and I hope your customers do. Was that it, then? Have you done something wrong?'

'If I had you'd be distracting me from putting it right, wouldn't you?'

'No need to speak to me like that, Terry. Just put my mind at rest and I'll leave you in peace. It's only me caring about you, assuming that doesn't annoy you too much.'

'Of course I'm not annoyed,' Terry said in a tone that suggested the reverse. 'We don't have to scrutinise each other's feelings every moment of the day, do we?'

'I don't need to scrutinise yours at all, not after all these years. That's what marriages are usually about, knowing what each other feel.'

'Then if you know you don't have to keep asking.'

'I wish you'd stop saying don't have. It makes you sound like an American, not that I've anything against them.' Sarah's gaze strayed back to the injured violin. 'That can't be the problem, can it? Don't tell me that's the problem.'

'Jesus *Christ*, Sarah, for God's sake, what?'

'The glue you use. Isn't that the kind they won't sell children any more? The way you were sitting when I came in, you looked as though you were inhaling it. You're never doing that at your age.'

Terry let fly a harsh snort which seemed to be intended to express mirth. 'No, I'm too old for that, like a lot of other things.'

'I didn't mean you would be doing it on purpose, but mightn't you get addicted without realising? If you laugh at me, Terry, I'll go away.'

'I wasn't laughing at you. I wasn't laughing, I was—' He expelled a sigh which resonated faintly inside the injured violin. 'Why are we arguing about whether or not I was laughing? What's the point?'

'We were talking about why you seem to be in such a state.'

Terry pivoted his chair to face her and took a long loud breath. 'All right, I'll tell you. I didn't want to in case it upset you. It's about the Lees.'

'What about them? They aren't splitting up, are they? Not them as well.'

'As well as who?'

'Mary and Herb Crantry, of course.'

'Oh, them. Of course, them. No, I don't see that happening to the Lees. It's mainly about Henrie, this, but obviously Jake as well.'

Terry pressed one finger against his lips and stared sidelong out of the window until Sarah prompted 'Is that all? Am I supposed to guess?'

'No, no. I'm just – I don't want you upsetting yourself when there's no need, that's all. The thing is – the thing is, she got pregnant.'

'Well, Terry, really, I'm disappointed in you.'

'In me? What do you mean, me?'

'For thinking I could ever be upset to hear that about a friend of ours or about just about anyone else for that matter. Maybe we don't know each other as well as I thought if you believe I could resent someone else having a child because we haven't had one yet. Why, not more than a few minutes ago I—'

She faltered, because he'd closed his eyes and was leaning his head back so that it hurt her to look at his Adam's apple. 'What haven't you told me?' she said.

He let his head sink. 'I said she got pregnant,' he mumbled. 'I didn't say she was going to have the child.'

'Oh.' Sarah fell silent, feeling as if she was doing so out of respect for the loss. 'You needn't have felt you had to keep it from me,' she said after a while. 'When did Jake tell you?'

'Jake? At the cathedral.'

'At your rehearsal last night? I thought you said he wasn't there.'

'Yes, well, not *at* the cathedral. I mean when he rang to say he couldn't make it.'

'Why, you told me you'd been expecting to see him there. I'm sure you did.'

'Expecting, that's right.' Terry fixed his gaze on her and said very slowly 'We were expecting to see him until he rang to say he wasn't coming.'

'No need to make such an issue of it, Terry. Who did he call?'

'It's you who's making an issue. What?'

246

'Who did he call?'

'Some, some – some priest, of course. Who else would you call in a cathedral?'

'Who said . . . ?'

'*What?* What now?'

'I was just wondering what the priest said.'

'What do you suppose? "Jake Lee can't come tonight and oh, by the way, his wife's going to have an abortion", something like that?'

'I don't think it's anything to joke about, especially when they're friends of ours. Maybe I should go and see her. It seems strange that Jake would tell you then, when he had to call you away from a rehearsal. Hardly the ideal time.'

'No,' Terry repeated, having already tried to interrupt her. 'I wouldn't, wouldn't go and see her just at the moment. Wait and see if she comes to you.'

'Terry, one thing you're not qualified to talk about is how women feel at a time like this. At least I may be able to imagine it, and I'm probably her closest friend here. If I'm intruding she only has to tell me to leave her alone.'

'I can tell you that. That's what she wants, at least for a while.'

'How—' For some reason Sarah found it hard to speak. 'How do you know how she feels?'

'The same way you do. It's as you said, we're their best friends on this side of the Atlantic.'

'No, that isn't what you're saying. You're saying you know her better than I do. Or did Jake tell you to tell me to stay away?'

'Both of us, until they get in touch.'

'At the cathedral.'

'Jesus, are we back at the cathedral again?'

'He called you last night at the cathedral to tell you we should stay away.'

'That's what I seem to have to keep saying. Where's the problem?'

'But you didn't tell me last night.'

'I've already explained that, and you can see why. I didn't want you upsetting yourself like you're doing now. Look, you're taking the news worse than you think you are. Why don't you go and lie down for a while?'

'To give you a chance to do what, Terry?'

'What does it look like? To string this.'

She wanted to believe him. Perhaps there was no reason not to.

If for a few moments she'd felt as if her body knew something her mind refused to acknowledge, couldn't that mean she was indeed experiencing Henrie's loss more deeply than she admitted to herself? 'All right, I'll leave you to it,' she said. 'I'll just make a phone call.'

'Fine.' He bent to the violin, so stiffly that she couldn't see what he intended to do to it. 'Who are you going to phone?'

'Jake, to find out how she is.'

'Ah, well. Ah, I shouldn't do that so soon. I'll call him later and find out for you.'

'You've already spoken to him. He can tell me if he thinks there's anything I can do.'

She was halfway to the phone in the hall when Terry's voice stopped her, the words jerking out of his mouth. 'No. Please. Don't. Call. Him.'

'Why not? Tell me why not.'

'Because, because—' Terry was shaking his hands, which he'd shaped into claws, on either side of his head. 'Because there's nothing you can do. It's her choice what to do with what's inside her. It isn't yours.'

Perhaps he meant the choice and not the baby, but that wasn't what she heard him say. Her midriff felt like a huge wound, as if everything she had been trying not to think had exploded in her guts. 'Whose baby is it?' she said.

'What a question, Sarah. Whose do you think? What are you trying to say?'

He swivelled towards her and turned up his hands and squeezed his lips into a wide smile and opened his eyes as far as they would go, and each of his questions and gestures made him seem more absurd and unconvincing. She waited until his posture and his expression began to waver, and then she said flatly 'Jake doesn't know.'

'Sarah, I wish I knew what you were—'

'Oh, don't you even know what I'm talking about now? Jake doesn't know about the baby. That's why you were afraid I'd call him.'

'I already told you why. Go on, call him. Ask him whatever you've got into your head if you don't think he'll already be upset enough.'

'You think I won't, do you? You think Sarah couldn't, she's too concerned about everyone else to do something on her own behalf for once.' She marched towards the door, only to discover that she felt as though she was giving in to a yearning to run out of the room. As she swung back towards Terry she glimpsed panic in his eyes, and realised that until then she had been hoping she was wrong. 'Just tell me one thing,' she said in a whisper that seemed to fill the room. 'Since when?'

'Sarah, you're only upsetting yourself. Try and calm down for both our sakes, and then perhaps we'll be able to—'

He shoved himself backwards along the workbench, nearly toppling his chair. He thought she was rushing at him, and at first she was. Instead she brought her fist down on the unstrung violin, splintering it like a skull beneath a hammer. 'Jesus!' Terry almost screamed. 'Are you mad? Do you know how much that's worth? I've got the father coming to collect it at four o'clock! What do you expect me to tell him?'

'I expect you'll think of something. You can be fathers together. You haven't answered my question. How long have you been seeing her? How long have you been . . . *screwing* her?'

'Sarah, if you think I'm going to discuss anything with you while you're—'

'Did you start in New York? Is that why you were so eager to persuade them to move here?' She ran to the cello that was leaning in the corner of the room, floorboards thundering like a stage beneath her feet, and grabbed it by the neck. 'Did you tell her it was the best night of your life like you used to tell me? Can you manage it with her without having to turn out the lights?'

'Put it down! Won't you be satisfied until you wreck everything?' When she gripped the neck with both hands and raised the cello like a bat, ready to smash it against the wall, Terry lurched off his chair and then, as she lifted the instrument higher, fell back onto the seat. 'All right, I'll tell you if it makes you happy. Not unless you put that down first, though.'

'Tell me or I'll smash everything in the room,' Sarah said with a calm that was only in her voice, and poised the cello above a violin.

'Twice! Just twice, all right?' He appeared to be pleading with her not to force him to say more, but her shaking of the cello prompted him. 'After they came to live here. I don't want you to get the idea it was planned in any way. You know what Jake's like, but when they're alone he can be worse. All I was doing was sympathising like you say I should do more often, and one thing led to another. I know twice is twice too much, but it *was* only twice, because the second time we nearly got caught, so we agreed it wasn't a good idea.'

Sarah seemed less to be hearing his words than feeling their weight gather, her mind and her body growing leaden. When he said 'Sarah' and wagged an admonitory hand at her she had no idea what he meant, not until her wrists began to ache; then she let the cello fall and heard it crush the violin. 'You silly bitch!' Terry shouted, leaping out of his chair. 'Why did you have to do that? What's the point?'

Sarah rested her hand on the neck of the cello and stared at him until she was sure he wouldn't dare to venture closer. 'Does there have to be a point?' she said and walked out of the room, down the hall to grab her handbag, and out of the house.

As soon as her feet struck the pavement at the end of her crazy-paved path she knew where she was going, not least because she saw a taxi cruising past the end of the street. 'Cab!' she called, and filled her lungs and produced the loudest shout of her life. 'Hey, cab!'

A middle-aged woman whose name Sarah didn't think she'd ever learned, and who was emerging with a bunch of three corgis on leads beneath the thorny arch over her gate, winced at the shout. 'Well, really,' she complained above the three-headed yapping.

'Yes, really. I'm real and I just didn't know it,' Sarah told her and ran, her kaftan and her body flapping, to meet the taxi. 'Eastgate,' she said, squashing herself into the back seat, and gave the young unshaven driver a look in the mirror to make it clear she didn't want to talk.

By the time the taxi had wended its way through the suburb and down to the river she thought her temper was under control. If she had to be reasonable to get what she wanted, she could be. As the traffic lights doled cars across the narrow bridge above the weir she was counting coins out of her handbag. When the floods of tourists spilling into the road let the taxi pass beneath the clock on the city wall she saw the Choral Store ahead. 'Here, this will do. Keep the change,' she said rapidly, slapping the coins into the driver's hand. Heaving herself out of the taxi, she ran through the crowd to the steps that led down to the shop.

Two teenage girls in black were coming up. 'There's no music in there, only singing,' the taller girl warned Sarah.

'I'll find what I'm looking for,' Sarah said, and hurried down before the door, which they'd left open, could swing shut. The window and the large white basement were full of scores and cassettes and compact discs and books about choral music and about the human voice. Jake was behind the counter at the far end of the shop, listing the serial numbers of recordings into a phone, and Henrie was advising a customer at the racks of compact discs along the middle of the floor. 'Sarah,' she said, glancing at her. 'Be with you in a minute.'

Sarah picked up a score at random and pretended to read it, though the swarms of notes appeared to wriggle like sperm, while she watched the Lees. She saw at once that for whatever reason – perhaps because Jake was engaging the phone – Terry hadn't called ahead. She thought Jake's preoccupation with the order he was phoning made him look unaware and stupid. Henrie kept pushing her red hair back to expose one ear and blinking her big grey eyes at the customer and smiling with her wide full lips as she listened to his requirements, and after only a few seconds of this Sarah had to stuff the score into the rack for fear of tearing it and turn towards the window. That didn't help much, because through the hymn that was floating in the air between the speakers mounted on the walls she could hear Henrie. 'I thought this performance was more, I guess I'd have to say sacred,' Henrie was saying, 'but the Bernstein is more passionate,' and all Sarah could do was stare at the red blotch that was the reflection of Henrie's head and clasp her hands together until the knuckles ached like teeth. She was seeing nothing at all when Henrie spoke almost in her ear. 'Hi, Sarah. Sorry, I didn't realise.'

Sarah succeeded in focusing her eyes. 'Didn't realise what?'

'Weren't you praying?'

'Oh, I see.' As Sarah wrenched her hands apart she remembered the prayer she had said not much more than half an hour, which felt like a lifetime, ago. Could the answer to it possibly be here? 'Perhaps I was,' she said. 'Where can we talk?'

'How about here? Jake needs me to stick around. Or isn't it something for men to hear?' Henrie brought her face closer to Sarah's, which was still turned to the window. 'Okay, I can see you'd rather it was just the two of us. Jake,' she called as a choirboy's treble began to hover in the air, 'we're going for a walk, all right?'

'Just hold on there for maybe two minutes. I'm nearly through.'

'Men,' Henrie said. 'What would they do without us?' When Sarah didn't answer, she set about tidying the compact disc cases in the racks. The telephone bell put an end to the rattle of plastic boxes, and Sarah thought Terry had got through until she grasped that it had rung because Jake had replaced the receiver. 'Okay, I'm being let out on parole,' Henrie said. 'Want to go for a drink?'

Sarah wanted nothing that might cause her to lose control. 'I'd rather stay in the open.'

'We'll do whatever you want to do.' Henrie held the door open for her and called into the shop 'We'll be as long as it takes.'

People were crowding into Sarah's awareness: a man whose nose had been transformed into a strawberry that was growing towards the left side of his face, a young woman who kept murmuring what might have been the same two opening notes of a melody as she traced a route through a street map in a guidebook with her fingernail, a boy repeating 'See the cross' as he wheeled a toddler in a buggy towards the monument where the old streets met . . . 'I know a place for us to sit and talk,' Henrie said.

She led the way up a flight of thick uneven steps onto the city wall, and Sarah felt as if the other woman was stealing the city from her. She mustn't let that matter – only her prayer did. She followed Henrie along the wall into the grounds of the cathedral, past the isolated bell-tower which was loading the air with the cry of iron. As Henrie stopped at a bench with its back to a flowerbed the bells ceased, and everything seemed silenced – the pigeons strutting across the mossy names on the flagstones, the tourists patrolling the walls, Henrie indicating the bench with both hands as though she was making Sarah a present of it. 'This do?' Henrie said.

Sarah supposed it would have to, though she didn't feel that Henrie was entitled to any of the peace which had returned to the cathedral grounds. She sat down at one end of the bench, where the wooden arm poked her in the side, and Henrie sat halfway along, turning towards her and crossing her long legs with a whisper of black nylon. The sight of her bottom, which was practically all that her red skirt covered, had infuriated Sarah almost beyond endurance as it had preceded her to the cathedral, but hearing her legs was worse. 'Gee, Sarah,' Henrie said, gazing at her face, 'don't torture yourself. Whatever it is, just go ahead and tell me. That's what friends ought to be for.'

In the course of their walk Sarah had thought of numerous ways to broach the subject, but now her feelings drove them out of her head. 'Terry told me your good news,' she heard herself saying.

'Oh, right,' Henrie said, but looked puzzled. 'About the store, you mean.'

'Doing well, are you? Glad you came?'

'We're doing great. We've had orders from all over England,

Britain, I should say. We're looking to do even better once we mail out a list of our stock. Finding out what people need and giving it to them, that's how to succeed. But listen, Sarah, we aren't here to talk about me, are we? Tell me how I can help.'

She held out her hands, and the bench dug harder into Sarah's side until she dragged herself away from the end, though not far enough to be within Henrie's reach. 'Keep still,' she said. 'Just listen. Don't interrupt until I've finished.'

'Sure, of course. Sorry, I'm interrupting right now. Go ahead.'

Sarah stared at her until she was sure that was all, then felt as if she had silenced herself. 'Let's get down to basics,' she said with a sudden notion of how to prevent Henrie from getting between her and her thoughts. 'The only one of the four of us who doesn't know what I'm talking about is Jake.'

It must have taken Henrie's expression only a few seconds to change from intent to enlightened to defensive to determinedly apologetic, but to Sarah it looked as though Henrie was shuffling expressions in search of one Sarah would accept. She watched Henrie's mouth open, and a small soft voice emerged. 'Sarah . . .'

'And he doesn't have to know so long as you do what I tell you.'

Now Henrie seemed prepared not to interrupt, which brought Sarah to a halt. 'What's that?' Henrie eventually said.

'You'd better hope I can forgive you. You'd better hope this helps. Wasn't Jake enough for you? Why did it have to be Terry? Didn't you realise you were giving him something I couldn't live up to, or didn't you care? Whose idea was it, his or yours?'

'Sarah, you if anyone ought to know why. I guess I was attracted to him for the same reasons you were.' Sarah was unable to speak, and Henrie risked continuing. 'It doesn't have to be like I know you're afraid it will be. I've seen marriages saved because one of the partners had a brief . . . you know. Last year some friends of ours in Brooklyn—'

'Every word you say is making me hate you more.'

'I guess I deserve that. I can't blame you, Sarah.'

'And I don't want to hate you, because it'll only get in the way.' At last she succeeded in moving her gaze from Henrie's face to her midriff, which was so flat beneath the orange T-shirt that Sarah felt suddenly as though its secret was hers alone. 'Maybe after you've done what I want you to do for me we can be something like friends again. I don't know.'

'I sure hope so.' Nevertheless Henrie paused before saying 'So tell me. I'm listening.'

253

'I haven't worked out the details yet. There'll be plenty of time for that. All I want from you now is your assurance that you won't do away with your baby. If you don't want it you can't object to giving it to me.'

Understanding crept like a shadow across Henrie's face, and her mouth opened very slowly. 'Sarah, I—'

'You weren't going to interrupt. I told you I've still got to work out the details. How can you expect me to have thought it through when I only found out what was going on this afternoon?' Sarah nearly touched the other woman so as to keep her quiet while she thought aloud. 'I don't care how you do it. I suppose you'll have to let Jake think it's his baby, unless not letting him will make things easier. As for me, nobody but Terry will know I haven't been pregnant. I've had people ask if I am.'

'Sarah, let me—'

'You can talk when I've finished. No need to look as if I'm suggesting something terrible when you were going to do away with the child. I wonder if you'll need to have it privately so that fewer people see it's yours. We wouldn't need to go through all these complications if I could just adopt it, but I'm supposed to be too old. Maybe if I fostered it for a while they'd have to see I was fit, if you could persuade Jake to let me do that. Otherwise we'll have to find a way to make him think you'd lost it, that it had died, I mean.'

'Sarah!'

Henrie's shout was so loud that several people on the city wall glanced about to locate the child she was presumably summoning. Sarah clutched at her heart, bruising her left breast. 'What?' she demanded.

'I've been trying to tell you if you'll only let me. It already has.'

'What already has what?'

'Oh, Sarah. The baby. Not that it was ever what you'd call a baby. I had it terminated as soon as I knew, because I thought that would be best for everyone. I can't believe Terry didn't tell you. I guess that's men.'

Sarah felt as though her guts had turned into a gaping wound. When Henrie ventured to reach out a sympathetic hand she backed away until the arm of the bench seemed to pierce her side. That intrusion of her surroundings shocked her mind out of the stupor into which it was retreating. 'I don't believe you,' she said.

'What don't you believe, Sarah?'

Sarah was almost too infuriated by Henrie's concerned

expression to be able to speak. 'I don't believe you could kill a child, whatever else you've done. I think you're just saying it because you don't want the trouble of having it, or is it because you don't want Terry's child? Either way you should have thought of that before you did what you did.'

'Sarah, listen to yourself. You're not making sense.'

'What sense does it make to kill your child when you know I'd do anything to have one?'

'Sarah, I'm truly sorry. If I'd known you would take it this way . . .' Henrie made a fist of the hand she was extending and shook it gently. 'I think you should check out the possibilities of fostering. Maybe you're right and that's the road you need to go down. Only Sarah, you have to accept I'm not shitting you about the termination. Look, I can show you the bill.'

She snapped open her handbag and leafed through a thin sheaf of papers, and Sarah was more convinced than ever that she was lying, because who would dare to write such a thing down? Even when Henrie withdrew a slip of paper and held it out to her she was sure it related to some other kind of surgery. Then she read the name of the clinic, and the ache at the centre of herself grew huger. She'd heard of that clinic, and knew what it did.

'Sorry. Okay? I'm sorry I had to do that, okay?' Henrie was holding the paper between them as if she couldn't replace it in her bag until Sarah responded, but Sarah was wondering dully whether Henrie was apologising for her abortion or for showing her the bill. So much of her seemed to be aching that she was hardly aware of rising to her feet until she found herself looking down at Henrie. 'Okay, Sarah? Can I put it away now?' Henrie said.

When Sarah only stood over her she slid the bill behind the other papers and closed her bag, and then looked up at Sarah. What she saw made her retreat along the bench before pushing herself to her feet. 'Maybe you need to be alone for a while, Sarah. I know I did after I'd had—'

'You killed my baby.'

Sarah didn't know how loud she said that: loud enough for people on the wall to glance at her, for Henrie to flinch and then brace herself. 'I really think you should take time to work out your feelings, Sarah. Maybe talk about them with Terry. I have to get back to the store,' Henrie said, and turned away.

Sarah watched her observe that the people on the wall were heading for Eastgate and decide to take the long way round the cathedral instead. As soon as Henrie disappeared beyond the corner of the building Sarah ran after her. A pigeon rose clapping into the air, its shadow shrinking on a dead name, as Sarah reached the corner. The thud of her feet on the stones caused Henrie to look over her shoulder. 'Sarah, this is getting us no place,' she called without breaking her stride. 'We need to behave like grownups. If you like I'll call you in a few days and then if you want we can meet for a talk.'

'My baby won't grow up, will he? Was it a he or a she? Do you even know?'

'I didn't check that out, Sarah. It didn't seem to matter.' Henrie had turned her head and was quickening her pace, faster still when she heard Sarah do so. They were behind the cathedral, in a narrow sunken passage which followed the outline of the building. Henrie dodged around a buttress onto the next short stretch, but Sarah had her in sight again before she reached the next bend. Sarah's breath was sawing at her lungs, her kaftan clung to her like a wet bath-towel. If she caught up with Henrie while there was nobody watching she didn't know what she might do. She lurched around the corners of the zigzag passage, each time seeing Henrie dodge out of sight ahead. She took a breath which seemed to pump up her head as well as her lungs, and flung herself into a sprint, labouring around a bend just in time to see Henrie slowing to a walk. She'd come abreast of a side door towards which sightseers were strolling down a ramp.

She thought she was safe. That sent fury coursing through Sarah's blood. For a moment she feared that her lungs weren't capable of drawing breath in time, but they did. 'She killed my baby,' she cried.

Half a dozen sightseers stared at her and then where she was pointing. Henrie attempted to outstare them and gestured at Sarah as though she was trying to grab an explanation out of the air, then she ran to the door and seized the iron ring with both hands and took refuge in the cathedral.

'No sanctuary for murderers,' Sarah breathed, and went after her. The squeal of the latch and the resounding slam of the door made Henrie look back along the dim stone passage, then flee towards a line of tall arched windows that stood above her like still flames, each containing a saint. When Sarah followed, shivering with the sudden coolness, Henrie dodged along the massive corridor to the nearest door into the body of the cathedral. Since two priests were emerging, she couldn't shut the door in Sarah's face. As Henrie ran into the nave beneath the towering vault,

Sarah was merely yards behind her. 'She killed my baby,' Sarah cried.

She heard her voice echo through the vault as dozens of visitors turned to stare at her and at the woman who was trying to leave her behind. Henrie could run as fast as she liked, there was nowhere beneath the vault for her to hide from Sarah's voice. As Henrie ran across the stone floor, the soles of her sandals flapping, Sarah strode after her, sucking in another breath. Then a priest hurried into Sarah's path. 'Please,' he murmured urgently. 'This is a church.'

'She killed my baby,' Sarah told him, but her voice was weakening. She made to pursue Henrie towards the main door, then she became conscious of where she was. It was as though the vault had stooped to frown at her. 'I'm sorry,' she mumbled, and wobbled aside into the nearest pew, where she fell to her knees on a cushion.

She had to pray, and then perhaps the ache would start to heal. As she heard the main door put paid to Henrie's running footsteps she closed her eyes and clasped her hands together. She needn't pray aloud, since for the moment she seemed unable even to whisper; she had only to frame the words in her head for God to hear. But all that was in there was her silenced voice, and all it was saying, again and again, was 'She killed my baby.' Perhaps she could pray if she opened her mouth, and so she did. She took a breath which tasted faintly of incense, and tried to form it into words. What came out, however, was a scream.

It summed up everything she'd learned that day and how what she'd learned made her feel. It seemed to fill the building until it sounded to her as though the cathedral itself, or something even larger, was uttering the cry of outrage, an effect which she found almost comforting. It easily blotted out the voices around her, even those which were trying to speak to her. Its echoes prolonged it when she had to stop for breath, and the more she screamed the more she thought she mightn't stop while she was able to breathe.

# Twenty-three

The offices of Singleton, Midgly and Sharp were on the ground floor of a building beside a canal which ran through Chester just outside the city wall. Richard Vale was twenty minutes early for his appointment in case he could use the time to inspect the computers, but Doug wasn't there, nor was anyone who wanted to take the responsibility for letting Richard past the reception desk. The receptionist, whose blonde hair was nesting on top of her head, kept giving him the same bright smile between answering the phone and typing letters on a keyboard which was half again as wide as her waist. He glanced at the clock as the minute hand prepared to win the race around the dial at just past two o'clock, and leafed through the glossy business magazines on the table which he persisted in forgetting not to bang his shins against, and gazed out of the picture window at the backs of a row of bungalows across the jade canal, and watched a woman with a dog stroll along the canal path, and watched another woman with a dog stroll by, and was rewarded with the sight of a barge painted all the colours of a fire. He was watching the last orange inches of the barge withdraw beyond the window-frame when the street door opened and closed with the thump and gasp of someone being punched in the stomach. He hoped to see Doug, but the arrival was an angular man wearing a grey suit and with untidy hair to match. His harassed look skittered around the reception area and fastened on Richard. 'Being seen to?' he said.

'He's waiting for Mr Singleton, Mr Midgly.'

Richard saw the scissors of the clock snip eleven minutes past two. 'Doug asked me to be here at two o'clock. He wants me to advise you on upgrading your computers.'

'Does he indeed? I wish he'd let me know these things. However, come through, come through.' Doug's partner darted towards Richard as though intending to haul him off the seat, then veered towards the receptionist. 'Anything on that intestacy case in the post? Buzz me if they ring, even if I'm with a client. I genuinely think some of these old folk take a delight in bequeathing problems to the world. This way, Mr . . .'

'Vale.'

'As in beer?'

'As in . . .' Richard felt as if he couldn't even grasp his own name – as useless as he'd begun to feel while the minutes clipped by – and then he saw the point. 'That's it, as distinct from something you put over your head.'

'Oh, indeed,' Midgly said, his thoughts having obviously dashed onwards, and with a gesture that came close to pushing him ushered Richard into an extensive open-plan office flanked by two interview rooms. 'I take it these are what you need to see,' he said, swinging a finger like a compass needle gone wild.

Richard made a tour of the computers on the eight large desks, most of which were presently unoccupied. 'You could certainly do better, and for not too much more outlay,' he said as he returned to Midgly's desk. 'For a start, these aren't IBM compatible, and you'd need a lot of extra hardware if you ever wanted to use a modem. For the amount of work you must get out of them I'd recommend machines with hard discs, and laser printers if you want less noise and more speed.'

'Muh?' said Midgly as if he'd been wakened from dozing, though Richard presumed he must have been concentrating on the papers in front of him. 'Off the record, and since you're a friend of my partner, money's not the object. If we're replacing our equipment we'd prefer to go for the best there is. Are you on commission?'

'No, I run my own business. At least – well, yes, I still do.'

'In any case, don't feel you have to stint yourself on our behalf.' Midgly favoured him with a preoccupied glance before lowering his brow over the documents. 'If you've finished, would you mind waiting in reception for Douglas? Have Janet out there make you a cup of something.'

It was now half past two by the clock above the receptionist's desk, but the time no longer bothered Richard, who felt the law firm was so much on his side that it would turn his life around for him. He was waiting for the receptionist to finish dealing with a call when the street door repeated its sound effects as it admitted Doug. 'Good God. Richard. Just be a few minutes. Sorry I'm late. Had to shoot over to my aunt's. Bear with me, as I expect you nudists say, while I make a call and then I'll be with you.'

The scythe of the clock straightened itself and began to reform, at which point Doug reappeared, though only to say 'Hasn't Janet looked after you yet? Give our friend a coffee, Janet, would you? Mine's black.'

During the next few minutes several people made the door gasp and hailed Janet boisterously before jostling into the office. A constellation of phone calls kept the receptionist busy at the switchboard until Doug put in another appearance. 'Richard,' he said in a tone he might have used to greet him in a hospital bed. 'You're not still dry, are you? Come through, don't be bashful. We'll have our coffee in the room by my desk, Janet. You can put through any calls.'

He held the door open just long enough for Richard to block its closing, then he dodged ahead of him between the desks, where the staff were swapping banter and earning themselves reproachful blinks from Midgly, who stood up abruptly and bore a stack of documents into the other interview room. 'We won't see much work done here this afternoon. They've been out celebrating the results of Estelle's pregnancy test,' Doug confided as he preceded Richard into the left-hand room. 'How about your lot? Jude well? Kids?'

'You'll see tonight at the school play.'

'Possibly. Some of us have to work, you know,' Doug said with a short deprecatory laugh. 'Maureen will be there so the next generation won't feel let down. Me, I'd rather watch professionals, I have to admit. Is it me, or do these school productions ever make you feel condemned to years of watching rehearsals for something they'll never get right?'

'It hadn't struck me.'

'Then Maureen must be right and it's me,' Doug said with unexpected sharpness. 'Incidentally, I wouldn't like you to think I was trying to weasel out of helping the charities. I've given them more than the price of a ticket. Still, we're not here to discuss me. Here you are.'

He was indicating his side of the table, which seemed to Richard quite long enough to accommodate a small conference. It and eight chairs were the only furniture in the plain white room, and Doug had spread his side of it with documents, starting with the lease for Computer Explosion and the letter Richard had received about it and continuing with papers Richard didn't recognise. Doug plugged a phone into a wall-socket and sat down at the middle of the line of documents. 'So it's you versus the council.'

'Just me?'

'Obviously not just you. Not that by any means.' Doug shuffled the papers into two piles with the lease on top of the left-hand stack. 'Well, the situation is— Hold on.'

Richard hoped he was telling the phone that, but he picked it up on the second trill. 'Yes, put him through, Janet . . . Mr Quinton, how are you? . . . Fine, and your mother? . . . Glad to hear it. You can tell her she's nothing to worry about . . . The end of next week, if memory serves. Just a second while I get the file.'

He lifted a finger and one corner of his mouth at Richard on his way to the outer office. Richard was tilting his head in an attempt to decipher Doug's notes when the phone began to issue sounds which suggested that the caller was relaying information to his mother at the top of his voice. Richard turned the sheet towards himself, but Doug's handwriting was as incomprehensible as the tiny shout. When he heard footsteps hurrying towards the room he skidded the page across the table, feeling ridiculously guilty, and grabbed his lease to peer at as Doug came into the room.

'I'll tell you about that right now,' Doug said, then picked up the phone instead. 'Mr Quinton? Mr Quinton? . . . Yes, as I thought, the tenants have to be out by the end of next week, and if they go anywhere near any properties belonging to your mother we can have the law on them . . . Oh yes, very definitely, children as well . . . If you find any damage we can certainly take the family to court . . . Don't mention it. That's what we're here for. There aren't many who care to stand up to us.'

He held the receiver between finger and thumb as he replaced it on its cradle. 'Sorry about that,' he said. 'In this business you have to be on the side that's paying you.' He lined up papers in the file he'd brought into the room and gazed at them for a few seconds before closing the folder and setting it aside. 'Anyway, Richard, as I was saying— Come in.'

When the door didn't budge, Richard opened it to admit the receptionist and the tray with which she had apparently been knocking. 'Leave it, thanks, Janet, I'll be mother,' Doug said, and as she reached the door again: 'Oh, there's the Quinton file for you to take. Black for you, is it, Richard, or half-caste?'

'White, please.'

'That's the man, no need to be ashamed of the word,' Doug said, his gaze straying after the receptionist as he topped up Richard's coffee with cream. 'Cane?'

'Sorry, what—'

'Sugar?'

'Not for me.'

'Sweet enough.' Doug gave the coffee a brisk stir as if he had forgotten it was Richard's, then pushed the cup across the table and filled his own. 'Well now, your disagreement with the council. I believe I can say we've looked at all the angles. I take it that was what you wanted.'

'I wouldn't have expected less of you.'

'Thank you for that.' Doug squinted at his notes until Richard began to wonder if he found them as indecipherable as Richard had. 'As I say, we've examined the situation from every angle, and our conclusion has to be that it's in order.'

'For me to stay in the shop, you mean.'

'Ah, well, no. I didn't say that, did I? No.' Doug sipped his coffee and peered at Richard through its fumes. 'No, I'm afraid I meant the council has the right of it, at least in law.'

'But not in – but not what else?'

'My partners did think you should have been entitled to more warning. It's a bit harsh to be chucking you out by the end of the month.'

'Can't you make something of that?'

'What would you suggest we make?'

'I don't know. An issue, a stink. You know more about the kind of tricks you can get up to than I do.'

'Those were some of the angles we discussed, obviously, but when you come right down to it, a lease is a lease. That's how we were able to get what our client wants in this Quinton case.' Doug turned his notes over, exposing their blank underside. 'You might try getting yourself into the papers, I suppose, but I don't know that that would buy you any time, and of course you'll only want publicity if the business is doing well. To be frank, my partners thought you were lucky to be paying such a low rent. We assume you'll have managed to save quite a respectable sum on that basis.'

The last thing Richard wanted to be reminded of was his and Judith's bank balance. 'You wouldn't know of anywhere else I could pay that kind of rent?'

'Not round here, no. Not for many miles round here. Maybe you should consider trading from home if the council will grant you permission.'

Even supposing that the council would let Richard move the business to the house, who would want to venture so far out of the city centre to a street where there was seldom room to park? 'What about compensation?'

'What about it, Richard?'

263

'Mightn't we be able to sue the council? You were saying people don't stand up to you.'

'That's people, but the council would. I'd advise you against going up against them, even if you've the capital to cover yourself in case you lose and get landed with costs.' Doug folded up the lease and glanced about, but failed to find an envelope. 'I'm sorry we can't offer you more encouragement.'

Not more so much as any, Richard thought and almost said. 'I'm sure you've done all you can.'

'Well, almost. I'll get you something to put this in on our way out.' That might have been the favour which his tone was promising until he said 'One thing I can do. Don't even think of paying our bill until you've moved out of your premises.'

'The bill.' Richard had been expecting the amount to be deducted from his own fee, but he supposed that wasn't businesslike. 'Have you any idea how much it will be? I mean, of course you have.'

'Well, not without working it out. Seeing it's you I'll throw in this chat for free.'

'Roughly, though.'

'Roughly a couple— Hold on,' Doug said, and interrupted the phone. 'Yes, Janet, I'll take it. Mr Vale is on his way out.' He put one hand over the mouthpiece and pushed Richard's lease across the table. 'This one's a bit confidential. Do you mind seeing yourself out? Get Janet to give you an envelope.'

'So it'll be about two hundred.'

'What will? Sorry, I won't be a moment,' Doug told the mouthpiece, and rearranged his frown to express amused reproof. 'Two *hundred*? I hope you don't think that's all we're worth. Two thousand, of course, or thereabouts. Not much more if I can help it.' He raised the phone to his face again, but covered the mouthpiece. 'Perhaps it sounds a little high for a week's work, but you must understand I had several of the staff on your case. You did say you wanted us to examine all the angles.'

'Two th—' Richard had to grit his teeth to prevent them from chattering. 'But how much are you expecting me to ask?'

'Forgive me, I'll be with you directly,' Doug assured the phone, and renewed his frown but not his amusement at Richard. 'I didn't catch that. What are you asking?'

'How high will you let me go?'

'I'm not getting this at all. Are we talking about some kind of payment?'

'Yes, for me to upgrade your equipment.'

'Good God, of course. I should have mentioned that before. Sorry, it went clean out of my head, what with the rest of my problems.' Doug clasped his other hand over the one holding the mouthpiece. 'The thing is, my partner had a firm in last week while I was away from the office, and, well, I rather fear we've accepted their estimate.'

'But he just had me do one.'

Doug let some of his impatience show. 'Who did?'

'Your partner. Mr Midgly.'

'Oh, him. I'm afraid he can be like that. Brilliant with documents but forgets Janet's name half the time. He didn't promise you anything, surely.'

Richard felt his fingernails bending as he dug them into the back of the chair with which he was supporting himself. 'Can't you call them back?'

'There'd be no point. We've already—' Doug said before realising Richard meant whoever was on the phone now. He gazed at Richard for some seconds, then relented. 'Are you still at my aunt's? I'll call you back in five minutes. Now, Richard, I don't quite see what I can do beyond apologise.'

'But you asked me first,' Richard protested, too desperate to care if he sounded childish. 'Doesn't that count for anything?'

'It would with me, but not with Sharp, who was the partner I was talking about before, you'll appreciate. I don't know another one like him for living up to his name. Though anyway, as I was saying, we've already signed a contract with this other computer firm. I hope you weren't banking too much on our business. Never advisable till you've got something on paper.'

Richard was trying to think what to do with the chair; if he sat on it he might never get up. 'I'll delay your bill for as long as I can,' Doug said, 'and on top of that you'll have thirty days.'

'And what do you think will have happened by then?'

'Something's bound to, Richard. Life's never that bad, not for people like us. Why not try getting yourself some financial advice? I've a card here somewhere, here.' When Richard didn't reach for it Doug snapped the accountant's card on the table like the beginning or end of a trick. 'Come to think, your bank ought to provide the same service for less. Do you mind if I return this call now? It's quite important. If I see you later I'll stand you a drink.'

Richard let go of the chair and picked up the lease and took hold of the doorknob. All of them seemed to be composed of some hostile substance that made his fingertips sting and flinch. As he opened the door several of the office staff burst out laughing, so that he wondered if the thought of the bank had distorted his face into a grimace of panic. Midgly was rummaging through a drawer of his desk, and Richard considered appealing to him, but what was the use? He stuffed the lease into a pocket, though he couldn't think why he was bothering, and wandered into the reception area. When he thanked Janet his voice sounded even flatter and more meaningless than he was afraid it would. He hauled the door open, and as he struggled past it he covered his ears, because its winded gasp expressed his feelings entirely too well.

He'd reached the nearest bridge across the canal, trudging as though the weight of his skull was dragging him forwards, when his emotions caught up with him. The canal and its parched banks, the bungalows and the unrelievedly blue sky, felt like spotlights that were trained on him. There seemed to be no more to him than the interior of his skull, a cramped stark place with just enough room for his thoughts to perform an agonised dance. Doug would find out that Judith couldn't get a job, Judith would have to be told they'd lost the shop now that Doug had given him no good news for her, the bank would be alerted to the fact that neither of the Vales had work if he tried to pay the solicitors by cheque. If he'd owned up to any of this sooner, could it have helped? That was one more thought to crowd into the dance that was jigging crazily around and around in his head. He dug his fingertips into his temples until his skull felt near to cracking, and leaned his elbows on the scrawny parapet. He leaned so hard that he dislodged a chunk of masonry, which fell into the canal with a dull flat splash.

He froze, but it appeared not to have drawn attention to him. Nobody came to the windows of the solicitors' office, beyond the larger of which he saw Doug at his desk. The masonry had vanished beneath the thick green surface of the canal, and soon there wasn't even a ripple to mark its passing. Nor did its fall appear to have harmed the bridge – in fact, he thought, now the bridge was less dangerous. Watching the canal wipe out all trace of the accident had calmed him, and even when he raised his eyes towards Doug's window he no longer felt as bad as he feared he would. It had occurred to him that the solicitors mightn't pursue the debt if he wasn't there to pursue. Perhaps not only the solicitors would take pity on the Vales if that didn't involve taking pity on him.

# Twenty-four

The proceeds of the school play were going to Save the Children and Help the Aged. 'I didn't realise they'd amalgamated,' David said, earning himself a dutiful grimace from Joelle but only a puzzled look from Gwendolen, even when he handed her a programme as he ushered her into the assembly hall. Perhaps she was confused by the title, *Thirteen Grandmothers*, or by the uproar of hundreds of families talking among themselves or to one another in front of a stage furnished with thirteen empty beds. Folding seats clattered as children jumped up to wave to friends and run to them if they weren't restrained by their parents, a teacher with a smile fixed beneath her wide-eyed frown stared hard at the beds before vanishing into the wings as though she couldn't remember what she was looking for, a small orchestra was beginning to gather between the stage and the audience with a rumble of settling cellos and a jangle of music-stands. Someone kept sneezing in exactly the same tone of polite surprise – 'Ish, ish, ish' – and a man as wide as two seats was saying loudly to his wife 'Education's too important to be left in the hands of the educated.' David was relieved to see someone the Owains knew. 'Look, there's Maureen Singleton near the front, and Rich and Jude Vale behind her.'

When he came abreast of the Vales he saw that none of the three was speaking. Maureen's stillness made her delicate face appear less at home than ever on her stocky form. The Vales noticed David first, and Richard dropped his jaw in his habitual way but didn't speak, while Judith's permanently amused expression, which for a moment had looked almost mask-like, regained some warmth. 'Where are you sitting?' she said.

'We aren't yet.'

Maureen turned until she found Joelle. 'You can sit by me. Doug won't be coming. Too many things on his plate.'

There was an empty seat beside her, and two by the Vales. David sat next to Richard and felt the row of seats stagger a little, though when Gwendolen seated herself it didn't stir. 'Time to go on a diet,' he said to Richard.

'That'll solve everything, you reckon?'

Usually David found the way Richard's face from the grey moustache upwards hardly ever moved amusing, but now it disconcerted him. 'I was meaning I need to lose weight, not you.'

'Maybe both.'

That sounded unambiguous, yet David had a fleeting sense that there was more to it, especially when he observed Gwendolen gazing at Richard as if she knew precisely what he intended. The teacher reappeared from the wings and surveyed the audience, who might have been extras she had to direct, before fleeing again. 'I take it she's Leonie Harrington,' he remarked to Gwendolen.

'Do you?'

'The lady who wrote this.'

He indicated Gwendolen's programme, but she seemed more puzzled than ever. '*Thirteen Grandmothers*,' he said.

Gwendolen stared at the programme in her lap and glanced at the stage and then back at the programme, and all at once David saw the problem: she couldn't read. 'Yes, she wrote and directed it,' he stammered. 'Is she anyone's teacher, any of your children's, I mean?'

'She takes Angela for English,' Maureen said without looking back at him. 'So as we were saying, Joelle, you haven't heard about Sarah Monk.'

'I was just wondering why the Monks aren't here, David, Angie being so irresistible.'

'At selling people tickets,' David clarified, and cursed himself for needing to do so. 'Doug's aunt isn't here either though, is she?'

'I can assure you she paid for a ticket,' Maureen said.

'I know, I was there when she bought it. I only meant—' David interrupted himself, not wanting to invite any more of Maureen's disapproval, which was as unexpected as it was unsettling. 'Anyway, you were going to tell us about Sarah.'

'I was telling Joelle, yes,' Maureen said, and lowered her voice. 'I hope this won't upset you, Joelle, but she's had a breakdown.'

'*Sarah*? Are you sure?'

'I wasn't till I checked. I heard it from someone she bought some antiques for who heard it from someone who works in the cathedral bookshop, and I couldn't believe it was Sarah myself at first. Apparently she started screaming in the cathedral and wouldn't stop until they got a doctor.'

'God, poor Sarah. Does anyone know why?'

'Well, yes, I'm afraid they do. That's why I'm hoping you won't be upset. The girl who works in the bookshop says Sarah was chasing some woman who she obviously knew, that's before she started screaming, only the woman told one of the priests she didn't know what Sarah wanted or even who she was. Maybe I'm old-fashioned, but I don't think I could tell a lie in a cathedral. She had an American accent, and the description sounds exactly like what's her name who the Monks brought to your barbecue.'

'Henrie? Henrie Lee?'

'Exactly. And apparently—' Maureen spoke behind her hand, presumably not realising that also sent her voice over her shoulder. 'Apparently, Joelle, Sarah accused her of stealing her child.'

'But she hasn't got a child to steal.'

'No, but— Actually, I've got it wrong. Not stealing, killing, though I suppose she feels it's both. Obviously as soon as I heard I went over to her house and refused to leave until Terry told me the truth, not that he seems to care who knows or care about much else. Sarah didn't have a child, but the American woman might have had, and not by her own husband.'

Maureen's voice had sunk almost to inaudibility, and now the Babel of the audience seemed to swallow it up. David wished he was sitting next to Joelle. He saw how her shoulders were moving, and as he waited for her to speak the hubbub felt like a sluggish fluid that was being poured into his ears. 'Joelle, you're upset,' Maureen murmured. 'I shouldn't have told you, at least not here. I just didn't know when I might see you again.'

'Often, I hope. But for heaven's sake, what's going on? Herb's dead, and Bill Messenger's scarred for life and doesn't want anyone to see him now he's out of hospital, and where's Sarah?'

'In hospital. I'll give you the address.'

'Sarah in hospital. What's wrong all of a sudden? What's next?'

For a moment David felt as though Joelle was accusing him, although it was Gwendolen who seemed not to know where to look. When he leaned forwards and massaged Joelle's shoulders Joelle put her hands over his and held onto them. She didn't let go until the overture began.

Even if it was newly composed by the music teacher, David didn't think it was intended to be quite so free in its use of quarter-tones. He staved off a tendency to wince by concentrating on the tympanist, a spindly girl whose long blonde hair flew up with every clash of cymbals. When the orchestra completed its labour more or less in unison and the applause and the chorus of summer coughs had died down, he found it harder to concentrate on the performance. At first he was relieved not to be able to identify Angie Singleton, neither among the old ladies who complained about gangs of children roaming the streets nor among the children who were equally wary of the old folk, whom they suspected were witches, but then he heard her speak. She was the oldest of the old folk, which was to say the most heavily made up, a sight he found close to dismaying without quite knowing why. Worse, he was glad after all that Joelle had her back to him.

The play seemed to take an age to convey its message – that the children and the old people had secrets to offer each other once they lost their mutual fears. When at last the final song and dance was over his clapping made his palms ache. 'What did you think?' he asked Gwendolen. 'Did it take you back?'

'To what, David?'

'Well, to . . .' He was suddenly aware how little he knew about her – so little that he felt momentarily as though a void was sitting beside him. 'I mean, was that the kind of thing you'd have been in at school?'

'I never was.'

'Didn't they approve of imagination?' When she gazed at her hands, which were folded on her breasts, he thought perhaps he should let her keep her peace, but impatience got the better of him. 'Are you playing word games with me, Gwen? You surely can't be telling me you never went to school.'

She raised her head and met his eyes, and he felt as if he was staring down twin tunnels which led to the truth – more truth than he might want to know. The heat and the uproar of the auditorium seemed to mass around him until they grew solid, walling him into some cramped place where the sense of light no longer reached him, trapping him with something he couldn't distinguish, only smell its dried-up ancient smell. The impression lasted no longer than it took him to waver, almost fainting with the onslaught of heat, and recover his balance on the seat, but now Gwendolen wasn't looking at him. She'd turned towards Angie Singleton, who was coming straight for him.

The sight made him grow even hotter; especially his face. It was more than enough to drive his momentary faintness, and whatever he'd imagined in the midst of it, out of his mind. Maybe he could blame the faintness on the strain of watching her performance. As he realised that of course she had been heading for her mother, not for him, he gave her a smile which he hoped wasn't suspiciously brief. 'You remember Angie, don't you, Gwen, from our barbecue?'

'I remember everyone.'

'Right, except she didn't look quite like this, did she? Amazing how makeup can alter your age.' He might have added 'Not yours, hers,' but drawing attention to the ambiguity seemed even more tactless. Feeling close to the void again, he turned to Simon and Olga, who were sidling rapidly along the row towards their parents. 'I wasn't out of tune, was I?' Simon protested. 'She keeps saying I was.'

Richard shrugged and turned his palms up. 'Not from where I was sitting,' Judith said. 'You didn't think he was, did you, David?'

'I didn't think anyone was.'

'See, I told you,' Simon told Olga. 'It wasn't me, it was Philly. I had to stick my finger in my ear so I couldn't hear him.'

'If you do that all you can hear is your own voice inside your head.'

'You don't know what I can hear inside my head, and anyway, so?'

'So you couldn't know if you were in tune with anyone else.'

'Now then, you two,' Judith intervened. 'Don't squabble or you'll have Miss Owain thinking you're as bad as Angie and the other old folk started out thinking you were.'

'Who's Miss Owain?' Olga said, then saw Gwendolen. 'We aren't really like that. You don't need to be scared of children round here, or anything.'

'I'm past being scared,' Gwendolen said, and gazed at David. 'There's no longer anything for me to be frightened of.'

'That's the way to be.' If she was thanking him, he couldn't imagine for what. Joelle was distressed and hiding it, he sensed, and surely that was all he needed to be aware of. He stood up carefully, as though he was poised at the edge of a very long drop. 'Let's head for home, shall we?'

He followed Gwendolen along the row, trying not to feel that she was leading him and then asking himself why on earth he should care, and was waiting for Joelle at the end when Richard lurched after him. 'David?'

'That's a relief. I thought you'd lost your voice.'

'No, I was just thinking,' Richard said, though the slowness of his voice and the dullness of his eyes suggested he'd forgotten what. 'Do you suppose we could—'

271

David waited, less patiently now that Joelle had joined him, with Maureen Singleton close on her heels. 'Go ahead, Richard, spit it out,' he eventually said.

'It's all right. It doesn't matter.' Oddly, the thought lent animation to Richard's face. 'It wasn't important.'

'Listen, if there's something I can do—'

'Would you men like us to withdraw so you can talk?' Gwendolen said.

'There's nowhere to go. Forget it. I won't be bothering David.'

'You've got my number if you want to use it,' David told him, but Richard was already turning to gaze after his family, who were shuffling away in procession along the row. The sight appeared to have a meaning for him, because he watched until Judith glanced back. When she called 'Aren't you with us?' he went after them, looking crippled by the narrowness of the gap between the seats.

'Are we ready?' Joelle said.

'I expect so.' Heading off another of Gwendolen's ambiguous comments was sufficient reason for him to answer at once. He might phone Richard if Richard didn't phone him. He led the way through the hot crowded corridors to the car park, where reversing lights and brake lights were firing in the dusk. As he sat behind the wheel of the Volvo while several cars were manoeuvred out of his way, the lights put him in mind of brands or torches that were converging to find him or to cast him out. That seemed wholly unlike anything he would think, but who else could be thinking it? He started the engine as soon as there was room for the Volvo to escape, and was glad to have to concentrate on driving through the twilight which was settling like an insubstantial fog into the streets.

Nobody had anything to say until they came in sight of the stone cross, which was exactly the colour of metal that had just been red hot, and then Joelle said 'Do you mind if we leave you now, Gwen? At the Shangri-La, I mean.'

'Or here if that's easier for you. David knows I'll be fine.'

He felt as though he'd missed the point again. He waited outside the Shangri-La while she walked across the dark pool of the lawn. As she approached the lit building she turned, having seemed slowly to catch fire, and raised one hand towards him. She might have been waving farewell, or indicating that they would meet again soon, or enjoining him to be silent about some matter, or even blessing him and Joelle. He felt entirely too preoccupied with her, and it was a relief to drive into the shadows and so home.

When he unlocked the front door a red slash glared at him out of

272

the dark: an I, a luminous vertical pupil, an indication that there was a single message on the answering machine. He switched the alarm off, the hall light on, and said apologetically to Joelle 'I'll just see who this was.'

The tape gabbled backwards at the pitch of a songbird attempting speech, then spoke. 'This is Doug Singleton. Will you call me as soon as you can? Thanks,' it said, followed immediately by a brusque click.

'He sounds as though he means business,' Joelle said.

'He can carry on meaning it for a while. I expect his aunt complained because I knocked off early.'

'It wasn't your fault you were supplied with the wrong – what was it exactly?'

'Try convincing her it wasn't my fault. Drainpipe.'

Joelle gave him a wistful look which said it had been too long since they'd played one of their games. 'Trousers,' she said without much conviction.

'Flies.'

'Lord.'

'Master.'

'Mistress.'

David went into the front room to draw the curtains, shutting out the sight of Mary Crantry entertaining friends or potential house-buyers in the room opposite. 'Domination,' he said.

'Bondage.'

When David heard some hesitation in her voice he turned, wondering if the idea appealed to her. As soon as their eyes met she said 'You'd never be unfaithful to me, would you?'

'How can you ask? More than one word, by the way. You lose.'

'I don't want to play any more.'

'You think it's time we grew up, do you?'

'We would have if we ever had a child.'

The confusion of tenses left him struggling to grasp what she was trying to say, then he remembered what must be distressing her. 'You're not comparing me to Terry Monk, are you? Because I'll never be getting anyone pregnant, and if there was anyone it would be you.'

'Not even someone younger and slimmer who hasn't given you the best years of her life?'

'Not even her, anyone like that. Anyway, who says they're the best years? All years are so long as I've got you.'

Joelle was by the door, and he was by the curtains with the night

273

breathing softly down his neck. Again he felt dizzy, because more than the room seemed to intervene between them. 'Aren't you tired of me and my dreams?' she said.

'Come *on*,' David said, and the words released him. 'Come on,' he said differently as he crossed the room to take her hand.

He wanted to lead her away from the subject of the Monks, but she continued talking as they went upstairs. 'If you ever did anything like Terry I think I'd kill you.'

'I wouldn't blame you.'

'If he had to do it, which he didn't, why did it have to be with someone she knew?'

'At least we didn't introduce them.'

'But we invited them all to the barbecue when we knew what was going on. I should have said something to Sarah.'

'What would you have said? She might have ended up hating you as much as them for telling her.'

'I don't care, I should have acted instead of hoping things would work out by themselves. If I'd told her in time there mightn't have been a child to kill.'

'By the time we knew it was probably too late. Anyway, I don't see what difference—' David hushed himself, knowing all too well the difference it made to her. He closed the curtains while she undressed as though her actions meant nothing in particular. He stripped more slowly, willing himself not to let her down when she was so dispirited. Then he was naked, and her torso looked more and more like a bearded face that was blankly observing him and his indifferent penis.

He lay beside her and stroked her and kissed the length of her body, but closeness didn't help. Her unresponsiveness felt like both a rebuke and a weight he was sweating to move. Even when she turned on her side and put her arms around him and raised her left leg to place it over his thigh, that only made him aware of the barrier of his unmoved penis between them. When she took it in her hand he almost flinched as though she'd found him out. He mustn't feel as though her expectations were rendering him unable to perform or that her mood or her need to talk about the Monks was doing so. It was Angie Singleton's fault, he thought, and at once his penis gave a tentative wriggle.

He resisted for as long as it took him to think, then gave in. If that was the only way at the moment he could ensure Joelle felt wanted— He remembered how his palms had ached from clapping Angie, and imagined their doing so from chastising her. His penis bulged in Joelle's fist, and she raised her left leg higher and pushed him deep into her warmth. Their contact threatened to deflate him until he visualised Angie's bottom under his hand, wriggling in a variety of costumes and eventually bare. Joelle rolled onto her back and squeezed him with all her limbs, and gasped as she managed to squeeze out his orgasm. She relapsed onto her side and closed her eyes and laid her cheek against David's until he dwindled out of her, then she turned on her other side and pulled his arm around her waist. From the moment she'd put him inside herself everything had seemed to happen at some distance from him, but now he realised how alone he felt, even before Joelle was asleep.

He told himself he hadn't been unfaithful to her, but he knew he had. Trying to believe he'd done it on her behalf felt like transferring his guilt to her. Having been unfaithful only in his head actually seemed worse than having done so in reality, because he'd done it while he was with Joelle. 'Never again,' he muttered, and was afraid he'd wakened her until she murmured sleepily and groped for his hand. For a time he was afraid to go to sleep in case he dreamed of Angie Singleton, especially when that thought caused his penis to stir. It was very dark, which was also how he felt, before he slept.

The shrilling of the phone wakened him. The machine could deal with the call. Then he realised he was alone in bed, and a flood of vague guilt rose like a stale taste into his head until he smelled coffee brewing downstairs and heard Joelle picking up the phone. It was already mid-morning. He sighed and let his body slump under the coverlet, and hoped the caller didn't need him to get out of bed. But Joelle shouted 'Are you awake, David? It's Doug Singleton.'

'Tell him we got in too late last night for me to return his call. I'll be down in a moment.' David shoved the coverlet away with his feet and eased himself off the bed, bearing an erection that was in no hurry to leave him. He waddled to the top of the stairs and waited for Joelle to look up so that he could mime the suggestion of dismissing Doug while they made the most of being alone. Then Joelle turned, and her words made his penis hang its head. 'I'm sure you're mistaken, Doug. He wouldn't have taken advantage of her,' she was saying. 'Here he is now. You'd better speak to him.'

# Twenty-five

At the end of ten minutes of waiting David wondered if Doug had forgotten the keys to his office. Across the canal a woman crowned with a multicoloured bouquet of curlers came to the window of her bungalow a third time to stare at David, who could only glance at his watch again and try to feel less like a criminal. He was starting to wish he hadn't agreed to meet Doug here, even if Joelle was still too edgy for him to want to talk to Doug in front of her. The last of the shade which the office building had afforded him vanished into the wall, and the sunlight began to accumulate on his scalp as a breeze presented him with the smell of rotten water. He would give Doug five more minutes, ten at the outside. A phone was ringing in the office, and that suggested to him that Doug was trying to contact him, though how could Doug expect him to reach the phone? He was attempting to impose some logic on his thoughts before he had to confront Doug when the woman opened the door of her bungalow. In the sunlight her head looked rather as though it was breeding luminous plastic grubs. 'Can I help you?' she called across the scummy water.

'Tell me how.'

'I can't hear you,' she shouted, and having waved her hands widely, used them in an attempt to waft him away. 'They're closed. Closed on Saturdays.'

'I know. I've an appointment,' David yelled, but she cupped her hands behind her ears. 'Appointment,' he roared.

'Not on Saturday,' she told him, and put her hands around her mouth. 'Sa. Turd. Ay. Shut. For. Week. End.'

'I know what day it is, you silly cow. It's about the only thing I am sure of.'

She augmented her ears with her hands again, but David had had enough. Besides, he might need to save his voice. He gave her what he hoped was an innocent smile as he pointed at his watch and mimed unlocking the door of Singleton, Midgly and Sharp, but she stalked to the edge of the canal. 'What do you want?'

277

'To know what the hell is going on,' David muttered before shoving his hands around his mouth so hard that his fingernails scratched his nose. 'Meeting a friend.'

'Who?'

'Would you know him if I told you? Jesus Christ,' David said, then realised she could see him muttering. He pushed himself away from the building and lurched towards the water. 'One of the partners,' he shouted. 'Douglas Singleton.'

As soon as he moved she backed away and retreated into her bungalow, closing the door with a slam that echoed across the canal. She reappeared at the window, and David saw her pick up a bone and raise it to her face. She must be making certain he saw it, because now he realised it was a white receiver on which she was buttoning a phone number. 'Go ahead, have me arrested, why not,' he said aloud, and heard a car door clunk shut on the far side of the office building. A few seconds later Doug came into view, looking breathless and determined. 'Sorry if I kept you waiting,' he said. 'I wanted to get the situation absolutely clear before we talked.'

'You might want to let the woman in that house there know we're supposed to be here. I think she's calling the police.'

'Is she? Why would she be doing that?' Doug unlocked the door without glancing at her and held it open until David followed him.

The door shut with a thud and a gasp. Through the window opposite the receptionist's desk David saw the woman in the bungalow putting her phone down. Presumably she hadn't called the police, yet he couldn't quite shake off the guilt she'd made him feel. Doug was already past the inner door, clearing his throat and gazing at a blank patch of the office wall as if he could see a clock. He needn't try implying that David had any reason to procrastinate. David took a breath which tasted faintly of carpet shampoo and strode after him.

There was little in the long pale room except wide empty desks, each of them occupied by the mound of a draped computer. Apart from a few shadows grey as dust behind the desks and in some of the corners, sunlight was everywhere. Though the place smelled parched, Doug didn't open a window or close the slats of the Venetian blinds, but stepped into a further room. 'We can talk in here.'

David didn't see why this was necessary; nobody would overhear them. Since this room had no windows it was cooler than the office, but it also felt as he imagined an interrogation room might feel. Doug sat halfway along the bare table and took out a notebook which he slapped down in front of him. David was taking a seat opposite him when he said 'Do you mind shutting it? Less distractions that way.'

David closed the door and sat down, dragging the chair forward with a screech of metal runners on linoleum. Doug's gaze flickered towards the sound, then he looked at the notebook and drummed his fingers on the cover. 'I hope we can sort this out, David.'

'I should think we can, don't you? That's why we're here.'

'Just the two of us, which could present a problem.'

'We could always go to the house, couldn't we?'

'The thing there is, to be frank, she doesn't want to see you. You know how she is. I don't know if neutral ground would make a difference.'

'Had you better ask?'

'Easily done, true enough.' Doug reached back and lifted a phone onto the table. Having gazed at it for a few seconds and tapped it shrilly with his fingernails, he pushed it aside. 'She's there if I need to check anything with her. Perhaps it's best dealt with man to man.'

'Whichever. I don't mind, but shall we get on with whichever?'

'By all means. I take it you don't want a drink.'

'What's on offer?'

'Only tea or coffee, I'm afraid.'

'It doesn't matter,' David said, then saw that it did: it was a way of fending off their gathering embarrassment. 'Unless you're having one.'

'I'm not.' Doug used the sides of his hands to line up the notebook with the edges of the table, then he said 'So what did I convey to you over the phone?'

'Just that she's not happy, that she feels she's being taken advantage of.'

'By whom?'

'By everyone in sight is my impression while I've been there.'

'Indeed.' Doug raised his eyes as though he saw an object hovering above David's head. 'Anyone in particular?'

'Well, you seemed to think she felt that way about you the time she called you over to see the dry rot I'd found in her house.'

'I seemed to think . . .' Doug mused, and appeared to be counting David's words on his fingers. 'The rot, yes. That's one of the issues we need to discuss.'

'With your aunt, you mean? You saw it.'

'I saw what you showed me, but not in the other two rooms where you put in new floors.'

'I didn't have to show you, did I? It's your aunt who's paying.'

'Oh, quite.' For a moment David thought it was resentment which had turned Doug's face patchily red, then he saw that Doug was embarrassed. 'And, well, I'm afraid I have to say this, David: I wouldn't like to think she was being asked to shell out more than was fair.'

'You don't, surely, even if she does.'

'It isn't quite so simple, David. I'm afraid she's been led to believe it.'

'Who did the leading?'

'I rather fear someone in your line of business.'

'I should have known,' David said, and felt it was safe to laugh. 'That's builders for you, you should know that. Show a builder another firm's work and he'll find something wrong with it, I guarantee it. That doesn't necessarily mean it's wrong, just that he'd have done it differently. I expect solicitors are the same.'

'I haven't found that. Not when it comes to the law.'

Doug's manner had abruptly turned so businesslike that David wasn't sure how to respond. 'You know more about your job than I do,' David said. 'Anyway, we were talking about mine.'

'I hope we won't find ourselves talking about both.'

David was beginning to feel confronted by someone he had never met before or, at best, hardly knew. 'Come on, Doug, there's no need for you to take that line, is there? You know me and you know my work. That's why you wanted me to fix up your aunt's house for you.'

'For her.'

'You, her, does it matter? What matters is whether you believe whatever this rival of mine is trying to say about me, and I'd like to know who he is.'

'He's the son of someone my aunt's father used to work with. She's only just found out he's still in your trade.'

'Meaning that if she'd known before you asked me to look at the job she'd rather have had him.'

'No doubt I would have tried to influence her on your behalf.'

'Don't make it sound as if you'd have been forcing yourself. You haven't told me his name yet, this friend of your aunt's.'

'Harry Jorrocks.'

'Jorrocks? I've heard of him, and nothing good either. Jorrocks the Bollocks, I've heard him called. The joiner who helped me put in the new floors at your aunt's was saying that last year—'

'David, you won't help your case by defaming his reputation.'

'That's what he's doing to me, isn't it?'

'Whatever you were going to allege about him is hearsay. That's the difference.'

'And what's he been alleging about me exactly, or don't you even know?'

'I'm afraid I do.' Doug laid his hand flat on the notebook. 'For a start, as I said, there was the rot.'

'If you don't believe it was there—'

'I'll take your word for that, but Jorrocks says you needn't have renewed the entire floors of those rooms.'

'He can say what he likes. He didn't see how far the rot had gone.'

'No, but you showed my aunt, you'll recall, and based on her description Jorrocks says you only needed to renew half of each floor.'

'I'm sure that's the way he'd handle it, and that's why nobody I know will work with him. Maybe you should know he specialises in tarting up properties so buyers and their surveyors can't see what's wrong with them. Call that hearsay if you want, but it's a well-known fact.'

'Show me any of plenty of those and I'll show you a misapprehension.'

'You would, though, wouldn't you? That's your living.'

Doug stared expressionlessly at him and then opened the notebook. 'Furthermore, there's the matter of the window.'

'Remind me.'

'The one whose frame you were going to let me examine, except it was carted away before I had the chance.'

'It's not my fault if your aunt told the bin men to get rid of it.'

'Jorrocks says he would have left it in the house for me to see.'

'He'd have left it rotting inside, would he? I don't think I need to ruin his reputation when he's so good at doing that himself.'

'You sound very defensive, if you don't mind my saying so.'

'How would you expect me to sound when I'm being attacked by some cowboy who spends his time giving his trade a bad name? Jorrocks, I'm talking about, not you. Go on, what else has he been saying?'

'I take it you feel there's more he could have said.'

'I feel—' David controlled himself. 'I feel he's trying to build up his reputation by bad-mouthing the competition, and if you think I am you ought to know me better.'

'I thought I did,' the solicitor said, and frowned at the notebook. 'Angela seems to think a lot of you.'

'A—' David felt his face change colour. Though Doug was intent on the notebook, it surely wouldn't take him long to sense that something was amiss. 'Angie?' David managed, but couldn't very well leave it at that, although he needed all his energy to drive out the detailed floodlit image of her that was forming in his head. 'Don't you trust her?'

'Are you saying I shouldn't?'

'No, I'm saying you should. Her and me both. What's wrong?'

David was trying desperately to pretend he didn't know, but what could have possessed him to link himself and Angie in that way? Doug had raised his head before David spoke, and his gaze seemed to be intensifying, even if so far only David's perception of it was. Eventually Doug said 'She's still a child, you know.'

'I'd have said a young lady,' David heard himself saying.

'A child. Perhaps if you had one of your own—' Doug looked embarrassed, and punched himself lightly in the mouth to muffle some of a cough. 'Anyway, your image of my daughter isn't the issue. I should have learned by now not to employ friends. It can cause more difficulties than it solves.'

So they had still been talking business, but Doug's abruptly brisk tone robbed that discovery of most of its relief. 'The scaffolding seems to have cost you a lot of time and expense,' said Doug.

'Blame the scaffolders for that, not me.'

'You'll appreciate what my aunt would say about the workman who blames his tools. Then again, it might be argued that if your judgment of the scaffolders was so faulty, your opinion of Mr Jorrocks and his firm could be.'

'Christ, Doug, I suppose working with that kind of language all the time has to rub off on you, but can't you say anything straight out?'

'If you insist.' Doug snapped the notebook shut and fixed David's eyes with his. 'Jorrocks says you've been somewhat promiscuous in your replastering.'

'He should have seen the walls before I fixed them. Why on earth would I have done more to them than I had to?'

'You'll forgive me, David, but since you ask, it was suggested you might have been giving Joelle more to redecorate.'

'You've got to be joking, except it isn't funny. Is Jo supposed to be in on the scam?'

'I can't say that, of course.'

'You better hadn't think it either. Say what you like about me but leave her out of it. On second thoughts, you'd better be careful what you say about me as well, and who to. I believe there are laws to protect people from, what's your jargon for it, defamation.'

'I hope we can dispense with the law, David. Jorrocks doesn't know who worked on my aunt's property. What we need to do is find a way of satisfying her.'

'Such as?'

'What would you consider to be honourable?'

'Honourable?' David repeated with a laugh which he meant to sound bitter but which, it infuriated him to find, sounded as though he was denigrating himself. 'If your aunt doesn't trust me I'd better stop work on her house.'

'That would seem inevitable. Mr Jorrocks has already undertaken to finish off all that needs doing.'

'So long as he doesn't try to blame anything he does wrong on me.'

'I'm sure there will be no likelihood of that. There remains the question of your fee.'

'There certainly does.'

'What would you be prepared to accept under all the circumstances?'

'What I'm owed, of course. I haven't brought the figures with me.'

'I would suggest you might want to forget them.'

'And do what instead?'

'I think you might consider asking for the fee Jorrocks would have charged for the work you've completed, less a significant discount for goodwill and to reflect the reduction you'll presumably enjoy in your bill from the scaffolders by reason of the inconvenience and loss of working days they caused. You may like to know that my aunt received complaints from her neighbours about unnecessary noise from a workman's radio.'

Out of all that, one word lodged like a red-hot jagged lump in David's mind. 'Goodwill?'

'Something you'd be well advised to do your best to foster.'

'I haven't noticed much of it coming my way this morning.'

'On the contrary, David. If we weren't friends, and if I didn't feel to some extent responsible for the situation, I should be obliged to adopt an altogether more hostile position. As it is, I'd like you to remember that I'm acting on my aunt's behalf.'

'In what?'

'In whatever may be necessary to achieve a satisfactory resolution.'

'And what are you saying is going to be?'

'That depends on what we can expect from you, David.'

'A bill. My bill for exactly as much as I'd have expected to charge for the job so far.'

'I'm disappointed to hear you say that, David. I hope you can be prevailed upon to see that you're in error.'

'You won't be prevailing, I can promise you that.'

'Perhaps Joelle may. Perhaps when you've had time to consider you will see this is best kept between friends.' Doug raised one hand as David shoved back his screeching chair: 'I shouldn't want you to say anything you may live to regret saying.'

'What are you threatening me with now?'

'With nothing, I hope. I should like to think that threats aren't necessary between us. All the same,' Doug said as David was turning away, 'please try and understand it would be inadvisable for this matter to see the inside of a courtroom. If the case should go against you, which I'm very much afraid it would, you'd end up ruinously out of pocket when the costs were awarded against you. I trust you appreciate I'm simply advising you as a friend.'

'I can't wait to find out what you do when you aren't one.' David marched to the door and jerked it open, strode past the hooded computers and through the reception area, setting a few specks of silver dancing in the air. He tried to slam the outer door behind him, but it was like pushing a mattress into a high wind. He stalked up the path which led from the towpath to the road and let himself into his car. He couldn't judge which was hotter, the sunlit city or the interior of his skull. He twisted the key in the ignition once too often and heard the starter motor grind, a sound which made him do that to his teeth as he drove homewards. Once he spoke to Joelle he would be able to let go of whatever was in his head. But when he stepped into the house and called her name, emptiness answered him.

Though he hadn't asked her to wait until he returned, he had assumed she would to learn the outcome of his meeting with Doug. Her absence let the shock of the morning's developments seize him. He went to the patio doors in case she was in the back garden, but the lawn was bare; the patch where the birds had fought was even barer. He poured himself a glass of water from the tap, and was sipping it despite its seeming to taste unpleasantly bitter when he heard a key scratching at the lock of the front door. He tipped most of the water down the plughole and went to meet Joelle in the hall. 'Jo, I wondered where you'd got to. Do you want to hear the worst?'

His voice trailed off, because she wasn't alone. The burly man, whom David felt he ought to recognise, pushed Joelle none too gently into the house. 'Here's your wife, Mr Owain. Maybe you'll want a word with her before I call the police.'

# Twenty-six

At first all David could see was Joelle's face. It was blotchy with shame or rage, and set stiff as a mask, which he understood was the only way she could stop her lips from trembling. For several seconds which he heard his heartbeats counting, she avoided looking at him. She glanced up the stairs, then into the front room and past him at the kitchen, as if she hardly recognised their home or didn't feel entitled to or was seeking a means of escape, and at last met his eyes. That was worse, because he seemed to be looking at someone he didn't know or who didn't want to know him. He started forward, trying to frame a question, and faltered, wondering if she had sensed he was being unfaithful to her. Then the door behind her slammed, destroying her frame of sunlight, and there was something else for him to look at, someone on whom to focus his uncomprehending fury – the man who had shoved Joelle into the house.

He appeared to have more greyish hair than he knew what to do with, dangling over his shoulders and down his back, turfing his cheeks and chin, coating the puckered lifebelt of his stomach above the death's head of his belt buckle, sprouting through the holes in the knees of his jeans. His broad face looked as though it had been flattened into shape, spreading the nose to almost half the width of his petulantly small mouth. The face, and the T-shirt which declared I'VE GOT THE HOBBIT HABIT, struck David as vaguely familiar, but his rage at the sight of this unkempt character leaning against the inside of the door after having manhandled Joelle gave him no time for reflection. 'Who the hell are you,' he said in a voice that sounded to him no louder than his heartbeat, 'and what do you think you're doing with my wife?'

'Maybe you should ask her what she's been up to.'

'I'm asking you. Don't tell us what to do in our own house. Where do I know you from?'

'Think about it, Mr Owain.'

That was almost enough to launch David at him with the

intention of throwing him out of the door, except that Joelle had sat abruptly on the third stair up. Either her legs had failed her or she was trying to keep out of his line of sight. He glared at the man, not knowing if it was the other's attention or his own that he was trying to distract from Joelle, and then he remembered. 'We did some work for you a while ago. So what?'

'Remember what kind of work?'

'Plastering, wasn't it?' All at once David remembered a roomful of games and plastic figures with swords, which he'd assumed was already a playroom but which had turned out to be where this man spent evenings and whole days with his friends – remembered helping the man clear the room while a baby howled, it had seemed almost constantly, somewhere in the house. 'And then Joelle put up some paper for you with teddy bears on it, only there didn't seem much point when you had to cover it up with all those shelves. I should think your son – Rutger, isn't it? – must be getting to the age when they look like a good place to climb.'

The last few words were unexpectedly hard to speak; he'd become aware that the man – Scott Pinnock, that was his name – and Joelle were listening to him with an intensity that disconcerted him. 'Are you two in this together?' Pinnock demanded.

'We're together in most things,' David said, which let him lean over the banister and hold Joelle's shoulder. Her stiffness was indeed the alternative to shaking, and she didn't yield even slightly to his touch, nor look up at him, nor move so that he could sit by her. If Pinnock had done this to her, David meant to ensure he felt a great deal worse than she did, though for the moment he was unable to let go of her. 'Did you have something particular in mind?'

'Ask her.'

'That's the second time you've tried that. If you've anything to say, spit it out or get out, or we'll be the ones who call the police.'

'I'd laugh if you did.'

'What game are we playing here, Mr Pinnock? One of these games you seem to spend most of your life playing?' David said, and succeeded in shifting his hand to the back of Joelle's neck, which felt so tense he could imagine it snapping. 'Jo, why don't you—'

'Ask her what she thought she was doing with my kid.'

'Nothing sinister, I'm certain of that,' David said, massaging Joelle's neck, willing her to respond to him somehow. 'Why don't you tell us what you think she was.'

'You haven't got any of your own, have you?'

'Any what?' David said, and saw Joelle gripping her hands between her legs.

'What do you think we've been talking about? Any brats. Any kids.'

'I can't be a father, if that's what you mean.'

'And maybe you don't know how she told our Hayley, that's my wife, how she wished you could. I'll tell you what, friend, you want to keep an eye on her. Women get peculiar when they can't have what they want.'

'Do you know, Mr Pinnock, I'm beginning to find you pretty offensive.' David had to continue, though his words seemed undermined by the way Joelle was behaving. 'I'd like to know what reason you think you have for insulting my wife.'

'I'm just trying to show you the truth you don't seem to want to look at, friend. Look at her.'

'I'm looking at you,' David said, unable even to glance at Joelle's face. 'You've shown me nothing, you've told me nothing. All I've heard are insinuations, and I think that's all you've got to offer.'

'She knows different.'

'My wife has a name, and we'd like you to use it as long as you're in her house.'

'All right, friend, let your wife explain this. Let her tell you where she was scuttling off to with our Rutger in his buggy.'

'Since I don't know the circumstances—'

'Come off it, friend. I reckon you know what I'm talking about. Our Hayley left him outside the front door for a couple of minutes, strapped into his buggy so he could get some sun on him, and your crazy bitch would have waltzed off with him if one of our neighbours hadn't caught her at it and wanted to know who she was.'

All of that had turned into a blur in David's head, except for the word Pinnock had used for Joelle, which was more than enough to get him thrown out of the house. David patted Joelle's shoulder, and was taking the first step towards Pinnock when she grabbed his hand. 'No, David.'

If she was going to admit anything in front of Pinnock, David didn't know whether he would be able to bear it. When he made himself glance at her face, however, there was a glimmer in her eyes. 'Answer me one question, Mr Pinnock,' she said almost steadily. 'Why was he dressed like that?'

289

'What sort of crap are you asking me?'

'I think it's a simple enough question, don't you, David?'

'Sounds like it,' was the best David could manage, even when she squeezed his hand. 'Dressed like what?' Pinnock demanded.

'Why, in long trousers and with those long sleeves and his shirt buttoned up to his neck.'

'He dresses how his mother dresses him. I reckon she knows more about it than anyone who can't have kids.' Pinnock stared at David, a challenge which seemed to contain the hint of a plea, then raised his voice. 'What am I justifying it to you for anyway? What business is it of yours, you interfering bitch?'

'It seems a strange way of letting the sun reach him,' Joelle said, holding onto David's hand with both of hers. 'I'd be inclined to wonder if there was anything you didn't want people to see.'

'I don't believe this,' Pinnock said as though he was addressing someone behind and above the Owains. 'I'm being accused of God knows what by someone who tried to pinch my kid.'

Joelle gripped David's hand so fiercely that it hurt. 'Isn't it time you called the police, Mr Pinnock?'

'Don't think I won't. Maybe our Hayley is right now, if she hasn't already.'

'Why don't you make sure? There's the phone in front of you.'

'What are you trying to make out, that I won't?'

'No,' David said, 'Joelle is saying that if you want the police involved you should call them right now instead of threatening her. And if she isn't saying that, I am.'

Pinnock grimaced at the phone. 'It's got some kind of bloody machine attached to it.'

'Don't let that worry you. The phone works just the same as any other. All it will do,' David added, with an inspiration which felt vague yet powerful, 'is record what you say.'

'You trying to make out that should bother me?'

'I thought I said the opposite.'

'Mess up what I say, more like, never mind recording it. Or maybe you will after I'm gone and make it sound like I said something different. Don't either of you start thinking I won't be calling them. I'd want to be sure I kept my wife under control in future, friend.'

'No friend of mine refers to Joelle as though she's some kind of animal.'

Pinnock opened his mouth and met David's eyes and closed his mouth again. He reached behind him and viciously twisted the latch. 'I'll be asking the neighbours what they saw. Don't go telling yourselves you've heard the last of us,' he said, nearly trapping himself with the door as he sidled clumsily out and dragged it shut.

For a few seconds David was able to feel that his leaving was a relief, and then he realised it was not, because it left him and Joelle with nobody to deal with except each other. When she stood up slowly and carefully he reached out to support her, but once she was on her feet she moved away quickly through the communicating rooms and into the back garden. He wasn't sure if she wanted him to follow her. He ventured far enough into the front room to watch her pace along the lawn, past the patch of dead grass, and pull a folding chair into the band of shade which was beginning to stretch towards the house from the wall at the end of the garden. The sight of her bumping the half-unfolded chair after her made her seem vulnerable as a child. She dumped it in the shadow and yanked it open and almost missed it as she tried to sit on it, and David lurched forward to catch her, forgetting the distance between them. She jerked the chair underneath herself and raised her head, and when she saw him he had to keep going, not least because she seemed to want to look away. As he carried another chair towards her through the sunlight which laid a burning weight on his shoulders she said 'Well, now you see what I'm capable of.'

'Nothing very bad under the circumstances. You don't need to tell me why you did it.' David sat beside her and took her hand, and they gazed at their empty house. The longer they were silent, the more of an effort it seemed they would have to make to say another word, and so when an idea occurred to him he blurted it out. 'You didn't have a friend at all, did you?'

'I thought I might still have you.'

'You know you have. At least, I'd have expected you to know. Only what were you trying to do with those letters?' When with some effort she looked blank he said 'That's what I meant about a friend. There never was anyone called Ellie.'

'Some of my friends used to call me that at school.'

'That was a long time ago.'

'You needn't remind me. I can see that every time I look in the mirror.'

'Then you shouldn't.'

'Shouldn't look?'

'Shouldn't think that.' For as long as this exchange lasted he was able to believe that nothing had altered between them, but then he felt it fail to reach her. 'I was trying to point out you're old enough to know better,' he said.

'Better than what, David?'

'Better than to think you couldn't talk to me. I understand why you wanted to do something about Rutger, even if I don't agree with how you tried to do it, but what was the idea of leaving those letters for me to find? Was I supposed to imagine you really had a friend who couldn't cope with her child?'

'You did until just now, didn't you?'

'And then? You were going to bring Rutger home and pretend he belonged to this Ellie and tell me what, that she'd left him for you to look after?'

'Something along those lines.'

'Didn't it strike you that I'd insist on taking him straight to the police?'

'Unless you didn't want to think of him being put into a home.'

'Even if I didn't recognise him, didn't you realise the police would be bound to come looking for him? Christ, Jo, I wouldn't have known what was going on, but they'd have thought the same as Pinnock did, that I was your accomplice.'

'Not once they saw the letters.'

David felt as if she'd gripped his heart and then relinquished it. 'Jo, you aren't saying that's why you wrote them.'

'Why can't you understand? I don't *know*. I don't *know*.'

'Because if it is . . .' Then her words caught up with him, and dismayed him. 'But you knew what you were doing when you tried to take Rutger.'

'Did I?'

'I mean, you must have had a plan.' When Joelle gazed through the house as though contemplating infinity he said 'Don't talk about it now unless you want to. So long as you know I'm still on your side, whatever it was.'

'Haven't I been talking?'

'Up to a point you have. I know it must be hard for you. It isn't easy for me either. I just want you to know I don't blame you. But before anyone comes, in case anyone does, I ought to know—'

'Then you should.'

'Well, that's what I've been—'

'Not trying to understand me. Blame me, for God's sake.'

'For what, Jo? Even if I wouldn't have—'

'Not for what I did, can't you see? For what I didn't do.'

'You've lost me.'

She turned and stared at him until he thought she had taken his words as a threat rather than a plea for clarity. He was about to explain when she said 'It isn't even as if I was so blinded by my feelings that I couldn't see it wouldn't work.'

'Then what, Jo?'

'I wanted to be caught so I'd be able to tell myself I'd done everything I could,' she said in a voice that sounded as though she was struggling to prevent it from rising beyond control. 'I just didn't admit it to myself. That's what the letters must have been for, and the way I tried to steal him in broad daylight, so I could pretend and have your sympathy as well. No, don't touch me, David, I'm not worth it any more.'

'Of course you are, and if you think I'm going to blame you while you're torturing yourself like this . . .' He took her hand, which at some point he'd released in order to make gestures he couldn't even remember. It was more inert and limp than ever. He did his best to stroke some life into it, but when she continued to stare ahead he looked where she was looking.

Through the series of windows, as if at the wrong end of a telescope, he could just distinguish Mary Crantry in her front room. At that distance she was too small to appear as anything except a victim. She stooped and picked up an object, putting David in mind of somebody finding a clue, then she dropped it on a chair and disappeared from view. He found himself recalling the dream he'd had the night before Herb's death, of the thin vigilant figure outside the house – recalling it so vividly that it no longer felt like a dream. For a moment he wanted to blame it for everything that had been going wrong since he couldn't quite remember when, but wasn't he simply trying to avoid feeling guilty? Then Joelle closed her hand around his as though to reassure herself he was still there. 'So what was the matter with Doug?' she said.

# Twenty-seven

As Richard stepped off the city wall into the Travellers Welcome he saw that everyone in the small crowded bar was staring at him. All of them looked stunned or dismayed; some of the women appeared to be close to tears. They knew, he thought, and found himself unable to move or think, even when the barman stopped serving long enough to throw Richard a glance that suggested he was about to ask him to leave. Then Judith and the children squeezed past Richard, and Simon turned to gaze over his head. 'Isn't that near where we go on holiday?'

The drinkers hadn't been looking at Richard after all. The harsh blurred voice which had sounded as if it was composed of gunfire, and which he'd sensed lowering itself onto or into his head, was the voice of a newscaster on a television mounted above the doorway. As Richard swung round, a sudden dizziness almost sent him staggering out of the pub. He focused on the faded picture above the sunlight through the doorway and saw women wailing, bodies on stretchers being carried away from exploded houses, young soldiers wearing white dust like makeup. So far as he was concerned this could have been happening anywhere, until he heard enough of the commentary to grasp that it was indeed Yugoslavia. 'It's the same country as our naked beach, yes.'

'Then it's a good job we aren't going this year,' Olga said.

He heard her trying to convince herself that in some way it must be for the best that they weren't going on holiday at all. His sense of the disappointment she and Simon had been more or less concealing for weeks was enough to distract him from the images on the screen before he would have had to understand why they seemed to have nothing to do with him and yet far too much. 'We don't have to go that far to have the time of our lives, do we?'

'Of course we don't, Rich.'

Judith meant to reassure him, but that only made him realise she couldn't know why he sounded anxious. He was heading for the

295

bar when a woman in a fluorescent orange track suit said 'Would one of you mind closing the door? We can't see a blessed thing.'

'On your way out,' the barman said.

'Don't move, I'll do it,' Richard said, then saw that the barman wasn't addressing the woman. 'You weren't talking to me, were you?'

'I'm sorry, I'll have to ask you to leave.'

Richard felt as though the television was dropping jagged lumps of sound into his skull. 'Why, what do you think I'm going to do?'

'Not with them.'

The barman grimaced and wagged one finger in a gesture which seemed to include Judith and the children, and again Richard couldn't move, not while the barman and probably everyone else in the bar was staring at him. Judith, however, had understood. 'We want to order lunch as well,' she said.

'Doesn't matter. Even if you're eating we can't let children in here.'

'But they were let in when they were younger.'

'Change of management. New policy, sorry. Nothing to do with me, love. If you don't like it, complain to the name you'll find over the door.'

Richard had a confused idea that the barman was referring to the bringer of tragic news until he remembered that the licensee's name would be displayed outside on a plaque. By now he had rediscovered his ability to speak. 'How old are they supposed to be before you'll let them in?'

'Older than these two look. Than he does, anyway. Never mind, kids, you can come back in a couple of years if you're still hungry.'

Richard was overcome by a shiver which he managed to disguise by flinging out his arms and ushering the family past him. 'If we're not welcome we're not welcome. You might want to think about changing the name of your pub.'

'They don't look as though they'll be travelling far,' the woman in the track suit told the barman.

Richard stepped back into the sunlight to rid himself of the chill, and found Judith reading the licensee's name. 'Don't let's waste the day,' he begged.

'I was just seeing who to blame.'

'We should complain about him saying I don't look as old as Olga. Some of my friends think I look older.'

Olga gave Simon her patented sceptical blink, then Richard

intervened. 'Where would you two like to go instead?'

'Somewhere by the river,' Olga suggested.

'That place with the burgers and popcorn,' Simon said.

'Isn't that dearer than we had in mind, Rich?'

'We can afford to do what they most want to do for one day, can't we?'

'I suppose so,' Judith admitted. Nevertheless she looked doubtful, especially when Olga said 'Can we go on the river afterwards?'

'Let's eat first and then take a vote. Though I think we know how it'll come out,' he commented to Judith as the children ran ahead along the wall.

She waited until their game of tag had taken them temporarily out of earshot. 'Do you know something I don't?'

'What sort of thing?'

'Some reason we can be extravagant just now.'

'Isn't it worth giving them a day they can go to sleep dreaming of? I do know something you ought to know,' he managed to add without, he prayed, too noticeable a pause. 'I know you're beautiful.'

'Am I? I haven't been feeling it. Being useless is getting me down.'

'Who says you are?'

'The education authorities, as if you didn't know.'

'They didn't say that. Too good for them to be able to pay you what you're worth, more like. And don't you think you're any use to us?'

'Sometimes I wonder.'

'Simon, Olga, come here a minute.' Judith dealt his arm a gentle punch, but he didn't lower his voice as the children ran back, vigorously tagging each other. 'Do you think your mother's any use?'

'Hmmm . . .' Olga mused with a finger to her lips, then snatched it away to show she was joking. 'If it wasn't for Mum the house would be a mess.'

'Like your room,' Simon said, 'except when she makes you do it.'

'At least *I* don't eat sweets in bed.'

'So? Only me has to sleep with the papers, that's what she said.' When Olga giggled at his solemnness he made to chase her, then recalled what he'd been asked. 'And she makes the best dinners, better than in restaurants.'

'Well,' Judith said, 'it sounds as though I'll have to get used to being a mere housewife.'

'And I liked you telling us stories so we'd go to sleep,' Olga said, 'only you never do any more.'

'I didn't know you still wanted me to. I thought you'd think you were too old for them.'

'I'm not.'

'Nor me,' said Simon.

'Perhaps I'll tell you one tonight before you get too old.' Judith took Richard's hand, at which point the children looked knowing and walked ahead. 'I'm sorry if I haven't been pulling my weight,' she murmured. 'I expect I'll be better now we've got something to help us sleep. And Doug Singleton may still be able to give us some kind of a hand, do you think?'

'I'm sure he will,' Richard said, feeling his innards cringe at the lie.

'And if he doesn't we'll carry on somehow. You're right, the next generation deserves a special day occasionally, and so do we. One day like this won't kill us, will it?' She tugged at his hand. 'Come on before we lose them.'

They caught up with Simon and Olga alongside the cathedral, where a breeze was stirring the plots of grass beside the inscribed path. It found the high notes of a choir, and Richard had the notion that the stones were singing. The idea was so childlike that he felt as though he was rediscovering himself. 'Do you want to go in and listen?' he said.

'We could. Simon, Olga, wait a—' But they were already chasing ahead through the crowd on the wall. 'Shall we come back later?' Judith suggested. 'I get the feeling lunch won't wait.'

Richard saw the children running beneath the clock that crouched spider-like over the wall. The closing of a door cut off the hymn, and he felt that the music and the yearning it had awakened in him had been crushed under the cathedral. 'It doesn't matter,' he said. 'It's supposed to be everyone's day. We'll do what everyone wants.'

They followed Simon and Olga down a flight of steps to a lawn occupied by bits of some old columns, beyond which a path led to the river, where a paddle-boat called the *Mark Twain* was pulling away from its dock. That, and the iron lacework of the Old Orleans restaurant which overlooked the dock, gave Richard a sense of straying between two worlds, each of which made the other seem unreal: old ladies being wheeled along the riverside, canoes racing towards the weir, the brass handle of the door he held open for the family, the aproned waiter who came to meet them. The jangling of an elaborate pinball drew Richard's attention to the far end of the long American bar. Sitting there were Jake and Henrie Lee.

Jake met Richard's eyes and raised a large glass of whisky towards him, and Henrie did so with a tall glass wearing a parasol. Perhaps they weren't sure how their gestures might be received, but to Richard they seemed more ironic than welcoming. 'Come on, children, our table's ready,' Judith said.

The waiter seated them in an alcove looking out on the river and brought them a dish of popcorn as Richard joined them. 'Did you see who it was at the bar?'

'I saw well enough, but I'm not about to say hello after what she did to Sarah.'

'You can't hold Jake responsible for that though, surely.'

'Can't we?' Judith squeezed a squeaky chunk of popcorn and raised it to her mouth. 'I don't believe anyone is that ignorant of what the person they married is up to.'

The return of the waiter with menus diverted her attention from him. The children ordered burgers while he and Judith went Creole. She raised her eyebrows when he asked for two bottles of Californian wine, then she gave him a smile so resigned he almost couldn't bear it or the thoughts it was threatening to rouse. 'I think I'll go and have a word,' he blurted.

'Can we come?' Olga said.

'I'm not stopping anyone,' Judith said. 'If you make it more obvious that I'm staying clear, so much the better.'

Richard's own motives were increasingly unclear to him. When he caught sight of the children in the mirror where bottles hung head down against their own reflections, they appeared to be following him into darkness. He turned hastily towards the Lees, and Jake said 'Giving the family a treat?'

'His wife is, you mean.'

'Sure, that's possible. Do you get this all the time, Richard, having to watch your mouth around women in case you say something incorrect?'

'Not that I'm aware of.'

'Got to be aware, old boy. God ain't gonna listen to no excuses like that when you get to her judgment seat, not from men, anyway.' Jake must have seen that some aspect of this theme was disturbing Richard, because he said 'So how's life with you?'

'As you see,' Richard had to say, 'we're making the most of it.'

'Only way to handle it. You'd agree with that, wouldn't you, Henrie my sweet?'

It became apparent to Richard that both the Lees were very drunk and that everything either of them said was designed to score a point against the other. 'If you guys want to talk,' Henrie said, making the first moves towards descending from her stool, 'I'll go and find Judith.'

'Ah, I think she's, um . . .' Richard was tempted to tell Henrie the bare truth, but then her feelings – everybody's feelings – seemed, unexpectedly, to matter. 'She's, er, a headache. Wants to be quiet for a few minutes. That's why we, er, though I wanted to say hello anyway.'

'Is that right, a headache?' Henrie hitched herself erect on the stool, using her elbows on the bar for leverage, and let her gaze stray to the mirror, where she appeared to see nothing that pleased her. 'Well then, I'll talk to your children, if that's okay with you.'

'That's what they're here for.'

'You're a lucky guy, I hope you know that,' Jake said, rattling the ice-cubes in his glass as though he was about to tip them out onto the bar for some kind of game. 'I guess there must be nothing like watching your children grow up.'

Though Richard could tell that was aimed at Henrie, it felt like a knife which Jake had driven deep into him. He heard Henrie say 'So how are you two using your vacation?'

Both children shrugged and looked vague, then Simon said 'Usually we go somewhere we can take all our clothes off.'

'Sounds like the kind of vacation that might appeal to my wife,' Jake said.

Olga regained Henrie's attention as she was preparing to glare at him. 'Only this year we can't because of the war.'

Henrie was having difficulty in focusing on her or on the answer. 'So you came to America instead,' she said as the paddle-boat glided by like a ghost in the mirror.

'I'd like to go to Disneyland,' Simon admitted.

'They should before they're too much older,' Henrie said, leaning one elbow on the bar so as to fix her gaze on Richard. He nodded and felt his mouth ache and saw in the mirror that he'd feigned a grin as Jake said 'Anyway, it looks as if you've figured out a way to make life work for you.'

Richard couldn't stop staring into the darkness that was his own eyes in the mirror. 'Maybe you can help us at the store,' Jake said.

That allowed Richard to turn to him and to the sunlight. 'Why, are you looking for an assistant? Because if you are—'

'Gee, no, I didn't mean that,' Jake said, visibly taken aback by Richard's burst of eagerness. 'I guess we can handle that side of the business between us, me and her. I meant advice on organising the financial side, seeing as you seem to have got yours together.'

For a moment Richard was convinced that the American was poking fun at him, then he succeeded in distancing himself sufficiently from his preoccupations to recall that Jake knew very little about him. He controlled his thoughts before the Vales' finances could begin their crazed dance in his head. 'You mightn't care for my solution,' he heard himself saying, which froze him until Olga interrupted her own conversation about Disneyland to say 'Dad, I think that's the waiter bringing our food.'

'Enjoy,' Henrie said, and demonstrated with the last inch of her cocktail.

'Stop by the store whenever you're passing. We're giving discount on requiems this month.'

'And tell Judith I hope she feels better soon,' Henrie said loudly enough to be heard in the restaurant.

'She will,' Richard said, and stumbled after the children, reaching the table as the waiter finished uncorking the wine. As soon as the waiter had moved away, Judith said 'Well, what did she have to say for herself?'

'She was talking to these two.'

'I hope it did her some good.'

'Maybe it will.' Richard wondered if he might have had some such purpose at the back of his mind. Being unsure confused him, but what did it matter now? He picked up his goblet-sized glass of red wine, and Judith said 'Here's to us.'

'Absolutely, to us.'

The children's glasses of Coca-Cola and the wineglasses met with a clink, and Judith added 'To better lives for us all. What's up, Rich?'

Simon giggled. 'Like Bugs Bunny.'

When his mother looked puzzled Olga had to explain, by which time Richard had manufactured an answer to the question. 'Can't it be the same one?'

'You know I meant that. We'll survive so long as we all stay together.'

'To staying together,' Richard said fiercely, taking so large a gulp of wine that it filled his mouth with a bitterness he had to wash

301

away with a drink of the white. As the warmth of the alcohol rose into his head, he and the family seemed to be surrounded by a benevolence suggesting that whatever might happen to them would be for the best. He had the impression that the light was intensifying to the point where he could taste it in the food, as though all his senses were illuminated from within. He could see it shining from inside Judith and the children, a sight which would have made him weep except that then he would have had to explain his tears. When he ordered another bottle of wine Judith looked resigned, and drank more than a quarter of it while the children lingered over ice-creams piled high. 'Well,' Richard asked them as they put down their spoons, 'was that the best meal ever?'

'Mm,' said Simon, and Olga agreed.

'Whatever we'll have to give up, it was worth it,' Judith said, and reached for Richard's hand. He gripped hers hard until she responded, and then he wondered how he would ever be able to let go. Eventually Simon said 'Can we go on the river now?'

'I don't know if they'll let us be in charge of a boat in our condition,' Judith said.

'But you promised. Didn't they, Olga? They said we'd have a vote, and I vote to go.'

Olga raised one hand as he did. 'We can go for a walk until Mum and Dad aren't so drunk.'

'I thought I was joking,' Judith said. 'Do they breathalyse you on the river, do you think?'

Richard let go of her hand in order to lift his. 'If these two row I can't see any problem.'

When Judith waved her hand to signify assent the waiter thought she was summoning him, and Richard asked for the bill. Its arrival was the cue for the rest of the family to head for the toilets. Richard opened his wallet and counted out notes while he attempted to decide whether to leave a substantial tip, since the waiter had certainly earned some appreciation, or none at all. He ought to keep the cash that was left over from paying the bill to spend on the family; it wasn't as though they would ever— As they reappeared he dumped the amount of the bill on the plate and dodged into the Gents, seeing himself skulking into the mirror and in due course out again. Flashing the waiter an apologetic grimace, he hurried out of the restaurant, past the bar where Jake and Henrie seemed to be trying to focus on each other's eyes, and followed the family down to the edge of the water.

His impression was that the sunlit ripples were simultaneously beckoning to him and recoiling from him. When he stepped off the narrow slippery dock into the rowing-boat, into which the rotund wheezing owner had already handed the rest of the family while dabbing his bald head with a spotted handkerchief, Richard felt the boat yield and sway beneath him. He fell next to Judith on the bench, and she steadied him as the man on the dock shoved the boat out. 'Are you feeling all right?' she said.

'As well as I need to.'

'I could go with them if you'd rather stay on the ground.'

He had a sudden vision of the boat capsizing as he watched helplessly from the bank, the family drowning while he ran back and forth like a rat in a trap. 'We ought to be together,' he pleaded.

'We're only talking about an hour, Rich, not a lot compared with the rest of our lives. I was just thinking of you, you know,' Judith said, touching his forehead. 'Have you been feeling a bit feverish today?'

'I'm feeling better than I have since I don't know when.'

'Well, you know best,' Judith said, settling herself more comfortably against him. 'In that case let's enjoy being Romans with slaves. You two can get in training for giving us rides when we're old and grey.'

That made Richard lean against her and close his eyes as the children steered the boat into the middle of the river. Sunlight on ripples kissed his eyelids, and he began to daydream that Judith and the children were doing so – that they had become the light, which was also the medium through which the boat was gliding. He kept his eyes shut and attempted to feel that he too had been transformed into light, or would be. The creaking of oars and the lapping of water slowed his thoughts to a stop, after which he knew nothing until Judith repeated some words close to his ear. 'Whuh?' he demanded.

'I was telling them our number's up.'

'Not yet,' he begged, struggling awake enough to realise that he'd heard the man on the dock shouting it across the water.

'Can't we pay for another hour?' Simon said at once.

'I wouldn't mind a walk,' Judith said, 'and I think your father might like one. You certainly slept, Rich. I hope you'll still be able to sleep tonight.'

'I will if you will,' he mumbled, thumbing his sticky eyelids open. At first all he could see was a blaze of light which was using the voices of his family to say several things he didn't understand; then he made out Simon and Olga in front of him, raising and extending their wings, from which flew feathers like shards of light. Then he saw that the wings were oars, and the boat grew uncomfortably solid beneath him, yet not quite solid enough. The eventual thud of the boat against the landing-stage seemed to lack conviction, as did the roughness of the owner's plump hand as it hauled Richard into the crowd on the river-bank. The sight of the family waiting for him under a gawky tree wearing a splint made him nervous, in danger of saying or doing something he wouldn't be able to pass off as innocent. Even if he remained silent, could he trust his face? He covered his mouth and held onto it as Simon asked 'What shall we do now?'

'It's Mum's and Dad's turn to choose.'

'Rich? I get the feeling you haven't done what you want to do.'

He exposed his mouth and turned hastily away from them. 'Go for a walk,' he said.

He was past the bridge by the weir before they caught up with him, and even when Judith took his hand he felt as if he was somewhere apart from them. For a while he had a sense of trying to walk himself awake, then it occurred to him that he was soothing himself into a state which allowed him not to think and in which he was able to believe he was avoiding thinking because that would aggravate the headache hovering in his skull. The river whose bank they were strolling grew increasingly deserted and featureless, and he was content not to speculate on what its placid unstoppable progress meant to him. One by one the luminous ripples went out, and he felt the chill of the water reaching for him.

He and the family were about halfway along an extensive curve of the river, between empty fields of unmoving grass, when Judith said 'Are we bound for anywhere in particular?'

He could no longer avoid realising that he was trying to postpone going home. 'You haven't had enough, have you?'

'It's lovely and peaceful, but I think these two may have. Remember they have to get up early tomorrow to meet their friends.'

'There'll always be something they have to get up for.'

'I certainly hope so.'

He hadn't meant what she assumed – he'd been talking far too carelessly to himself. He felt in grave danger of being aware of too much too soon. 'Shall we find somewhere we can have a drink by the river?'

'All right then, a last drink.'

Richard felt as though he'd lurched awake at the worst hour of the night. Some small creature emerged from a field onto the path ahead, then darted back through the hedge. He would have pointed it out except that he believed it was fleeing in terror of him alone. He stared along the darkening river until Judith said 'Shall we look for one on the way back?'

'Go ahead,' he told her, unable to turn until they had their backs to him. As he matched his pace to theirs he found himself struggling to understand whether he was herding them home or protecting them from the darkness he sensed gathering behind them. Now that they were retracing their walk it seemed to have been dismayingly pointless, especially when the sight of the children plodding onwards brought to mind activities they would have enjoyed more. 'I'm sorry,' he said.

He thought he'd kept his voice low, but the three of them looked back. 'What on earth for, Rich?' Judith said.

'Dragging you all out here.'

'Don't talk daft. We wouldn't have come if we hadn't wanted to, would we, you two?'

'No.'

'Suppose not,' Simon said, so dutifully that Judith and his sister laughed until he had to grin.

'Now stop looking as if it's the end of the world,' Judith bade Richard. 'You're only feeling the way you're feeling because you've had a lot to drink. Don't worry, we'll have another so long as you promise not to get maudlin. That's the last thing we need right now.'

Richard succeeded in concealing most of the shiver which his effort and the chill of the approaching darkness sent through him. 'I promise.'

By the time they returned as far as the weir, the lamps beside the river were lit. Couples were strolling under thin trees whose leaves were coated with light. As the Vales passed a silent bandstand Richard remembered vaulting onto it and pulling Judith after him and threatening to sing at the top of his unmusical voice unless she got engaged to him. She must be remembering too, because she squeezed his hand as they headed for the riverside pub where they had celebrated their engagement once he'd slipped a rubber band onto her finger for her to wear until they chose the ring.

She had a gin and tonic again while Richard bought himself twice as much whisky as then, drinking half of it before manoeuvring the tray through the crowd inside the pub. At the table outside there seemed to be little to do except drink and gaze at the reflections of the lamps, which were coming to resemble flowers hanging head down in the water, dead yet luminous. When Judith had sipped most of her drink he said 'Another?'

'I think we'd better move. I see someone not too far from nodding off.'

'No I'm not,' Simon protested, and when Olga laughed at him, gave the table a kick that made the glasses jump.

'I was talking about both of you. Come along now and no arguments, or you won't be going anywhere tomorrow.'

As she moved away from the table Richard drained the remains of her gin. That and the whisky felt capable of numbing his thoughts for a while. Halfway up the passage which led from the river-bank to the nearest main road he glanced back at the pub, but a dark curve of the passage had extinguished its lights. The family was waiting for him at the top, beside the ruins of a church. All at once he didn't think he would be able to face the trudge home, not least because it was likely to sober him up. 'Who's for a taxi?'

'I think we've spent enough for one day, don't you?' When the children began to complain, Judith relented. 'I expect my feet are aching as much as anyone's. I wouldn't mind taking them to bed.'

'Not just your feet, I hope.'

'We'll have to see,' Judith told him as the children exchanged amused glances. 'Meanwhile, what's this I see coming for us?'

Richard looked over his shoulder and saw the blackness between two streetlamps swelling towards the family as though the night was squeezing itself solid. The light from the foremost streetlamp washed silently over the roof, and he identified the blackness as a car, which seemed to take more time than it should to emerge into the light, as though the vehicle itself was longer than a taxi. That was only because it was slowing now that Judith had hailed it, but the impression meant more to him. He watched the beacon above the windscreen go out, and the family climbing into the back seat, and the driver's heavy pear-shaped face gazing at him over the meter. 'Where to?' the man said around the stem of the dead pipe in his mouth.

Richard couldn't remember. He was about to panic when it occurred to him that as long as he couldn't the family would be safe. He might tell the driver just to keep driving, and once their money ran out—Then Judith gave the address, and the driver took hold of the wheel. 'Is he joining you?' he enquired, the pipe-stem clicking between his teeth.

Was Richard being given a last chance to reconsider? He

306

imagined Judith discovering in the midst of her and the children's grief that he had left them nothing but debts, that even if their grief caused Doug Singleton's firm to relent, their day out had left their bank account raw red; that Computer Explosion was full of merchandise which the manufacturers refused to buy back but which had to be moved out of the dusty shop by the end of the month . . . He would be taking a coward's way out, he decided anew, and the thought put him back on course. 'We're together,' he said, and pulled the door shut behind him.

He had to sit with his back to the driver. Every time the taxi passed beneath a streetlamp, Judith's and the children's faces glowed like masks in a ghost train. Their eyes lit up and were immediately extinguished, and another light raced away behind them down a road deadened by the night. Now Simon's eyes were no more than glinting slits, and the next lamp showed that his eyelids had abandoned the effort. As the taxi swung off the main road into the darker side streets, Richard saw him almost waken and attempt to blink at the dimness before subsiding into sleep. The sight brought him close to panic again, so that when the taxi turned along their street he found he couldn't speak. He saw their unlit house sail past the family as though the street had become a dark river, and no longer wanted to speak. But Judith said 'This is it. Can you stop, please?'

The sudden halt threw Richard forward. As he flung out his arms he felt that he was gathering the family to him or trying to prevent their leaving the vehicle. His face almost collided with Judith's, and she gave him a quick secret smile which was a promise. 'All right?' the driver said.

'As we'll ever be,' Richard heard his own voice say, and shoved himself back so that the family could get away from him. He watched them trudge like sleepwalkers towards the dead house, and it wasn't until he saw Judith unlock the slab of darkness and switch on the light in the hall that he felt compelled to leave the refuge of the taxi. He peered at the digits on the impatient meter and dug out the contents of his pocket, and discovered that the notes and coins had ceased to mean anything to him. 'Is this enough?' he said, dumping the money in the driver's hand.

The driver removed the pipe from his mouth and poked at the cash with the stem. After a few seconds he asked with some reluctance 'Are you sure you want to tip me all this?'

'You came when we needed you. Take it with you, it's no use to me.'

'It's very decent of you, I must say.' The driver glanced past him at the increasingly lit house. Richard was afraid he might insist on consulting Judith about the amount or on knowing Richard's motives, but then the driver said 'I'll remember you.'

'That's all any of us can ask for.'

'I mean, whenever you need a cab just call this number and ask for Malcolm.'

'I appreciate that,' Richard said, and stood with the card in his hand while the taxi swung towards the opposite pavement and back again before speeding away to the main road. Once it was out of sight he posted the card down the nearest kerbside drain and made for the house. It seemed to him that by accepting all his cash the driver had left him nowhere else to go, no other plan. He stepped into the house, which met him with the faint smell that always reminded him of some herb he couldn't put a name to. He was gazing at the dark street which looked distant and unfamiliar and irrelevant to him when he heard Judith say 'Don't start that now. You'll have plenty of time next week.'

He pulled the door shut and made himself let go of the latch and hurried into the main room. 'What's the trouble?'

'None, I hope.'

She was in the front part of the room, which was crowded with a fat flowered suite and a hi-fi system and a television capped with a videorecorder, all of which had seen better years. Beyond the sliding doors with which David Owain had replaced a wall, the children were huddled rebelliously around the computer next to the mismatched dining suite. 'We were going to start our tournament,' Olga said.

'If you start it now you won't be able to sleep when you go to bed. That's right, isn't it, Rich?'

'I'm a, I'm afraid so.'

'I think we could all do with as early a night as we can manage. Who's for hot chocolate?'

'I'll make it. I'm just going upstairs first,' Richard said, and hurried to the main bedroom, switching on all the lights he could reach, though even then the house seemed dimmer than it ought to be. He felt he was fleeing Judith's and the children's eagerness to have a bedtime drink – at least, he did until he switched on the bedroom light and saw there was nowhere to flee, no more time to waste. He slid open the door on his side of the unstable Scandinavian wardrobe and hung up his jacket with a clash of distorted coat-hangers, and slid the mirror in front of them again, confronting himself with himself. He could see nothing in his eyes, nobody at all. He turned away and went to the head of the bed.

There was barely enough room on either side of it for a small table. Beside the Ruth Rendell paperback with its spine broken by a bookmark on Judith's, and on his otherwise empty unmatching table, stood an opaque bottle of sleeping tablets. He stared at his bottle, and when he discovered that staring changed nothing he picked it up and pressed hard on the cap to unscrew it, reflecting as he did so that there was no longer any reason for the container to be childproof. He emptied the bottle, which was almost full, into the pocket where the money had been, then he replaced the cap and stood the bottle on his table. There was just room in his pocket for Judith's tablets as well. He screwed the cap down and set the bottle by the paperback, and was heading for the stairs when he saw that before she fell asleep Judith would realise what he'd done.

The prospect froze him, and he couldn't think. Now that he'd arrived at the moment he was going to fail. He stared at the empty bottles, almost desperate enough to pray for inspiration. He dug his hands into his pockets and felt the tablets crawling insect-like around his fingers, and at once he knew what to do. Catching two tablets between finger and thumb, he laid them on top of the paperback. He was on his way to the door again when he realised his mistake and ran back to leave a pair of tablets next to his side of the bed. He couldn't tell if he was really making mistakes or secretly trying to delay himself, and so how could he be certain that there weren't any more errors lying in wait for him? If he lingered until he was certain, he thought he would never move. He sent himself out of the room, one hand flat on his pocket to muffle the rattling, and ran down to the kitchen. Judith was there, standing in front of the cooker.

She turned away from the large saucepan to place two empty milk-bottles on the windowsill. If he didn't manage to speak before she looked at him she would know something was wrong. He saw himself beyond her, waiting behind her in the night. 'I said I'd do it,' he blurted. 'You go and sit down and I'll bring them.'

'I was just putting the milk on. Don't you want me with you?'

'Of course I do, only . . .' Richard stuffed his hands into his pockets to keep them still, and felt the tablets shifting restlessly. 'Only I thought you wanted to sit down after all that walking.'

'I can always sit in here.' Judith took four mugs two at a time from the draining-board and stood them on the table, then she considered the working surfaces where she often perched. 'I suppose my feet could do with a chair,' she admitted, sounding less than entirely convinced, and wandered into the hall.

When he heard her with the children Richard closed his hand around as many tablets as he could grasp. Then he was at the saucepan, and there was a moment when he hadn't tipped the tablets into the milk, and then a moment when he had. He gathered the last few tablets from his pocket and dropped them into the saucepan in case they made a difference. He found a spoon and stirred the milk fiercely, crushing the tablets and feeling as though he was killing a nest of insects beneath the surface of the milk, until the heat of the saucepan reached through the spoon to sting his hand, then he turned down the heat and grabbed a tin of drinking chocolate from the cupboard above the sink and dug a thumbnail under the lid to prise it off. As he spooned chocolate into the mugs he saw them more vividly than he could recall ever having seen them: Judith's bearing two cartoon snakes which appeared to be trying to glimpse each other around the mug, Simon's which had been part of a promotion for a computer game and which showed robots pursuing an endless chase, Olga's that was inscribed 'Save Our World', his own which Simon had bought him for his birthday years ago, its rim so chipped by now that he had to drink out of the wrong side, and which he would have unobtrusively lost except that its motto was 'World's Greatest Dad'. He turned away from them as the milk started to bubble like the contents of a cauldron. He turned off the gas and took hold of the handle of the saucepan, only to find that it felt as if he'd seized the bar of an electric fire which hadn't long ceased being red. He closed his other hand around his fist to steady his grip and poured the milk into the mugs, and gazed at the white scum which was all that was left in the saucepan. He dropped the pan with a clang into the sink, and pressed his tongue against his reddened palm until that aggravated the stinging. He turned on the tap with his other hand and filled the saucepan with water, in case Judith might wonder why he'd neglected to do so, then he arranged the mugs on a tray. The pain in his hand had stabilised enough for him to be capable of lifting the tray, which he carried into the front room.

Simon was leafing aimlessly through a computer magazine. Olga had given up reading a book, instead erecting it like a tent on her lap, and was humming a song to herself, unaware that her mother was watching her. It was a moment Richard would have liked to prolong, but as soon as he stepped through the doorway Judith said 'Why don't you two take your drinks up to bed? I'm going to.'

'Will you tell us a story?'

'You said you would,' Simon added.

'Not tonight. Maybe soon. I don't know about anyone else, but I'm too tired to think. Are you going to stand there, Rich, or are you giving us our bedtime drinks?'

Richard moved as though he'd been pushed from behind, and knew he was about to drop the tray, not least because its edge was scraping his injured palm. He fell to his knees in the midst of his family and let the tray down, and Judith seized it just in time to prevent most of the contents of the mugs from spilling. 'What on earth have you done to your hand?' she cried.

'Nothing worth mentioning. Soon I won't notice it.'

'You should have let me make the drinks. You look even more exhausted than the rest of us. I think it had better be straight up to bed for everyone. We'll all feel more ourselves tomorrow.'

She rose with a sigh like someone much older and went to the kitchen for a roll of paper towels with which to dab the bottoms of the mugs as they were removed from the tray. 'Just do your teeth and then I should get into bed,' she told the children as they claimed their mugs and each took a tentative sip. 'Hold on, Rich, before you drip everywhere. Do you want some of mine?'

'I've plenty.' More of his hot chocolate than of anyone else's had ended up on the tray, but the idea that Judith might drink less than himself dismayed him almost as much as the spectacle of the children beginning to drink before he did. He gulped a mouthful, which was so hot he couldn't taste it, and barely managed to hold it in his mouth until it was cool enough to swallow. He seemed to be watching himself as well as the rest of the family swallowing, all of them taking the only course left to them. He saw Judith mop her mug and stand it on the mantelpiece, and drop the wad of paper towels in the metal bin inside the wicker basket by the television, and carry out the wet tray. Simon risked a larger sip of his drink, and Olga said 'Will you come and say goodnight in a few minutes, Dad?'

'Of course I will. Don't I always?' Richard found himself scrutinising their faces, which appeared only as tired as they had when he'd entered the room. 'I'll just wait for your mother,' he said.

Once they were out of the room he topped up Judith's drink from his. He'd experienced a sudden terrible vision of her wakening in the lonely dark. He listened to the children plodding up the stairs, and it seemed to him that they might never reach the

311

top, though he couldn't tell whether they or his perceptions were slowing down. At last he heard their bedroom doors opening, Olga saying 'Bags the bathroom first' and Simon responding with a mumble that suggested he was too exhausted to argue, and then Judith came back. She picked up her mug and took a sip, and another, and grimaced. 'Does it taste all right to you?'

Richard gulped again. 'I don't notice anything,' he said, tasting only the scalded roof of his mouth.

'Don't you think the milk's going off?'

'It might be. It's drinkable though, isn't it?'

Judith sniffed at the steam rising from her mug. 'Just about, maybe.'

'Have mine if you like,' Richard said in desperation, 'and I'll finish yours.'

'It isn't the mug, it's the drink. You didn't put anything different in mine, did you?'

'No, how could I? I mean, what could I have?'

'I don't know. Maybe you scraped the tin too hard. I certainly won't be recommending this brand. You shouldn't have insisted on trying it. Oh, Rich,' she said with a laugh, 'don't look so anxious. If you can finish it I expect I can. Are you coming up now?'

'Yes, let's go up.' His panic when he'd thought she was going to leave her drink had blotted out everything else, but now he realised that he couldn't hear the children. When had he last heard them move? 'Are you two out of the bathroom yet?' he called, too shrilly.

'I am,' Olga responded.

'I nearly am,' said Simon from his bedroom, and ran across the landing. Richard heard him stumble, and his own heartbeat stumbled too. As he followed Judith out of the room he turned off the light, and felt as though the darkness had wiped out part of the house. Judith was starting up the stairs when she switched the mug to her left hand and grabbed the banister with her right, and he lurched after her to steady her, almost spilling the rest of his drink. 'Are you feeling—' he said, and couldn't go on.

'Just overtired. I'll be fine once I sleep.'

'We all will,' Richard said like a prayer, and saw Simon grope his way around the bathroom door, foaming at the mouth. The sight made him want to cry out and run, though he didn't know if he would run to Simon or away, until Judith said 'Wait, Simon. You've got toothpaste all down your chin.'

'Sorry,' Simon mumbled, rubbing his chin with one bare arm.

'Come here. Look at you,' Judith said, reaching behind her to her larger buttock, which became proportioned as she pulled a handkerchief out of the back pocket of her jeans to wipe Simon's face. 'I wouldn't call that hair brushed. Well, leave it for the morning now. Did you drink your drink?'

'Yes,' Simon said, and grimaced.

'I haven't,' Olga said beyond her door. 'I heard you saying it tasted off.'

'Just leave it if you don't want it,' Judith said.

Richard sidled past her and slipped into Olga's room. She was in bed, her knees propping up her daintily flowered quilt, a different book half-closed around one finger. 'I think it tastes all right,' he said, swallowing a mouthful of his own drink.

Olga wrinkled her nose, but he kept his face neutral, although now he could detect a faint stale taste that reminded him of some previous occasion. He had no time to remember. 'Try it again for me,' he made himself say. 'We don't want you waking in the night.'

'What if it makes me sick?'

'It won't. How could it?' Richard said, appalled by the possibility. 'I thought chocolate was your favourite nightcap.'

'It was when I was little. You and Mummy never ask me if it still is.'

'Well, we'll—' He was afraid that he couldn't go on. He gulped from his mug and succeeded in saying 'If you drink that up now, next time we'll get whatever your favourite is.'

She gave a teenage sigh and looked ready to argue, then tiredness got the better of her. Dropping her book on the narrow strip of carpet between the bed and the plasterboard wall that David Owain had constructed to give her and Simon separate rooms, she waved her hand about in search of the mug. She was going to knock it over, Richard thought; even when she found it her grip on the handle was precariously loose. He darted forward and lifted the mug for her. 'Thanks,' she said, and had a token sip.

'It isn't bad, now is it?'

'It tastes funny.'

'Then laugh.'

She made a face instead and took almost a mouthful. He thought she was considering returning it to the mug, but after a few moments she swallowed it. 'Night,' she said.

'Don't I get a kiss?' When she raised her face, the mug beginning to sway unnoticed in her hand, Richard said 'Finish your drink first, or you'll be falling asleep.'

She looked prepared to make him wait, and his legs no longer felt too firm. Even when he pretended to drain his mug she didn't respond. 'Careful,' he blurted as hers tilted further. He saw her focus on it and grab it with her other hand and tip it into her mouth. She didn't lower it until it was empty, though she screwed up her face. 'Night,' she repeated.

He felt she didn't want him in the room. She put down her mug with a dull clunk and then appeared to have to remind herself to let go of the handle before lowering her head onto the pillow. Richard was beginning to experience a dullness which he struggled to fight off. As he stooped to kiss her forehead, the dividing wall and its display of her paintings, some of them years old, seemed to topple towards him. His lips touched her warm dry smooth skin, and he imagined the room without the wall or the paintings or her. 'I'll send Mummy in to see you,' he said unevenly, and turned away so fast that her paintings became a blur of colours. He was about to look back at her from the landing when Judith emerged from Simon's room, easing the door shut behind her. 'Don't go disturbing him. He's just about asleep.'

'I only want—' Richard only wanted to say a goodnight that would be a goodbye, and having missed his chance distressed him so much that he could hardly speak. 'Can't I give him a kiss?'

'I shouldn't think he'll notice,' Judith said, and glanced into Richard's eyes as she headed for Olga's room. 'Go on if you must. If he doesn't notice I don't suppose it can matter.'

Richard pushed the door open less quietly than she would have liked. Whereas Olga's side of the halved room was strewn with clothes and books and cosmetics containers which she insisted on keeping even when they were empty, Simon's collection of computer magazines and old undefeated conkers on strings and toy guns, most of which had ceased to work, was tidy enough for Richard to be able to walk along either side of the bed. Simon was lying with his left cheek buried in the pillow, his hair sticking up like a tuft of grass which a lawnmower had failed to tame, his left hand splayed on the pillow with the thumb an inch or two short of his mouth. He didn't move when his father entered the room or even when Richard walked slowly towards him, deliberately vibrating the floor and bumping into the bed. Richard grabbed the headboard, uncertain whether he was supporting himself or intending to shake it so as to rouse some sign of life. Then Simon's lips parted and closed, having released an inaudible breath, and a few seconds later they did so again, allowing Richard to breathe.

He leaned down gradually, feeling in danger of overbalancing onto the bed, and brought his lips close to the boy's ear. 'Simon?'

'Mm.'

'Can you hear me?'

'Mm.'

The sound was too drowsy to qualify as a protest or to be expressing anything else. 'Can you, Simon?' Richard pleaded.

'What?'

'Hear me.'

'Mm.'

Richard told himself that Simon's single word, resentful though it had been, was enough. 'Sweet dreams,' he murmured.

'Mm.'

Richard kissed the boy's forehead, which felt utterly calm. He was straightening up when Simon's paintings on the wall ahead of him appeared to blaze with colour, to become the brightest things in the world, and he felt as if Simon was in them on his way to somewhere else. He kept his eyes on Simon while he backed towards the landing, and it seemed to him that the boy had started to glow with a light Richard had never seen before. He switched off the light-bulb and inched the door closed, and when it had shut his son away from him he moved to Olga's door. 'Sweet dreams,' he said through it.

Olga just about responded. 'Dree' was the only syllable he recognised, and he knew she was practically asleep. Though he would have liked to see her and her pictures beginning to shine, he didn't need to. He turned off the light above the landing and let himself into his and Judith's room.

Judith was sitting up in bed, her arms folded across her breasts, her head leaning against the plush headboard. She still bore her habitual expression of sleepy amusement, which struck him as more meaningful than usual, especially when it fastened on him. 'What's—' he said, and felt it best to stop.

'Are you anxious to put me to sleep, Rich?'

He felt his hand raise his mug to his lips as if to hide them. He drained the chocolate, which was cold and tasted stale and bitter, and realised what she was referring to. 'The pills, you mean? I thought as long as I was putting mine out ready for the night I'd get yours out as well.'

'I was only teasing, you know. Thanks, but I don't think I need any tonight,' Judith said, and groped for the bottle to put the tablets in.

Richard stumbled forward and managed to catch her hand just before her fingers would have found the bottle. 'I know what you need,' he said indistinctly.

'I think I'm too tired, Rich. Shall we save it for the morning? Do you mind?' When he shook his head, whose contents seemed to continue moving after he stopped, she said 'Just hold me.'

He would have to let go of her hand in order to undress. 'Shall we leave the tablets out in case we wake in the night?' he made himself finish saying.

'If you want, but I know I won't need them.'

He knew that too. He pulled off his clothes and hung them over the back of his bedside chair with a neatness which he couldn't justify to himself, especially since it might give Judith time to fall asleep before he could join her. But she was still propped against the headboard with her eyes open, and when he approached the bed her gaze shifted to greet him. She slid down the bed as he climbed under the quilt. He dug one elbow into the pillow to support himself, though it felt as though the support was about to collapse, and touched her tongue with his in the midst of a long kiss. 'Sweet dreams,' he said, and tugged the light-cord, and put an arm around her.

'Sweet dreams.' She reached one hand back and held his penis gently, and he had never felt so close to her. His penis and her hand seemed almost to have merged. In a very few minutes he couldn't distinguish his breathing from hers. He saw them and the children naked in a garden so extensive he believed it might never end, and in the moment before he ceased to be aware of breathing he thought he and Judith were about to share that dream.

# Twenty-eight

It was Sunday afternoon when David found the photograph. He and Joelle had wandered through the remains of Saturday in a state where their emotions seemed to be just out of reach. They'd gone to bed early but had been unable to make love, not least because David had put Angie Singleton firmly out of his mind, although having to do so had caused him to feel as guilty as letting her in. He'd stroked Joelle's stomach, which usually calmed her when she needed calming, while she'd used his other arm as an extra pillow, but she had been less calm than inert. 'What's happening to us?' was one of the very few things she'd said before falling into an uneasy slumber, and it had kept David awake for an hour or more without his even being able to grasp the question. Had she meant their relationship or some external influence? The distinction had been as vague in his mind as the random phrases and fragments of memory which had eventually led him to sleep.

On Sunday morning he and Joelle stayed in bed late, again failing to make love. He was starting to fear that she might grow suspicious, of what he imagined must be his preoccupied expression if not of his strenuous attempts to prove his love for her, when she said 'Give it time, David. Maybe you don't think you know me any more.'

'I know you better, that's all, and I haven't stopped loving what I know. Maybe it's the other way round.'

'Which way is that?'

'Maybe you feel there are things you don't know about me.'

'Should I?'

He glimpsed a hint of the old seductiveness and willingness to experiment in her eyes, and then it was gone, leaving him even less sure how to respond. 'It's all right, you needn't invent any-thing this very minute,' she said, and laid her cheek against his shoulder. 'I expect we'll be able to come up with a few surprises to keep each other going if you don't find you've had enough of me.'

317

'Never,' David said, feeling guiltier than ever. He stroked her face and listened to bells announcing the beginning or end of a church service. After a while he said 'What would you like to do today?'

'What are you offering?'

'We could go for a drive if you like.'

'Or visit someone we haven't seen for a while.'

'Anyone in mind?'

'How about the Vales? They're always fun to be with, especially Richard.'

'When he doesn't go over the top, you mean.'

'On second thoughts, they can look after one another. I wouldn't mind finding out how Bill Messenger is getting on.'

'Best to let him know we're coming, would you say?'

'You can while I have a shower.'

David found he viewed the task without much enthusiasm. Once Joelle had padded to the bathroom he put on the black dressing-gown they shared, and let himself be diverted into making coffee. He took Joelle a mug and left it for the veiled blur of flesh she'd become in the steamy bathroom. 'Is it late enough to call him yet, do you think?' he said.

'I will if it bothers you.'

'Don't worry, I will. I'll do it right now.'

David fetched his mug from the kitchen and wandered along the hall, trying to understand why he felt he was being forced to acknowledge some kind of responsibility for Bill's condition. Perhaps he was feeling so guilty that the feeling attached itself to anything it could relate to, but the explanation didn't satisfy him. He sat on the stairs with the phone on his lap and fed himself another gulp of coffee before dialling the actor's number. The phone at the other end rang seven pairs of times, and he was about to give up when the sound was terminated by an outburst of rattling followed by a creak of plastic. 'This is the answering machine of Bill Messenger,' a flattened version of Bill's voice announced.

'Bill? This is David Owain. Are you there?'

'This is the answering machine of Bill Messenger.'

'It's you, isn't it, Bill? You rather than a machine. Jo and I were wondering if you were seeing people yet.'

'If you wish to leave a message, please speak.'

'If I do, will you call me back? You can't blame us for worrying about you. We were thinking of coming round to see how you were.'

'Mr Messenger does not wish to be visited at present.'

'Then can we talk at least? You've a good routine there, Bill, but I'm finding it a bit unsettling, to tell you the truth.'

'Please continue with your message.'

'What's wrong, Bill? Is there something that's stopping you talking to me? I don't mean to presume, but surely you don't need to keep this up. If you're doing it for me, it's impressive but I've had enough.'

David heard Bill's phone creak and rattle, and thought the actor was about to cut him off. Then Joelle emerged from the bathroom, naked and towelled pink. 'Would you rather speak to Jo? She's here.'

'There is no limit to the length of your message.'

Joelle halted at the top of the stairs. 'What's Bill saying?'

'I wish you'd speak to him in case that makes a difference. He's pretending to be a recording, only it's as if he can't stop.'

A single drop of bathwater ran down from her navel and wound its way through her bush, and glittered for a moment between her legs before falling to the carpet with a tiny plop. 'You don't want me to talk to him while I'm like this, do you?'

'Why not like that? He isn't seeing anyone.'

She gave David a look halfway between reproachful and amused, and he said into the receiver 'She's on her way. She'd very much like to have a conversation with you, Bill.'

'Mr Messenger is only able to converse in this fashion at this time.'

Joelle nestled against David and held the receiver so that he could hear Bill's voice. 'Bill? It's Joelle. How are you?'

'Mr Messenger is attempting to recuperate.'

'I'm glad to hear it, but how does talking like that help?'

'Mr Messenger . . .' There was a pause troubled by restless static, and David thought she'd managed to break through Bill's defence. Then Bill said 'This is the only way Mr Messenger is able to tell the truth.'

'How, by acting like a machine?' Joelle demanded.

'Mr Messenger has found that identifying with a role appears to satisfy his need to lie.'

'That's your job, but aren't you taking it too far? What happens if we come to see you? You don't carry on like this when you're with people, do you?'

'Mr Messenger is unable to receive visitors at present.'

Joelle swung the receiver away from her face as though to slam it down, but then she brought it back. 'Will you call us and let us know when you're receiving?'

This time the pause was longer, and David hoped she'd got the better of Bill. Eventually the actor said 'If Mr Messenger were to call it would be impossible to identify—'

'Don't be silly. We'd know it was you. We're your friends.'

Bill was silent, and she clutched her forehead. 'I'm sorry, Bill. What were you going to say?'

'Mr Messenger may welcome further such calls in the future.'

Joelle glanced at David to see if that satisfied him, and he could only shrug. 'You're getting out though, aren't you, Bill?' she insisted. 'You're keeping yourself fed?'

'Mr Messenger has arranged a supply of provisions.'

David sensed that she'd had enough but didn't know how to finish. When he reached for the phone she gave it to him. 'Goodbye for the moment then, Bill,' he said. 'Make sure you look after yourself.'

'Goodbye, Bill,' Joelle said in the tone of a comment to herself.

They heard a click like the switching off of a machine, then the dialling tone. Joelle took the receiver and dropped it on its cradle and sat on David's lap, pulling some of the dressing-gown around her. 'How long has he been like that, for God's sake? How long is he going to be?'

'More to the point, what's made him that way?'

'What do you think has?'

'I can't tell you,' David said, feeling unexpectedly and disconcertingly accused. 'Better leave the diagnosis to someone who can deal with that sort of condition.'

'How can they if Bill won't see anyone?'

'He'll have to sooner or later. We aren't his only friends, you know, and certainly not his oldest and closest. We can't be responsible for everyone we know.'

No sooner were the words out of his mouth than David saw they could be taken to refer to the Pinnocks' toddler. He hugged Joelle and stroked her warm flat stomach, and she leaned her head back to brush her cheek against his and then, having captured his hand, moved it up to her breasts. The moment her fingertips touched his penis it rose to the bait, and he felt her groin mouth on his lap. As she raised herself, clasping his hands to her breasts, his penis rose with her. She turned deftly and straddled him, and was gazing into his eyes as she grasped his penis and lowered herself onto it when it began to fail.

It mustn't, not now. He tried to be conscious that they were making love on the stairs for the first time, but although that had helped to begin with, it no longer did. As Joelle pushed him up into herself he lifted his hips, but felt the tip of his penis falling short of any goal. All he seemed able to do was channel his anger, of which he discovered he had quite a store, into his penis, as long as he wasn't directing it at Joelle. 'Take this for your father,' he heard himself telling Angie Singleton to her bottom, so fervently that for a moment he was afraid he'd spoken aloud. He pressed his tongue against Joelle's as he reared up inside her and she began to ride him and pump him. Somehow the antics of their tongues and the activity at his groin got mixed up with Angie's struggles across his lap, and when he came like a fountain he didn't know for several seconds where he was. At least his gasps were in time with Joelle's. He kept his cheek against hers until his penis sagged out of her, then he raised his head. 'What are you thinking?' she asked.

'Nothing worth mentioning,' David said, and even more hastily 'Except, I mean, I love you.'

'Then I wish it made you look happier.'

'Like this, you mean?'

'Like you used to.'

'Don't I ever still?'

'I expect so, but I don't remember when. If it's something about me—'

'It isn't, and that shows you're feeling like I'm feeling. I read somewhere once that we're supposed to be sad after sex.'

'Just us?'

'Not likely,' David said, unsure how much she'd meant it as a joke. 'Every creature in the world.'

'God help any that are alone and feeling anything like this.'

David experienced a surge of guilt which felt capable of making him say too much. 'It's that bad?'

'It's as bad as I let it be.' She took hold of his hands in order to stand up. 'Maybe it means it's time for breakfast, and you've earned a large one if that's what you want.'

'Shall I stay with you?'

'No, you have your shower and let me be alone and think.'

Given what she'd said about being alone he wasn't sure that was advisable, except that she had presumably meant a solitariness more profound than this. He gave her the dressing-gown and made for the shower, only to feel as if he was avoiding talking to her or was trying to wash away the secret he'd kept from her, though that would take more than all the water in the world. He plunged his face into the onslaught and spat out a mouthful, which seemed to taste staler than even hot water usually did. He ducked his head and imagined the shock of being baptised, and wondered if he ever had been, which set him thinking of babies, not a topic he welcomed just now. In any case, the idea of the newborn having to be cleansed of a sin which they hadn't committed, in case they died with the guilt of it on their souls, struck him as primitive in the extreme. Wasn't there some even more superstitious and probably more ancient ritual to do with sin? He was going over himself yet again with the shower, and thinking with no sense of urgency that the answer must be buried somewhere in his mind, when Joelle called 'It's ready when you are.'

He could scarcely believe that his musing had kept him so long in the bathroom. 'I wouldn't call that a breakfast,' he said to Joelle as he uncorked the bottle of sparkling wine she'd placed in the cooler on the table. 'It's more like a brunch.'

'It must be the American influence.' She helped herself from the various platters and chewed a few mouthfuls, each one more slowly. He sensed that she was going to get up before she did so. 'You carry on,' she said. 'I just want to make a call.'

David guessed where she was calling, and overhearing her side of the conversation left him ready to be positive when she came back. 'Sarah isn't seeing anyone except Terry and her parents,' she complained.

'She must know what she needs, or the hospital will.'

'Are you trying to tell me she needs Terry after what he did?'

'Who knows what people need? I'm not defending him, you understand.'

'You better hadn't be,' Joelle said, though he could tell the retort was automatic. 'But Bill's seeing nobody, and Sarah almost isn't. What's happened to them?'

'Hardly the same thing.' When Joelle looked unconvinced – all the more stubbornly because, it was clear, she didn't know why – he said 'Never mind, there are still lots of people who'll see us.'

'I'm not feeling outcast, David. That's not the point at all.'

'How are you feeling, Jo?'

'Oh, David, don't tell me you have to ask.'

More than simply reviving his guilt, that multiplied it, and he could only look chastened and understanding and shove food into his mouth. They had finished the meal and cleared up and were sipping the last of the wine, not having said anything else, when a black car drew up outside the house.

The young couple were either just married or shortly to be, judging by the way they held hands as soon as they emerged from the car. Joelle watched, tying the cord of the dressing-gown tighter about herself, while they crossed the road and rang the doorbell opposite. After a brief conversation with Mary Crantry they returned, looking disappointed, and drove off. Mary came to her gate and stood gazing past the For Sale sign, then she caught sight of Joelle, who raised one hand impulsively. 'I'm going to speak to her.'

'Do you want me along?'

'Up to you, David. I can't tell you what to do.'

He left the front door open as he stepped into the sunlight that was laden with scents and birdsong and a low ragged chorus of mowers. By the time he reached the gate Joelle was across the road, and Mary was holding her hands stiffly by her sides, fingertips pointing downwards, like an actress restraining a tendency to gesture. She seemed to be withholding all expression from her face. 'Is it sold?' Joelle said.

'Why, are you wondering when you'll see the last of me?'

'No, we just saw you turning some people away.'

'Oh, I thought you might be keen for me to move.'

'Why should you think any such thing?'

'Well, not from anything you've said.'

Mary gave her a long look which David would have described as entirely blank but which Joelle was apparently able to read, because she said 'I'm sorry we left you alone for so long. We ought to have come over to see how you were.'

'I had to get used to being alone.'

'Well, you don't need to put up with it any more as far as we're concerned, does she, David?'

'Absolutely,' he said, though the reversal was happening rather fast for him.

'So how is the house going, Mary?'

'It was nearly sold, but then the buyer let me down. I've been trying to decide how I felt about that. I've been thinking of taking it off the market, to be truthful.'

'No need to sound so defensive about it, has she, David?'

'None at all.'

'It's kind of you both to say so, and I don't think the neighbours on either side mind me staying.'

'I'm sure they won't if this is where you feel at home.'

'I do. I've found I do. At first I didn't think I could bear to live here after . . .' Mary retreated a couple of steps, and David thought she was about to take refuge in the house, but then she controlled herself. 'Will you come in for a drink? I wouldn't mind talking.'

'I'll come. How about you, David?'

'Another time if that's all right with you, Mary. I'd better find out what my next job is going to be.'

This was true, but he also sensed that the women, Mary in particular, would prefer to be without him. He went back to the house and up to the spare bedroom, which was both a guest room and as much of an office as he and Joelle required. He took the diary out of the lightweight metal desk that was tucked into one corner of the large room and went downstairs to phone the pencilled numbers, but for whatever various reasons, Sunday brought him no responses. Eventually he left a message on an answering machine, which put him in mind of Bill Messenger.

As he returned the diary to the shallow drawer he wondered when if ever Joelle had resigned herself to never using the room as a nursery. Thinking of her secret reminded him of his, which made him feel not only guilty but banal. He was about to quit the room when he recalled what he'd been intending for some time to locate, and lifted down his and Joelle's first, now dusty, suitcase from the top of the old wardrobe. Springing the rusty catches, he sat on a slab of sunlight which smelled of the bare mattress and opened the uppermost photograph album on his lap.

This had to be the one. It had belonged to his father's mother, but his parents had let him have it because they owned copies of most of the photographs. The most recent pictures showed him and Joelle at the register office, first posing as though impatient to kiss and then ducking a shower of confetti. On subsequent pages David grew younger: twinning straw hats with Joelle on a Turkish holiday before she disappeared into the past; standing with his parents beneath the Eiffel Tower and on an Alp and surrounded by skulls under Rome; almost lost in a series of school photographs; sitting on a bicycle which he still remembered being about to fall off; beaming out of a pram which he didn't recall . . . By now he was squat and fat, and two pages later he felt almost as though he'd imploded, leaving his parents to continue their rejuvenation. Their clothes progressed from shapeless to exaggeratedly shaped, the fading of their faces denoted how ghostly their youth was. As the past swallowed his mother the photographs began to acquire a scorched look, and increasingly to be surrounded by auras of glossy blankness as if they were being engulfed by the past rendered tangible. The distorted slab of sunlight crawled away from David, who felt compelled to crouch over the album as he found the photograph Gwendolen had shown him on the island.

Except that it wasn't quite the photograph. There was his father's mother as a child in a confirmation dress, surrounded by two ranks of relatives, the outermost of them fading into the edges of the oval iris: but there was no sign of Gwendolen.

David bent closer as though the encroaching blankness was dragging him down, then he straightened up. Of course the photographer must have taken more than one picture of the occasion, no doubt because this one had failed to include the child at the left-hand edge of the family gathering. David stared at the photograph to see if he could coax forth a hint of Gwendolen's presence – and then he felt his memory and the past rushing towards him like a huge vague flood, because his mind had betrayed him. The pale dim figure he remembered seeing on the margin of the photograph which he'd been shown on the island had not been a child. It had been Gwendolen as she was now.

He peered harder at the photograph, refusing to let himself blink, until the dead appeared to shift and dance. The notion that Gwendolen in some form was about to sidle into view among them made him recoil, shaking his head and squeezing his eyes shut and telling himself not to be childish. He'd had so little sleep on the island that it was hardly surprising if, then or now, it affected his mind. He needn't feel isolated with his mistake, because hadn't Joelle seen Gwendolen's photograph too? He disengaged the corners of the picture from the cardboard page and dropped the album in the suitcase, which he replaced on top of the wardrobe before hurrying out of the house.

Joelle and Herb's widow were sitting in the front room opposite, and Mary had covered her face with her hands. Joelle shook her head at David and waved him away, and he knew where to go instead. He indicated that he was going for a walk and headed for the Shangri-La.

Several of the residents were sitting on chairs on the lawn, deploring reports in the Sunday papers to one another. An old lady wearing the edge of the shadow of a parasol like a flat cap pushed high on her grey scalp greeted David as if he was a long-lost relative. 'How's it going?' he said, vaguely enough to let her think he recognised her if that was what she needed, and crossed the lawn to be met by Brenda Mickling, who came out of the lounge. 'You aren't here to visit, are you, Mr Owain?'

'Gwen, yes. Isn't she here?'

'She went up for one of her snoozes, didn't she, Clorinda?'

'What she calls a snooze,' said the old lady who had greeted David.

'Clorinda is your Gwen's new neighbour.'

'Next door to her, Brenda means.'

'That's what I thought.' David was trying to grasp how he'd felt when he had momentarily assumed that Gwendolen had in some sense gone away. 'What would you call what Gwen's doing?'

'Beg pardon?'

'You were saying she calls it a snooze.'

'I expect that's what it is. When you get to our age you take your rest however you can.'

'You don't mean she hangs by her feet from the ceiling or anything like that.'

'He's a card, this one. You ought to book him for the Christmas do, Brenda, to buck us all up.' Clorinda interlaced her fingers over the unshaded patch of her scalp. 'No, it was just that when I went to introduce myself she was lying on her bed with her eyes open, and I thought – well, it gave me a bit of a turn, that's all, like they give a pig on a spit.'

'But then . . .'

'Beg pardon?'

'What did she do then?'

'Well, I told her the bell had gone, the one they ring for dinner, and I was taking my old bones down when I heard her behind me and we started getting to know each other.'

She shuffled her chair backwards under the parasol as though she was retreating from any further questions. 'What did you think she was doing when you first saw her, though?' David pursued.

Clorinda glanced at the other nearby residents and lowered her voice. 'I think she was making her peace.'

He might have pointed out that he'd asked for her first impression, not what she thought in retrospect. 'That's what you think she's doing now, is it?'

'I wouldn't disturb her, that's all I'm saying. None of us are here to be disturbed.' Clorinda fanned herself with a Sunday tabloid whose front page promised a feast of sin. 'Good grief, it's hot as hell out here. If you'll excuse me, I'm going in.'

'Here's my arm.' Brenda turned to David as the old lady arranged her limbs preparatory to standing up. 'Shall I tell Gwen you were after her when she appears? Was it anything special?'

'Just this,' he said, handing Brenda the photograph. 'I suppose I could leave it for her and ask her about it when I next see her.'

'Look, Clorinda, does it take you back? Why, there's a little girl who looks just like Mr Owain, and you can see his face here too, and in this one – why, in half of them. Is that what you want Gwen to see?'

David thought of a question which it suddenly seemed he ought to have asked quite some time ago. 'Do you think she looks like me?'

'Not as much as these do. As a matter of fact, not really at all, but then you and she are only distantly related, aren't you? That's what she gave us to understand.'

'I thought so,' David said, struggling to think. 'Actually, I'll hold onto the photo. I can always show it to her again.'

'It'll be safe with me, I assure you.'

'I know.' David was tempted to let Brenda keep the photograph, since he couldn't think how to retrieve it without seeming rude, but then he saw a way. 'I was meaning to show my wife. She hasn't seen it, at least not for a while.'

'I'll mention it to Gwen, shall I?'

'You may as well leave that to me.'

'Whatever you think best.' By the sound of it Brenda thought he was behaving oddly, which he supposed he was. He didn't want Gwendolen to be forewarned, that was all, though about what and for what reason? He took the photograph, which curled around his hand as though trying to hide itself, and wandered out of the gate. Since it was unlikely that Joelle would yet have left Mary's, he walked to the main road.

As he reached the memorial a bunch of shrill birds tumbled out of the grove and screeched over the face of the cross, leaving the shadows of foliage fluttering on it like ghosts unable to disengage themselves. A van swerved off the forecourt of the petrol station and roared into Chester as if the driver was fleeing a crime. David walked as far as the railway bridge, beneath which goods wagons were clanking together, then turned back as if the memory of Herb had prevented him from going any further. He had the impression, infuriating in its vagueness, that everything around him – a group of teenagers sprawling on the forecourt of a hotel, the shouts of children in a side street, the trail of a jet plane cutting a bloodless

327

wound in the blue sky – was either about to yield up a secret or hindering him from perceiving one. A breeze made the photograph tap the back of his hand feebly as he strolled towards the memorial, not wanting to go home until Joelle was there to talk to. He was almost abreast of the cross when a woman with a toddler in a buggy dodged out of a side street ahead, shouting indistinctly at a man behind her. She was Hayley Pinnock.

She shoved the buggy a few yards along the pavement, continuing to argue as loudly even though the man had caught up with her, and then she saw David coming towards her. At once her expression, which had been blazingly righteous, changed to a look of trapped fury, and she darted into the side street which separated her from him. 'Keep that on,' she screamed at the toddler, who was tugging at the waist of his long-sleeved pullover. By the time David arrived at the corner she was hundreds of yards distant, and the man who had followed her was turning away, pushing his thick hairy lips forward in a resolute grimace. 'Excuse me,' David called to him, waving the photograph as he ran across the intersection. 'Hold on a minute.'

The man waited without bothering to alter his grimace, and folded his muscular sunburned arms. 'Do you mind telling me what that was all about?' David said.

'Who's asking?'

'Just an interested party.'

'Pity there's not more of those around,' the man said, sucking some of his moustache into his mouth to chew, apparently as an aid to reaching a decision. 'All the same, what's your interest?'

'My wife and I have reason to know the Pinnocks and their son.'

David was afraid he might have identified the Owains too precisely until the man let the moustache retrieve itself from his mouth. 'As long as you know them, you can tell me what you think of this. Our Mag's no older than their Rutger, and Hayley Pinnock tried to make out Mag beat him up.'

'Why would Mrs Pinnock want to do that?'

The man lowered his left eyelid and peered narrowly at David. 'You're not a social worker, by any chance?'

'That's not my job, no.'

'Pity. It would have saved us a phone call. As long as you're asking I'll tell you this much. All our Mag was trying to do was help him get his pully off because he kept complaining he was hot.'

'He would be.'

'And then his mother comes out and starts screaming at him to put it back on, but not before Mag's mother sees how he's covered with bruises.'

'And his mother accuses your daughter of having made them.'

'Mag and then some woman who tried to take him for a walk the other day. Somehow I don't think the Pinnocks will be having the law on her. We thought at the time they were making too much of a row about telling the police instead of doing it. We thought we might know why, and now we're sure.'

'Do you think the woman you mentioned might have been trying to rescue him?'

'You wouldn't know her, by any chance?'

'It's possible.'

'Well, I wouldn't be surprised if what you said was true.' The man rubbed his glistening moustache with one forefinger. 'And one thing I can tell you. The way the Pinnocks behaved over her confirmed some suspicions of ours, and tomorrow we're going to be talking to the people who should know.'

'Thank you,' David said, having restrained himself from saying 'I'll tell her', though this was almost as unequivocal. He grinned at the man, hoping that didn't look too conspiratorial, and stepped off the pavement into the path of a speeding car.

The brakes screamed, and he thought the car had pulled up short of him. He waved gratefully as the car veered across the middle of the road, and the photograph slipped out of the hand he was waving. The wake of the vehicle snatched it and flung it onto the tarmac. He was lunging after it when the moustached man grabbed his arm. 'Road,' the man warned, as no doubt he would speak to his daughter, and the wheels of a lorry thundered over the photograph.

'Thanks again,' David told him. When it was safe to cross he picked up the photograph, only to discover there was nothing worth picking up. The gloss had cracked and flaked away as though the age of the photograph had caught up with it, and all that remained on the cardboard was the skeletal imprint of a tyre. Once he reached the far pavement he dropped the remains into a wastebin. Given the good news he had for Joelle, the photograph no longer seemed worth mentioning.

# Twenty-nine

To begin with, all he knew was that he couldn't waken and that there was a reason why he . . . but even that drifted away into the vagueness he'd become. He'd be forgetting his own name soon, he thought, then realised he seemed to have done so. It might be broad daylight or the middle of the night, because his inability to hoist his eyelids left him uncertain how much of the light was inside them, how much of the uncomfortable heat was a product of himself. If anything was capable of rousing him, his unsureness would – that and his heart, which kept leaping and subsiding like a dying animal, with an irregularity which disturbed him. Perhaps he would feel less uneasy once he saw himself. If he succeeded in locating his hands he could use them to force his eyes open, but his hands were so distant that the task of shifting them seemed beyond him, especially while he was failing to grasp whether he had reason to awaken or to dread awakening. He couldn't tell if that uncertainty had caused his heart, which felt somehow both softened and jagged, to give another uncontrollable leap. One ill-defined hand responded with a twitch at the end of his impression of an arm which lay on what he supposed was the sheet, clammy and wrinkled now, that was spread over the mattress. For an indeterminate length of time the twitch seemed to be all that his hand could produce, then it began to crawl about in a vague quest which felt wide-ranging but which equally could be exploring no more than a few inches of the mattress. In any case he appeared to have, or want, virtually no control over its progress. It wandered back and forth as if attempting to count the wrinkles of the sheet, and his fingertips encountered a body next to him.

It must be Judith, but she felt wrong. His heart jerked so painfully that for some prolonged moments he was unable to think or to judge the nature of the wrongness. She felt dressed, that was it, though they always slept naked. With an effort which sent a wave of heat through him he slithered his hand away from him until

331

it succeeded in resting against her side, and after a pause he made it hitch itself towards her upturned stomach.

As it did so it undressed her. She wasn't wearing a nightdress after all, only the sheet which was meant to cover the mattress but in which she'd tangled herself at some point in her sleep. His hand splayed its fingers on her midriff, which was warm and gently pulsing, and he wondered why he should have expected her to feel any different – and then he remembered. 'Din,' he said thickly and with difficulty, opening his lips against the pillow, which was sticky with saliva. 'Dint work.'

The implications of this began slowly and randomly to catch up with him. His unpredictable heartbeat and the overheating of his flesh and the stale taste in his mouth kept threatening to make him sick. Too little of the drug must have ended up in each mug. When Judith awoke, or at some time in the future, he was going to have to confess what he'd done. Even if she couldn't forgive him, even if she left and took the children with her, his failure had given them another chance – and perhaps she mightn't leave him; perhaps they would grow as close as they'd once been. He dragged his fat slack glove of a hand towards his eyelids and struggled to arrange for the other to meet it. 'Jude,' he mumbled.

He wasn't surprised when she didn't respond. She must be as asleep as he had been and almost was, and he ought to be careful how he wakened her, in case her heart was as unsteady as his. He fumbled at his glued eyes, scratching the lids before he succeeded in pinching the lashes between his fingernails. While he scraped the eyelashes clean he couldn't avoid poking at his eyes, setting off explosions of dull light in them, and so when they flickered open, the darkness was a shock. He waved one hand above his head as though he was drowning in the blackness, and succeeded at last in capturing the light-cord. As he tugged it he used it to haul himself upright against the headboard, gritting his teeth as the plastic knob at the end of the cord chafed his palm that was raw from having held the saucepan, and he was looking down at Judith when the light came on.

Though she was lying on her back, her face was turned away from him. She was reaching for something on her bedside table, perhaps the mug which she'd knocked to the floor. Despite his not having heard the thud he had the impression that the mug had only just fallen, because her hand was resting on the table, palm upwards and fingers slightly curled, as if she was waiting for whatever she required to be placed in it. 'Jude,' he said, and cleared his throat, aggravating the stale bitter taste. 'I'll get it for you. What do you want? A drink?'

His blood was so loud in his ears that he couldn't understand her whisper. He felt as though the waves he heard were swaying back and forth in the top of his skull. He grabbed the headboard, which emitted a creak as sharp as the stinging of his palm, and stretched out his other hand to stroke her face. 'Say it again,' he told her, trying to judge how loud his distant voice should be, and a shiver overwhelmed him. Her cheek was as cold and flabby as a piece of meat in the process of defrosting.

'Don't,' he pleaded. She couldn't really feel like that, since only a few minutes ago her stomach had been warm and alive, but the illusion bewildered and dismayed him. 'Say something else,' he coaxed her, and leaned over to gaze at her face.

The headboard started shaking because his arm was, and he felt that any moment the support might give way, but he couldn't straighten up. Judith's eyes were open, staring ahead as though they had given up trying to focus on whatever she had reached for, and her mouth appeared to have slackened while attempting to grimace, exposing her clenched teeth. 'Why are you looking like that?' he said wildly, and laid his free hand on her stomach. It was as cold as her face.

'No. No, you can't . . .' he begged, and at once he could feel the warmth and the pulse. He moved his hand up to her left breast and searched for her heartbeat. There it was, except why did it feel exactly the same as the pulse in her stomach? He didn't want to dwell on how flaccid her breast had become, nothing like the firmness he loved – but he had noticed, which brought the rest of the truth with it. The warmth and the pulse which he'd imagined he was finding in her body were the sensations of his own hand.

'I don't care,' he said as if he had only to be fierce, 'you spoke to me just now.' He hung onto the shuddering headboard and digging his other hand beneath her cheek, his fingers pressing the sodden spongy pillow, turned her face up to his. 'You did, you did,' he insisted, but that failed to unfix her empty gaze from the ceiling. He could no longer postpone the realisation that he'd only heard the sound of his own blood. 'It doesn't matter,' he cried at the top of his voice, and stooped dizzily to fit his mouth over hers.

It tasted full of stale bitterness, and it felt like kissing a fish. He was unable to make himself breathe into it before he recoiled, sobbing dryly. 'I'm sorry,' he blurted, apologising as much for how she'd made him feel as for what he had done to her, and heard his voice going nowhere. Then her hand slid off the bedside table, its knuckles thumping the carpet. His convulsive movement had shaken the bed.

For a moment he was appalled by the possibility that the noise might bring one or both of the children to see what had caused it, and then the equally terrible notion struck him that they might be past awakening. As he clung to the headboard and stared at Judith's vacated face, her stillness seemed to form itself into a rebuke so silent it was deafening. She was rebuking him for leaving Simon and Olga by themselves, he thought. He heaved his legs off the mattress and levered himself away from the headboard and staggered towards the door.

As soon as he gained it he hung onto the doorknob. It wasn't just his dizziness which had brought him to a halt, it was dread. What could he say to the children? 'Your mother is . . .' he heard himself mumbling. 'I've . . .' Then he saw himself dawdling when he might be able to save them. He tugged the door open with both hands, almost tripping himself up with it as it lurched towards him, and grabbed the edge of the doorframe so as to sway onto the landing.

He caught the switch for the bulb over the stairs with his injured palm and, in the indifferent glare, saw the two closed doors side by side ahead of him. They made him think of two coffins standing on end, and he was falling towards them before he was ready to see what they concealed. Three helpless running steps took him to Olga's door, through which he blundered, bruising his chest, wrenching his shoulder as he threw out a hand for the light-switch.

Olga was lying face down on her bed amidst the chaos of her room. She had kicked off most of her quilt, exposing the mole at the base of her spine, a mark that always made her self-conscious for the first few hours at the nudist beach. She looked as though she had been swimming in a dream, her legs drawn up to begin a last kick, her arms spread out and raised, perhaps to dredge herself out of her sleep. She'd dug her face into the pillow, too deep to be able to breathe. 'Don't lie like that,' he said, 'you'll . . .' and stumbled forwards, unable to avoid treading on one of her favourite books and tearing the cover. 'I didn't mean it,' he cried and fell on his knees beside the bed, crushing more books. He brushed her hair away from her face until he could see one of her eyes. It was half open, and the half was entirely white.

'Don't do that,' he told her with all the authority he could summon. 'You're scaring me.' He seized her upper arms and shook her, although they were limp and chill. When her face began to quiver lifelessly he let go and shuffled backwards half the length of the bed before managing to reel to his feet. He felt himself trampling on her favourite things, and it no longer mattered. He lunged away from the multicoloured blotch that was all her paintings were now, and along the landing to Simon's room.

He had to slow himself down by punching the wall on either side of the door. At least he hadn't floundered into the room and trodden on any of Simon's treasures in the dark. He held onto the wall outside the room with his aching hand and groped for the light-switch. He said a prayer, which he couldn't hear for the jagged drumming of his heart, and then he turned the light on.

At first he couldn't see Simon, just the mound of the quilt over him. It was very still. That was only how it looked, which needn't mean anything, especially at that distance, Richard told himself. As he advanced to the foot of the bed, his knees bumping into the end of the mattress, he saw the quilt stir. He was opening his mouth to call out to Simon when he caught sight of the boy's hand. It was dangling over the side of the bed, its fingers pointing at the floor.

'Don't play games, Simon,' Richard said – loudly, as far as he could tell. 'Don't hide from me just now, there's a good boy.' While he realised that was nonsensical, he didn't care what he said so long as it wakened Simon; he didn't think he would be able to venture any closer until he saw the boy move. 'Simon, wake up now. Please wake up, son.'

When there was no response he bowed forward and grabbing two fistfuls of the mattress, began to shake it and saw Simon waving to him. 'Here I am, Simon,' he called, and sidled alongside the bed, scraping his bare shoulder against the wall. Once he was close enough he lowered himself onto the bed and took the boy's hand in both of his. If anything, it was even colder than Judith and Olga had been.

Richard held onto it for a long time, rubbing it as though lending it some of his own warmth might bring it back to life. He was talking to Simon, and after a while he heard himself say 'Don't leave me all by myself.' Suddenly he was brimming over with self-loathing, not least because he knew that deep down he was concealing some relief at not having to tell any of his family what he'd done. As he flung himself away from the bed his heart pounded louder, as if to mock him with his being left alive, and at once he was determined to stop it. He reeled out of Simon's room so carelessly he almost plunged down the stairs instead of ending up in the bathroom.

The light, or as much of it as there appeared to be, fell about him when he tugged the cord. He'd thought he was alone now, but as he lurched past the bath the culprit stole into view in the mirror, furtive and slack-faced and caught in his own shadow. 'There you are,' Richard screamed, 'but not for long,' and saw his reflection stretch out a hand. It couldn't prevent him from picking up whatever he was reaching for, but what could he use? His fist closed around a handle and swung the safety razor towards his face, but when he focused on the minute twin blades embedded in plastic he hurled the razor away from him, cracking the fibreglass of the bath. They would take too long – so long that he might weaken before he could finish. 'Coward,' he snarled, and seizing the bottle of bleach that Judith used – had used – to clean the toilet, he wrenched off the plastic cap and upended the bottle into his mouth.

Though even the smell of the contents made his eyes stream, he managed to force the neck of the bottle past his flinching lips and grind it against his teeth before tipping his head back. Bleach poured into his mouth. The next moment a convulsion wrenched the bottle from between his lips and sent it out of the door to tumble downstairs, pretending to rest and then falling down another step like a toddler learning how to descend. Richard felt as though he'd stuffed his mouth with red-hot coal. He couldn't swallow, and when he spat in the face of his reflection there still seemed to be as much left inside him. He saw himself choking and searching for a cry that would sum up how he felt, he saw the inside of his gaping mouth seared white, and then he dashed out of the bathroom as if his heart was a bludgeon that was driving him helplessly onwards, although what he was trying to outdistance was the atrocious pain in his mouth. He ran into the main bedroom, where Judith's mouth had fallen wider in sympathy with his, but as soon as he saw her he swerved away from her, because how could he compare what he'd done to her with the little he'd done to himself? Now he could see them both in the dressing-table mirror, and he looked as though he was trying to imitate Judith, to persuade himself that he'd suffered enough. He rushed to the window and tore the curtains apart, and there he was again, mouthing in agony. 'Not for long,' he tried to scream in a whisper that felt like another mouthful of bleach, and butted himself in the face as hard as he could.

He felt his forehead crack. He wasn't sure if it was his or the reflection's, but either way the sensation was a promise. He smashed his face into the window, and again. At the fourth blow the pane gave way. A patch of glass at least twice as wide as his head clanged into the night and shattered dully on the lawn. He toppled forward, and his chin came down on the edge of the hole in the glass.

He thought that might have done the trick, especially when he dragged his head back over the glass and saw trickles of blood worming their way down towards the sill, but if he was able to stand, that meant he hadn't finished. He shoved his chin onto the glass and sawed his head back and forth. He'd thought his mouth was giving him as much pain as he was capable of experiencing, but two dragging slices of the glass edge proved him wrong, and his heartbeat was more persistent than ever. He jerked his head up and staggered back against the bed.

He thought he'd lost control of his bladder until he realised that a stream of blood from his throat had reached as far as his legs. He still had a great deal of blood to lose, and it was taking too long and causing him too much pain. Before he could hesitate, he launched himself at the broken window with all the strength remaining to him. His shoulder crashed through the glass, the windowsill tripped him, bruising his ankles, and he fell into the dark.

The night snatched his breath. He might have felt he was ceasing to exist if it hadn't been for the gaping wounds of his throat and his mouth. The ground came rushing up to break open his head as he'd broken the head of his reflection. He had only to let himself fall, he mustn't attempt to protect himself – but one arm tried to ward the ground off. His fist struck the earth with an impact he thought should have shaken the world, and he heard his arm snap.

In the moment when his body sprawled after it with far too little force, crunching fragments of glass beneath him, the pain wasn't as hideous as he would have expected, and then it was worse, and worse still. He thought he might faint, but he couldn't even achieve that. He pushed himself up with his uninjured arm until he was on his knees, which had started to throb with the fall, and swayed to his feet, every motion of his broken arm multiplying the agony in it. He wasn't going to attempt to lessen that when it was driving him to finish himself off. He ran almost blindly, trying to scream with breath that seemed to be spilling out of too large a mouth, looking for a way to end himself.

The street and houses and parked cars were still. Not a window

337

was lit except for the broken one above him. He felt cast out by the world. At least there was nobody to see him, naked and streaming with blood from his throat and half a dozen other wounds, but equally his surroundings seemed to be offering him no means to destroy himself. Then he heard a car droning along the main road.

It took him five minutes to get there, the uneven pavements digging into his bare feet, the bones of his snapped arm grinding together. Twice he had to stop and lean on a fence or a wall as the loss of blood began to catch up with him, but then he shoved himself onwards. He heard another vehicle speeding along the main road, and wished he had been there to meet it, and prayed for another to be ready to meet him. He was afraid that someone might look out of a window and try to stop him, because by now he was too weakened to fight them off. But the street held its peace, and there was nobody in sight when he stumbled onto the pavement of the main road.

He barely saved himself from sprawling headlong by clutching with his good arm at the nearest lamppost. Its light was out, which seemed both an omen and the first thing to have helped him. It looked as though it might be alone in that, because he could hear no vehicles. If one didn't come soon he would collapse, and someone might find him in time to save him.

Straining his ears only filled them with the sound of his heart as it pumped the blood out of him – he thought it might even be causing his heart to pound faster. It wasn't until he gave up that he heard another sound, and thought he was delirious. What would a bus be doing on the road at this hour? If it was as close as it sounded, why couldn't he see it? Then its headlights swung around the bend a couple of hundred yards away. Its windows were dark, its destination panel was blank, and it was the most welcome spectacle he'd ever seen. But when he tried to push himself away from the lamppost he discovered he couldn't let go.

He was too weak from loss of blood. If he managed to launch himself he would fall short of the bus, which was close to the middle of the road. Already it was less than a hundred yards from him, and wasn't the driver leaning over the wheel, having noticed him? Richard scraped his hand down the concrete pole, skinning his fingers, as if one more pain might lend him strength, and then he lost his balance. He was falling towards the pavement, away from the road and the bus.

At the last moment he managed to hold onto the lamppost. He swung himself around it and let go, and the impetus which twisted his broken arm carried him into the road. He lowered his head like a bull, feeling his mouth and his throat merge into a single wound, as the brakes screeched, too late. The front of the bus smashed his head and rammed him into nothing more than darkness.

# Thirty

Perhaps David was trying too hard to be positive. 'They may end up having to foster him.'

'That's a long slow process, and who says it's best for him?'

'I thought you would have.'

Joelle took so much time to consider this he regretted not having kept it to himself, but then she said 'Somehow I don't think we'd have much of a chance.'

'To foster, you mean? If people realised how much you care . . .'

'The trouble is I let too many people realise. No, David, I've lost my chance. So long as I didn't lose Rutger his.'

'Gave him another, more like. And maybe his parents too.'

'That's assuming they deserve one.'

'Don't we all?'

'How have they been acting?'

'Accusing each other for the neighbours' benefit of being too rough on him is the way I heard it. The social workers haven't taken him away yet, but they're keeping an eye on the family, that's for sure.'

'Is it enough?'

'And supposedly counselling them.' Alarmed by the way her face almost crumpled at that, he said 'That can't be bad, can it?'

'I'm not sure what's good or bad any more.' She pirouetted before the dressing-table mirror and looked over her shoulder to examine the back of her dark suit. 'Don't take any notice of me. I was just wondering if a social worker could have helped Richard and, and . . .'

'Maybe, but we couldn't have done anything.'

'We'd want to think that, wouldn't we?'

'That doesn't mean it isn't true, and it wasn't just us who didn't notice much was wrong.' Had they had the opportunity at the school play? He tried not to think so. 'And besides . . .'

'There's always a besides, isn't there.'

'I don't believe we could have done much about whatever got into Richard, that's all, or any social worker could have either.'

'Who, then?'

He found he had no answer, and a shrug would have been callous. After a silence he said 'Shall I fetch Gwen?'

'I may as well come down with you, then we can go straight on.' Joelle dabbed at her eyes in front of the mirror. 'Is that supposed to be sticking out?'

'Only for you.'

'Later,' she said as if she meant his automatic joke as well as the proposal. 'The tag at the back of your neck.'

'In case you want to hang me up. Put it in for me if you like.'

He was beginning to feel incapable of saying anything that wasn't loaded and at the same time excruciatingly banal. Joelle's fingertips touched the back of his neck, and she gave him a brief dry kiss that might have been a token of forgiveness before they made their way out of the house. Along the pavements, birds were singing in the trees plated with sunlight. 'Mary's definitely not coming, then,' he said.

'She feels she didn't know the Vales that well. If anyone ever really knows anyone.'

'Present company excepted, I hope. You can understand her not wanting to go to another funeral so soon after . . .' Saying that made him feel surrounded by death and secret vices. 'I wouldn't have expected Gwen to want to go.'

'Maybe it reminds her.'

'Of what?'

'Of the inevitable. Or that she's still alive. Or maybe she just likes going to funerals. I wouldn't know, would I? Why don't you ask her yourself?'

Having waited for Joelle to fasten her seatbelt, David started the car. 'What did she say to you?'

'Just that she felt she ought to be there. I wasn't in a state to do much talking, especially in the middle of the street. No, really, David, if it bothers you, why don't you ask her? She's your relative, after all.'

'We've only the photograph as evidence of that. As a matter of fact, we haven't even got the photograph. You saw it though, didn't you?'

'Which photograph was that?'

'Of her with the family when my grandmother Owain was a child.'

'If you say so.'

'I thought you saw it that night on the island.'

'I seem to remember seeing a photograph, but not with her in it.'

'Are you sure? Try and think what you saw.'

'I've just told you. You might remember I was half asleep. If it was a picture of your family that's good enough, isn't it? I don't understand what you're trying to say.'

'I can't figure out what made her show me the photograph in the first place. For the life of me I can't recall saying anything to make her realise we were closer than just sharing a name, and come to think of it, who says we even do?'

'You said, or she did. You've lost me, David. What are you trying to get at?'

'Suppose she made it all up just so we'd take her off the island?'

'Made all what up? The photograph? She'd have to be pretty special to be able to do that, I should think.'

'Maybe she is,' David retorted, though he was beginning to sound absurd to himself. 'Maybe we both only imagined we saw it.'

'What else do you think she's capable of putting in people's heads? I can't wait to hear what you're going to ask her. Here we are.'

'I know that,' David said, and got out of the car, feeling confused and resentful and apprehensive. Was he so guilt-ridden that he was trying to turn Gwendolen into some kind of scapegoat? He'd hoped Joelle would help him clarify his thoughts, but she had left him uncertain what to say to Gwendolen, indeed afraid of what he might say, of even coming face to face with her. He crossed the lawn and made himself ring the doorbell, which brought footsteps to the door more promptly than he would have liked. When Brenda Mickling opened it, however, she seemed to be mirroring his confusion; then her expression cleared. 'Of course, you want Gwen for the funeral.'

'It's not how I'd put it, but yes.'

'Is it very important for her to go?'

'I wouldn't say exactly important. I don't see how it could be. Or do you mean important to her?'

'If you know.'

'I shouldn't think so. She only met these people once, the family who died, that is. Why, is anything wrong?'

'I don't know if wrong's the word. Only she told me not five minutes ago she was going up for a rest.'

'What, again?'

'People of Gwen's age do need their rest, you know.'

'I appreciate that. Shall I just look in on her?'

'I expect she'll be fine.'

'I was meaning in case she's forgotten about the occasion and would like to be reminded.'

Brenda looked stubborn, but then she stepped back for him. 'She's your family.'

So he kept being told, David thought, less sure of his own motives than ever. As he climbed the wide stairs under the bright skylight, having mimed to Joelle that he didn't intend to be long, muffled happy music followed him up from the lounge, and an outburst of rapid hammering which, in some confusion, he took to be the sound of nails being driven into a lid until he gathered he was hearing a tap-dancer in a musical. At the top of the stairs he hesitated outside Gwendolen's room. The rule of the house was to knock before entering, and it would be wholly unreasonable of him to open the door without announcing himself first, except wasn't he simply trying to avoid disturbing her if she was asleep? He closed one hand around the ridged brass doorknob, which felt momentarily soft as a rotten apple, and inched the door open.

Gwendolen was lying on top of the quilt on the bed in the impersonally cheerful room, her face upturned to the sunlight through the window. It occurred to David that she never acquired any colour, no matter how much direct sunlight she took; her hands, which were folded on her chest, and her face seemed bleached as white as her long dress. She was lying quite still – he couldn't even see her breathing – yet he had the impression that she knew he was there. If that was the case, did she appreciate how she looked to him, as though she was deliberately parodying a corpse at a funeral? A surge of unexpected anger almost sent him into the room. He controlled himself and eased the door shut and hurried downstairs, wiping on his sleeve the hand which had touched the doorknob.

Brenda Mickling met him in the hall. 'Satisfied?'

'I just wanted to be sure,' David said, which made him realise he was anything but. He had the notion that some element had been missing from the tableau of Gwendolen on the bed. Then sunlight and the smell of cut grass outside the house overwhelmed him, and he saw Joelle wondering why he was alone, and gave up ransacking his mind. 'She's decided she needs her rest,' he said.

'That's understandable. Maybe she only said she ought to come because she felt I expected it of her.'

As David ducked to climb into the Volvo, a light probed his eye, and he thought Gwendolen had opened her window to watch him. The light came from there, but it was his own movement which had trained the reflected sunlight on him, causing the pane to glare like a huge burning eye or the entrance to a furnace. By retreating into the car he was trying to leave behind the impression that the light or something within it was aware of him. 'Did you ask her?' Joelle said.

'She didn't seem to be awake.'

'Then I expect she wasn't, don't you?'

He heard Joelle telling him that he was being as unreasonable as he kept feeling he was. He twisted the key in the ignition, and she said 'I was thinking while you were in there . . .'

He didn't speak until the car was on the main road. 'Yes?' he said impatiently.

'I won't tell you if you don't want to hear.'

'Don't do that on top of everything else. Go ahead.'

'Well, I was thinking – just suppose Gwen did pretend to be someone she wasn't so that she'd be saved, which I don't believe for a moment, where's the harm in it? She hasn't been any trouble to anyone, has she?'

He hadn't known how much he'd been hoping that Joelle would explain away his fancies until he heard her reinforcing them. He was going to have to confront Gwendolen, no question of it. 'I can't argue with you,' he said, and drove to the crematorium.

Flowers still weren't permitted on the grass, but the graves were as florid as ever. Above the trees that surrounded the low concrete building, crows tore the air into harsh black fragments. Having found a parking space, he and Joelle hurried into the chapel. In the long room beyond the wooden door which an undertaker's assistant opened for them, the pews were almost full, and he had to sit across the aisle from Joelle. Music murmured an intimation to the mourners that they should keep their voices and their emotions down, and so he was conscious of swallowing loudly as he caught sight of the four coffins, one pair slightly smaller than the other. He let his gaze drift around the chapel, whose paleness struck him all at once as the colour of innocence, in search of people he knew. There were the Greys, Archibald and Agatha, on their knees, and both the Monks ahead of them, Sarah wearing her black tent. He nodded to indicate them, but Joelle had already noticed them and was frowning over how she ought to feel. Further up the chapel he saw Doug and Maureen Singleton, and was wondering uneasily why Angie wasn't there when the priest went up into the pulpit and leaned forward over his clasped hands as if the sobs of the bereaved were drawing him towards them.

He was older and sadder than the priest who had said the last words over Herb. 'Sometimes a tragedy can be so great as almost to cause one to doubt the existence of a loving God . . .' He spoke with a gentleness which promised reassurance, and which David was certain was what Richard's and Judith's parents needed, but it was falling short of him. 'Even if the pressure of circumstances made Richard lose all hope at the end, my faith tells me that does not mean it will be denied him . . .' Archibald Grey emitted a sharp disagreeable cough, which earned him several hostile glances, but David wasn't sure that Archibald was wrong; he felt that Richard had reduced himself and his family to nothingness in boxes, a non-existence as banal as it was terrible, a void which even the priest's faith couldn't people. The sobs of the parents sounded as though they were on the way to being comforted, however. When the service was over and the curtains drawn, and he was able to rejoin Joelle, he meant the thanks he gave the priest along with the handshake.

The two sets of parents hadn't received sympathy from everyone when Judith's mother fled into the black limousine. She was followed by her husband, who had to be helped in by Richard's father. Soon the Vales retreated into the car, which cruised away, leaving the rest of the congregation standing awkwardly among the wreaths. The Monks and the Singletons were smiling at each other with a restraint which presumably was meant to acknowledge the occasion but which looked like wariness. Eventually Maureen said to Sarah 'I'm glad you felt able to come.'

'I read about them in the paper.'

Sarah's voice was so slow and toneless that Maureen hesitated before smiling more firmly. 'At least you're feeling better than you were when you didn't want to see anyone.'

'I'm not ill. There just isn't much of me apart from the too much you're seeing.'

'You mustn't put yourself down, must she, Terry?' Doug protested, and when his heartiness failed to communicate itself to either of them, went on: 'I hope you'll be receiving visitors now. Maureen was afraid we'd lost you when you wouldn't let us come.'

'I'll be home soon. He'll tell you when.'

'They said soon at the hospital,' Terry said as though he was almost too ashamed to speak.

'Bring your daughter, won't you? I was expecting to see her today.'

Maureen stared hard at Doug, who cleared his throat and said 'The lesser spotted teenager had one of her tantrums.'

'Only because you wouldn't let her come,' Maureen told him.

'Which proves I was right to forbid her.'

Joelle had been ignoring him, but now she turned on him. 'Simon and Olga were her friends.'

'Exactly,' Maureen said.

'She wasn't able to convince me that she would control herself.'

'Then she has my sympathy,' Joelle said, 'because I know what a job people have to convince you.'

David thought it was time he intervened, until Doug squared his shoulders and faced him. 'This may not be quite the place for it,' Doug said, 'but I'd like to settle our differences.'

When he stuck out a hand David wondered if he was proposing a fight, but the hand was open and empty. 'If you'll send me your bill for the work at my aunt's house,' Doug said, 'I'll see that it's paid without argument.'

'Well, that's . . .' David shook the hand, which refrained from clasping his. 'That's very decent of you.'

Joelle wasn't letting Doug off so easily. 'What can we thank for the change of heart?'

Doug looked away quickly at the wreaths. Into his silence Archibald said 'You'll forgive my saying so, Douglas, but I think you were well advised not to bring the child.'

Maureen stared at him while she selected her mildest response. 'I take it you're going to share your thinking with us.'

'Certainly. Would you prefer a private word?'

'It won't be the same if you don't let everyone hear.'

'As you wish,' Archibald boomed, and lowered his voice, but not much. 'I simply feel that the lack of moral guidance shown on this occasion would have made it unsuitable.'

'Shown by whom?'

'Why, the priest, of course. In his position I should have felt bound to point out that Richard committed the unforgivable sin.'

'Then thank God you weren't.'

'Despair is the sin against the Holy Ghost, and I trust you won't mind my hoping you take some such message home to your child.'

Maureen opened her mouth, but a mime of disbelief was the extent of her response. It was Agatha who blurted 'You're a fine one to talk about sin.'

'Now, Agatha, I hardly think this is the appropriate—'

'No, I don't suppose you'd like me to tell our friends what you did.'

'I hope I have nothing to be ashamed of.'

'That's you, forever hopeful. Do you know what he did to me?'

She stared at each of them in turn, but when she came to David the most he felt able to risk was a shake of his head. Nobody else had singled themselves out when Archibald gripped her arm. 'Agatha, I really must insist—'

'You've insisted long enough, or I've let you think you can.' She yanked herself free, almost bumping into a wreath. 'This paragon of virtue spent all our money without telling me, all our savings for when we retire.'

'As long as that has been made public, I feel justified in mentioning that it went to Christian missions in countries some of us still regard as heathen.'

'That's the trouble with you, you always feel justified.' Agatha glared at a group of mourners, who quickened their pace towards the car park. 'I don't begrudge the missions some money, but that isn't the point. You took all the money that belonged to both of us. That's called theft, and it's supposed to be a sin, and there's a few more of those involved in what you did.'

'Call me old-fashioned if you like, but once upon a time the wife's possessions—'

'Once upon a time is right. You're living in a fairy tale.'

'I thought we were both attempting to live as God requires us to live.'

'Then it's about time you thought again. We've been living as *you* think we should.'

This gave Archibald pause, and Doug took advantage of it. 'If there are any legal issues either of you want to consult me about—'

'Leave them to it, Doug,' Maureen said, steering him away. 'I think it's about time we were going, because you've got things to say to Angie, and I'm going to tell you them.'

'We're off too,' Sarah said. 'But some of you call us soon.'

'I will,' Joelle promised, and followed the exodus that left Archibald and Agatha stranded among the wreaths. Once she was in the car she said to David 'It's just as well Gwen didn't come.'

'Think so?'

'She'd hardly have wanted to see people at their worst.'

He turned the key to start the car, startling a crow and some kind of white bird out of a tree. 'I expect she's come across worse in her life,' he said, and almost knew.

# Thirty-one

As David drove out of the crematorium grounds the sky began to turn to slate. On the way back to Chester the fields and roadside verges glowed as though they had just been painted, the cars on the roads seemed about to burst into flames. By the time the monumental cross came into view, the sky was squeezing all the colours from the houses and hotels. In the shadows under the luminous foliage the cross had grown spiky with blackbirds, as if it was reverting into a more ancient symbol. The mass of birds splintered into the descending blackness as David swung the car off the main road. Residents of the Shangri-La were quitting the lawn while the staff carried chairs after them. Something struck the roof of the Volvo with a soft flat urgent thud as David located Gwendolen's window, which looked walled up with slate, secret and enigmatic, the focus of the imminence he sensed all around him. He had to drag his gaze away from the expectation of a shape appearing out of the rectangular darkness and concentrate on the road.

Another heavy raindrop struck the car, exploding on the windscreen and separating into drops which streamed in defiance of gravity over the glass as he braked outside the house. While Joelle dug in her purse for her keys and sprinted to the front door he watched the flagstones of the pavement grow piebald, then black. Joelle must be opening the door, although he couldn't see her for the shattering of water on the side window. As he climbed out the drumming on the metal roof transformed into the dousing of his scalp. Rain danced on his hand while he locked the door, rain chased him as far as the hall, where he discovered that Joelle had continued through the house and was standing outside the patio doors, her face upturned to the downpour. Her sombre clothes darkened, the bare patch of the hissing lawn beyond her seemed to gulp the rain yet stay as parched. David went to hold her and share her enjoyment, but he had the impression of trying to wash away something without knowing what it was.

When the noise of the lawn diminished to a whisper, and their faces began to grow wetter with the rain in their hair than with the wake of the storm, Joelle withdrew her arm from around his waist. 'Time for a shower and a change.'

'You first, and then I'll be up.'

She fingered her hair away from her forehead and blinked at him, looking years younger. 'Don't go catching pneumonia. I'd hate to lose you.'

'Not much chance of that so far as I'm aware,' he said, and faced the garden while he waited for the silence to complete itself. He heard rain dripping from gutters, and then he only saw drops trembling at the tips of leaves, gathering as though the twilight which the storm had left behind was growing solid. The world seemed paralysed by imminence. When the shrilling began inside the house it made him suck in his breath.

He hurried through the patio doors as the phone rang again. 'I'm getting it,' he called up to Joelle, but instead he loitered at the foot of the stairs, his hand sinking away from the receiver, until the call triggered the answering machine. The click was followed by the faint squeaking of the spool of tape, a sound which snagged his nerves. Then a voice said 'Hello? David? Joelle? Anyone listening? Anybody there?'

He was calling to take back what he'd said, David thought, picking up the receiver. So much for virtuousness. 'Yes, Doug.'

'You're there. Right,' Doug said rather sharply. 'Is Angela, by any chance?'

'Is Angie . . .'

'There with you.'

'With us? With me and Joelle? Not since, you know, the barbecue. Should she be?'

'Not so far as I'm concerned, but I've just spoken to my aunt and she suggested I try you.'

'I can't think why,' David protested, wondering if he should be able to. 'Is anything wrong besides you not knowing where Angie is?'

'She was told to be here when we came home.' Doug sounded as though he was rehearsing the tone he would use on Angie, but David heard Maureen say 'Tell whichever of them it is, Doug, or I will.'

'If you must know, David, she left some kind of a note. The sort of thing you'd expect from a girl of her age. She probably got most of it out of the books she reads.' Perhaps he took David's silence

352

for scepticism, because he said defensively 'If you strip away all the melodrama, I suppose she was more upset by our not letting her attend the funeral than I could have imagined she'd be.'

'By your not letting her, you mean.'

If Maureen hadn't said that, David thought he might have. 'But what did she actually say?' he said.

'It depends what you mean by actually. What she wants us to think is that she's run away from home.'

'You don't believe her.'

'I'm sure she has temporarily, and I'm growing surer by the moment that at least one of her friends isn't telling the truth.'

'And what will you do when you find her?'

'Need you ask? She won't be able to sit down for a week.'

David felt as though Doug was proposing to act out his fantasies, but the reality had no appeal for him. 'If you do that, Doug—'

He never knew how vehemently he might have stood up for her, because Maureen spoke, so loudly that she must realise he could hear. 'If you lay a finger on her, Doug, we'll both be leaving you for good.'

'For heaven's sake, Maureen, you're starting to sound as melodramatic as your daughter.'

'Then I suggest you listen to both of us, and while you're about it, stop sniping at her all the time and making jokes at her expense, and let her grow up. Then maybe she won't mind living with us a few more years. I'm not anxious to see the last of her, even if you are.'

'Of course I'm not anxious—' To judge by the clatter Doug was gesturing with the phone, which presumably reminded him that they had a listener. 'If by any chance she should turn up on your doorstep, David, I don't need to tell you to let us know at once.'

'Can I tell her she needn't be afraid to go home?'

'If you must,' Doug snapped, and cut him off at once, leaving him holding the receiver like a weapon that had abruptly grown useless. He became aware of his sodden clothes, which seemed to be weighing not only on his body but also on his mind. He reunited the phone with its cradle and trudged upstairs, hoping that he hadn't simply managed to antagonise Doug. He was peeling off his clothes in the bedroom when Joelle came in. 'Who was that?' she said.

'Guess.'

'Bill Messenger.'

'Don't you wish. No, it was Doug Singleton.'

'That was never just a show he put on at the funeral to make himself look good.'

'Now, Jo, one cynic in the family's enough. No, he was looking for Angie. She's done a runner.'

'I can't say I blame her. Why did he think she was here?'

'Apparently the aunt thought she might be. Don't ask me why.'

Suppose Joelle did, would he tell her? Confession was meant to be good for the soul, but he didn't see how his could be for her. As Joelle frowned he tried to prepare what he would say, but she wasn't pursuing that question. 'Will Angie be all right, do you think?'

'She's looked after herself pretty well up to now,' David said, and wondered whether at that very moment she might be breaking her promise to him. That threatened to revive his fantasy until Joelle said 'Don't stay wet. Have a shower while I find something for dinner.'

David finished stripping and stood under a hot shower, though the experience felt frustratingly aloof from him. Before he left the bathroom he was aware that Joelle had decided on chili con carne for dinner. He dried himself and shrugged into a bathrobe and went down to find her making garlic bread. He opened a bottle of Merlot, and they sipped a glass while the chili simmered. Perhaps it was simply one of those interludes when there seemed to be nothing to say nor any need to speak, but David felt as if he was marking time – as if something was, though if Joelle was unaware of it, who was to say it existed at all?

As they ate dinner the night took away the garden. Whenever he looked up he saw himself beyond two of Joelle, her face and the back of her head. He wasn't sure why the sight made him uneasy: perhaps with its impermanence, or his being unable to read his own eyes because they were so far away. Even the tastes of the meal seemed to be, and he clinked his glass against Joelle's more than once in attempts to feel closer to her.

Washing up after the meal gave them more opportunities to touch, and showed him an insubstantial version of the two of them above the stain on the lawn. He finished at the sink and dried his hands and crept them around Joelle's waist and up to her breasts. She leaned back against him and rubbed her cheek against his, but when he began to squeeze her breasts she lifted his hands away. 'Not on top of garlic bread and chili, David. Let's save it for the morning.'

'What else would you like to do?'

'Let's wait and see what Sunday brings and decide then, shall we?'

David didn't know why he had been trying to fix Sunday in advance, but he was troubled by the notion that she had somehow abandoned him. Not making love had left him unable to determine if he could do without his images of Angie Singleton. He rather thought he couldn't, which made him feel irredeemably banal, shrunken by his secret. 'So what do you want to do now?'

'Can't we just be together?'

When she sat on the couch he joined her there, and she swung her legs onto his lap. He slid one arm behind her shoulders and began to stroke her legs, as he remembered doing the first time they'd shared a couch at her parents' house and he hadn't known how far she would let him go. As she nestled against him, the warmth of their bodies uniting, he sensed that she was remembering too. They were in a place beyond words, a place they had built together over the years, except that part of him wasn't – was alert for a knock at the door or the window, or the sound of the phone, or some other intrusion he couldn't begin to define. As for Joelle, she was soon asleep.

David sat without moving for over an hour, feeling as though he was holding the future still. When a nod wakened him before he realised he'd dozed off, he carried Joelle upstairs and deposited her on the bed. He locked the house for the night and went through the rest of the bedtime ritual, then he undressed Joelle, who murmured drowsily as he stretched out her legs to slip them under the quilt. 'Come to bed,' she just about pronounced.

As he reached up to tug the light-cord, having inserted himself beneath the quilt, she put a sleepy arm across his chest, pinning him on his back. He lay gazing up at the almost invisible activity on the ceiling, tattered shadows growing as they merged and then falling apart before he could put a name to the shape they formed – shadows of the foliage above the streetlamp whose light seeped through the curtains. In time the passes which the shadows made over one another seemed to grow more regular, increasingly hypnotic, and before long he forgot to reopen his eyes.

He awoke on his back in darkness. The shadows had almost stopped moving, but the elongated disintegrating fingers appeared to be reaching stealthily into the room, groping in search of him. Joelle had turned away from him and was breathing to herself. When he eased himself out of bed, he thought he was heading for the window in order to show himself that only the tree was out there, that nothing was summoning him. Or perhaps he already knew. He took hold of the curtains with both hands and parted a gap wide enough to look through.

A figure was standing beneath the tree outside the gate. He had the impression that it might have been waiting there for some time, because only its long white dress stirred as a breeze tousled the foliage. The leaves prevented David from seeing its face. He gripped the handfuls of velvet, wondering whether Gwendolen would wait for him if he let go and ran out of the house. Then she stepped forward, and he saw her face break apart like a swarm of pale moths emerging from the neck of the dress. The next moment he realised that he'd seen shadows of leaves clustering on her face, which she tilted up to him, smiling faintly if at all. She raised one hand in a gesture of farewell and turned away into the dark.

# Thirty-two

David went down on his knees so as to bring his mouth in line with the opening beneath the sash. 'Gwen, wait,' he called, and pushed himself to his feet at once. As he grabbed the bathrobe from the floor at the foot of the bed Joelle moaned almost wakefully and stretched out her arm beneath the quilt towards his half of the mattress. 'I'm not going far,' he told her in case she could hear, and ran downstairs.

His keys were in a pocket of the robe. He shoved the key into the control panel of the burglar alarm so urgently he was afraid it might set off the bell and the siren. The system held its peace, however, and he raced to the front door to slide back the bolts. He was grasping the latch to pull the door open when he wondered if the sight outside the window had been the last of a dream – as much of one as the figure he'd seen outside Herb's house on the night before Herb's death.

Gwendolen was there. She was moving away, so slowly that she had only reached the adjoining garden fence. As the hallway spread its light onto the path she turned and looked at him, the left side of her face crawling with shadows of foliage. She stood like a monument, her hands folded on the bag in front of her body, while David padded as far as the pavement, his feet wincing at the stony chill. 'Why are you about so late, Gwen?'

A breeze set her cheek fluttering, or at least the shadows on it, and tugged her dress against her body, of which there appeared to be dismayingly little. 'It's my time,' she said.

'Excuse me, but time for what?'

'For me to go back where I came from.'

'You don't mean the island, surely.'

'Further than that,' Gwendolen said with a smile as subdued as her voice.

'But how do you mean to get there?'

'However I can.'

'Aren't you happy where you are?'

357

'I have been. Never think me ungrateful,' Gwendolen said, and stepped into the road.

'You can't go now, Gwen. Not at this time of night. I don't want to frighten you, but you don't know who you might meet or what they might be capable of.'

She raised the bag in front of her as if she was preparing to enact some kind of rite. 'Believe me, I do.'

'Won't you at least wait till daylight? Then I'll take you if you like.'

'That's kind of you, David, but I haven't time.'

At that point he had to acknowledge he wasn't being unselfish: the prospect of her departure had made him realise there were questions he wanted to ask her, if he could frame them. 'If you'll wait while I get dressed,' he said, 'I'll take you now.'

'As you wish, David. It's your choice.'

Perhaps she resented his having undermined her self-confidence, he thought, reminding himself that emotions might be more fragile at her age. 'It's the least I can do,' he said. 'Come in the house.'

He thought he would have to insist, but the invitation moved her at once. As she glided onto the path the shadows streamed off her face, exposing it to him. She looked enlivened by the dark hour, but then he understood that old people often were. The slate discs of her pupils gleamed, her long oval face appeared to seize light from the hallway. As soon as she stepped over the threshold he closed the door, shivering with a sudden chill, and switched on the light in the front room. 'Have a seat. Can I get you anything?'

'I have everything I need, thank you, David.'

'You'll want to stop off at the Shangri-La, will you?'

'There's no call to waken anyone. I've left Brenda a note.'

'I was meaning' – which to some extent was true – 'to pick up something more for you to wear.'

'That won't be necessary,' she said, lowering herself into the nearest chair and interlacing her fingers on the dark lump of her bag.

David was afraid to push his interference any further in case the threat of it drove her away while he was upstairs. 'I'll be two ticks,' he said, as his grandmother used to, and padded swiftly up to the bedroom. He'd halted in the doorway to allow his eyes to adjust to the dimness when Joelle mumbled 'What are you doing? Come back to bed.'

'Actually, Jo, I won't come back. Not just now. I'm taking Gwen home.'

358

'Oh dear, is she wandering?' Joelle said in a voice which sounded about to go back to sleep. 'Don't be long, then. Leave the alarm off until you get back.'

David paced into the room, where vague disintegrating shadows gestured over their heads. 'I won't just be walking her up the road, Jo. I'm driving her back where she came from originally.'

Something began to tap like a fingernail against the wall. It was the weight at the end of the light-cord, which Joelle succeeded in capturing after a few seconds, sending the shadows out of the room. 'What, now?' she protested, and fumbled for the bedside clock. 'It's four in the morning.'

'I know that, but maybe Gwen doesn't,' David said under his breath. 'Anyway, I don't mind. I expect it's the last thing I'll ever do for her.'

Joelle propped herself on one elbow, squeezing her eyes shut so as to open them wider. 'How far are you supposed to be going?'

'As far as it takes. She hasn't said.'

'Is she here now?'

'Downstairs, yes.' As Joelle kicked off the quilt he said 'Why?'

He hadn't intended to speak so curtly; he couldn't think why he had. 'I just thought I'd say goodbye to her,' Joelle said. 'Any objection?'

'I'm sure she'd want you to. Go ahead, and I'll be down as soon as I'm dressed.'

While he did so and tugged a brush through his hair he heard murmurs of conversation downstairs. He was following Joelle when he overheard her asking 'Why have you got to leave now, Gwen?'

'Don't mistake me, but there's no longer anything to keep me here.'

'Money, do you mean? Have you run out of coins?'

Gwendolen looked away from her as David reached the doorway. 'Here's your husband. Time to say our farewells.'

Joelle tried another question. 'But where do you feel you have to go?'

'Who knows what it may be called these days? All I can promise is that I'll know the way. I've already told David that he needn't take me. I'm used to finding my way by myself.'

She seemed almost to be appealing to Joelle, who, David saw, found this as confusing as he did. 'I'm sure you are, Gwen,' he said, 'but I know we'll both feel happier if I take you.'

'I should like you to feel so, of course.' Gwendolen stood up abruptly, as though she'd made an offer which had been rebuffed. 'Let me say I'm glad to have known you, Joelle, and the same goes for David.'

Joelle rose also, visibly feeling superfluous. 'How long are you likely to take, do you think?'

'It's been so long I wouldn't care to say.'

'Will you phone me when you get there, David?'

'The first phone I see. And how will you spend your Sunday? Not hanging around waiting for a call, I hope.'

'If I'm not here I may be over at Mary's. There was something she couldn't quite bring herself to say about Herb, about the train crash. Anyway,' Joelle said awkwardly, 'have a safe journey, Gwen. Look after yourself. Write to us if you like.'

Gwendolen met this suggestion with a gaze so patient it was all but expressionless, and David saw Joelle remember that he'd told her Gwendolen couldn't read. She stepped forward and clasped Gwendolen's hands in hers, then she hugged her shoulders. Their cheeks touched for a moment before Joelle stepped back so quickly she might have been recoiling. 'Send him back safely, won't you?' she said.

'Of course, if it's within my power.'

It occurred to David that he would have expected Joelle to do her best to dissuade Gwendolen from leaving, but presumably she had tried while he was upstairs. He went to her and held her face and kissed it. 'Don't worry. Whatever it is, don't worry, all right?'

'Just come back soon,' Joelle said, and trailed behind him, holding his hand, as he went after Gwendolen, who was already making for the car. He felt as though they'd become a ritual procession into the otherwise deserted night. Joelle relinquished his hand as he unlocked the passenger door, and gave him a sudden fierce open-mouthed kiss while Gwendolen arranged herself, rustling dryly, on the seat beside the driver's. 'That'll be waiting when you come home,' Joelle told him.

'It's all I need,' he said, giving her hand a final squeeze before climbing into the Volvo. The engine caught first time, and he waved to her in the mirror for the moments before she shrank and was withdrawn out of sight around the bend in the road. He was still thinking of calling at the Shangri-La, but every window he could see there was dark. As he turned onto the main road the trees flexed their branches above the cross. Then it was in the mirror, dwindling rapidly, growing dimmer before the trees closed around it as if it had never been there at all.

# Thirty-three

They were still in Chester when the buildings began to vanish. The hotels had given way to selections of suburban architecture, but the side streets which multiplied these were growing shorter by the minute. A few hundred yards down each street, the houses had been demolished by fog. It was further away on the main road, where it kept producing streetlamps and the occasional glistening tree, and beyond the roundabout which marked the edge of the suburb it was indistinguishable from the fields on either side of the road. Only the smoking of the headlights of lorries thundering towards Wales revealed its presence on that route, and David thought it was nothing like an adequate excuse for turning back, even if he had been searching for one. 'That's the way, is it?' he said.

Gwendolen nodded once. She was sitting stiffly upright, her bag nesting in her lap, her fingers interwoven over it as though at prayer. A stray car swerved off the higher road, its headlamp beams scything through the Volvo and catching her face. As David glanced at her he thought the irises of her eyes resembled discs of fog inserted into the whites. 'Just tell me when I have to turn,' he said, and sent the Volvo up the ramp.

The dual carriageway afforded him a view of not very much: fields that seemed undecided whether to shrink; clumps of trees which shone darkly as the passing of the car made them pirouette; infrequent isolated houses, their lights guttering in the fog. Every few miles the fog on the carriageway beyond the limit of the headlamps released a blue looming which developed into a sign for the next exit. Several of these had sailed by when Gwendolen murmured 'Here.'

'You want me to turn off, you mean.' David had had a fleeting impression that she already wanted him to stop. The monotony of the road and of the constantly withheld imminence of the fog must be telling on him. He glimpsed her nodding beside him, and swung the car onto a road which led south.

361

The fog rose to meet him, and he had to brake. Usually, even at night, he would have been able to distinguish the first mountains on the horizon by now, but the most the lowland fog offered him was a sample of the road to examine with his headlamps. The lights of the outskirts of Wrexham briefly smudged the murk, and some species of leviathan rumbled past him, splashing the tarmac red in its wake, at a speed which made him renew his grip on the steering wheel. Then there was only the song of the road beneath the car, and the endless unspooling of the roadway, which had narrowed itself by half. Whenever he attempted to peer a little further ahead than he could, he saw Gwendolen's face hovering above the lit stretch of road as though she was beckoning him onwards, a reflection illuminated so faintly by the glow from the dashboard that he kept thinking he was dreaming it. Then the fog sprouted a signboard with the warning ARAFWCH NAWR, and the road began to protrude ribs to ensure that he did indeed slow down before the roundabout. 'Looks as if we're over the border,' he said.

There was no response, either from the shape propped at the edge of his vision or from the faintly sketched mask sailing unimpeded through the fog. He needed conversation to keep him alert, because the early start and the featurelessness of the journey appeared to be making him fanciful: he kept feeling that if he glanced at Gwendolen he would see only the outlines of a pale mask above the white garment. He steered the car around the roundabout and picked up speed, then turned to her. She was gazing ahead as though she could see far beyond the fog; she didn't seem to have altered her position since she had strapped herself in. 'So what shall we talk about?' David said.

'Whatever you think is called for.'

If that was an invitation to ask anything he liked, it didn't so much clear his head as empty it. At least a mile had trailed beneath the Volvo when he said 'Tell me about where we're going.'

'What about it, David?'

'Anything you remember.'

She was silent for a few seconds. He pressed the buttons to ensure the electric windows were shut tight, since a chill and a hint of staleness seemed to have insinuated themselves into the car. Gwendolen's sketch of a mouth opened in the fog ahead, and she said 'A funeral.'

'Not your own, I hope.'

It had been the unexpectedness of her response that provoked the comment. 'No, not mine,' she said with, he thought, a suggestion of wistfulness.

'If you don't mind my asking, whose, then?'

'I don't mind, but nor do I remember.'

'Nobody close to you, in other words.'

'Only in a way.'

The reflection of her face appeared to be growing fainter along with her meaning. 'Why do you remember it?' David said, feeling his impatience begin to escape his control.

'Because it was the last thing I saw before they made me leave.'

'Who made you leave?'

'The people.'

A sudden inspiration came to him, and though he had no idea what it might imply, he blurted 'Is that what's happened now?'

'Not this time, David. People have forgotten, most of them. Now there's nothing to keep me away from where I began.'

Her reflection was unquestionably becoming more obscure – so much so that he was compelled to glance at her to reassure himself that only her reflection was. He was almost certain that her face was too blank to be innocent, which infuriated him. 'Maybe you can tell me this,' he said, clenching his fists around the wheel. 'What were you doing at the funeral?'

'Something they used to believe someone had to do.'

He might have grasped it then, but his anger was too quick. 'How long have you been playing games with me, Gwen?'

'Why, ever since we met. I thought you and Joelle liked to.'

That sounded like another winning move on her part. Her face above the endlessly paid-out stretch of road was almost invisible now, because daylight was starting to seep into the fog. The brightening emphasised the obscurity into which he was heading and made him feel insufficiently awake. 'Why don't we play that game, then,' he said, 'and see where it takes us.'

'Which game, David?'

'The one from the island.'

'Who shall start?'

'Ladies first.'

Her hands shifted in her lap. 'Bag,' she said.

'Cat.'

'Stroke.'

'Poke.'

It was a response he would have been happier to say to Joelle, but Gwendolen appeared to be unruffled by it. 'Pig.'

'Porky.'

'Dirty.'

'Thirty.'

'Pieces.'

'Whole.'

'Dig.'

It was beginning to resemble a word-association test as much as a game, and he felt it leading him deeper into the murk. 'Up,' he said.

'Higher.'

'Rise.'

'Dead.'

'Soul.'

'Judgment.'

'Day,' he had to answer, willing that to manifest itself as more than a solidification of the fog. He couldn't shake off the impression that although he had proposed the game Gwendolen was in control of it, guiding him to some end. A few miles back they'd passed a Little Chef, and now he wished he'd stopped for coffee to help him awaken. Peering ahead in the hope of another roadside café, only for the fog to yield nothing more substantial than the occasional layby, was giving him an embryonic headache. 'Day,' he repeated in case she hadn't heard.

'Last.'

'Everlasting.'

Perhaps she wasn't as much in control as he'd thought; he was beginning to hear some weariness in her responses. 'You win,' he said. 'Do you mind if we stop for breakfast next time we see somewhere?'

'I've done with eating, but you do what you have to, David.' She let the bag loll forward in her lap, its strung mouth opening. 'We could have gone on.'

She sounded reproachful, as if she would have liked to hear his next response. The notion of her using him as oracle as well as chauffeur was no kinder to his headache than the fog's unending mockery of deference had been. He drove doggedly onward, his ankle beginning to twinge from his having no chance to press hard on the accelerator, and after too many miles of unveiled tarmac and drenched grass verges he became convinced that the fog was hiding signs for roadside services from him. 'Listen,' he said, 'do you mind if we pull over for a while until this lifts?'

When she didn't reply he peered at her. Her eyes were shut; the lids looked fragile as a moth's wings. They, and her cheeks and wrinkled lips, appeared to have sunken inwards. 'Gwen?' he said uneasily.

Her hands clutched at the bag. 'Could we go a little farther? Just until you feel you can't,' she said in not much of a voice.

He was already near to feeling incapable, and if she was as worn out as her appearance suggested, he didn't see how his continuing to drive could help. On the other hand, he would feel happier once he found a petrol station – the needle of the gauge was sinking close to the red zone – and there was always the possibility of finding a café in the same place. He sat up straighter and hung onto the wheel and swivelled his foot back and forth on the pedal to ease his ankle. His straining to see ahead made the fog appear to flicker, like the outline of Gwendolen's face at the edge of his vision, but more and more of his awareness was being drawn to the needle twitching closer to the danger zone. If he halted now it would achieve nothing, not least because he felt there was a question which he ought to ask Gwendolen and which he wanted to define to himself before they were alone with the silence of the car. The convergence of the needle and the red wedge kept the question out of reach, and he could only crouch over the wheel and drive into the fog, the fog, until without warning the fog blazed red.

If he hadn't been so tired he would have seen that it wasn't an accident ahead in the fog, only the rear lights of a juggernaut in a layby. His foot jerked on the accelerator as though it was fastened to the pedal before it managed to locate the brake. He thought he was overtaking the lorry on the wrong side of a dual carriageway, and braked so hard that he stalled the car. 'That's it, I'm sorry. I need a break,' he said, and risked reversing the Volvo as far as the entrance to the layby. He bumped one front wheel over the narrow strip of kerb and parked behind the lorry, whose red lights were extinguished as he did so. 'Excuse me a moment,' he said to Gwendolen. 'I just want a word with this chap.'

He clambered out of the Volvo and supported himself with one hand on the roof while he flexed his ankle gingerly. Alongside the layby he could see the edge of a bedraggled field beyond a hedge interrupted by a stile which looked rotted by the fog. When he'd finished groaning and wincing he limped as far as the cab of the lorry, a trek of at least twenty yards, which allowed him plenty of time to notice that the name of the town where the lorry came from seemed to be composed of bunches of Ls and little else. 'Hello up there?' he shouted as he reached the cab.

There was no answer that he could hear. Asking whether the driver spoke English would be less than diplomatic. 'Anyone alive in there?' he called.

'Yeah. Yeah, yeah,' said a Welshman's voice attempting to sound rougher than it was. 'Trying to get some kip.'

'Sorry to disturb you. Can I get petrol near here, would you know?'

'Up ahead if you keep going.'

'I should think that follows. Would you have any idea how far?'

'Five miles, give or take . . .' the voice growled like a dog roused from slumber. 'Five miles,' it said with more resentment than conviction.

'Thanks. You and your confectionery get some rest,' David said, having been dwarfed by the image of a cake on the side of the vehicle. He limped back as far as the tailgate and stopped short. He'd realised what he had to ask Gwendolen.

Now that the engine of the Volvo was switched off, the windows had clouded over, and he couldn't see into the car. He leaned across the bonnet and wiped the windscreen clear over Gwendolen's face, collecting the chill sweat of the glass on his palm. He thought of clearing the window set into a coffin to reveal the face within. Gwendolen's eyes turned their foggy pupils towards him, though no other part of her papery face moved. He shoved himself away, the print of his hand on the bonnet immediately beginning to drool into a less recognisable shape, and climbed in beside her, wiping his hands on his trousers. 'I'm just going to rest for a few minutes and then we'll get some fuel. The chap in the lorry says we shouldn't have to go far.' He hesitated and said 'If I hadn't brought you, were you thinking of hitching a lift?'

'Such was my plan.'

He hadn't yet asked the question he had to put to her. He wiped his hands again and took a breath that tasted stale and cold. 'It was what you did at the funeral that made them throw you out.'

That led to the question which perhaps he couldn't ask. His words had brought her head nodding around towards him as though they had released her from holding herself still, and he was suddenly able to read a great deal in her eyes: sadness, a mixture of relief and apprehension, a sense that he ought to realise everything now. She let her head fall back against the headrest, and he heard a dry crumpling – of her hair, he supposed, or her dress. When her eyes shut he wondered if she was continuing to play her game, making it more difficult for him to question her, but he wasn't sufficiently certain of that to trouble her further. He leaned his head back and closed his eyes, and memories of events since he and Joelle had gone down to the abandoned village began to swarm: Gwendolen wolfing down breakfast at the hotel as though she'd forgotten what food was like, her reluctance to enter the churchyard, the deaths which seemed to have clustered around her – Herb's, Richard and Judith's and Simon's and Olga's, Naomi's . . . It had been a while since he'd thought of the woman who had shared Gwendolen's floor at the Shangri-La and presumably her confidences, but all at once he knew what she had tried to tell him. 'Thirty pieces,' he breathed. 'Nothing to do with dirty people or saving anyone. Thirty pieces of silver. All those coins you had.'

Gwendolen made no sound, but he knew she could hear him. He didn't need to look at her, and keeping his eyes closed was allowing him to think. 'They paid you for what you did at the funeral, didn't they,' he said. 'They paid you to go away.'

Her silence was an answer which he no longer even needed, except – 'You had more than thirty coins, a lot more,' David said, and solved that problem at once. 'You kept on doing it. It was what you did in life.'

He was almost asleep, in that state where thoughts were free to put themselves together or emerge from secret places of the mind. He suspected that one of the windows mightn't be properly closed, because the chill and a stale smell were intensifying in the car, but this didn't bother him enough to make him look, which was too much of an effort. Putting his ideas into words used up all his energy, though the ideas themselves didn't bother him. 'You took away the sins of the dead, didn't you. You took their sins on yourself.'

The silence seemed not merely to be agreeing with him but to be encouraging him to think further. 'They paid you to do it because people were afraid to die with some sins on their souls – and that's what you've been afraid of.'

There came a sudden coughing roar as if some huge and savage beast had sprung out of hiding. The juggernaut was moving off. David must have been putting ideas together more slowly than he'd realised if the lorry-driver had had time for a nap. He listened as the unseen vehicle receded, prolonging its thunder like the first rumble of a storm, at last relinquishing a silence which felt intimate, a guarantee of frankness. More thoughts had gathered in the meantime. 'Did being frightened keep you alive somehow, Gwen?' he mused, then wondered if at last he'd reached the question he was nervous of asking. 'What could make you so scared?'

Just as he decided that the protracted silence was telling him to find the answer for himself, he sensed movement close to him, coming closer. It was so discreet that he didn't feel compelled to look, even supposing that he would be able to raise his eyelids, even when a soft object touched his mouth. The crumbling object pressed gently but insistently against his parted lips until the taste of it reached him. It was one – presumably the last – of Gwendolen's cakes.

Was it meant as the answer to one or both of his questions, or as a reward for his groping towards the truth? He seemed to have come to the end of his thoughts, and his reflexes took over. Hardly aware that he was doing so, he opened his mouth and bit into the cake.

He felt his teeth sever a portion and set about chewing it. He had the impression that his jaws were considerably more distant from his mind than usual. That suggested he was at least to some extent dreaming, which might explain why the texture of the cake reminded him of flesh as much as of confectionery, though did he think the dough had been transformed into flesh or vice versa? Then the taste penetrated his consciousness fully, a taste not simply stale but ancient, and he was seized by an instinctive panic which felt like the beginning of comprehension. He groped frantically for the window release with one hand, the door-handle with the other, while his eyelids struggled to unglue themselves. The door swung away from him, and he almost sprawled on the tarmac in his haste to rid himself of the contents of his mouth.

His eyes faltered open, and blinked and winced. The fog had retreated at least a quarter of a mile, and the sunlight fired the drying tarmac, but that wasn't the only reason why his eyes were vulnerable: he felt as though he was about to be able to see far too much. He became aware of a chill that smelled stale at his back, and he made himself turn to confront it, made himself overcome the temptation to close his eyes tight. It was only the fog which lingered in the field beyond the passenger door, which was wide open. Except for Gwendolen's bag, gaping emptily beside a cake with a bite taken out of it on the seat next to him, he was alone in the car.

# Thirty-four

As David stared about in search of Gwendolen he began to experience his surroundings with a clarity which unnerved him. He heard water dripping from the upper bar of the stile onto the lower, a tiny irregular hollow plopping, and the repeated single note of a bird that sounded as if it was sharpening its beak on the steely fog. He saw the fossil imprint of tyre tracks fading from the layby, and seemed to be able to perceive the molten silver coating of the road as separate from the surface of the tarmac. He was aware of the dance of the fog, trailing moisture over the fields as it inched back and forth, and beyond it he sensed mountains massing towards the hidden sky. When he felt drops of water too small to be visible settling on the hairs on the backs of his hands, he slammed the door and lurched across the passenger seat to pull the other shut.

The twin sounds cut themselves off, two chops of an axe, and he pressed his spine and the back of his head against the seat in an attempt to narrow his sensations down to himself. The smell of something older than he wanted to imagine was in his nostrils and insinuating itself into his mouth – he couldn't delude himself that it was only the fog. Trickles of condensation sketched enigmatic symbols on the windscreen, and he saw that he'd failed to shut anything out. He was apprehensive because the clarity was reaching deep into him.

Perhaps he was simply reclaiming information he'd heard or read somewhere, but it seemed vivid as a memory. The bereaved would lay out food beside or on the corpse, and by eating the food the sin-eater was believed to consume the sins of the deceased. David could almost see a stark room, a supine body whose hands had been placed together on its chest, the grim faces of the mourners ostracising the outsider as the coins were handed over to signify the end of the transaction. It was clearly an ancient tradition, one which he felt sure must have died out long ago – but that wasn't what made Gwendolen unique. Had every sin-eater been afraid to die? If not, why only Gwendolen?

He could feel his innards twitching with a confusion of emotions, of which the strongest for the moment was anger. He'd released her from the island and introduced her to his and Joelle's friends, and she'd fed sins to them. That much seemed clear to him so instantly that he tried to be suspicious of it: did it really explain his feelings about Angie Singleton, or was he determined to shift the blame? If everyone whom Gwendolen had fed at the barbecue had acted out a sin, just what sins had they been enacting? He felt trapped in his head with his speculations, and was beginning to feel that he would prefer not to be released by the truth, but he no longer seemed to have that choice. He sucked in a breath which intensified the ancient taste, and stared at the retreating fog as if his stare could call it back or blot out the thought he'd just had. Surely it was crucial to the tradition that sins could only be passed on if they were taken from a corpse.

The thought might have paralysed him, except that he sensed Gwendolen receding from him, taking the answer with her. He snatched the key from the ignition and scrambled out of the car. As his soles hit the tarmac, momentarily surrounding themselves with a penumbra of moisture, and he locked the door, he felt as though he was about to leave behind everything he'd taken for granted. The chill of the road penetrated his shoes and sent a shiver twisting up through him, and he translated the involuntary movement into a step towards the hedge. The drumming of water on the lower bar of the stile had become slow and regular, and seemed to have a meaning for him. When he came to the gap in the hedge he saw where Gwendolen had walked.

The upper bar of the stile sweated in his grasp as he climbed over. A grass-blade hitched itself minutely more erect, and then two others did, leading his gaze along a track that vanished into the fog. On the track through the grass beaded with rainbows he was sure he glimpsed the faintest traces of bare footprints. As he started to follow them he found he had to stride in order to equal their reach. Before long he was running.

Rainbows shattered around him. The ankle-deep grass wept on his trousers. The uneven ground challenged him to predict whether it would yield or try to trip him with a hummock or meet his next step with a half-buried rock. He could smell grass, wild flowers, different mixtures of earth, all the smells exaggerated by the fog. Once a bird clattered out of a hedge, emitting a series of shrill sharp notes as if it was chipping its way through the murk.

There was a stile in this hedge too, half a mile from the Volvo, and the prints of Gwendolen's bare feet led to it. It gave a moist creak as he vaulted over it. His heels dug into the ground, and the fog backed away from him.

At the far side of this second field, where the grass grew shaggier, a hill or a mountain began. The lowest slopes were jagged with heather and ferns and bare spiky slate. Though the field was at least half a mile wide, David could see Gwendolen's footprints in the sunlit grass, leading to the foot of a path. There was no sign of her up to several hundred yards, where the fog merged with low cloud. It occurred to David that she was climbing towards the light, and the notion suggested a finality to him which he didn't like.

Perhaps it was because he was stretching out his senses in an attempt to locate Gwendolen that he seemed to be aware of all the life around him. Insects scarcely large enough to be visible hopped away from him as he followed her glistening footprints, and once he was convinced he felt an insect die beneath his tread like a spark extinguished by his heel. He thought he could feel worms squirming in the earth. He hadn't time to be disconcerted by the impression, because there was movement on the slope. Rock scraped against rock somewhere in the murk, and then a fragment came skittering down, stopping short of the hem of the fog. He drew a breath which tasted like a head cold, and wondered if Gwendolen was as conscious of him as he was of her. Instead of calling to her he dashed through the wet grass to the foot of the path, where he thrust his fingers into rough grooves in the rock and stared up.

The mountain came alive with glittering as though his eyes were causing it to crystallise. The heather was sown with globules of sunlight, the ferns nodded and dropped them to shatter and trace cracks in the rock. Several hundred yards above him, where the vegetation paled as if trying to camouflage itself as slate, he saw Gwendolen clambering into the fog, which perhaps was the reason why her skin appeared more pallid than ever, and glistening. The sight dismayed him. 'Gwen, wait,' he shouted.

He thought he'd caused her to fall, and his own hands clenched on the rock-face. He saw her cling to handholds above her head before glancing down at him. He couldn't read her face, a pale oval which appeared to be merging into the same white mass as her hair and her dress. Was that an effect of the fog? He hadn't drawn another breath when she turned away and began to drag herself

371

upwards. Perhaps she was on a steep stretch of the path, but she seemed to be climbing straight up the rock.

David scrambled onto the path, a narrow strip of thin earth overgrown with patchy turf, and tramped after her. Now his heightened awareness felt as if it was slowing him down with the presence of so much life, the intricate translucent symbols of spiders' webs among the bright green spikes of heather, the globes of water coursing from frond to curled-up frond of the layers of ferns, the swarming world hidden in the vegetation, a world that verged on the next, the microscopic. At least he was still aware of Gwendolen, although the fog had lowered itself to meet her. She was climbing without pause, and it struck him that wherever she had come from, it could hardly be up there. She must have felt that he'd brought her as far as he could. She was seeking the light with all the strength remaining to her, and the thought drove him upwards to reach her before it, or whatever she was expecting, did.

While the path was by no means straight, at least it confined itself to this side of the mountain. It sloped upwards for stretches of anything between a few yards and a few hundred before turning back on itself. Each turn frustrated David, adding to the burden of sweat and fog that was settling on him. The thudding of his feet on the path was louder than any sounds Gwendolen was making, but he sensed her climbing faster than he was. In a couple of places he tried dispensing with the path, only to discover that slopes which looked easily climbable were slippery and thorny and composed, under the vegetation, of rubble which his weight was sufficient to dislodge.

Perhaps half a mile above the field which had sunk into a residue of fog, and at least twenty yards above one of the narrowest stretches of path, the mountain crumbled under the length of his body, sending him slithering on his face down the almost vertical slope. Neither the sodden ferns nor the chunks of rock they hid seemed capable of slowing his fall. He felt his heels strike the path, jarring his knees so hard he thought they had collided with the rock. He bent them belatedly and staggered backwards over the edge of the path.

As his feet skidded into nothingness he threw his arms forward, digging them and his fists into the thin mossy earth until he could drag himself, panting and cursing and shaken, onto the track. There he had to rest, massaging his legs, telling himself that every moment he felt unable to climb took Gwendolen further away from him. But as he pushed himself gingerly out of his crouch he saw that the cloud had lifted far enough to show him a white shape lying still on the path several hundred yards above him.

Was his impression that Gwendolen was receding from him an illusion? He began to toil up the track, wiping moisture from his forehead with the back of his hand, gripping his thighs to help himself up the steeper inclines. By the time he reached the first stretch above the point from which he'd fallen, the mountainside had intervened between him and the white shape. He imagined ranging back and forth on the mountain while Gwendolen outdistanced him. But no, he glimpsed white, still in the same place beneath the cloud that was raising itself towards the sky, exposing tracts of shining slate and dazzling vegetation. Each time David crossed the mountainside he managed to locate at least a hint of the white. He was beginning to will it to move – beginning to grow afraid of what he might find. The ferns overhanging a stretch of path obscured his view, but he was nearly there now. As he leaned on his thighs and shoved himself onto the incline where the object was lying, a wind stirred the cloud and trembled the heather around him, rearranging the millions of drops of water with a chorus of minuscule liquid notes he was certain he heard, and the white shape raised itself feebly to meet him. But it wasn't Gwendolen, only her dress.

So his sense of her continuing to climb was no illusion. For a moment the sight of the dress seemed like a trick she'd played on him, and then the implications caught up with him. He must be most of a mile up by now, and she was somewhere above him, climbing naked through the cloud whose chill he was experiencing from a hundred feet away. Was she trying to hasten her climb or her death? He stared up the glittering tufted slate that was smoking with fog, and filled his lungs, and shouted 'Gwen, wait. Tell me where you are. Let me help.'

There was silence except for the dripping of vegetation, stillness apart from the restless shifting of the lower edge of the cloud. How had he sounded to her – like the huge blurred voice of the cloud? He was taking another chill breath, though he wasn't sure he ought to call to her, when the hovering whiteness as wide as the mountain thinned momentarily, and he saw the peak.

It was at least half as far above him as he had already climbed, but the slope was gentler. Near the top of the enormous overgrown mound, whose outline put him in mind of the crown of a skull, patches of earthbound whiteness clung to the grass, and among them a figure was crawling on all fours up to a last stretch of path.

Something about the figure made David think of icicles – because it looked so thin and brittle, or white as ice, or melting? Surely some or all of its appearance was an effect of the blinding snow or the drifting cloud, and he was about to call her name at the top of his voice when he saw that she was naked even of hair. The next moment the cloud thickened, cutting off his view of the peak.

He wanted to believe that Gwendolen didn't actually look as he had seen her, but the impression was as vivid as everything else he was experiencing. When he sent himself onwards, it was mostly because he wanted to prove himself wrong. The track was wider now, its traverses of the slope more prolonged, and he forced himself to run wherever its steepness didn't defeat him. By the second zigzag he was panting harshly, by the third his heart sounded as loud as his footfalls, but he hadn't time to rest, even when the sight of long white strands – sometimes ragged clumps of them – that were caught on the vegetation made him falter. He felt trapped in his own exertions, weighed down by sweat and the residue of the cloud, deafened by himself. He could only trust his impression that he was overtaking Gwendolen and try not to imagine what he might stumble upon. The cloud had thickened stubbornly as though to delay the revelation, and he wasn't sure how close he was to the peak. Certainly a change was looming above him – the open sky, or something even vaster? If he tried to define the impression he would lose momentum, and so he continued toiling upwards at little more than an uneven trot, although he was beginning to feel as if all that kept him going was a refusal to acknowledge his fear. He was almost at the turn onto the final quarter-mile of path when the sky blazed, filling the grass with crystalline light, and he heard Gwendolen cry out on the peak.

It wasn't just her cry, in which triumph and terror were inextricably mingled, that halted him. He'd craned his head back at the sound in an attempt to find her, and for a breath he did. The cloud had sailed away all at once as though to expose her to the sky, and David glimpsed her silhouette. Perhaps it was the distance and the onslaught of light which made her limbs look thin and blackened as spent matches, but that was as much as he saw. Then her cry disintegrated as if her mouth had turned to dust, and she collapsed like a figure composed of sticks and vanished beyond the peak. He felt her merge with the blaze wider than the world or be engulfed by it, and he tottered against the sodden grassy wall of the bend in the path to support himself.

So she was gone, and he would never be able to ascertain

whether she had been afraid to die because she'd eaten the ultimate sin. Or could what she'd taken upon herself have kept her alive? He pressed his forehead against the chill grass, and listened to the delicate cracking of snow as it melted on the peak, and felt the sunlight strengthening on him. When he was able to breathe easily he pushed himself upright and headed for the top of the mountain, telling himself that she might have left some kind of sign for him.

The peak was perhaps fifty yards wide, and as flat as an altar. Apart from its covering of grass and minute starry flowers it was bare. As David set foot on it he felt his sense of the world expanding vertiginously around him. He tried to tell himself that was only because the clouds were racing away across the landscape, but he already knew better. The ancient taste was in his mouth. He didn't know how much he'd eaten – perhaps a few crumbs sufficed – but Gwendolen had left him more than a sign. He paced to the edge of the peak and raised his eyes.

There were bones in the grass below him, though they were so crumbled that the skull was hardly recognisable as such. They no longer seemed relevant except to lead his gaze out to the landscape. He was surrounded by mountains shining with all the colours of vegetation and limestone and slate, and growing brighter. He felt as though they had upheaved themselves to meet him, but he was most aware of an absolute stillness which encompassed not only the seasons that would change their colours but also the ages it had taken to create the mountains themselves, a timelessness in which the world appeared younger than newborn and yet a juggernaut speeding through a valley in the distance seemed capable of taking forever. The stillness was within him, and then it felt like the essence of him, and he thought he was seeing what God must be seeing. If this was the ultimate sin, he would have said it was no sin at all.

He stood for a while on the peak, stretching out his hands to let the wind run through his fingers and the sunlight gather on his palms, then he turned back to the path. He had no idea where he would go when he came down from the mountain, nor when or how he might return home, but for the present it seemed not to matter. He would go wherever his instincts led him. Just now he felt capable of taking away the sins of the world.